A Simple AVALANCHE

NICOLE SHARP

This book has some strong language, drinking and sex. Enjoy!

A Simple Avalanche by Nicole Sharp
Copyright © November 2023 The Writing Moose
All Rights Reserved

eBook: 979-8-9859257-8-4
Print: 979-8-9859257-9-1
Cover by **A. M. Rasmussen**
Editing by **Ariane Kimlinger** at Owl Focus Editing

The WRITING Moose

For more information visit: https://nicolesharpwrites.com

The Simply Trouble Series:

Big Trouble in Little Italy
Simply Protocol
Worth The Trouble
A Simple Avalanche

Standalone Books

The Italian Holiday
La Bella Luna
Surviving Thirty

Novellas

Let It Snow
The Museum Guide

For the archivists who painstakingly preserve the past.

And for those who wish Cassie to be their
spirit animal; and those "trying to figure
out how to have 'alone time' with Benji."

But mostly, for my Grandpa Sharp,
who lied about his age to join the
U.S. Navy in World War II.

A Simple AVALANCHE

ONE OF THE DEEPEST IMPULSES IN
MAN IS THE IMPULSE TO RECORD, TO
SCRATCH A DRAWING ON A TUSK OR
KEEP A DIARY... THE ENDURING VALUE
OF THE PAST IS, ONE MIGHT SAY, THE
VERY BASIS OF CIVILISATION.
-JOHN JAY CHAPMAN

Chapter One

I t was almost time.
Cassandra Dodd's breathing was jagged and shallow.

Every few seconds, she'd gulp as deep a breath as she could to inflate her lungs, in the hopes it would settle her nervous system.

It didn't work.

She glanced at her phone again: one minute.

She began to cough, a mingled result of her damned nerves, erratic wheezing, and the stupid aridness of her mouth. She rolled her eyes at the rising of emotions pressing against her chest. No one could truly ready someone else for moments like this, no matter how many detailed conversations were had. And no one ever mentioned that such overwhelming emotions could render a woman unable to create saliva. The thought turned the cough into a barked laugh.

Another glance at the time; any second now.

Cassie attempted another deep cleansing breath in through her nose, but the abrupt exhale of hot air was an exercise in breathlessness that overpowered the attempted calm.

Her irregular heartbeat was in charge now.

The faint squeak of floorboards, just outside the door, electrified every last nerve her body housed; she flung the front door open and blew out the name "Benji" as she greedily soaked in the vision of the man standing before her: bearded; tired rings around his eyes; rumpled polo, untucked yet still hugging his well-toned frame; jeans, and black and white Adidas. Every inch of the man's entire six foot three frame was wonderfully, ridiculously sexy.

His fatigued features brightened at the sight of Cassie and his own greeting was an incoherent mixture of a groan and garbled "hey" as he dropped the duffle bag he carried and reached for her in the same instant she reached for him.

They crashed into each other, desperate to make up for the last three weeks of lost time. Lips and hands fumbled as they claimed territory they'd been parted from for far too long. They were animals, moaning and clawing at each other.

"Oh my God," a laugh called, "get a room."

Cassie reluctantly pulled away and turned to stare daggers at her sister, Jessica, who had chosen that precise moment to walk by and disrupt the heated display.

Cassie took in her sister's appearance; dishwater blonde hair pulled into a loose bun, wearing a T-shirt and yoga pants on a frame that stood a fraction shorter than her own five nine. She was mildly irritated at how 'at home' Jessica looked. "I have a room," Cassie grumbled. "In fact, we have an entire apartment. Maybe *you* should get out."

"I can't. *Our* place is being fumigated." Jessica's blue eyes sparkled as she mocked Cassie's anger.

Agent Benjamin Stills—Benji to his girlfriend; Stills to the rest of the world—moved his bag just inside the apartment, used his foot to close the door, then urged Cassie's attention back to him.

When she met his amber gaze, the fog of frustration dissipated as his fingers splayed across her hips, then moved up to her waist and pulled her closer so she could feel the heat radiating off him. He winked and finally uttered the greeting she so needed, his voice low and velvety. "Hey Dodd."

Saying her last name, which had become an alluring endearment over the past two years, melted her against him and refocused her. "I missed you," she sighed.

He leaned his forehead against hers and breathed her in as she wrapped her arms around his waist. Abruptly, she stepped away and held his face gently in her hands. Stills raised an eyebrow as she turned his head slowly to the right and then left, narrowing her gaze in a study of his face.

"What are we doing?"

"Seeing if you're hurt." Cassie was searching for cuts or bruises, or any other signs. Satisfied with his face, she pulled his hands from around her and studied his knuckles; no bruising or cuts.

"I think I'd tell you if I'd been hurt."

"Would you?" She slipped her hands under his shirt and spread them across his muscular chest, watching his face for a reaction that might give away any serious injury. His eyes darkened with the attention, but there was no sharp intake of breath. She continued her tactile search, slipping her hands around his powerful back and shoulders, running them along the broad span.

"Is there something else I can help you with?" Stills didn't disapprove of having her hands all over him.

"Are you okay?" Finished with the upper part of his body, she crouched, apparently in an effort to continue searching his lower extremities for wounds. Stills crouched down, mirroring her, and gripped her hands in his. "That's enough," he said gently.

She sprang into a standing position, pulling him up with her; worried eyes searching his. "Did something happen to your legs?"

"Dodd ..." He nodded across the room. "I'd prefer that intimate part of my pat-down to happen without your sister present."

"But you're okay?"

"I'm okay," he promised.

Cassie squinted as she tried to ascertain exactly what he'd been through by examining his bloodshot eyes.

For the past three weeks Stills had been on the longest assignment he'd been given in the last two years. But if Cassie was certain about anything when it came to this man; he was careful, calculating and damn good at his job. He didn't work in the field often, and the few times it couldn't be avoided had only been assignments lasting two or three days. This trip couldn't be helped and Cassie found herself in the precarious position of trusting his judgment and intuition while going about her day-to-day life, then having to ward off unfounded worries late at night.

She ran her fingers along his chin. "I really like the beard."

"Oh yeah?"

She lowered her voice as she admitted, "I have a few itches I think will benefit *tremendously* from it."

"Do you want me to leave?" Jessica called from the sofa where she was dramatically turning up the sound on the TV.

Cassie's eyes widened before she turned all her attention toward her sister. "Yes." She put her hands on her hips. "You and your *husband* should leave."

"He's not my husband."

"You're getting married in four months." Cassie waved exhaustedly. "And you never got divorced from your Vegas wedding, so on paper, you're still married."

"It's not the same." Jessica muttered her lame defense.

"Yes. It is. And you know what else? You and your husband bought a house together. So you should go back to your *home*."

Jessica rolled her eyes. "I *want* to, but we *can't*."

"Just tell the fumigator to ... fuck off," Cassie insisted.

"Cassie, the house is still tented and it's not my fault everything is taking longer than anticipated. And we would have stayed with Mom and Dad, but Mom's the one who found the two for one coupon in the first place."

Cassie opened her mouth but before she could continue, Jessica added, "And *you're* the one who said it was fine if we stayed here." She pointed while mocking the invitation Cassie had given— "It'll be nice to have company while Benji's away."

"And *you* said you would only be here for *three* days." Cassie pointed back. "It's been ten. *Ten* days!"

"We'd stay in a hotel, but we just bought a house!" Jessica bit back at her older sister. "We need to save money."

Stills laughed and tugged on Cassie's arm, propelling her back to him. He slowly lowered his lips to hers, and when he was a mere fraction away, whispered, "If she gets uncomfortable, she can leave the room."

"I thought you said you didn't want to do anything intimate in front of my sister."

"Well ..."

Just then the door flung open and slammed into Stills' side, parting him from Cassie, and forcing her back a few steps.

"Dammit!" Stills growled.

The offender, Jessica's non-husband, Parker Salvatore, glanced a disheveled sandy blond head around the door. "Shit, sorry man."

Cassie rolled her eyes, shrugging as she mumbled, "Welcome home, Benji."

Chapter Two

T he alarm screamed, jarring Cassie out of a deep sleep. Her head throbbed in time with the electrified beep, beep, beep. She swatted at the nightstand until her hand made contact with the phone. While trying to turn it off by mindlessly pressing the side buttons, it slipped to the floor, still screaming—though its position under the bed helped muffle the sound a bit.

"Why do you have it turned up so loud?" Stills asked groggily.

Cassie slipped her torso off the bed, her fingers crawling along the floor in search of the phone. "I don't sleep well when you're away. Then I fall asleep late and ..." She found the phone and pulled it and herself back onto the bed. Trying to focus with only one eye open, she dismissed the alarm. "I don't always wake up to the quiet alarms." Closing her eye, she leaned back, laying the phone on her chest.

Stills rolled over onto his elbow. "What do you mean you don't sleep well when I'm away?"

Cassie let her head fall to face Stills and smiled as she opened one eye again.

"I worry," she stated.

He reached out and pushed a strand of her short wavy hair behind her ear, smiling at the early morning wildness. "You don't need to."

She rolled her body toward him, blinking her tired eyes open as her phone slipped between them. "I know."

"But ..." he led.

"Do you worry about me when you're not here?"

When he didn't answer, Cassie gave a soft laugh. "I know you don't worry about me because you have a lot going on. And I'm not trying to trap you into some bullshit argument."

He gave a shrug. "I don't worry about you. My Cassie is pretty badass. I just wish you wouldn't worry about me; it doesn't do any good."

"Yeah, I know." He was now going to launch into one of his favorite quotes, so she figured she'd beat him to the punch: "'If a problem is fixable, if a situation is such that you can do something about it, then there is no need to worry. If it's not fixable, then there is no help in worrying. There is no benefit in worrying whatsoever.'"

"Dodd, the Dali Lama has a point." He traced her jawline with his fingers.

Cassie grunted. "Benji, I've never been in love like this." She took his hand and held it. "I've never been with a man who has a job like yours—even though I'm not supposed to know what you do for a living. So while I understand that worrying is futile, and I *do* trust you and your training ..." She licked her lips as she tried to explain, "It's just that the longest you've been gone for work over the past couple of years was four days." She sighed. "I need to figure out how to make it through the longer assignments."

"There won't be too many of them," he reassured.

"How was it?" she asked, knowing he couldn't tell her much. As he inhaled deeply, she knew he was about to tilt his head to the side and utter an apology; in order to avoid it, she continued her line of questioning. "Did you have any good pastries?"

His face softened. "Maybe."

"Were they prepared with a lot of butter?"

"In the recipe?" he asked, confused.

She smiled as she elaborated. "Did you know a lot of French pastries use tons of butter? Also, I would go ahead and make the assumption that many recipes in South America use more milk. Like flan and tres leche. Now, the ancient Assyrian dynasty of the eighth century," she gave a mischievous wiggle of her eyebrows, "which is home to modern day Lebanon, Turkey, and Egypt, are more honey heavy in their recipes. So Benji, would you say the pastries you *might* have had were more butter, milk or honey?"

"Very clever Dodd." He studied her for a few long seconds. "Are you a fan of pecans?"

"Pecan pie? Traditional, *southern* pecan pie?" She was thrilled that his reply was an obvious act of trust; while he wasn't divulging where he'd been, somehow the willingness to give her a broad area helped.

"Maybe one day you can look up a recipe for a cinnamon bun pecan pie."

"Oh," she ran her tongue along the inside of her teeth, "that sounds really sweet."

"Yeah, well, it's nothing compared to how sweet you taste." He slipped his hand around her waist and used her body as leverage to pull himself against her while his lips sought her neck.

"You were tired last night," she whispered, tilting her head so he could have better access.

"I was." He reached for the hem of the tank top she wore, tugging it up; she in turn let her hand drift into his tight, black boxer briefs.

He grunted, then pulled the sheets back as they became a whirlwind of clothing removal. Cassie's panties were the last item to launch across the room, but neither saw where it landed as Stills maneuvered her naked body beneath his; becoming a twist of limbs and passion, moaning as the thrill of naked skin melded together.

Cassie wiggled under him, anxious to position him where she wanted him. But he shook his head and trailed his lips in between her cleavage, using his body weight to keep her from having a more active role this morning. She let out a frustrated moan and he laughed, the vibration echoing inside her chest, sending waves of electricity up her arms.

She arched against him as the abrupt, high-pitched scream of an alarm tensed Stills and shocked Cassie into sitting up. The quick motion caused her chin to clip Stills' forehead, sending her backwards with an "oof."

"What is that?" Stills asked.

"The apartment complex's fire alarm." She rubbed her chin.

They were unwinding from each other when the door to their room was swung open by Parker, pulling a sweatshirt over his head while loudly yelling, "Come on lovebirds. Time to evacuate."

"Jesus, Salvatore." Stills grabbed a pillow and threw it toward the door as Cassie pulled Stills' body against hers to hide the parts she wasn't interested in her brother-in-law seeing.

Parker laughed as he closed the door. Stills looked down apologetically at Cassie then lightly touched her chin and—so he could be heard over the unrelenting screech—raised his voice. "I guess we need to evacuate."

"Unless ..." Cassie tried.

"Dodd, I want you so bad I could finish pretty quick. But that doesn't seem fair to you."

"I could finish quickly too," she said, but the act of yelling the sentiment dowsed any flames they had built.

Stills laughed. "Dodd, if you really think this sound isn't ruining anything, I'll try."

She growled and rolled off the bed. "Damn apartment living."

"This might be the sign we needed to finally start house hunting."

"You're right," she yelled as she pulled on a shirt, "I'm properly motivated to start looking now."

Cassie tugged on pants and a hoodie, tucking her phone in the sweatshirt. Then she opened her closet, grunting as she liberated a large duffle bag from the dark confines.

"What is that?" Stills asked having finished dressing and collecting the bag he'd been living out of for the past few weeks.

"My go bag," she called.

"Really?" He crossed the room to help her but when he picked up the bag, he cursed under his breath from the weight of the beast.

"It's my mom's influence," she admitted as he looped the handle over his head and arranged the weight of the bag across his shoulder and chest.

The bedroom door swung open again; this time it was Jessica yelling, "We gotta go!"

"I'm getting my bag," Cassie replied loudly.

"Parker went to see what's going on," Jessica added before she hurried away.

Cassie's stomach fluttered anxiously as she shoved her laptop in its bag then glanced around her apartment as Jessica and Stills quickly collected their own chargers, phones, laptops and bags.

Parker returned saying, "The unit at the east end of the hallway on the first floor is on fire." He finished collecting his own things.

She stared blankly at the walls. What else should she bring? It was just stuff. Everything could be replaced, couldn't it? If it had to be? But this was her home. She'd never been in a position where she had to decide in a moment's notice what she should save.

"Dodd ..." Stills called to get her attention, then gave a nod of understanding that propelled her into action while at the same time, comforted her.

She took a breath as the realization of the things she'd hate to lose came to her. As the others filed out into the hall, Cassie hurried into the kitchen and pulled out the rolling pin Stills had bought her on their first date, and the book of handwritten recipes she'd gathered from her two grandmothers, her great-grandmothers, as well as the great-greats.

She gave one more fleeting glance around as she shouldered her purse and computer bag. "Okay," she called as she joined them, pulling the door shut behind her.

Parker and Stills were quick but not rushed. There wasn't an air of chaos or hurriedness about their actions. Cassie assumed that was the various training kicking in that they'd received over the length of their careers. She'd heard that firemen, EMTs, nurses and doctors, were trained the same way; to stay calm. That's why you never saw them running. After being together with Stills the past two years, she'd come to appreciate his calm when it seemed everyone else was hurried.

The sounds of sirens outside joined the alarm and flashing lights in the hallway of the complex. The smell of smoke was apparent now. At the end of the hallway, in the entrance of the stairwell, there was a fireman giving instructions to everyone exiting. "Slowly, folks. Head to the front door and across the street."

Once in the designated area with the other tenants, they watched as the firemen fought the smoke coming out of the first floor.

Cassie chewed her lower lip as the scene unfolded. Stills pulled her to his side and pointed to the overweight bag he'd escorted out of the apartment. "What exactly is in a 'go bag' inspired by your mom?"

Cassie accepted the attempt at sidetracking her.

"Barbara Dodd," she stated her mom's name, "saw a special 20/20 television program when she and my father first moved to California. It talked about earthquake preparedness."

Jessica laughed, adding, "And our mom believes in being prepared for anything. You received your airplane readiness bag last year." She referred to the family trip they'd all taken to Italy and the gallon size baggies her mother handed out filled with candy, granola bars, wet wipes, printed copies of the itinerary and a euro coin for a pay phone just in case anyone got separated or lost, *and* their phone died.

"Well," Cassie continued, "the moment we bought our own cars, Mom made sure they were equipped with earthquake bags. And when we moved out, she made us put together 'go bags.'" She pointed at hers. "That bag contains my birth certificate, Social Security card, an extra pair of clothes and an old pair of running shoes. Emergency blanket. First aid kit. A few bottles of water. Disinfectant wipes. A USB with copies of important bill information, photos, and other documents."

Stills chuckled. "Your mom is amazing."

"No ..." Cassie groaned.

"Take that back," Jessica chimed in.

"I *admire* her," Stills corrected. "I can't help it."

Jessica shook her head. "Don't ever tell her, okay?"

A fireman positioned himself in front of the crowd and caught everyone's attention before he addressed them. The fire was almost out. It had not spread, but it would take the rest of the day for them to make sure the apartment building itself was still structurally sound. That was protocol for such fires. If people needed to get into their apartments to gather items, they could be escorted in one at a time, but it was highly suggested that the best course of action would be for the tenants to find different accommodations for the night.

Stills turned to Cassie with a raised eyebrow.

Jessica asked, "Where should we go?"

Cassie winked at Stills and turned toward her sister.

"Jess, I'm calling in sick to work. Benji and I are going to check into whatever hotel you are NOT checking into. Then, I'm going to spend the rest of the day having sex with my boyfriend."

"TMI." Jessica laughed.

Cassie doubled down on making her sister uncomfortable. "The dirty kind."

Jessica put her hands over her ears but grinned at her older sister.

"Okay, principessa," Parker announced to Jessica, "let's give these two some space. See you around, Stills."

"Salvatore," Stills returned, then inclined his head toward Cassie and asked, "Dirty sex all day long?"

"Hell yeah."

He jerked his head in the direction his car was parked. "Then what are we standing around here for, Dodd?"

Chapter Three

Cassie reached above her head, spread her fingers wide and stretched, doing an impressive backbend in her ergonomic chair as she let out a loud yawn.

"I see your boyfriend made it home safe from his trip and you two are making up for lost time?" Tina, her coworker and friend, called from her desk across the office space they shared. "You two are like rabbits." She laughed, sitting back as she pushed her green glasses—that matched her green eyes—atop her black pixie cut.

Cassie grinned as her arms dropped down by her side. "How would you know?"

"I am a student of human nature." She pulled at the hem of her Aerosmith T-shirt innocently. "When you're this exhausted at work, yet smiling, it means you're having *relations*," she drew out the word, "and relations that border on the side of ridiculous to your coworker who is single."

The two women had worked together for eight years and shared the same large office space for the majority of that time. They both wore the title "Senior Academic Historian" at Ancestry Home, a genealogy company that supplied clients with DNA testing and historical documentation in order to give detailed, personalized reports on their ancestors.

Cassie had been recruited right out of college for the job when the owner of the company was laying the groundwork. The founder understood early on, that helping living relatives discover their ancestors wasn't enough. She wanted to give clients the option to have a deeper understanding of the life one's ancestors lived. So, rather than simply presenting dates and names in a chart, the company placed their research findings against the historical backdrop, as well as the social context, of the lives the ancestors had lived.

Enter Cassie. She worked on in-depth projects referred to as 'Full-service research packages.' Sometimes the research was a deep dive into one specific relative and their life story; other times it revolved around an entire family tree.

Regardless of the task, Cassie was always fascinated. When she described her job, she'd often say she was a bit research assistant, a bit public records clerk, and a splash storyteller. And she couldn't imagine working anywhere else. The people she worked with, the culture, and the assignments that differed from project to project, year to year ... it all continued to keep her absorbed and captivated.

Unless she was exhausted from late nights with Stills.

Or early mornings with Stills.

"How is Mr. Sexy?" Tina's question produced a physical reaction in Cassie, she was so sleep deprived and well-loved that her body hummed.

"Good," she offered.

Tina leaned forward in mock exasperation. "Jeez, Cass. I need more than 'good.' I'm single again and I need to live vicariously through someone."

Cassie eyed her friend as she pursed her lips, then sat forward. "It's been over two years, we've been on vacation with my family and his family and we live together and apparently we're going to start looking for a house together and I've never been with someone who sees me and loves me for me and he still turns me on and makes my legs go all wobbly."

Tina sat back in her seat and held an imaginary cigarette to her lips; taking a 'deep drag,' then holding her breath she said, "Yeah, that's the stuff." She blew out the air. "House hunting? Things are getting serious."

"The fire alarm went off at the apartment complex the other morning, and Jess bought a house and I've been a bit jealous of that ..."

Tina pointed a mock accusatory finger at Cassie. "But you *never* wanted a house. You never wanted to get married or settle down. You wanted to be a gypsy and travel the world with no ties." She regurgitated Cassie's past claims.

"I never knew Benji was in the world."

"God! He's made you yearn for domesticity? Holy shit, I never thought I'd see the day."

"No ... well ... no. I just want a house." Her eyes sparkled as she reasoned, "That way when I scream and moan I don't have to blush when I see the neighbors the next morning." Cassie almost made it through the ridiculous explanation with a straight face, but broke halfway through.

Tina laughed. "Well, whenever Benjamin Stills proposes, just know that I'll be ready and willing to help in any way I can."

"Who said anything about proposing?"

"Me. Everyone who's ever met you two. Your mom."

Cassie groaned. "Please don't talk to my mom."

"She sent me a really sweet card for my birthday last month," Tina defended.

Cassie grunted.

Tina walked her chair closer to Cassie. "Tell me the truth, haven't you thought about marrying him?"

"I mean, *of course* I have." Cassie shrugged. "But you know me, a ring wasn't ever my end goal. This is so different and new, and unexpected. I'm just trying to enjoy it."

"Well, I'm enjoying it," Tina said. "I'd enjoy it even more if you'd pin up some shirtless pictures of him or find a brother of his that *isn't* married."

"Whatever," Cassie tisked, "and don't give me the living vicariously through me bullshit. I know your life. You're headed to Paris in two weeks for three months. For *work*. To play around in the National Archives?"

Tina fanned her face and preened. "I guess–"

"And someone set you up on a date with some tall handsome Frenchman."

"Three months in a dimly lit room with an archivist and my passable French." Tina pouted.

"Nice try. You won't even notice what kind of room you're in cuz you love the research and you made the mistake of showing me a picture of the 'friend' you're being set up with." Cassie laughed but it turned into another yawn.

"Oh my God, did you get any sleep?"

"No." Another stretch and Cassie stood up. "C'mon, let's go get coffee. I need to ask you a few questions about Colorado and mining anyway."

"Oh, is this for your latest project?"

"Yeah, there isn't a lot of information online." Another yawn struck as Cassie grabbed her computer bag and purse.

Tina did the same, shaking her head. "Cassie, what is he like in bed? I mean, is it acrobatic or ridiculously competitive? Should I worry? Should I help you invest in long-term healthcare just in case your back goes out?"

"Jeez," Cassie laughed, waving away the mock concern, "I'm simply tired."

Settled with midmorning coffees at the café across from their office building, Cassie pulled out her laptop and opened the notes for her current project. Then taking a swig of her four-shot latte, she smiled as the hot goodness seeped into her veins from the inside; even if it wasn't medically possible, she needed the illusion today.

With another yawn and a shake of her head, she nodded toward Tina. "Okay, Colorado."

"One of the fifty states in America,"

"Mining," Cassie continued.

"What do you need to know?"

"Well, you worked for the Denver Historical Society before you moved here."

"I did?"

Cassie flicked her friend on the arm. "I'll talk this through first."

Tina sat back and hugged her cup between her hands. "Oh good, I was worried you were going to ask for the history of mining in Colorado."

"I mean, if you have a PowerPoint ready ..."

"Sure," Tina laughed, "and while we're at it, is there anything else you want to discuss? Perhaps the cause and effect poor plumbing had on the downfall of the Roman Empire?"

"Poor plumbing?"

Tina shrugged. "It's a working hypothesis."

Cassie gave a humph in reply.

"Okay, let's talk it out. This is Eden, Colorado?" Tina verified.

"Yeah, small mining town turned tourist town in the southwestern part of Colorado." Cassie pulled up a map of the town on her laptop.

"I know the area, but most of the work I did in Denver was in Colorado Springs and Cripple Creek, the other side of the state."

"Well, as you know, the smaller towns don't have the manpower to keep websites updated or even deal with the influx of information they continue to receive. Eden barely has a handful of their photographs and history online," Cassie explained, but it was more rhetorical, as they both understood the world of archives and researching history.

"Have you ever wanted to be in a documentary?" Tina asked.

Cassie shook her head with a laugh, used to Tina's off topic questions.

Tina sighed. "You'd be good in a documentary. I would love to be in one. Sitting in front of a bookcase, glasses in place; I'd probably wear something that screams collegiate doctorate—you know, white shirt, vest, sweater."

"And what would your specialty be?"

She winked at Cassie. "The cause and effect poor plumbing had on the downfall of the Roman Empire."

"I'd watch that."

"Of course you would." She waved the idea away. "So you're headed to Eden for a little research and *a lot* of honeymoon time."

"Tina," Cassie chided.

Tina held up her hands in defense. "Did I say honeymoon? I meant a little stale, boring *vacation* and a lot of research. In the middle of that wilderness that you and Benji seem to like so much." She gave a shiver and wrapped her arms around herself. "I hate the wilderness."

"So you've informed me. Many times."

"Okay," Tina smiled, "so you're headed into the wilderness for some sex and research."

"I think we found the title of your biography, once you make it big on the documentary touring circuit."

Tina held her cup aloft and toasted it in Cassie's direction. "I love it."

Cassie pulled up a file, took another deep drink and began her story as succinctly as she could.

Chapter Four

"Theresa Moss is the client I'm working for. She lost her father, William, two years ago; her mother several years before that; but she's only interested in her father's history."

"Theresa Moss," Tina verified. "Who does she want the history for? Her kids? Grandkids?"

"She alluded to an ex-husband, but no kids," Cassie said. "She's a realtor in the greater LA area. Really put together, nails, hair and outfits are always done up; very tidy but there is something about her face that reminds me of a ferret, like she's always figuring the odds."

Tina rubbed her hands together. "Continue."

Cassie pursed her lips, feeling bad about the description, but it was on point. She and Tina had figured out long ago, if they could pinpoint the personalities of their clients, they'd be better equipped in handling their expectations. Certain clients called every other day to check up on the progress being made. Then there were those who continually added to the stack of work some new item of family history found in the attic. And still, others who conducted their own research online simultaneously.

"She's too busy to be hands-on and is willing to wait as long as it takes to get a complete story." Cassie shared the character trait she felt was most pertinent to their job. "Of course, I'll meet with her in two weeks, before we head to Eden."

Tina bobbed her head. "So Theresa is curious about her dad's life."

"William Moss was a respected English professor at UCI. He wrote a memoir about his time in the Army during World War II that was well received, and as I understand it, was one of the catalysts for him getting the job as a professor. He taught for years and was prolific in his publishing."

"Ew, English professor publishing? I'm sure they were riveting articles."

Cassie clicked around on her document and read a few titles of the good professor's work: "European backgrounds for English literature," "How allegory and symbol set wide resonances with literature after 1945," and my favorite– "Somerset Maugham and his highly idiomatic and fluent characters."

Tina gave a grunt of a laugh. "That was English?"

"Yup."

"Okay, so that's the surface story, right?" Tina asked. They'd done this job enough to know that often, when someone hired their company to do research on a single family member and the story started this dryly, there were always a few interesting skeletons in the closet.

"Yes. Last year, after giving Theresa proper mourning time, the university reached out and asked her if they could add any letters or writings he might have left behind to their library collection. They were mostly interested in any war correspondence. When he retired he did a lot of volunteer work with veterans."

"Ah..." This was par for the course when it came to these stories. "Is that when Miss Theresa went into the proverbial attic?"

Cassie gave her friend a knowing grin. "She didn't just find a few letters, she found boxes upon boxes of writings and recordings."

Tina wiggled her eyebrows and sang, "Dun dun dunnnn."

"William Moss was helping veterans in various ways, but it turns out he was also interviewing them and documenting their time in war. He'd even written several papers on war and cultural studies."

"So William Moss was an amateur historian?"

"Yes, and when Theresa told the University what she'd found, she said they were peeing down their pants in excitement."

Tina nodded. "Because if they have an archive of veteran histories that no one else has seen or heard, it'll attract attention and money to their university."

"You got it." Cassie took a drink and cleared her throat. "So that part is pretty cut and dry."

"I figured as much. What else ya got?"

"Okay, the history I was able to piece together so far ..." Cassie scrolled through her research and began, "William Moss was the youngest of three kids, two boys and a girl. Born and raised in Chicago, their parents died, leaving them orphaned, but the kids were never sent to an orphanage. If I had to guess, I figure they were old enough to know if they stuck together, didn't get in trouble and took whatever job they could, they could stay together."

"And out of an orphanage."

"Exactly. Then, in 1941, America joins the war. William was seventeen, so he lied about his age to join. His older brother, James, joined as well. Theresa shared a few letters she found between her father and aunt who wrote she was grateful for the money that the brothers continued to send to her in Chicago. So more assumptions I'm making here; James was continuing to look out for his younger brother and the draw of a paycheck also prompted him to join."

"Stage is set," Tina said.

"Stage is set," Cassie agreed. She took another sip followed by a deep breath. "So, Theresa always assumed her father went straight to California after the war. But among his papers, she found that William and James were in Eden, Colorado. For five years. How does she know this? Mining claims. Fifteen mining claims in either James' or William's name, with dates between 1947 and 1951 on them."

"Cassie," Tina said excitedly.

"I know!" This was what excited Cassie about her job. While she worked hard to respect the lives and stories of those that came before and what they lived through, she absolutely loved the research required of her to piece the narrative together as completely as possible.

"So, this is why you get a sexy trip to Colorado."

"It's not going to be sexy-"

"Sexy," Tina interrupted, drawing out the word.

Cassie rolled her eyes. "Yes, this is why I'm headed to Eden, but you *know* this story gets better."

"Do I?"

"Theresa found a marriage certificate for one William L. Moss. Of Eden, Colorado. In 1947. Several years before he married her mom."

"Has she done the DNA testing? Are there relatives?" Tina's

excitement paralleled Cassie's.

"Those results haven't come back yet." She cleared her throat. "When I did a preliminary birth and death certificate search, I found the death certificate for the uncle, James Moss. In 1949 in Eden."

"What happened?"

"Don't know," Cassie said before she continued. "And here is another random puzzle piece. Theresa found letters between her parents, tucked into one of her mother's old purses. They are dated between 1965 and 1970, when William was in Eden, Colorado."

"He went back?"

"Theresa said she remembers a time when her dad wasn't around, but he came home for all the holidays. She said she was too young to understand where he really was, and when she asked, she was told he had to work."

"Do you think he went back to his first wife?"

Cassie gave an excited, conspiratorial shrug. "That's another question I hope to answer while I'm there, but how about one more mystery to heap onto the pile?"

"Yes please."

"I found a mining claim in Eden, Colorado from 1962. In the name of James Moss."

"He used his brother's name?"

"It would seem so. Or James wasn't dead?"

"I do believe Cassandra, that you have quite the ball of yarn to unravel."

"It would seem that way." Cassie smiled happily.

Tina sat back. "So what do you really need from me?"

"In your work in Denver ..." she led.

Tina grinned. "You want to talk about boring mining claims, huh?"

"I don't know anything about mining claims."

Tina took a drink and cleared her throat. "Okay, Cass, people get all excited when they hear they are inheriting a mining claim. Visions of gold deposits dance in their heads." She laughed and wiggled her fingers above her head, "But a person isn't rich because they inherit a mine. A lot of paperwork and red tape comes with that territory. Literally." Sniggering, she went on. "First, a lot of people think; they get a mine, they get land.

That's not the case. The land a claim is on is not private property, only the mine itself is. And there are different rules and permits and laws depending on if the mine is located on state land or federal land. And then, when all the i's have been dotted and t's crossed and ownership has been transferred, people forget they have to go to the claim and mine the damn site."

"This sounds pretty boring," Cassie admitted.

"It's … interesting."

"So where do I start to research mining claims?"

"I'd start with the southeastern department of the Bureau of Land Management. And then when you're in Eden, go to the county clerk and recorder's office. The claims Theresa has will have enough information for them to point you in the right direction. They can also find out if the claims are transferable to next of kin. But when it comes to mines and rights, Colorado is a big state; they've been mining that country since the 1890s."

"I know."

Tina shrugged, she understood the unraveling that Cassie was beginning. "What are your main objectives in Eden?"

"Find information on William and James' lives in Colorado. Find the first wife. Find out how James died. Find out what William was doing in Colorado from '65 to '70 and finally, find out if the mines are inherited and if they are worth anything."

"They probably aren't," Tina supplied. "I'd tell Theresa not to hang any hopes on those. Mining claims these days are merely interesting pieces of paper to frame and use as a conversation piece."

"Thankfully, Theresa Moss seems to be the type of woman who isn't dying to inherit millions. I think she only wants to piece together her father's life story." Cassie couldn't hold back another yawn.

"But Cass, if I may suggest one important step before you start this adventure?"

Cassie raised an eyebrow in question.

Tina winked. "Take a nap first, sister."

Chapter Five

"**D**odd, your mom just called, they're on their way up." Stills was in the living room as the timer on the oven went off.

"I'll get the oven, you get the door," Cassie said as she headed toward the kitchen. "And when we get a new place, we're not giving anyone our address."

"Agreed," he said from across the room then supplied, "I called the realtor Salvatore used. She wants to set up a meeting with us."

"Then set it up, Stills." She laughed triumphantly just as her cell began to ring. She pulled out the lasagna, slipped it on the stove and took the phone out of her pocket to see who was calling. After a few seconds she made a decision and answered without saying hello, then after a moment gave a frustrated growl as she walked into the living room. "Whoever you are, I'm telling you this is the wrong number. Now stop calling. Take me off the list. I don't want what you're selling."

"What the hell is that about?" Stills asked with a concerned frown.

"Nothing. A wrong number ... or someone is trying to sell me something and the automated recording isn't working."

"Are you getting a lot of weird calls?"

"Benji, it's spam," she soothed. "Twice a week, Tuesday and Thursday, at the same time. Like clockwork. I only answer when I'm bored or want to yell at someone."

"Always those days at the exact same time?"

"Yes, like a company has a bot spamming me."

Stills held up his hands defensively. "You're probably right."

"I'm probably right," she parroted.

"Why did you need to yell at someone?"

The answer rushed through the open door then, arguing. "I am *not* a bad driver, Walter, you are. You never use your blinker and you have a blind spot you never check and that's how we're going to die, going ninety-five miles an hour on the freeway, hit by a semi because you don't signal." Her mother gave the fortune-telling information with her chin in the air.

"You can't even get up to ninety-five on any of the freeways around here," her father defended.

"You can, because you always find a way to speed, no matter how many times I tell you I don't like my car to go over seventy miles an hour."

"Hi Mom." Cassie reached her mom, took her purse and planted a kiss on her cheek in an attempt to defuse whatever ridiculous argument this was.

"Something smells good," her dad offered as he shook hands with Stills.

"Lasagna," Cassie supplied as Stills passed her, and winked, on his way to the kitchen to get the wine and glasses.

"Oh dammit. I forgot the bread." Her mother pursed her lips. "Walter, you made me forget the bread." What came out as a harsh criticism was followed by a strange giggle.

Cassie tilted her head; a silent question. Barbara Dodd took a breath and gave the sing-song explanation, "We're late because your father got a little handsy."

"I have bread," Cassie announced loudly.

Her mother laughed as Stills appeared and handed a glass of wine to each of Cassie's parents.

Called by the large open road atlas, Walter wandered to the kitchen table to see a map of Arizona.

Her father tapped on the northern part of the state. "Are you going to take the 40?" He asked about the route she and Stills would follow on their upcoming vacation. The ten-day trip would span several states with the bulk of time spent in southeastern Colorado.

"Yeah, to the Grand Canyon." Cassie joined her father and began pointing out the planned route.

"Dodd." Stills smiled, amused.

She held up her hand in defense. "I know I could do this all on my phone, but there's something about the oversized map that takes up the whole table and tracing the route with a finger that gets me excited." She elbowed her dad. "I get it from him."

"How long is it from LA to the Grand Canyon?" her father asked.

Cassie followed the wandering yellow highway. "Seven hours, then we'll camp around the south rim area."

"We've lost them now." Barbara sighed.

"I'll go make the salad," Stills said as Barbara followed him, asking, "How's your family doing? I talked to your mom last month. Did she ever get the dog to the dentist?"

"She talks to his mom?" Cassie muttered.

Her father nodded. "Of course she does. When you girls don't answer, she calls your mothers-in-law."

"I'm not married, Dad."

"Don't tell your mother. I don't think she knows."

A conspiratory laugh erupted between them as her dad sat down in front of the map. "Where will you go after the Grand Canyon?"

"To the Four Corners Monument, roughly another four hours away." Her father traced the route as she continued, "Then to Mesa Verde; another hour further and we'll be there for two nights. Then it's on to Eden, Colorado for the rest of the trip."

"That doesn't look far from Mesa Verde."

"Three hours, not bad."

"Should be good weather." Of course he already checked the weather, and he had probably already pulled out his own atlas to study the various routes they might take; not that there were too many other options.

"Yup." She smiled. "Right now the forecast calls for a bit of rain, but nothing too bad. Springy weather."

Walter tapped the map. "That'll be a good trip. I think your mother and I are going to drive up to Canada this fall."

"After the wedding?"

"Lord knows we'll all need a break after your sister finally gets married. Again. Your mother ..." he shrugged and reiterated, "we'll all need a break."

"She's in heaven planning this wedding," Cassie supplied. "Canada would be a fun trip."

"Yeah," he sat back and pointed to the map again, "but *that's* going to be a great trip. I'm jealous."

"You and Mom go on trips all the time."

"I know, but it's been a while."

"Dad, we went to Italy last year."

"That was last year. I'm just saying I like going on trips. And I'm ready for the open road again."

"Even though you came in yelling at each other about how you drive?"

Her dad rolled his eyes. "You'll understand one day." He pointed to the road into Eden; on the map it looked like the lines on a heart monitor. "This road looks a little rough."

"I talked to the archivist who lives in Eden and who'll be helping me. She said there are a few twisty areas and there's still snow on the ground, but the road crews have everything cleared. So long as we drive cautiously, we won't have any problems."

He squinted at the map. "Is that the only road into Eden?"

Cassie nodded. "That's it. Any other roads are dirt paths and used primarily for four-wheeling in the summer and snowmobiling in the winter. There's only this one highway that leads into and out of town."

He gave a grunt then advised, "Call when you get there. I'll worry about you on that part of the trip."

"You honestly think Mom'll let me go a full week without talking to her?"

"I think *you'll* try to go a full week without talking to her." There was laughter in his voice. "Look, it doesn't matter if you're sixteen or thirty, we worry. So let us know when you get to each destination."

"I'll be with a CIA agent," Cassie said dryly.

"Yeah, that helps a little, but now we worry about him too." He sighed. "I now have four kids to worry about."

"Then I'll make sure to at least text."

He tapped the map again. "A helluva trip, kid."

"I think so," Cassie affirmed just in time to overhear her mother suggest to Stills that double weddings weren't unheard of and there was still time for him to propose.

Chapter Six

"Thank you for calling the Eden County Historical Society. This is Elizabeth."

"Elizabeth, this is Cassie," she exclaimed, sitting back in her desk chair.

"Cassie! Are you ready for your trip next week?"

Cassie chuckled; Elizabeth was the head archivist for the Eden County Historical Society. The woman's easy, outgoing nature was palpable over the phone.

"So ready," Cassie said. "I'm just double-checking all our reservations and thought I'd give you a call."

"I'm so glad. I'm so excited to meet you in person and I know Marsha is too." Elizabeth referenced the proprietor of the rental home that Cassie had reserved. "I've pulled a few files, but it's been so busy. The historical society is planning their annual heritage festival and the museum is finally putting the finishing touches on a book they've been writing for the past three years; which means they suddenly know exactly what kind of photos they want so I've been pulling all those for them." She took a deep breath and laughed. "Not that you needed to know any of that. The point is that I'll be caught up by the time you get here and since you know what you're doing, I figure together we'll unearth what we can."

"Perfect," Cassie said. "I appreciate everything."

"You'll probably end up helping *me*. I might be the hired archivist, but the gaggle of volunteers who help out here all have different ideas on how to organize this place. And since my husband and I are only here a few months out of the year, it seems most of the work I do is unraveled by the time I return."

"I understand. And I realize that just because someone lived in Eden and you have an archive doesn't mean I'm going to find the information I need."

Elizabeth gave an audible sigh. "You have *no i*dea how refreshing it is to talk to someone who understands that little fact."

Cassie smiled to herself. "I went to a preservation conference last year and they said that the National Archives Collections will never be more than five percent digitized."

"Because the amount of documentation and the manpower it would cost to keep up the collection can't even begin to even out," Elizabeth supplied.

"Exactly."

"I get it, this week alone I've had seven donations."

"Boxes?" Cassie asked.

"Boxes and boxes and boxes," Elizabeth confirmed. "Seven donations, and I now have twelve new boxes of photos and who knows what kind of documentation and paperwork."

"Unorganized?"

"Uh-huh."

"God that sounds like so much fun," Cassie admitted.

The kindred joy in Elizabeth's voice was tangible as she replied, "A fun headache."

"Okay, I don't want to keep you too long, sounds like we both need to get back to work. I can't wait to meet you and see what we can dig up."

"Travel safe and call me once you get into town; or if you need anything at all while you're on the road."

After the phone call with Elizabeth, Cassie left the office for lunch with Theresa Moss. One of the perks of the full-service package were three updates throughout the project. This was number one. And while Cassie usually conferenced her clients on the phone, Theresa asked for an in-person meeting. They'd agreed to meet for lunch.

Theresa entered the Mexican restaurant across from Cassie's office building with the stature of a model who was still waiting for her shot. With palazzo pants swinging around her thin hips, and a billowy white shirt that screamed less *Pirates of the Caribbean* and more early spring in Los Angeles, she paused and gave a slight twist of her stylish heeled boots.

With pursed red lips she studied her surroundings, slipping her large frame sunglasses atop her head. Seeing Cassie, she gave a half wave and made a beeline.

"I'm so sorry I'm late," she breathed out. "Have you found out anything more? Do I have ... family in Colorado? Was my father a polygamist?"

"Unfortunately, I haven't made any headway on the Colorado questions. As we discussed, the archives in Eden are understaffed and they don't have enough of their collection online. I've done preliminary work on your father's career in the military and found the birth records of your uncle, aunt and grandparents."

"All dead." Theresa sighed then waved a waiter over.

After they ordered, Theresa tented her manicured nails. "Miss Dodd, do you think it's strange that I am so intent on uncovering all my family's ... skeletons? No matter what we find?"

"Not at all," Cassie replied honestly. "A lot of people feel more complete after they've found a connection with their past."

"Yes. Complete." She pointed at Cassie as if she'd pinpointed the idea herself, then retracting her hand she continued, "That's part of it. But I have no family left. So I fear that now, in order to live my spinster life to the fullest, I must live in the past."

Cassie tilted her head, trying to come up with something helpful or encouraging to say. Her father's favorite phrase, 'it ain't over til it's over' came to mind, but she didn't think it was the kind of thing that would make Theresa Moss feel better.

She was saved from answering as the woman held up her hand. "It's simply an interesting prospect. To think that the father and mother I knew, might not have been the people I thought they were. I'm seeing this as an opportunity to maybe not be who *I* thought I was as well."

"That's a good attitude to have."

"It is, isn't it?" Theresa ran a hand through her hair. "So, what *can* you tell me?"

"I think the story really starts when your father and uncle joined the army. We know your father lied about his age, so he was seventeen in 1942 when he enlisted and his brother James was nineteen. They went through bootcamp together at Fort Bragg, North Carolina."

"Dad mentioned that in his book, that there were so many men who signed up so quickly that the military put them wherever they had room."

"Correct. Now, during the war years, basic training lasted about fourteen weeks."

Theresa gasped and pressed a hand to her chest. "They were just babies."

Cassie nodded emphatically; she'd told this story before—babies suddenly adult enough to go fight.

"I never read my father's book until he passed away. Have you read it?" Theresa didn't wait for an answer. "He kept a journal when he was over there. When he met my mother, in English classes at the university, he shared the journals with her. She was the one who encouraged him to write about his service. And I always thought there was an element of romance to what he wrote ..."

"It is very romanticized. I got the impression he sugarcoated some of his ordeals. Did you know, many veterans from the war weren't open to sharing their experiences? A lot of them wanted to forget it. There were only a handful of memoirs published from that time. And that's why your father's collection of personal interviews is so interesting. Even though the interviews happened much later, he was able to get stories from a generation that tried to forget."

Theresa's spine seemed to straighten with pride. "He was a quiet, stoic man. Not very forthcoming, unless you wanted to know about metaphors in turn-of-the-century literature."

Cassie laughed. "I came across several of your father's papers and articles he published. Pretty ... university-level stuff."

"In other words, English wasn't your favorite subject in school either." Theresa winked.

The waiter delivered their meals and as Theresa took her first bite, Cassie continued, "At the end of May 1942, your father and uncle were deployed with the 39th Infantry Regiment. It was a pretty well-known regiment."

Theresa shook her head. "You could tell me any number and military insignia, and I wouldn't know the difference. I don't have a head for those things."

Cassie gave a polite smile. "That's fine, thats why I have a job. The 39th Infantry were the first Americans to land in northern Africa on November eighth, 1942."

Theresa's face screwed up in confusion. "I thought he was in Germany."

"Not right away."

"But ... he never said anything in his book about Africa." She sighed. "Then again, he never said anything about Colorado either."

Cassie pasted an apologetic smile to her face; she'd just found a copy of William Moss' memoir and was halfway through, but in the first pages he wrote that he chose to only write about the end of the war, as they closed in on Germany and their forces finally fell.

"From November 1942 to February 1943, your father and uncle were part of the campaign to secure Tunisia, the northernmost country in Africa that's closest to Sicily." When Theresa shook her head, looking puzzled, Cassie continued her explanation. "To put it into context, whoever had control of Tunisia, could control the Mediterranean Sea. And no one wanted Hitler doing that."

Theresa gave a shake of her head, her eyes wide, as she dabbed at the corner of her mouth. "Do you just know these things?"

Cassie shrugged. "I've always loved history, the stories, the cause and effect. But if I'm being honest, I've researched many stories that take place during this time period, so I suppose at this point, I do just know these things."

"Fabulous." She waved for Cassie to continue.

"Okay, in July of 1942 your father's regiment participated in the allied invasion of Sicily."

"Sicily?" she breathed out with a frown.

Cassie pulled out a pen, took one of the extra napkins the server left, and did a rough drawing of Europe, Africa, and England, explaining, "Hitler and his allies had control of most countries in Europe, inland, when the United States entered the war. So, they couldn't head straight into the conflict, they had to fight back forces in the surrounding areas. It wasn't until 1944 that they made headway in defeating Germany."

"You should teach or something, I've never understood any of this stuff before now."

Cassie smiled, it wasn't the first time she'd been told that. "I like to make history accessible. We don't understand our relatives, or their actions and beliefs, unless we can put their lives against the background of what was happening in their world at the time. We can also understand books, movies and the culture of the day more when we better understand the landscape."

"How do you know where my father was during those years?"

"Thankfully, the United States military kept pretty pristine records."

"So did he stay in Italy?"

"No, he was shipped back to England and from there, his platoon crossed the channel, went through France, and in March of 1945, he was among the US forces that crossed the Rhine River and fought back the retreating Germans."

"I thought the war was over in 1944."

"The official surrender of Germany happened on May seventh, 1945."

"Wow."

"In October of 1945, your father and uncle's enlistment came to an end. They left Europe and the next record we have of them is the mining claim in Eden, Colorado, January 1946."

"And you have to go to Colorado to do the research there on everything," she verified.

"Yes."

Theresa sat back with a heavy sigh and shake of her head; whether or not it was from being impressed or overwhelmed at the idea of all the work, Cassie wasn't sure.

After a moment, Theresa announced, "I found something else." She pulled two books from her purse, but held them on her lap for a few moments, summoning the courage to show them to Cassie. Finally, she handed them over. One was her father's memoir, and the second was a green book with embossed letters, covered in a yellowed plastic that dulled the title: *Subsurface Geologic Methods.*

"These were the two books by my father's bedside when he died." She held them tenderly. After a few moments, she opened the geologic book and pulled out a note from the back. "I found this." She handed it over. "And I'm sorry I didn't give it to you with the original documentation. I didn't know what to make of it ..."

Cassie read the note and tried to control the emotions that wanted to flash across her face.

"Cassandra," Theresa said softly, "what happened in Colorado?"

"That's what I intend to find out."

Chapter Seven

Cassie and Stills stood by the open storage facility that butted up to the back of their assigned parking area.

"When we get a house, we can park the cars in the same spot where we store all this crap," Stills said.

"I'm sold on the house idea, you don't have to keep pointing out what's going to be handy about it."

"And we can make sure we have *space* for all our crap."

"Crap?"

"Amazing vacation accoutrement," he corrected.

Cassie grunted.

"I'm also willing to make sure we find a house with a deluxe chef's kitchen."

She laughed. "What's a deluxe chef's kitchen?"

"One with about five ovens and seven burners so that you can stay home and bake for me all day long."

"And will you be able to get out of the house after you eat all the food I'm supposed to supply?"

"Well ..."

"Let's focus on a normal house with a garage and space to store all this *crap*." She smiled, turning her attention to the list she was double-checking.

Understanding they would run a gamut of various climates as they drove from tepid Southern California to a chilly small town in Colorado in early March, she made sure to pack their winter camping gear.

She was muttering and making second check marks next to the items she'd already checked the night before. "Sleeping bags, tent, ground cover, sleeping pads, stove, propane, camping tote, laptops, phone chargers–"

"Dodd, we have everything."

"Cooler, clothes …"

Stills pried the list and pen away from her and mocked checking off his own items. "Sexy ass girlfriend, baked goods she made for me, a reminder to not tell her she's being just like her mother …"

Cassie elbowed him in the side.

"Oof." He put a giant check mark across the whole page. "Let's get on the road, Dodd."

"Okay, we're as ready as we'll ever be," she agreed.

With to-go coffees and pastries purchased from the nearby coffee shop, La Petite Café; weighted down with winter camping gear, ten days' worth of clothes, a cooler and a full downloaded list of music, they finally set out at six fifteen on a Monday. If Cassie had learned one thing about traveling, it was that off-days in the off-season meant fewer people on the road and at tourist attractions.

She gave an exaggerated, excited wiggle. Stills glanced at her with a raised eyebrow.

"I'm so excited. I'm excited you got the time off, I'm excited for you to see the Grand Canyon, I'm excited to see Colorado–"

"I just want to get to Mesa Verde," he said, his voice soft and sweet and velvety.

An electric current shot through each nerve ending in Cassie's body as the memory of the fantasy he told her of when they first started dating interrupted: *I want to take you camping in the Mesa Verde area and make love to you under the stars.*

She leaned across the center console and brushed a kiss on his cheek, then settled back. "I'm so excited."

The drive became an extension of discovering even more about each other. Beloved songs were turned up and sung along to while others brought about memories and stories.

When a particularly sexy R&B song came on the shuffled mix, Stills began to laugh.

"What?" Cassie asked.

"This was the song I got my ear pierced to."

"Excuse me?" Cassie sat up. "How have you never told me this story?"

"Summer between my sophomore and junior year of school," he began, "my best friend had his cousin visiting. His girl cousin. He was supposed to entertain her, but he had a girlfriend that summer and his mom said he couldn't go anywhere without his cousin, so he invited me most of the time. Which meant *I* was the one who ended up 'entertaining' his cousin, while he got to awkwardly make out with his girlfriend in the middle of the mall and darkened movie theaters. Meanwhile, his cousin and I did *not* get along; she thought I was boring and I thought she was stuck-up, which she was. So, I suppose out of boredom, and not liking each other, we just started daring one another to do stupid things. Steal a pen from that counter, stuff as many fries as you can in your mouth all at once. Eat that gum from under the table …"

"Ewww."

He laughed. "*I* dared *her* to do that."

"Eww," Cassie reiterated.

"So one night when we were in my friend's basement—he was basically dry humping his girlfriend while this song was playing—our game reached its pinnacle when she dared me to let her pierce my ear."

"Oh no."

"Yup. And we did it the old-fashioned way. Good old ice cube for numbing, cork held against the back of the lobe, and a needle sterilized with a lighter."

"You thought you were the shit after, huh?"

A half-grin pulled at the corner of his mouth. "I bit the inside of my cheek so I wouldn't even flinch in front of her and when it was done, she took out her own cubic zirconia stud and put it in my ear. And yeah, Dodd, I thought I was the shit."

Cassie reached up and traced a finger against his lobe where the tell-tale sign of the earring hole had been. "Did it get infected?"

"Nope. She was so impressed, she gave me a bottle of peroxide."

"That's a good story."

He winked in reply.

"I was seven when I got my ears pierced," Cassie began. "I begged my mom for weeks. She finally agreed and when the first earring was punched through, I was shocked at how much it hurt."

Stills glanced at Cassie and said, "But you didn't cry, did you?"

"Of course not. I was the one who'd made the big deal over getting it done. So, when Barbara Dodd hitched her purse on her shoulder and raised an eyebrow at me—Mom's typical challenge—I gritted my teeth, and refused to flinch when the second hole was done. And the next day, when I looked at myself in the mirror, I knew it was all worth it."

Stills' phone rang and they both glanced at the display on the center console; it was his brother Dan.

"Dammit," he sighed.

He and Cassie had a relationship that was stalwart and sexy and continually interrupted by family. It was a fact they joked about often, but this was the first time they'd been able to plan an extended vacation, *alone*. And Stills told his whole family that he didn't want any interruptions while Cassie had threatened hers within an inch of their lives. Yet here they were.

"Just get it." She didn't hide the laughter in her voice.

He answered with a frustrated "Yes?"

"Uncle Ben?" The ten-year-old voice of his niece softened the edges of his annoyance.

"There's my favorite girl!" he exclaimed.

"I need to talk to Aunt Cassie," she said excitedly.

Stills gave a dramatic roll of his eyes that involved his head as he muttered "I'm chopped liver," at the same time Cassie shifted toward the speaker and called, "Hey Olive! I'm right here!"

"I made a goal yesterday!" Her voice cracked on the announcement.

"What?! That's amazing. Tell me everything." Cassie's grin spread as she stared blindly out the window and listened to the welcomed soccer report.

"So I play in the front, but you know I'm a forward. My team had the ball, well, the other girl in the middle, Taylor, she had the ball. And she got closer to the goal and I was running next to her like I'm supposed to so I don't get offsides and then she passed the ball and I took a deep breath because no one was covering me and I took the extra step like you always say you can do if you look up and see you have time and I knew I had time and so I dribbled and then I knew, like, I just *knew* where to kick the ball and I did and scored. We won the game cuz of my goal!"

Cassie clapped and gave a "Woo hoo!"

"So," Olive took a deep breath, "I wanted to call you yesterday but we had a pizza party and then I had to do homework, but dad said I could call you this morning on the way to school."

"Oh, *thank you* for calling and telling me. I love it."

"Aunt Cassie, when are you gonna visit again? You can come to my next game."

"Well, Uncle Ben and I are on vacation but when we get back, I'll look at our schedules and talk to your mom."

"Just move to San Diego. That would be better," Olive offered.

In the background Cassie and Stills heard his brother Dan loudly agree, "Have babies and move here!"

"Oh, we just pulled up and I see Taylor," Olive said. "I gotta go." There was a fumble with the phone as it was passed to her father.

"I didn't want to interrupt your love fest," Dan oozed a fake apology, "but your niece was dying to tell you the good news."

"*She* can call us anytime," Stills offered. "You can't."

"Have you made it to Mesa Verde yet?" Dan asked, his voice laden with a cheeky sarcasm.

Stills glanced at Cassie and shook his head. "No, Grand Canyon first. Go away."

"Have fun you two," Dan sang, then hung up.

Cassie sat back. "I love that you're Uncle Ben, it's so ... seventies prime-time TV."

He grunted in reply with a purse of his lips.

Cassie mimicked the sound then said, "Well, I love being an aunt. And I love being the *favorite* aunt."

"How do you know you're the favorite?"

Cassie sat up, gesturing to herself with both hands as she half-incredulously, half-wholeheartedly asked, "Really?" She then sat back and with a nod, verified, "I'm the favorite."

There were no more interruptions as they continued their drive. Stills pulled over to the side of the road at a few historical sites that also happened to have stunning vistas. They lingered over brunch at a kitschy diner that was plastered with Route 66 signage, old wagon wheels and retro red booths with ripped laminate.

When they were only an hour away from the Grand Canyon, they gassed up and fortified themselves with Swedish Fish, peppered jerky and Cheetos.

"I don't remember any of this from the last time I was up this way," she said as she zoomed out on the GPS. "The roads, the landscape ..."

"You were younger then," Stills responded., "As you get older, your memory starts to go."

"Watch it, you're three years older than me."

"But you keep me young, Dodd."

She rolled her eyes and changed the subject. "We'll be there in time for the sunset. Actually, we'll have a few hours to explore first."

"And you said the campground is about five minutes from the visitors center?"

"Yeah. We have time, so we *could* set up the tent first," she offered.

"Nah, let's get wild Dodd, test our skills as a couple and campers by doing it in the dark."

"I thought that was the point of this trip, to do it in the dark. *A lot.*"

He growled low in his throat. "That is *exactly* the point of this trip."

She laughed as he rearranged himself in his seat and changed the subject. "How long does it take to hike from rim to rim?"

"As a round trip, it's forty-five miles with elevation change and heat and tourists. The trail, when you go up, takes a lot more time and energy. I know a few people who hike down and up in one day, stay on the north rim and then return the next day, from the north rim, down and back up to where they started. But that's fifteen-hours, two days in a row, and they were in great shape. If I was going to do it, I'd do four days."

"Then that's what we'll do when we come back and hike it."

She glanced at Stills, a soft smile on her lips, that feeling of disbelief and warmth filling her—she knew he meant it. He was a man of his word and the one thing they hadn't done was play games in this relationship. "That's what we'll do when we come back," she reiterated.

"Tell me about this project. This is the professor, right?"

"Yes." She angled herself toward him as she began filling him in, ending with the best part. "So now there's a treasure trove of oral histories from World War II veterans, a first wife, and secret years spent in Eden, Colorado."

Stills glanced at her as a grin spread across his face. "You know your eyes turn a brighter shade of blue and sparkle when you get excited about this kind of stuff?"

Cassie felt a familiar flutter against her ribs, and rubbing the area, she replied, "Your eyes get dark and narrowed when you get excited about me being excited."

"Because it makes me want to get into your pants." He reached out and rubbed his hand on her mid-thigh.

"You know, we haven't passed very many cars, we could pull off the road ..."

"We could. And I'm game, but have you also noticed that the only thing surrounding us for miles and miles, is unobstructed, open land?"

Cassie leaned over the seat, let her hand slowly float up his thigh as she whispered. "It's up to you, Benji. You're the one driving."

He slowed, pulled off the road as far as he could, slammed the car into park, and unbuckled her seat belt. She laughingly pressed the power button to lay her seat back as far as it would go with one hand, while the other helped her shimmy out of her pants.

The air in the car heated with need as Stills pulled his pants down around his knees and with laughter and heated kisses, maneuvered himself as they executed the most awkward rearranging of bodies and arms and legs so they could come together.

Stills kissed Cassie's neck and said, "If someone pulls up to see if we need help, we aren't getting out of this tangle very quickly."

"Then hurry." She turned her head so she could capture his lips, and together they enthusiastically and excitedly sought their release.

Stills had moved back into his seat and was finishing zipping his pants when the first car pulled behind them to see if they needed help. He rolled the window down, gave a thumbs up and a wave to indicate that everything was okay and the good Samaritan could move on.

Cassie was still laying down, wiggling and rearranging her clothes. "That was timed quite well, sir."

He started the car with a smile, and once Cassie clicked her seat belt back into place, pulled back onto the road and asked, "Now, where were we?"

Cassie stretched as she waited for the automatic seat to raise her once more into a seated position and answered, "Making me happy."

"Do I?"

"Seriously? You don't know how happy you make me?"

"I know how happy *you* make *me*," he said.

Cassie gave a shudder of the effects Stills continued to have on her, "you make me very happy, Benji."

"Good."

"Yeah, good."

"Okay," he slapped the steering wheel, "you interrupted the story you were telling me in order to use my body. You can continue now."

Cassie grunted. "But if I tell you, I'll get some magical twinkle in my eye and you'll have to pull over again and we'll never get to the Grand Canyon."

"I promise to behave myself for the next twenty minutes."

She gave another grunt, and he laughed before relaying the last bit of information he recalled. "You found mining claims and a secret family in Colorado."

"I'm not sure about the secret family, but found some interesting discrepancies."

Stills chuckled and when Cassie raised an eyebrow at his reaction, he explained, "I may or may not have found myself in a meeting or two in my life, describing the results of my research as interesting discrepancies."

"Are you saying you'd make a good genealogist?"

"Maybe I'm saying you'd make a good agent."

Cassie shook her head and continued to tell Stills her favorite part. "I had lunch with Theresa this week and she gave me a book she found on her father's nightstand. It's a copy of a book called *Subsurface Geologic Methods*."

"That's a mouthful."

"Isn't it? While she was flipping through the book, she found letters circled here and there. On random pages. And there was also a letter in the back of the book. Old, worn, and it had one sentence on it." Cassie's grin grew and she studied Stills' face. He didn't show any emotion other than an eyebrow raise.

She waited, allowing the excitement to build, waiting for him to ask what the letter said. Instead, he goaded, "You know you're dying to tell me."

"Maybe I won't." She sat back as if she could truly not tell him.

"Okay."

She waited almost a whole minute before she blew out a theatrical sigh.

"C'mon Dodd, tell me."

She sat forward excitedly. "Okay. It said: *He hid it. And now that I'm dying, you'll never find it.*"

"Ah, intrigue."

"So much intrigue!" Cassie sat back in her seat again.

"Did you figure out what the circled letters meant?"

"Kind of. When I wrote them all down in order, it spelled out Salerno Wall."

"Salerno Wall?"

"It's the name of something," she shrugged, "maybe a mine. But I'm not sure if you name mines or how that works. That's where the archivist in Eden comes in."

"What happens to a mining claim after a family member dies? Does it go to the next of kin?"

Cassie splayed her hands out. "Turns out mining claims are a whole thing. Everyone in Colorado's got one. But you have to be made out of some strong stuff to actually work the mines. And in Eden, the large operations are all closed down and only serve tourists now."

"Will we get to visit the mines?"

"I think we have to so I can really immerse myself in the history."

"That's quite the story," Stills remarked.

She gave her best game show imitation. "But wait, there's more. Elizabeth found a newspaper article that said James Moss was gunned down. Gunned down in the 1940s in an old mining town."

"Really?"

"She emailed me that she'd found his obituary and was putting the information with everything else she had for me, so I don't have all the facts on that yet."

"In my experience Dodd, people don't often get gunned down for no reason," Stills surmised.

"I know. There's a lot to unpack with this one. Secret wives, brothers killed in gunfights, secret messages in books, mining claims ... and because I'm pretty good at research, I get a working vacation with my boyfriend to figure it all out."

As if on cue, Cassie's phone rang; it was her mother. She held up the call screen to Stills.

"And a trip far away from our families who can still get in touch because of modern technology," he added.

"Why do they have to love us so much?"

Stills barked out an unexpected laugh as Cassie ignored the call, and instead texted that they were pulling into the Grand Canyon.

Chapter Eight

The flat desert of northern Arizona gave way to small bushes and scrub. With a slight elevation gain, the bushes turned to juniper trees, then Douglas firs, and finally towering ponderosa pines.

The trees on either side of the two-lane road secreted the final destination; the canyon wouldn't be visible until they were right up next to it.

Cassie pointed out the exit for the campground they'd reserved as they passed. Stills continued driving saying, "I think I want to see this big hole in the ground first, Dodd."

"I get it."

They followed the signs toward the 'Visitor Parking and Overlook.'

Open parking spaces abound and there was no need to crawl along in order to dodge other tourists. "I love how empty it is," Cassie muttered as Stills got a spot as close as he could to the edge and saw his first view.

"You said off-season was the way to go." His words were muttered, his body reacting to the scene in front of him. He was pressed back into his seat as he parked, his mouth opened to comment, but the words stuck. The canyon—wide, sprawling, unattainable in photographs—flaunted all her beauty before him.

Cassie's grin grew as she watched Stills take it all in. She was just as excited to see the Grand Canyon again as she was to share it with him.

"Cass ..." He was finally able to utter a word as he pointed, as if she hadn't seen it yet.

Vibrant red earth arched its way out of the ground. In the distance, striped mountains showing off their various stratus levels were an explosion of earth tones against a subtle blue sky, filled with rolling, billowy clouds.

Stills slowly climbed out, never taking his eyes from the visual feast before him. Cassie followed and stretched; there was a chill in the air, so she grabbed her sweater and Stills' lightweight jacket. She approached his side where he was standing between the car and the open door, one arm on top of the roof, his head shaking slowly in disbelief.

She stepped beside him, slid her arm around his waist as he let his hand drop to her shoulders, pulling her into his side as he finally uttered an impressed, "Damn."

"I knew you'd like it."

"Pictures don't do it justice."

"Nope."

He accepted his jacket, then closed the door and clicked the lock. They had time before the sunset, and Cassie knew if he was impressed by this view, he'd love what was to come.

"C'mon." She led the way to an asphalt path with large rocks on either side. Pinyon trees with twisting dark trunks held on to the edge of the canyon, and shorter bushes and junipers used the pinyons as cover from the elements.

When the path had taken them even closer to the very edge, she held her arms out wide and took a deep breath. It smelled of cold and dust, pine and earth. Some of the best memories of her youthful endeavors had been made here.

"It's remarkable," he said, still in wonder. "I've already said that, huh?"

"Yeah, but I get it," she agreed as she gestured to the path on their right, a silent invitation to continue walking.

Stills reached for Cassie's hand and they allowed themselves to become lost in thoughts about the minute lifespan of the human versus the wide expanse of Mother Nature. They slowly made their way to an area with a sign that designated a trail that would lead to the bottom of the canyon.

Cassie pointed. "This is the trail I took when I hiked it."

"You know I want to hike it more now than ever, right?"

Of course she knew once he saw it, he'd be inspired, just as inspired as she was to hike it once again, but that wouldn't be this trip. "It's challenging and I was in my early twenties when we hiked this."

"Yeah, now that you're an old woman, it might be difficult."

"Said the pot to the kettle," she muttered. "But c'mon, let's put a little distance on the trail. That way you can say you hiked in the Grand Canyon."

Stills readily agreed; of course, hiking down something was a breeze. The cool dry air, different from the slight humidity they woke to this morning, wafted around them. They twisted back and forth down a few switchbacks, stepping over tree logs that'd been half buried across the trail every hundred feet or so to deter rain water from eroding the path. And at one point they had to press back against the side of the cliff wall as a train of donkeys carrying up bundled riders passed.

"Oh yeah," Cassie said, "you can take a mule ride down. And when you're on your fourth day of hiking this thing and you're headed back up, legs tired, toes bruised, and you keep having to step to the side for the animals, and a rider jokes for you to hop on ... Let me tell you, Benji, there's nothing you can do but force a smile at the joke you've heard eight times and hope you don't actually kick them off because the offer is so damned tempting." She laughed.

They came to a wide outcropping with another unobstructed, perfect view of the canyon. While standing in awe, they arrived at a silent agreement that this was as far as they'd venture today, knowing they still had to retrace their journey.

A strong gust of wind brushed Cassie's hair around her face. She leaned into Stills as she tried to tame it with a free hand. He hauled her up against his side, as if this was going to be the photo they took together, or an invisible artist was standing nearby, ready to capture them in oils for the rest of time; and Stills wanted to make sure she was as close to him as possible.

He gave a grumbled laugh. "I know it took millions of years for the water to carve away at this, but I'm wondering how many people stand in these spots and wonder the same things, feeling so infinitely small in comparison to this."

"All of them?"

Stills gave a humph in reply.

"I mean, one or two probably don't really care." She attempted to tuck another free-flying hair behind her ear.

"Those are the people you need to look out for in this life," Stills warned.

"Noted. I refuse to be friendly with anyone who doesn't stand at the edge of the Grand Canyon and think it's spectacular."

They watched the final rays of bright orange sun release a burst of illumination, imbuing its energy into the red walled limestone, as if the final flare was what gave the stripes of red that ran the length of the canyon its power.

Begrudgingly, they made their way back to the top. Dust kicked up under them, and their exertion became staccato bouts of breath. Cassie grinned, wanting to wrap the whole experience: Stills, the canyon, the hike, the cool breeze, the smells— wrap all of it up so she could hold it in her hands.

Arriving at the top, Stills stopped and stretched with a loud, happy yawn. He pointed to the steakhouse with a view of the canyon a few hundred feet away and said, "Dodd, I don't know about you, but I'm hungry and that sounds good. Can I take you to dinner?" To sweeten the offer, he added, "I'm not done with this view."

"I suppose." She smiled.

"It won't ruin what we had scheduled for dinner tonight, will it?"

"Nah, it was just chicken fried rice."

He paused and glanced between the view and the steakhouse. "The really good chicken fried rice you make that I love?"

"You love everything I cook." She prodded him into action. "Let's go have a steak and keep our eyes on this view until there's no more light left."

The Pinyon Steakhouse was the first floor in a large three-story 'lodge.' Two, extra wide, floor-to-ceiling doors welcomed them into an oversized room with dark wooden beams crossing the ceiling's wide expanse. A full-length river rock lined fireplace had a veritable bonfire warming the room and a check-in desk stood against the back wall.

There were indigenous designs represented in earth toned frescos toward the top of the walls and a large elk horn chandelier hung in the center of the room. To the left of it all was a grand staircase that led to the second floor, the bannister made of rough-cut birch, smoothed and shining.

The concierge greeted them with a polite smile as they crossed the distance. "May I help you?"

"We're checking in," Stills said.

The comment whipped Cassie's attention to him. "What?"

"Benjamin Stills." He gave the concierge his name.

"Ah yes, here is your reservation. We have you in The Juniper. A superior cabin."

Cassie, mouth agape, eyes wide in disbelief, tried to catch Stills' attention.

He waited a few seconds, until he couldn't contain his smile and asked the concierge, "Will you excuse us for a moment?"

"Of course."

Stills took Cassie's hands in his as he backed away from the desk, pulling her with him. "Dodd, did you know they have separate cabins here? With rooms right on the rim? One of them even has a hot tub. And if the pictures are any good, said cabin might be the perfect place to watch the sunrise and not miss a moment."

"When did you ... what if I'd insisted on stopping to set up camp first?"

He shrugged. "I would have let you, just to keep the surprise."

Her eyes glistened. "What if ...? How? When did you do this?"

He laughed and brought her fingers to his lips, brushing a kiss across them. "I planned this two weeks ago when we finally set the dates for this trip."

"I don't mind camping," Cassie muttered.

"We're still going to camp, but I wanted the Grand Canyon to be special."

"Benji, just being together makes this special."

"I know," he said, "but this is our first real vacation together."

"We went to Italy together." She laughed, giving another disbelieving shake of her head.

"With your whole family. This is the first trip that's just the two of us. Not two days to go see my family in San Diego. Not two days for a quick overnight trip. Dodd," his eyes softened as he admitted, "I love all the firsts we get to have together. And this trip will have more firsts, so I thought why not have a first cabin stay on the edge of the Grand Canyon?"

"I suppose this *has* been a day of firsts." She beamed. "I mean, first trip to Arizona, first time pulling the car over to make love and first argument about what's better; Orangina or Fanta."

"Dodd," he looked down his nose, "Fanta is the definitive answer."

"Benji, Orangina is far superior." She grinned, repeating the line she'd used to defend her stance when they both reached for orange sparkling drinks, but not the same brand.

He slowly pulled her toward him. "First night at the Grand Canyon requires a candlelit dinner, hot tub, and romance." He studied her eyes and shook his head. "I don't know what's more breathtaking, that you're in my life or the view out there."

"Fine," her voice was still wobbly as she agreed, "take me to a fancy dinner and a fancy cabin."

His smile grew. "Dodd, we have to; it's protocol."

"Well then Benji, I suppose we'll have to follow protocol."

"Excellent." He returned to the counter to finish checking in.

Chapter Nine

"I was worried I wasn't dressed for this," Cassie whispered as the hostess led them to a table she claimed would be 'out of the way.'

They walked through the first front room where two tables had been pushed together for a large family reunion. As they passed, a young woman rocking a crying baby looked longingly at Cassie and Stills' entwined hands. The table was a raucous event, with kids crying, chasing each other and being hissed at to sit down, while straggling members at either end shifted their confused gazes back and forth in an attempt to catch any of the turbulent conversations whirling around them.

Next was a group of older women teetering as the handsome waiter inquired about their needs. When he left, they gushed and laughed, falling over each other and talking at the same time.

The hostess rounded a corner into the back of the restaurant, where voices and sound didn't carry. She gestured to the table next to a window and repeated with a knowing smile, "Out of the way."

Stills held Cassie's chair as the hostess set black leather placards with the evening's specials in front of their place settings.

Cassie put her elbows on the table and rested her chin atop her clasped hands as she reveled in the remarkable, unobstructed view of the canyon and the last light of day that slowly drew a blanket of darkness across the earth.

She glanced at Stills out of the corner of her eye, not realizing she would be so caught up in his reaction. Anyone giving Stills a passing glance would miss his stoic excitement, but Cassie knew the little things—a clench of his jaw, the pull of a smile at the corner of his mouth, the way his shoulders rested open instead of in a stressed rounded slump, and how his eyes scanned ever so slowly when he was impressed.

And he was impressed.

The world stopped, as it often did with him; as it often did in these moments, when her family and friends were happy and healthy, and *she* was happy.

A few years ago, when Jessica's life had been in danger, Cassie came away from those rough few months with an openness to adventure and taking life, especially the good times, as it was presented. And she'd tried since then to not take anything for granted.

"What are you thinking about?"

"You," she admitted.

"What about me?"

"How comfortable you are in your own skin. How self-assured you are. How cool it's been to see the Grand Canyon through your eyes."

The helpful waiter sidled up to them and gave recommendations for meals and wines.

Cassie agreed to the elk burger, reasoning, "I was inspired by the chandelier." Stills ordered the house special, a filet mignon served with a gorgonzola cream sauce, a vegetable medley and house garlic potatoes.

"And two glasses of the red wine you suggested." The comment was more of a question for Cassie; she nodded in agreement. When the waiter left, Stills said, "My grandfather is spinning in his urn."

"Because we're at the Grand Canyon?"

"No. About what I ordered. He was a mean old son of a bitch who thought slabs of meat should be served *only* with a bit of seasoning, and when we went to dinner with him, if our slab of meat was slathered in sauce, he'd snarl at the plate all night and continue to bemoan 'such a good cut of meat, wasted.'"

"You loved him," Cassie said with a tilt of her head.

"Loved him," he agreed. "Doesn't mean I have to agree with his take on food."

The wine glasses were delivered, and Stills smiled over the rim of his. "He would have liked you."

"For my cooking?"

"For your sassy argumentativeness."

"I'm not ..." She cleared her throat. "I *am* sassy."

Stills touched his glass to hers then sat back and let his attention be drawn by the nearly imperceptible last bit of light.

With full stomachs they walked the softly lit canyon rim trail back to the car and drove the slight distance to the other side of the lodge, where the cabins were located.

The cabins sat at stair-step angles to maximize the space and amount of privacy each had. The landscape of trees and tall bushes surrounding each unit helped magnify the isolation. At the end of the loop they drove, they arrived at The Juniper. The small log cabin of redwood was illuminated in soft yellow that glowed throughout the entirety of the property.

Cassie took the key Stills handed her and bounded up the front walk. She opened the door and shook her head in wonder; only one bedside lamp was on, but trios of flameless candles flickered around the room.

"Benji ..." She walked into the large studio room of white stucco walls and hand-hewn exposed beams, ran her hands along the cozy, sage green throw at the foot of the king size bed. Across from the bed was an off-white loveseat facing a fireplace, but most intriguing was the back door that had been left ajar, and the humming sound coming from beyond.

Cassie turned to find Stills leaning against the front doorjamb, his arms crossed, eyes hooded, a soft smile in place.

She jerked her head to the back door. "Wonder what's out there?"

He shrugged so she peeked to find the soft whirr was a hot tub, fenced in on three sides and open to the stars that had begun to appear by the hundreds as the land soaked up the darkness.

She went back into the room, mimicked his stance and dryly informed him, "Benji, there's a hot tub, a table with more candles and a chilled bottle of prosecco and a ton of stars out there."

"Oh really?"

"I didn't bring a bathing suit," she said matter-of-factly.

Stills closed the front door of the cabin, pulled the drapes on the front windows, then reached for the hem of his shirt, pulling it over his head as he started crossing the distance that separated them.

Cassie stood her ground, pressing her crossed arms against her chest excitedly in reaction to the muscles that had been revealed. The muscles that rippled with his action. The muscles she so desperately wanted to feel under her hands.

Stopping partway, he unzipped his jeans, leaving them open, but not removing anything else. Cassie licked her lips as she studied the trail of hair that dipped down in a vee into his jeans.

"Cassandra ...?" He said her name as both a question and expectation.

"Oh," she righted herself, "was there something over here you wanted?"

"Hell, yes." His voice was a deep rasp.

She tilted her head. "But I was admiring the show so much. Maybe when it's finished, we'll see what I can do for you." She bit her lower lip.

Stills stepped out of his shoes, then slipped his jeans and boxer briefs off in one motion. When he stood, his need for Cassie was hungrily apparent.

She swallowed hard. She *never* got tired of this sight.

Eyes riveted on him, she mindlessly reached for the hem of her shirt but Stills growled "No." It paused her action and her smile stretched across her face in the time it took him to finish crossing the room and sweep her up into his arms, attach his lips to hers and carry her to the bed.

"I thought you wanted me to take my clothes off," she said into his mouth in between kisses.

"I changed my mind, I want to do it."

She laughed as he deposited her on the bed and pulled her clothes from her body. The laughter gave way to hurried, charged wanting, shallow breathing and desperate caresses.

Cassie stretched her tired limbs that were simultaneously sore from the long car ride, vibrating from love making, and completely loose from the extended hot tub session under the stars.

She glanced over at Stills, sleeping on his back, the covers pulled up under his chin. His forehead was relaxed, the bridge of his nose—that sometimes gathered with the stresses he couldn't talk about—was smoothed, and his deep breathing was edging its way into a soft snore.

She was caught in a daydream studying his strong chin, olive complexion, and the short-trimmed beard darkening his cheeks. She pressed her lips together as well as her legs at the very recent memory of how that beard felt against the inside of her thighs: tantalizing, sensual, and hot as hell.

An excited shiver rushed through as she slipped out of bed. She quietly pulled on her discarded clothes, grabbed the large, extra blanket off the back of the sofa and crept out the back door to sit in one of the overstuffed wicker chairs on the porch next to the hot tub. She would wake Stills up shortly, but for now he needed the sleep.

Cuddled up in the blanket, she watched as the predawn light yawned, illuminating the backdrop.

She didn't know how long she watched the world awake. A long stretch of clouds subdued the orange yellow glow of the sun. As it rose the canyon first showed a beige palette. Cassie let her gaze do a slow scan of the horizon; the orange of the sun seemed to be slowly contagious, coating the tops of the cliffs red, the distant cloud coverage pink.

She needed to get Stills, he'd want to see this.

As if he knew, his whispered "good morning" from behind her was as soothing as the sun warming the early spring desert.

"Morning," she sighed as he brushed a kiss on her cheek.

He'd dressed in jeans and a soft blue T-shirt that hugged the muscles on his arms; she hated the sweatshirt he was pulling over his head, covering her favorite sight.

He positioned the other chair close to hers. "Why didn't you wake me to watch the sunrise with you?"

"You looked so peaceful and you don't get a lot of sleep as it is."

"Your fault."

"*Your* fault," she corrected. "I was actually just going to come get you."

When he was settled, she offered him some of the blanket, knowing the chill would linger with the cabin and surrounding area covered with trees.

She found his hand under the blanket and held it as the sunrise continued to impress them, painting the earth in various shades of reddish-brown, dreamy caramel and wheat cream.

Two squirrels suddenly screeched their chatter and ran between the chairs, almost getting caught in the blanket. Cassie lifted her legs straight into the air, grunting, "Damn rats." She looked both under and around her chair to make sure they were gone.

"Rats?"

"I'm not a squirrel fan," she admitted.

Even though the little rodents had moved on, Cassie didn't lower her legs; nor did she stop studying the dirt next to her chair.

"What's going on?" Stills asked.

"I don't know ... nothing," she replied, pulling her legs under her, but keeping her attention on the ground.

Stills extended his torso over her to see what she was looking at.

"It's the footprints ..." she pointed, "they stand out. Who has a snake on the bottom of their shoe?" She snorted a laugh. "Probably something the Italians would do," she answered herself.

He chuckled. "The Italians *would* do that. Probably someone who wanted to be a cowboy, so bought a nice pair of leather boots with a snake emblem on the bottom."

She turned her attention to her own footprints she'd made in the dust this morning. "This is the only sign we'll leave that shows we've been here."

"That's pretty profound for this early." He slipped his arm around Cassie's shoulders, readjusting the blanket around them.

"I'm having all sorts of fanciful thoughts on this trip. I love it. I keep thinking how so many people have been here ..." She let the canyon draw her attention back. "And sure, we all have pictures and souvenirs, but the only tangible proof are these footprints we leave, and even those won't stay."

Stills agreed with a sound in his throat, then added, "We could go farther and talk about how our prints, placed on top of those snake shoe prints, means we're all a complicated spiderweb touching each other's lives." He glanced down and looked for proof of their footprints covering others.

"You're right, we are getting into the deep end this morning."

Stills grunted uh-huh, *his* continued attention on the ground this time.

"What is it?"

"Nothing." He shook off the question. "Now where were we?"

"Grand Canyon," she smiled, "gorgeous sunrise after a gorgeous night."

"Ah yes, next to a gorgeous woman."

"Making widely philosophical theories out of footprints."

Chapter Ten

A sea of rolling clouds accompanied the complimentary breakfast, muting the red tones, heightening the green. A final goodbye from the vast canyon, as if it was making sure Stills and Cassie had viewed each dramatic colorful offering the landscape was capable of.

Cassie was holding the cooler halfway out the trunk, allowing the water from the melted ice to drain as Stills rearranged their bags, then helped to add more ice.

Cassie pulled on a sweater over her long sleeve shirt. "Can you toss my rain jacket into the backseat?"

He tossed both coats before closing the trunk. Cassie pulled him into her arms and pressed her face into his neck, mumbling into his familiar warm smell, "Thank you for this."

He kissed the top of her head until it was time to reluctantly bid farewell to the magic of the Grand Canyon.

"Four Corners, here we come," Cassie said as she slipped a headband on to tame her hair.

"Four Corners, four hours." Stills started the car.

If Cassie's skin had hummed that morning, the open road and the promise of the coming evening made her a veritable ball of light.

"Okay Dodd, time to come clean."

"About?"

"How many of your past boyfriends did you go hiking and camping with?"

"Not counting you?"

"Not counting me."

"One." She snuggled into the seat that was slowly heating up.

"What?"

"And he didn't take me camping, *I* took him."

Stills pulled out of the visitors parking area and onto the main road. "Story time, I believe," he said as he draped his arm around the back of her headrest.

"Not much of a story really. It was the wrong person, wrong time. I was prepared, but it began snowing. It wasn't really that cold, and our sleeping bags were rated for cold weather and had hoods, and I had insulated sleeping pads for us ... but he complained the *whole* time. About everything. From carrying a backpack, to the three-mile hike, and the snow and cold."

"Three miles?" Stills sounded disgusted that someone couldn't backpack three little miles.

"And for some reason, after we got back, he said he didn't feel he could give me what I needed in a relationship." She mocked the past memory.

He gave a humph. "I'm glad the asshole didn't have any staying power."

"Who said he was an asshole? I simply said he complained."

"Dodd, he was with you for two days, he was an asshole." An electric current ran up her spine at the offhand compliment.

"I must admit, Agent Stills, your personal camping technique is quite tremendous."

"Is it?"

"And your romance game is on point."

He winked at her, as a flash of memory captured them both: An opulent 'glamping' trip in the Joshua Tree National Forest, where Stills had a friend set up a massive ten-person tent for them, the inside decorated with a real bed and champagne. A catered dinner amidst twinkle lights had topped off the whole week. It had been the most sleepless, overexerted, romantic trip of Cassie's life.

With the Grand Canyon now running a close second.

The man could pull off romance. That was for sure.

"I ..." she cleared her throat, "you know how much I love everything you do for me, right?"

His hand slipped down from the back of her headrest and he brushed his knuckles along her cheek. "I do. And I hope you know how much joy I get from surprising you and treating you the way you deserve."

Unexpected tears formed, along with a tight knot in the back of her throat. She reached up and took his hand, giving it a squeeze, knowing it didn't hold the multitude of feelings and things she wanted to say, but hoping he would understand. She cleared her throat again. "Your turn Benji. How many camping trips with past girlfriends?"

"One."

"No, really?"

"Really." He began his tale, "I'd just gotten out of boot camp for the Marines. Something happens to you after those first few months when you're young and stupid and shown your limitations, as well as what you can excel at and what you can push through. I thought I was untouchable, but I was also homesick and needy."

"Didn't you go to Pendleton for boot camp? Near San Diego. Where you're from?"

"Well, it was the kind of homesickness where you realize you can never go back to who you were before."

"Ah."

"I went out to a bar and the first girl that smiled at me, I literally pounced. After a dinner date she said she wanted to do something special; I told her I knew exactly what to do." He shrugged, the one Cassie had come to know as his embarrassed shrug.

"Ooo, this is gonna be good."

"I thought we'd go camping. I'd spent the majority of my training in the hills surrounding Pendleton sleeping in my clothes on the ground, so what difference would it be to take a girl to the beach and sleep on the sand?"

"You probably weren't thinking much about sleep though, huh?"

"I was ill-prepared and presumptuous." He gave a soft snort of breath, thinking back on the awkward time. "I brought with us marshmallows, a bag of chips, a twelve pack of cheap beer and one sleeping bag."

"Presumptuous," Cassie repeated.

"I took her to an area of the beach that I thought would be private. We parked, then had to walk probably a mile to get to the actual sand and water. Once we did, I built a fire and laid out the sleeping bag, like a young idiot, and gestured to the whole scene as if it was the best thing she'd ever been presented with."

"It wasn't?" Cassie mocked her surprise.

"The cops pulled up ten minutes after I built the fire. I'd missed the area very close to us where we could have parked; you know, the one that said no overnight and no fires. The cops wrapped up the date pretty quickly."

Cassie shrugged. "That doesn't sound *so* bad ..."

Stills sighed. "The young woman forgot to inform me that her father was a San Diego police officer, and the cops who interrupted us knew her. So instead of a warning, we were escorted to the police station. Needless to say, we never saw each other again and I only went camping with friends after that."

"Look at us," Cassie gestured between them, "without interruptions and work, look at all the little nuanced things we find out about each other."

"Dodd," his lowered voice was serious, "you jinxed us. I swear I can feel your mom picking up her phone to call you right now."

An oasis of craggy mountains jutted brown, gold and red, reaching skyward, growing out of the sandy, beige desert floor. Early spring clouds—heavy, white, surreal—created shapes that twisted and puffed as they drifted across a shocking azure.

They turned off the main road and drove a slight distance to the Four Corners Monument. An open, four-sided building was topped with a red roof. Flags that represented the states and Tribal Nations of the area, fluttered in the wind.

They walked into the center of the monument accompanied by the hard flick of the flags snapping in the wind. In the center was a bronze disk embedded into the ground. Around that, four concrete pie sections bearing the name of the states on which land they were laying.

"Okay, Benji. Get your phone out and let's take the obligatory photo of us in four states at once."

"How do you want to do this?"

"Awkward Twister style," she said as she planted a foot in New Mexico and Arizona, then leaned forward to place one hand in Colorado, the other in Utah.

Cassie strained her neck as Stills backed up and fumbled with his phone several times, keeping her in the awkward position.

"Benji." She laughed and he finally took the photo. As they traded spaces he calmly said, "I think I would have rather had a photo of that fine ass."

She licked her lips and swallowed the immediate need built by the comment and muttered to her coworker, who was hundreds of miles away, "We're not rabbits."

Stills lay on his back, Vitruvian Man style, spreading his arms and legs to make sure a different limb was in each state.

Cassie attempted the same ruse with him, but instead he called out, "Dodd, I could stay here all day."

They lingered, reading the information about the Tribal Nations and the unique cultural elements of the sacred region. She pointed out the Trail of the Ancients Scenic Byway. "There is just so much to see and not enough time."

It was a sentiment that didn't require a response. Merely a squeeze of the hand; the reassurance that Stills felt the same.

They parted ways to use the facilities and when Cassie found him again, he was standing outside the monument, slowly scanning the area, methodically; the way he'd been taught to pay attention.

A spark of panic rose like bile in her throat. "Benji?" She called his name softly when she was close enough.

When he turned and smiled, the panic melted. He pointed to the ground where a snake indent from a shoe had been made in the sand. "We're following our leather-booted Italian friend."

Cassie glanced around and dramatically whispered, "Or, he's following us."

Stills matched her tone. "Probably."

"Because it couldn't be that we're stopping at the most iconic tourist stops along a very heavily tourist-traveled path ..."

"That's my assumption as well."

"And a print like that is going to stand out."

"Like a sore thumb." He nodded. "Is there anything else you want to do here?"

"Um, did you see the sign on that building?" She pointed to their left where a well-loved shed had been built as an entrance in front of a parked RV; simple black letters on the outside of the shed spelled out: Grandma's Frybread Shack.

"Oh, hell yes," he growled hungrily.

The hot puffed dough, filled with air pockets and dripping with honey, was a dream. Stills handed the first piece to Cassie, but she laughed and pushed it back. "You're dying to try it."

He took a bite and closed his eyes appreciatively.

A laugh came from the window as the kind, weathered face of the woman, who Cassie assumed must be 'Grandma' of Grandma's Frybread, handed over the next hot bread and said, "He must be fun to feed."

The idea had never been presented to Cassie that way, but she accepted the bread, then tilted her gaze on Stills as he took a giant bite, winking at her as he licked the sticky honey from his lips. She laughed. "He *is* fun to feed."

"You like to cook?" The older woman leaned out and crossed her turquoise jewelry laden arms on the small table built for cash transactions and holding plates of fry bread.

Cassie nodded. "I do. I love baking the most."

"This is wonderful," Stills said, taking the last bite. "I think I need to get another one."

Grandma laughed. "I knew it." She winked at Cassie. "You know the secret to baking?"

"I don't think so," she answered honestly; because had someone asked her before this moment, she would have said 'proper measurements.'

The woman pointed to her head then tapped her heart. "You just gotta be calm and put love into it. If you're mad and doing it wrong, it won't come out right."

Cassie stared, in awe of the woman in the simple RV setup, as her age carried her in a wobble to the stove, and watched the patience and calm in action.

Cassie would say she did *receive* those two things from baking; as she sometimes put in her worry and fears, but at some point, the process always transmuted those, turning them into calm and love.

"You two found each other later," the woman affirmed, handing over another order to Stills.

"We did." He appreciatively bit into the bread and gave another moan.

The woman laughed delightedly and gazed between them. "You are strong together. That's good. My husband and I, we're strong together."

"I think you're probably one of the most interesting women I've ever met." Cassie almost whispered the compliment.

The woman waved her hand. "No, no. I'm just Grandma."

Cassie glanced at Stills, her eyes screaming the million questions she had and the propriety and timing of them.

But before she could voice any, 'Grandma' eyed Stills and asked, "Where did he take you on the first date? A good restaurant I think."

Cassie smiled. "Yes. It was called Le Stelle: The Stars."

"Ahhh," she breathed and gave Stills an approving wink, then pointing at Cassie's earrings, said, "There are stars in your earrings, he gave you those too?"

Cassie rubbed the blue star sapphires. "For our one-year anniversary."

"Good." She tapped the table. "You found your symbol. The stars. They will keep you strong."

Cassie's eyes widened, but behind her a family had gathered. She felt the multitude of compliments and words she had stuck in her chest, but in the end, all she could think to do was lamely smile and give her a genuine, "Thank you so much. It was truly wonderful meeting you."

The woman's eyes crinkled around the edges as she nodded in reply.

Cassie twisted her head around, coming back to earth after a strange out-of-body experience.

Stars.

They *had* become their symbol. For the restaurant, the earrings, and when they were in Italy, Cassie had set up a private tour called Rome Under the Stars.

"I love her," she whispered as she dreamily took Stills' hand in hers and they made their way back to the car.

Chapter Eleven

"Y‍ou okay?" Stills' voice was barely a whisper, floating around her, over her.

They were returning to earth, dazed, luxuriating in the inability to catch their breath. Cassie shivered, but nodded that she was alright.

"You cold?" He turned so they were facing each other, connected at as many points of skin as possible; locked together, keeping the world firmly removed.

"No." She blew the word out with a grin as the earth gathered under her once more.

"Cass ..." There was concern in his voice.

"I love you," she let out shakily.

The momentary worry faded as he brushed back her hair, wild with that natural curl that fell against her cheeks, then returned the heartfelt emotion, "I love you too."

She clutched herself to Stills as another shudder erupted. Cassie wasn't hurt, she wasn't cold, she was alive and full. She was lost in the echoes of their lovemaking. Lost in the brush of his hand against her hip, the feel of his breath on her neck, the grunt of their mutual exertion.

She was fully and wholly lost in this moment with nothing more to do than appreciate that they were two souls adrift on a raft made of time; all the time in the world.

The tent had become a fortress against the cold and dark. A small LED flashlight slipped and fell in the corner, becoming an awkward beam of light angled across the opening, an extra bolt against reality.

"You promised me ..." Another arresting shiver, she laughed at the reaction. "You promised me *this night.*"

"You aren't disappointed?"

She shook her head and brushed a kiss on his warm, soft lips. Slowly, tenderly. She traced his hip with her fingertips, making lazy circles while his large hands splayed against her back, warming her.

She ended the kiss and tried to press herself closer, tucking her head against his chest, wrapping herself around him, but it still wasn't close enough.

His contented sigh echoed in his chest, and in a faint low tone he asked, "I take it you're impressed with Mesa Verde?"

"So damn impressed."

They'd arrived at Mesa Verde National Park in the early afternoon, greeted by gathering clouds and cooling weather. After setting up their campsite they drove around the park that encompassed an imposing 52,000 acres.

Cassie never expected to be captured in the unexpected embrace of reverence and awe as they explored. She shook her head endlessly, words and descriptions continually failing her.

The obvious comparison was to the Grand Canyon, mainly because they'd just come from there. From a distance you wouldn't know the green plateau mesa of land had been eroded in various areas by water over hundreds of thousands of years, creating natural valleys cut at various angles and designs. It was as if giant fingers had reached out of the sky and dug into earth, drawing wobbly canyons.

The smell of sage and pinyon pine filled the air; and archeological finds—which numbered in the thousands—were tempting attractions around each corner.

They pulled into the parking area for the Cliff Palace where restrooms and signs directed people to the start of the tour.

Not sure when they would actually arrive or what they would feel like seeing, Stills had purchased tickets for the last tour of the day.

They followed a paved path that wound toward the edge of a valley, surrounded by small twisting pine trees. After descending several steps, they came to an overlook with a sign asking tour groups to wait there for the ranger, who'd serve as their guide.

Cassie stepped into Stills' side. "Is this our tour group?" She excitedly whispered the rhetorical question of the three other people there, who smiled, patiently pacing and taking photos of their surroundings.

The ranger appeared and after filling the small group in on the park's history and the archaeological work still being carried out; he gestured with a wave for the group to follow him. They quietly started heading down a flight of metal stairs that had been built around rock walls.

He wordlessly allowed the group to wonder at their surroundings as they reached another man-made path and followed it along the canyon ridge; large red boulders on their left, gnarled trees with new vibrant green growth on their right. When they came to a ten-foot vertical ladder made of wood, Stills seemed ready for Cassie's beam of excitement, winking just before she began to scramble up.

Another few steps and Cliff Palace, the most famous dwelling of the Ancestral Puebloan, came into view.

"Benji ..." She breathed his name as if that alone would relay everything she was thinking and feeling.

Built in an alcove below the rim of the mesa, the dwelling was made of stacked sandstone bricks which created towers held together with mortar and wooden beams. The crumbling high walls and darkened windows dotting here and there, ignited the imagination. A true palace, the whole structure had 150 rooms and was reminiscent of something medieval; primal and inspiring.

Their guide pointed to the alcove overhang. "This is why we have these keenly preserved seven-hundred-year-old structures to study today, because they've been continuously kept out of the elements."

There was more information given, but Cassie missed it all. She was on beauty and information overload. When the ranger gave them time to ask questions or take photos, Cassie shook her head in wonder. "I didn't realize how expansive the park really is."

By the time she and Stills arrived back at the car, the sun was on a quick decline for the night.

"Is that all we can see today?" Cassie asked.

"We have all day tomorrow," Stills said as they headed back to camp, which was twenty miles from where they currently were.

Cassie was in a trance, finally feeling completely relaxed. As Stills pulled into the campground, headed to the backside of the last loop—a space they'd chosen for privacy and the view—they only passed two other claimed spots for the night. One campervan and a tent camper, far away from them.

Cassie made quick work of dinner as Stills made a fire. They sat on padded seats with adjustable backs, legs spread out in front of them. She set her empty plate beside her and took a long drink of air, tilting her head back in the darkness and frowning up at the gray, cloud-covered sky.

"You okay?"

"So okay." She took another deep breath and added, "I love this smell."

"Campfire?" Stills asked.

"Yes, no. These trees, the cold, the dust, and ..." she took an experimental breath trying to pinpoint the other smells, "sweet grass and you."

"I think that's the smell of coming snow."

"No. You think? It might be rain, but not snow."

"There will be snow in Eden," he acknowledged.

"On the ground, but if we have any weather it'll be rain. I kinda thought that here we'd have ..." She glanced up at the sky again. "Did you know the night sky is filled with four quadrants that cover the sky for six hours each?"

"I can't say I did." He looked up at the twisting figures of clouds.

"I wish there were stars out tonight."

Stills put his plate down, leaned over and brushed a kiss on her cheek, then moved to her ear so he could whisper, "Cassandra, I'll make it my sole mission in the next few hours to make you see stars."

"Jesus." She hissed out the word. "Then what the hell are we still doing out here?"

They laughed as they fumbled out of their seats, put the food in the car and contained the dirty dishes and rest of their supplies away from any midnight critters.

Stills shoveled dirt onto the fire to douse it as they scrambled into the tent.

And Agent Benjamin Stills did right by Cassandra Dodd; making sure the fantasy he promised, came to full and complete fruition.

Chapter Twelve

T hey slept in and woke with the sun. Once Stills had made the fire, Cassie dressed quickly against the cold morning then snuggled in front of the flames as the percolator and camp stove hurried to caffeinate them.

The sky was scattered with clouds, the sun attempting to break through here and there. After two cups of coffee and a generous amount of sunlight finally shining down to help warm them, Cassie pulled out a few ingredients and began making a breakfast of pancakes, sausage and eggs.

Stills offered to help, but his hands continually reached around her waist and up her shirt, while his mouth sought her neck. She laughingly slapped him away with the spatula she was using. "Do you want to eat or not?"

"I found *my* breakfast," he teased.

"Do you want it burnt or not?" She rephrased her question and turned in his arms, attaching her lips to his, then after a round of heated making out, pushed him away so she could get back to work. "Get some plates."

He set the plates, a roll of paper towels and their coffee cups on the picnic table and sat down close to the stove.

"Why Mesa Verde?" she asked as she flipped a pancake.

He tilted his head in question.

"I see why you would love it here, but when a person wants to share their favorite place with someone, there's usually a reason. So what is it about Mesa Verde?"

He stretched his legs out and crossed his feet at the ankles. "Didn't I ever tell you this?"

"Nope."

He raised an eyebrow, glancing around at the surrounding trees and bushes that secluded their campsite. A slow inhale accompanied his gaze as it continued to scan the horizon until it finally landed back on Cassie. "You know I was shot several years ago."

"I do."

Eight years ago he'd been shot in the left hip during one of his operations for work.

"I was angry afterwards and it affected my work and attitude and the relationship I was in at the time. It was strongly suggested I take some time off and see a therapist. I went to several sessions and then one day, I was suffocating, so I took off and started driving." He rubbed his hands together. "I went to Texas to see a friend from my military days, but he was a drunk and not what I needed. I thanked him for the hospitality after one night and didn't wait for him to convince me to stay. I went to get gas so I could get as far away as possible. I was in a hurry, agitated; I was in line to buy some drinks and food and gas but the woman in front of me was continuously having her credit card declined.

"I offered to pay for her gas and the things she was buying, not because I was being nice, but because I wanted to get the hell out of town." He gave a slight laugh. "The woman followed me to the car and thanked me over and over and I was getting really angry. I told her pretty firmly it was no big deal and that's when she put her hand on my arm to get my attention." He mindlessly rubbed his left hip and shifted his position. "Dodd, I hadn't actually looked at the woman, but when she put her hand on my arm, I frowned and was about to yell at her, but then when I saw her we just kind of ... looked at each other. And for the first time in a long time, a very long time ..." He cleared his throat. "Well, I felt seen. After a few minutes, she nodded and said 'Go to Mesa Verde. It will start healing everything.'" He shrugged. "And since I didn't have anywhere to go, I came straight here—fifteen hours."

Cassie realized this was indeed another link that would tighten their bond, another opening of his past pain.

"So I got here, went straight to the visitors center, with a chip on my shoulder mind you, and got a map of the park then did the only thing that seemed to make sense. I started hiking this place. All of it, as much as I could. My leg still hurt and I wasn't taking any medication for it; you know, I decided that wasn't the way to go. So I walked slowly. For a week I camped and walked through as much of this land as I could because a stranger at a gas station told me to come here."

Cassie brushed a tear away.

Stills winked. "I cried a bit too."

She watched him stare off into the distance as the smell of pancakes and sausage filled her nose and she knew, all of these smells and even the weight of the cooking utensil she held in her hand would sear the memories they were making into her mind; this would be how she remembered this place.

He continued, "This land Dodd, it's different from any other place I've ever been. It's living and breathing. And I know that might sound stupid, because it's land, and there are animals and trees so yeah it's alive, but it's more than that. Everywhere you go here is an untold story."

She turned off the burner and went to stand between his legs. "Benji, I am the one person who completely understands that."

"I know. That's why, when I first met you, I thought bringing you here would be the ultimate culmination of why a stranger in a gas station in Texas told me to go to Mesa Verde."

After a leisurely breakfast they filled a daypack with lunch, snacks, and water, then headed out to explore the vast park.

They dressed in long pants and donned windbreakers to walk the Petroglyph and Spruce Canyon loop. When registering their hike with the park service, Cassie picked up the suggested brochure while the ranger explained it was an interpretive trail with numbered markers, then mentioned points of interest worth seeing. Studying the map on the brochure they saw that each hike, each ruin, required hiking down first into various valleys.

On the petroglyph path, they walked over steps made by the forest service, turned sideways to move through slots carved out of large muted red boulders, all while the dusty trail wafted up.

Signs with arrows marked the trail as they edged their way along high canyon walls. They didn't pass another soul for the entirety of the steep, rocky loop. There were ruins in many of the alcoves they passed, not as well preserved, but the signs of history still provoked a feeling of awe.

"The brochure said this is the same trail that would have been used seven hundred years ago," Cassie said as she carefully maneuvered over a loose rocky section on the edge of the cliff of the canyon.

They rounded a curve and the trail thankfully widened to a larger space featuring a cliff face with a petroglyph panel that covered an area about thirty-five feet wide. There were human and animal figures, spirals and handprints—the statement of a people who declared 'I was here' in the language of their time.

"Wow." Cassie shook her head.

Stills stood next to her as she pulled out the brochure and pointed out the different markings. They sat off to the side of the trail, to have a snack and water as they studied the panel.

No words were needed, they simply listened to the wind and the rush of birds calling to each other.

"You can't be afraid of heights when you come here, huh?" Cassie asked as they started walking once more.

"I never asked if you were," Stills said. "I just assumed you weren't."

"I'm not. My dad is though."

"Ah," he scratched his beard, "that explains it."

"Explains what?"

"Why he was pale and sweating so much as we walked to the top of the Vatican dome."

"Yeah, he loves doing that stuff, but the heights get to him."

Still laughed. "Dodd, I was worried he might have a stroke."

When they reached the top, where the path deposited them back to the parking area, Cassie caught her breath and looked out over the canyon, at the red and white layers across the distance, the green topped mesa; at the whole wondrous spectacle.

They went to the archeological museum then the post office to mail postcards to their families. They drove to the western most part of the park, had lunch on a shaded picnic table and joined a sparsely filled tour of a ruin called the Long House, another cliff dwelling that rivaled the Cliff Palace they'd seen the day before.

The ranger who led the tour was a member of the Laguna Pueblo; she shared with the small group the history of the land and buildings. And before they walked into the Long House, she asked everyone to stop for a moment. "When we enter these dwellings, I like to ask permission. It is a sign of respect. We are not here to interrupt or defame our ancestors' memories. We are here out of reverence." She smiled and continued into the well-preserved sandstone brick buildings, saved from the elements by the cliff overhang and the fact that it took twelve miles of winding roads to get to this area of the park.

As they hiked and listened throughout the two-hour tour, what stood out the most for Cassie were the words of the kind ranger: "If you listen closely, here, on this land, the ancestors whisper their wisdom to you."

Maybe that was why a stranger in a gas station in Texas told Stills to come here.

Chapter Thirteen

They leisurely drove back toward camp, their bodies happily depleted from the exertion of the day. As the road curved past the Far View, where a hotel, restaurant, and visitor center were located; a sign for a gift shop and hot coffee made Cassie give an appreciative groan. "Can we stop? I'd love some coffee right now."

"Sounds good." Stills slowed and pulled into the parking area, asking, "So what do you think?"

"Of what? The park? Or the ruins? Or the stories?"

"All of it."

She sighed. "I knew it would be cool, but I don't think I really understood exactly how large the park was. And I definitely didn't expect that this would be a doorway into a new area of history I want to know more about."

He nodded in understanding.

"What's been ..." she trailed off and waved her words away.

"What?"

"I was going to ask what your favorite part has been; but if you asked me that question, I wouldn't know what to choose."

"Being here with you." He filled in the answer quickly.

"Sure. Take the easy way out," she joked as they climbed out of the car, both stretching their tired muscles.

The new green growth was a sea among the paved road, and as the name indicated, there was indeed a view as far as the eye could see atop the mesa.

"What's for dinner?" Stills asked as they walked to the store.

"I think sausage and tortellini soup," she said distractedly as she took in her surroundings.

"Really?"

"Really."

"I guess I wasn't expecting something that sounded that good."

Cassie laughed. "What *did* you expect?"

"I don't know ... something more campy or freeze-dried?"

"You're with me baby, and I can do some amazing things with camp food."

He slung his arm over her shoulder and stood taller. "I'm getting hungry."

"You're always hungry. Making up for all those months and days without home-cooked meals before you met me, huh?"

"That I am Dodd. That I am."

They meandered through the store. Cassie picked out a delicate vase made by a local artisan, a hoodie for herself, a book on the history of the area and postcards showing off Mesa Verde's starry night sky; silently fighting her frustration that she and Benji had not been able to see it the previous evening.

They bought coffees and cookies then sat next to the wall of windows that offered another unobstructed, staggering view.

"It's pretty amazing," Cassie said, unable to stop herself from pointing out the obvious.

"Are you tired?" Stills asked.

"Yes, but in a good way."

"Do you think you have one more stop in you before we head back to camp?"

"Sure, the question is do *you*? I'm not the one already thinking about dinner."

"I'll be fine. And where I want to show you, it's a little walk from a parking area, nothing too long or strenuous," he promised.

She popped the rest of her oatmeal raisin cookie in her mouth and mumbled, "Ready when you are."

They continued driving in the direction of the campground, but Stills pulled off at one of the several designated scenic overlooks. Once parked, he grabbed the daypack and a blanket.

Cassie tilted her head in question but all he offered her was one of his 'you'll see' smiles.

A dirt trail led from the parking area to the edge of the mesa then dipped down slightly. After another quarter of a mile, they came to an opening off the path that was flat. There was a picnic table and bench but Stills sidestepped both, opting to lay out the blanket in front of them instead.

The sky stretched so far that the horizon twisted; the distance between the end and where they sat became visually incomprehensible. The clouds created a ceiling of gray and white, allowing the slight blue to only peek between them. The sun was puffed up on the skyline, readying itself for the final descent of the day.

Stills set the daypack between his legs, reached into the bottom and pulled out two plastic champagne flutes and a small bottle of prosecco.

Cassie shook her head. "I don't even know how you're pulling this stuff off." She held the flutes he handed her and with the back of her hand touched the bottle; it was cool as if it had somehow been chilled. "Is that a Mary Poppins bag?"

"I have my ways." He poured into both cups then took his, holding it toward Cassie.

"To Mesa Verde?" she asked.

"To you," he replied.

Cassie touched her plastic flute to his. "To us," she corrected.

She arranged herself so she was lounged against his side, legs stretched out in front of her as she surveyed the wide expanse that extended down the cliff, continuing into a carpet of green and sage that twirled together with earth and sun-bleached rock.

In the distance, at the edge of the world, was the beginning of a mountain range, all of it still covered with snow.

"Dodd," Stills said softly, then amended, "Cassie."

She turned her smiling face toward him in question. He hesitated and then reached into his pocket. Cassie caught the quick glimmer as he held, between his thumb and forefinger, an offering.

A vintage floral ring. A white gold filigree band grew into a small round crown that held aloft a solitaire, soft pink stone.

Everything from the blood running through her veins to the sounds surrounding her froze as she stared in awe at the ring.

Time stood still.

The air ceased to matter to her lungs.

Tears marred her vision and light was trying to escape from her chest and explode radiance into the whole world.

"Cassandra Leigh Dodd ..." he began, his voice shaking, his hand slightly trembling.

Cassie hastily set her drink onto the dirt then reached out and cupped the side of his face, smiling into his eyes that were glistening with emotion. He licked his lips. "There was so much I wanted to say ... but now that I'm here ..." He took her left hand and slipped the ring onto her finger. "I love you."

Her voice cracked as she declared, "I love you too."

Holding the ring in place, Stills widened his eyes and softly, reverently asked, "Will you marry me?"

Cassie grinned and whispered his favorite phrasing, "Hell yeah." She joyously wound her arms around his neck and pulled him to her.

Everything she wanted to convey at that moment, she tried to express in that kiss. And as Stills pulled her onto his lap so he could be as close as possible, she realized he was doing the same.

Her laughter interrupted the kiss. "I'm sorry." Her face was afire from delight, burning her cheeks, inflating her heart. "I'm just so ..." She pulled her hand back and looked at the ring with a shake of her head. She pointed at the stone. "What is that?" she asked breathlessly.

"I didn't think you'd like a diamond, but when I saw this ring, with this stone ..." He held her hand and ran his thumb over it. "It's called morganite, and when I saw this ring, everything about it screamed it belonged to you."

"It's beautiful." Another delighted laugh escaped. "You're beautiful." She brushed a kiss against his lips. "Everything about this damn trip has been beautiful. I ..." She swallowed the urge to declare that she didn't deserve him, and instead looked into his eyes and told herself that she sure as hell deserved to be romanced and loved and cherished; just as much as he deserved the same.

"I'm going to marry you," she announced, and when another laugh escaped, she turned toward the land in front of her and loudly declared, "I'm gonna marry him!"

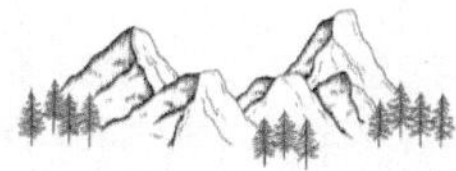

They watched the sunset and would have stayed longer if a park ranger hadn't been doing his nightly rounds to make sure visitors were abiding by the expressed park hours.

Cassie held up her hand so the ranger could see her ring and said, "We just got engaged."

His stern disposition softened. "Congratulations. I'll give you a few more minutes but then, if you don't mind heading out ..."

"Of course," Stills said.

They packed up and walked hand in hand back to the car. Although Cassie was convinced she was floating.

On the road back to the camping spot, Cassie continued to touch the ring with her thumb; it felt strange on her finger, and amazing, and promising.

"Just so you know Dodd, I'm not having a double wedding with Salvatore." Stills smiled in the darkened car.

"Good, cuz I'm not having a double wedding with my sister." Cassie wrinkled her nose at the very idea. "My life isn't some modern-day *Sense and Sensibility*."

"What?"

"Don't worry about it." She laughed off the comment and made a mental note to tell Jessica about the joke; she'd get a kick out of it. After leaning over and brushing a kiss on her fiancés cheek, she whispered, "By the way, *this* has been my favorite part of the trip."

Chapter Fourteen

T he next morning, when Stills went to take a shower at the nearby facilities provided for the campground, Cassie pulled her cell phone out of her pocket, excitedly scrambled into the tent and sleeping bag, then called Jessica. Her face was cracking with a wide smile and the need to share the news.

"Yellow." Jessica drew the word out.

"He proposed!" Cassie screamed.

"What?!" Jessica matched her enthusiasm.

Cassie held her hand up and studied the ring. "Last night, at sunset, in Mesa Verde, he had champagne and he proposed and the ring is a morganite stone and it's soft pink, kinda looks like rose quartz, and it's vintage looking and classy and has a history to it and I'm not getting married with you." She sucked in a deep breath after the long-winded announcement.

"Why didn't you call me last night?"

"Because we had to make dinner and I was so elated and he was all handsy–"

"Gross."

"And it was late and … I'm engaged!" she yelled again.

"I'm so excited. Send me a picture of the ring."

"Oh!" Cassie lowered her phone, positioned it for a close-up over the ring, took several photos and sent them to Jessica before she put the phone to her ear again. With a breathless grin in place, she waited to hear her sister's reaction.

There was a muffled sound on Jessica's end and then the scream of "Oh my God, it's so perfect and so you!" When Jessica got back on the phone her voice was thick with emotion and tears. "Cassie ..."

Cassie also welled up. "I know."

They laughed as they cried happy tears for each other. Jessica demanded Cassie tell the whole story again.

"This place is magical Jess, and it's felt that way from the beginning, but now, it's even more ... What's more than magical?"

"I have so many questions."

"Okay, but I need a favor."

"Don't tell Mom?" Jessica filled in the favor.

"Please," Cassie begged.

"Of course not. You think I have questions; she'll have a mountain of them."

"I don't want to ruin your wedding," Cassie said.

"How can you ruin my wedding? I'm already married."

Cassie let out a groan. "So convenient how you're married one day, but not the next."

"Isn't it?"

"Listen, when we get back to town, I'll tell Mom and Dad and my friends. But you had to be the first to know." She smiled and muttered, "Although you weren't technically the first."

"What?" Jessica gave the mocking offense.

"I told a park ranger last night."

Jessica snorted. "Okay ... I'll let that one slide."

"Jess, I'm so overwhelmed and full and tired and happy."

"Good! I love this, everything about this. I love it! And I won't tell Mom and Dad."

"Thanks."

"But I am going to tell Parker."

"As long as he doesn't tell anyone else."

"Who is he going to tell?"

"I don't know, Benji and Parker work at the same place and know the same people ... And what if he told his sister? The last thing I need is for him to inadvertently tell his sister, who'll tell her mother, who'll tell *our* mom."

"I'll swear him to secrecy as if this was one of his top secret operations."

"Perfect."

"Get off the phone, go be with your fiancé and have a great trip."

"Fiancé," Cassie repeated, the giddiness apparent in her voice, so Jessica said it again, "Fiancé."

"Okay, I'll go." But she didn't hang up.

Jessica laughed. "Go then. And call me the second you get back. I want to see that ring in person."

Chapter Fifteen

"I don't want to leave. We didn't have enough time," Cassie said as the signage thanking them for visiting Mesa Verde National Park winked goodbye.

"We'll be back."

"We'll be back," Cassie confirmed his assured declaration.

The high desert landscape of flat top mesas decorated with silvery sage and juniper, began to morph into grass-covered hills as trees grew once again into towering pines.

It was only a forty-minute drive to Highland, the last city before they headed into the mountains for Eden, but cell service was spotty. As they neared the city and the signal returned, Cassie's phone vibrated endlessly with messages. She checked and laughed at the fifteen GIFs Jessica sent of congratulations along with the information that she'd told Parker, who also sent his congratulations.

"You know, you and Parker are going to be brothers-in-law now," Cassie reminded Stills.

"It's the reason it's taken me so long to propose," he muttered.

"I told Jessica when you took your shower," she admitted.

"I know."

"How?"

"Dodd, I heard you scream that you were engaged all the way in the shower room."

Cassie blushed and scrolled through a message from her mom wishing her a good trip, from Tina wishing her a *very* good trip, and two email notifications from work. She tried to open them, but the signal wouldn't cooperate.

"When we stop in Highland I need to pull out my laptop for a minute and check these emails; they won't open."

"Lousy vacation signal," Stills mocked.

"Hey, I'm not complaining. But you know, I bet you've got some sort of CIA device that would boost the signal for me."

He gave a humph in reply.

Cassie turned her body toward him. "Is there really something like that? And do you have it on you? Can I use it?"

"Dodd ... I'm on vacation."

"So am I."

"I didn't check out any special equipment for this trip."

"You mean you could have? And you have to check it out? What's that process like?" She was intrigued by the parts of his job she wasn't privy to.

"I didn't think we'd have need for anything CIA-ish on this trip."

"Well ... that's not true."

He raised an eyebrow in question as Cassie gave a nonchalant shrug, then settled herself back in her seat and muttered, "I wouldn't have said no to a pair of handcuffs or something."

"Dodd," his smile was evident in his voice, "we don't use handcuffs anymore; it's all zip ties, and if you need to be tied up, I can buy those at any local hardware store."

An unexpected thrill ran through her and she had to swallow several times to push down the visions of being under Stills' complete and utter control.

"Well ... I'm sure the reason you can't bring your CIA 'go bag' with you is because you're with a civilian."

He shook his head and sighed. "What do you think it's like for me at work?"

"Insert the movie *Spy Games* here."

He laughed.

"Were you ever a Boy Scout?" She glanced up at the sudden thought.

He shook his head in answer.

"That's okay. I was a Girl Scout." She went back to holding her phone up at different angles, as if that would somehow boost the signal.

"How many years of selling cookies did you put in?"

It was her turn to grunt. "There's a lot more to the Girl Scouts than Thin Mints."

"Interesting." Stills drew out the word.

"Benji, the Girl Scout organization being made up of more than cookie selling is *not* comparable to the CIA being more than spy games."

"You're right, because it isn't spy games."

"Said the spy."

"Dodd."

"Stills."

"What you need to do is start drawing parallels of the work you do on a daily basis to the work I do," he offered. "We actually do a lot of the same things. We look at research and apply our best educated guess to the background in order to make sense of what information we have."

"Whatever." She held her phone up to him. "But seriously, you can't do something spy techy right now and help a girl out?"

"We've only got fifteen more minutes to town."

She sighed. "I wanted to get into your bags and see if there are any other surprises waiting."

He reached out and brushed his thumb against the ring. "You'll never find out."

"Benji, I don't think I can take too many more surprises."

Chapter Sixteen

Highland, Colorado was a happy marriage of two distinct styles: Southwest—represented in shops that sold leather, suede and desert-colored clothing; and the Old West—defined by wooden walkways, Victorian style buildings, and a saloon with tinny piano music vibrating into the streets.

Elizabeth had advised them to stop for groceries in Highland as it was the nearest town, and the grocery store in Eden was more expensive and had limited offerings.

But before stopping at a grocery store, they decided to explore the downtown district.

It was an easy decision to decide where they were going to stop as the main street of Highland boasted an excess of restaurants and pubs, coffee shops and art galleries, western wear stores, southwestern jewelry and touristy T-shirt stores.

They took their time wandering up and down the main thoroughfare that was alive with visitors and locals. Cassie laughed at a display and dragged Stills into a store where she bought T-shirts for his three nieces and two nephews that read 'My favorite aunt went to Colorado and all she bought me was this lousy T-shirt.'

"My aunt bought me a T-shirt like this on one of her trips when I was around the kids' ages, and I thought it was so funny," she reasoned. "Besides, I'm trying to solidify my place as 'favorite aunt,' so I gotta start somewhere."

"I think getting engaged is a good step."

She swung her attention to Stills, eyes wide. "I'm gonna be an aunt! For real."

"Yes, I made an honest aunt out of you."

"The T-shirts will be even better now. But you know what would really solidify my case?"

"Candy?" He smirked.

Cassie pointed at him. "Yes, candy."

As luck would have it, the next store in the lineup was the aptly named Rocky Mountain Chocolate Factory.

The large front window framed employees creating caramel apples.

"Here we go, chocolate to solidify my place."

"It would win me over," he admitted as he held the door open for her.

"I think any food would win you over."

She had tubes of rock candy tucked under one arm, crystalized sugar sticks clutched in her left hand, and she was handing over small cloth bags stamped 'Gold Mine Gum' to Stills.

He leaned down and whispered in her ear, "Dodd, I suddenly have an urge to lick chocolate off your entire body."

Without saying a word, she turned away from him, marched to the counter with her purchases and gestured to the large chocolate display, asking the clerk, "Which of these chocolates will melt the fastest?"

Cassie's grin grew when she heard the unexpected laugh from behind her. The young girl helping her glanced at the strange reaction of the man setting the bags of gum down, but answered Cassie's question.

"I'll take a dozen of those," Cassie said.

"Dark or milk chocolate?"

Cassie turned a smart-ass questioning look to Stills.

"Milk," he requested.

With purchases wrapped and bagged, they headed to the door. Cassie was drunk on both chocolate and the scene by the front door, where the work space had been angled in such a way that shoppers could watch whatever candy making process was happening. Today it was an employee dipping a large caramel apple into a vat of milk chocolate while the coworker across from him had a lineup of strawberries she was dipping in fresh, glossy chocolate.

Cassie opened the door, her attention on the chocolate as she mused, "Maybe we should have gotten the strawberries ..."

One second she had a hold of the door, the next, she was twisting her body out of muscle memory as she fell to the ground, having tripped over a man who'd chosen the spot right outside the door to stoop over and tie his shoes.

Stills did his own awkward stumbling trip and dropped the bags that had their purchases as he called out, "Dodd!"

Once he righted himself he knelt next to her prone body. She lay on her side, her purse and its contents sprawled next to her.

He gently began to run his hands over her to check for damages. Her hair covered her eyes and her shoulders were shaking. Stills' heart hammered in his chest, worried she was truly hurt until she rolled over onto her back, her hair slipping off her face to reveal that she was laughing.

"You okay?" Stills asked.

"I'm okay." She laughed.

The man she tripped over was kneeling on the other side, frantically apologizing. "I'm so sorry. I'm such an idiot, I don't know why I decided to tie my shoe right there. I could have moved."

Two employees from the chocolate shop joined the concerned group, offering water and ice. Stills accepted both.

Cassie took a deep breath and began at her head, checking her neck, shoulders, arms, hands, and legs for pulled or twisted muscles. Stills was doing the same visual assessment while the man continued his apology.

"I'm truly sorry." He began to sweep up the contents of her purse.

Cassie held out her hands to Stills who pulled her into a seated position. "It's okay," she said to the man. "I would have seen you if I wasn't transfixed by the chocolate."

She was ready to try to stand, so at her urging, Stills hoisted her up and she shook out each leg and moved her hips from side to side.

"You okay?" Stills asked again.

"Soccer for the win." She referred to her continual soccer playing that taught her how to do rolls when she tripped over opponents—a thing that had happened often in the years she'd been playing. She rolled the right shoulder that took the brunt of the fall.

Stills swallowed the initial onset of fear and turned to the man who was worriedly clutching her purse against his chest. "I'm sorry," he repeated.

"She's okay," Stills reassured.

"I'm just glad it was wood and not concrete," Cassie admitted.

The man shook his head. "I feel so awful ... Can I do anything?" He held out the purse to return it. "I feel like I should buy you a drink or a pound of chocolate?"

Cassie shook him off with a smile. "It was an accident."

Now that they were face to face, Cassie saw he was in his late sixties maybe; about five eight, same height as her; salt and pepper hair cut short; a nose that had been broken on more than one occasion; and brown eyes, circled with creases. He wore a button-down maroon, plaid shirt tucked into dark jeans.

"I'm Lou Macon. I'm in the insurance game." He took a card out of the front pocket of his shirt. "If there's anything I can do, or if your injuries end up being worse later, please let me know. And I promise, I'll make sure I take note of my surroundings before I tie my shoes next time."

Cassie laughed. "And I'll never let chocolate sidetrack me again."

With handshakes and apologies finished, the employees returned to work and the insurance man walked away, his shoulders slumped in embarrassment. Stills made Cassie sit down on a bench close by and squatted in front of her. "You sure you're okay?"

"I'm gonna have a bruise on my shoulder, but other than that, I'm fine," she promised.

He rubbed her knees. "Did you mean what you said?"

"That I'm okay?"

"No, that you're never going to let chocolate sidetrack you ever again ..." His voice lowered in register.

She felt the heat from his hands on her knees begin to throb its way up into her core. "Well, maybe I misspoke, I probably need to give those quick melting chocolates a chance."

His amber eyes sparkled. "Dodd, we probably need to get on the road and get checked in stat."

"Then what are we doing sitting here?"

The last leg of their journey would be seventy miles of twisting, turning road that would take them from rolling hills to climbing pine trees and snow-topped mountain ranges of 12,000 feet until finally, they would arrive into the small town of Eden.

The meadow land they passed was covered with the first blushes of spring. Yellows and purples were pastel sprinkles in the unkempt, bright green fields. Their vibrancy was illuminated by the almost blinding sun in the surreal blue sky.

As they gained elevation, the green was lost, turning into hillsides covered in white and brown aspen trees; their leaves tiny buds on the branches.

Twists and hairpin turns took them higher and higher in elevation. Aspen trees gave way to pine, and snowdrifts collected along the forest floor then built up walls on either side of the road.

After they reached the top of a pass they began their descent; around two wide corner turns, the scenery opened into a sea of dark green pines topped with snow shimmering in the bright sunlight, all of it backed by the eerie, billowy, dark gray clouds, quickly sailing across the blue.

"Oh man," Cassie sat forward in her seat, "I don't know where to look."

"Damn." Stills whispered his impression, slowed the car and pulled over into a cleared emergency area.

"What's going on?"

"We need a picture. No one is going to believe us when we tell them about this place."

Cassie's hands fumbled with the seat belt, then threw the door open at the same moment he did.

Phones in hand, they took deep drinks of the air and began to cough from the coolness. After clearing her throat several times, Cassie laughed. "I don't know if I've ever had such fresh air in my life."

Stills snaked his arm around her waist and pulled her close to his side. "Do you think we might be allergic to fresh air?"

"Why? Because we're from Southern California?"

"Maybe our lungs have been conditioned to need a hit of smog."

She took another deep breath, this one having gone better than the last, then shook her head. "No, I think we need to clear out the smog first. You know, before this new clean stuff can work properly."

He took her phone from her hand, turned the camera to selfie mode, and held it out as they both grinned, their heads touching as the vast, snow-covered detail behind them preened.

Chapter Seventeen

The last few miles of road into Eden was a harrowing switchback of asphalt that lacked a guardrail. Cassie's hand tightened on her seat belt as Stills shifted into a lower gear.

"Jesus…" she whispered as he gradually made the hairpin turn of a corner and met a semi coming toward them, causing Stills to hug as much of his side of the narrow road as he could. Which wasn't much.

Another twist and below them was a valley of flat land, wherein the center of the nature made bowl lay the ant-size town of Eden, Colorado.

Steep mountainsides rose up in each direction on the edge of the town to form massive, awe-inspiring peaks. The simple grid layout of the town was barely visible among the layers of snow that blanketed the streets and houses, but one thing was for certain, the town had expanded as far as it could in each flat direction. If they were going to build any more, it would be up onto the sides of the surrounding hills and mountains.

When Stills reached the level road, he gave an audible release of breath.

"Good job, Benji." Cassie patted his knee, letting her foot off the phantom break.

"Damn Dodd, that was something else."

They pulled off onto the only exit that would take them into Eden, the road aptly named Main Street. The snow had been cleared and plowed into random piles every so often along the street, but what was left was still travelable, having been packed down from all the other drivers over the season, still travelable.

They went slowly, and as one-story buildings became two they were transported back into the early nineteen hundreds.

"Have you ever seen anything like this?" She whispered the question out of a strange reverence for the history now engulfing them.

It was a motley collection of building styles and colors that helped define the very essence of the Old West. There were buildings constructed simply from brick and stone; some with a hint of decorative, gothic elements; others had colorful wooden storefronts—pastel purple, sunny yellow, faded red—with vertical facades and square tops. All of it made for a platter of overwhelming eye candy.

They came to a stop sign halfway down the street, slowly slid partway through the intersection, the brakes shuddering with the ice under the tires.

"Good thing no one else is out here," Stills said.

"Look at that." Cassie pointed to their right at a grand three-story, early Victorian building made from simple red brick, with elaborate detailing around the windows of the second floor, while the third-floor windows had steepled frames around each one and were enhanced by decorative, ornate trim. Across one of the large front windows facing the street on the first level was the name of the hotel painted in gold in a typical late eighteen hundreds typography: The Mining King Hotel.

To the left was a bank building, a two-story structure made from red brick with rough red sandstone trim.

Cassie was awestruck as she said. "Did you know that bank buildings were intentionally built to look stalwart and strong?" The question being rhetorical, she continued, "In the days of the Old West, they were built separate from other structures to look imposing, so people would have as much faith in the building as they did the safes inside that kept their money."

"I can't say I knew that," Stills responded.

He slowly gave the car gas and they crept down the street once again, their heads on bobbles as they glanced back and forth between the different sides of the street, as if they were watching two opposing tennis matches. A handful of people walked down each side of the street, exiting and entering the open stores.

"There." Cassie pointed to the right ahead of them, where a swinging sign jutted out from a dark maroon, three-story wooden Victorian building with the moniker, The Grand Rose B&B.

Elizabeth suggested that Cassie and Stills stay in a rental home while they were visiting; to really settle into the feel of the town and have the privacy a hotel or bed and breakfast wouldn't afford.

Turns out the proprietors of The Grand Rose B&B also handled the renting of five small homes for the owners who were seldom in town.

A bell chimed as they walked into the small entryway. Dark wood paneling covered the walls, while the ceiling was decorated with replicated tin tiles with diamonds and flowers pressed into the metal. The stairs were blanketed in maroon carpet and large paintings of Victorian roses hung on the walls. To the left was a small reception desk with a note on a bell that instructed visitors to 'Ring for service.' Cassie gave the bell a ring and from a room off the front hallway, a woman loudly called, "I'm on my way."

After a few moments, a matronly woman in a long flowing skirt, with weathered skin and a large smile, floated into the front room. "Well hello there! I'm Marsha. This is my place," she began. "And you must be the Dodds?"

Cassie grinned, sparing a quick glance up at Stills as she confirmed, "We are."

His only reaction was the upturn of his lips.

Hands shook in greeting, Marsha pulled out a spiral bound notebook from under the desk labeled "The Hideout," along with a rose keychain with two keys attached.

"Since you said you were here to do some research, I put you in The Hideout." She tapped the binder. "It's the closest property we have to the archive building. It's actually only two small blocks away, and you're on the edge of town, so you'll get a real feel for being out in the middle of nowhere. You two will have *plenty* of privacy."

"Thank you," Cassie said.

"You're gonna love it. It's the perfect retreat for two young people." She winked at them but didn't give them time to react as she grabbed a pen while pulling out a map of the town. She pointed. "Okay, you can't get lost in this town. The whole thing is on a grid system; north to south streets are numbered, east to west have names. You are here." She first circled The Grand Rose in red then a house labeled The Hideout. "That's your home away from home."

She slipped the map under the keys and glanced between Cassie and

Stills. "If you're interested, we're open for breakfast every morning from seven to eleven. My husband, Edwin, is the chef, and folks in town will tell you he's one of the best. Because you're staying in one of our properties, breakfast is free, but don't feel obliged." She pursed her lips in thought. "Let's see, what else? Oh, the town's not in the full swing of tourist season yet, so if there's a shop you're interested in looking at and they aren't open, you just let me know. I can contact the owner and get you in. And no one cares about letting you window shop. Don't feel like you're being an imposition."

She opened the binder to a section called 'Restaurants.' "We've got some great restaurants in town, most are open, but if you only have time to eat out once or twice, I would suggest going to The Western for at least one meal. Good food and great décor."

Cassie's smile widened at the whirlwind that was Marsha. The woman's personable air was addictive, though the only interactive option she left was for Stills and Cassie to nod their heads as she spoke and asked questions.

"There's more snow in the forecast," Marsha went on.

This time Cassie made sure to interrupt. "Really?"

"Happens that way. The news'll say we only have ten percent chance of rain and the next thing you know, we've got a snowstorm upon us."

Cassie glanced nervously at Stills and Marsha caught the look. "Don't you worry. The roads are well maintained and you have time for a storm to come and go."

Another round of nods.

"If we get a little dusting, there's a shed in the back of the house with cross-country skis and snowshoes. They're yours to use while you're here." She opened the binder to a section entitled 'Snow preparedness.' "This will answer any snow questions you have." She leaned her hip against the desk and tapped her lips with the pen as she thought, and then shrugged. "I think that's everything. I have you booked for five days, four nights and everything is paid for. So all I need from you is a signature ..."

After Cassie signed the paperwork, Marsha handed over the keys and map of the town then opened the notebook to a section called 'The damned fireplace.' "We started the pellet fireplace for you, it does a better job heating the house than the old heating system and you'll find instructions on that here. These buildings are old, mind you. We've done our best to update them, but the ghosts that haunt our little town keep us on our toes, so there's always tricks to making things work." She flipped to a page titled 'Suggestions for a great stay' and pointed to the second tip down. "If you want a full hot shower, don't run any other water at the same time."

After verifying Stills and Cassie understood her directions, she closed the binder and handed it over. "I'm sure you want to get on your way. Just know that I'm available night and day if you need anything, and you're never imposing. With the weather coming, you'll find that your cell signal and internet service aren't that reliable, but there's a landline in the house. Best to use that if you need to contact anyone in town. All the numbers you need are in the binder."

Marsha took a deep breath and blew it out. "Oh wee. I know it's a lot, but you look like capable kids, you'll get on just fine." She winked and shook her head in wonder. "Has anyone ever told you what a gorgeous couple you make?"

"Thank you." Cassie smiled.

"I'm sure I'll see you around, so I'll let you be on your way."

Stills offered his hand and thanked Marsha.

She walked them to the door and held it open for them. Once they were in the car, she gestured in the direction they were to go. Cassie gave a thumbs up and Marsha disappeared back into The Rose.

"So ..." Cassie said, gripping the notebook between her hands.

Stills put the car in drive and as they drove away, they both began to laugh.

"Did you get all that?" Stills asked.

"Benji, I feel like we were just given a mountain of information and now we're going to be tested on it and I'm not sure I understood *anything*."

He reached over and tapped the binder. "We've got the ever-important book, I'm sure we'll be fine."

They continued down Main Street, away from the direction they'd driven into town. Off Main, the rest of the town was made up of homes; a lot in the Victorian style, many of which had been refurbished and looked brand-new; a few run-down homes that might never be updated;

along with everything in between.

They turned and heading toward the end of the street, Cassie pointed to a two-story white home with blue trim, surrounded by pine and aspen trees—it did indeed look secluded from the neighbors.

Stills pulled to a stop in front of the house, a quaint looking half-house, more long than it was wide from the front. The snow had been shoveled off the walkway and the three steps that led up to the covered porch. Above the steps hung a yellow sign with black lettering denoting it was The Hideout.

Cassie fumbled with her seat belt once again before throwing the car door open and bounding up the steps with the keys and notebook in hand. She inserted the key into the brass Victorian plate above the faux glass doorknob on the simple mahogany door.

Nothing happened.

Stills caught up as she tried the other key; it didn't fit, so she switched keys and tried again; and again nothing happened.

As she looked for other possibilities on how to open the door, Stills took the book from her, flipped through the pages and began to read, 'How to open the front door.'

Cassie righted herself as he read the instructions. "Don't put the key all the way in the lock, leave it out a fraction and be gentle."

Cassie snorted and Stills muttered, "Dirty mind."

"You read it." She pointed to the book in defense. Stills continued reading and laughed. "What is it?" she asked.

He cleared his throat. "If you are too forceful with the key and lock, the spirits who guard this hideout will refuse to let you in. Best to introduce yourself as you try to open the door."

Cassie let go of the key in the door and went to look over Stills' arm at the book. He pointed to the section he was reading. "I'm not making this up."

She shook her head as she read but Stills elbowed her and instructed, "C'mon *Mrs.* Dodd, better introduce us."

"You know when I made the reservations I used my name. Marsha was the one making an assumption."

"I figured as much, and I don't mind ... the Dodds are good people."

"So you'll take my name when we get married?"

"I think we should both hyphenate, then you'd be a Dodd. Still." He winked at her but didn't hold back a chuckle as Cassie rolled her eyes.

She turned her attention back to the house and dramatically called, "Hello Hideout ghosts. I'm Cassie. This is Benji. We mean you no harm."

She began to gently work the key in the lock again. "I'm here to do research and Benji is finally taking a well-deserved vacation."

The door opened and she glanced over her shoulder, surprised.

"We've been accepted," he said. "Probably should be honest about the rest of our trip."

"What do you mean?"

He leaned into the door and called out, "We're going to be having a lot of sex too. I kinda can't keep my hands off this woman and we just got engaged, so we'll be respectful but maybe you could pause all hauntings and suspicious activity when we're busy, okay?"

"A lot of sex?" she asked as they stepped into the house.

He pulled Cassie against him, his eyes gone smoky, the tell-tale sign he wanted her.

She dropped the book on the ground as he pushed the door closed. Neither of them gave much notice of the layout of the house as they raced upstairs, and with labored, excited breathing, lost layers of clothes along the way until they found the bedroom. By the time they reached the bed they were hot and naked so Stills picked Cassie up and pressed his lips to hers as she wrapped her legs around his waist; then once guiding them onto the bed, he pressed himself inside her the moment he had leverage.

Chapter Eighteen

"We need to get the groceries out of the car." Cassie stretched her naked limbs and yawned. "God, you make me feel good."

"It isn't hard, you *do* feel good." Stills' velvet voice drifted over her skin as he brushed his hand against her exposed stomach.

She turned toward him as her cell phone began to ring and his stomach growled. She raised an eyebrow.

Stills laughed. "You answer that, I'll bring everything in so we can have something to eat."

Cassie retraced her steps and found her phone in the pocket of her discarded jeans outside the bedroom door. It was Elizabeth.

"Hello!" Cassie answered, genuinely happy to hear from the woman. She grabbed a blanket laying on the back of the overstuffed chair in the corner, wrapped it around herself and sat down.

"So, you've arrived," Elizabeth announced. "And before you ask how I knew that, let me say that this is a small town, where news travels at the speed of light."

Cassie smiled. "I'm charmed, I have to admit. Just driving in on the main street, meeting Marsha and having seen this house ..."

"I completely understand. It was that way for me the first time I came here. Cassie, I didn't mean to bother you as soon as you arrived, but talking to you, I have a feeling we're kindred spirits, so I'm just excited."

"It's no problem at all. We're going to unpack the car, get organized a bit and then do a little exploring before the sun sets."

"Sounds good, and if you're up for it, my husband Aidan and I were wondering if you wanted to join us for a drink after dinner. After you get settled?"

Stills was walking through the bedroom door, with a suitcase in each hand, and one of the cookies she'd made for the trip in his mouth. Cassie hit the mute button on her phone. "Feel like going out for a drink tonight with Elizabeth and her husband?"

"Sure," he muttered around the cookie.

She unmuted. "That would be wonderful. When and where?"

"How about eight? At the Silver Creek Hollow? It's behind the fire department on Main Street, easy to find."

"Sounds great, we'll see you then."

They said their goodbyes and Cassie smiled up at Stills. "Do you need help?"

"I've almost got everything."

"Want to have a snack and then go explore this town?" she asked.

"What kind of snack?"

She held the blanket around her as she stood and crossed the room to him. Still smiling, Cassie looked up at him and stretched up on her tiptoes to brush a kiss across his lips. "A snack." She grinned. "Then maybe we'll go out to dinner tonight?"

"As long as I can have my dessert here. Or did you forget the chocolate we bought?"

She wiggled her eyebrows at him and opened her suitcase to find some clothes. "C'mon, let's go introduce ourselves properly to the ghosts."

The Hideout was a narrow, long, rectangular house with a front door at one end and the back door at the other. Over the years, upgrades and improvements had been made so that the first floor, which was once divided by walls, was now an open space. It consisted of a galley style kitchen with a bar separating it from the small dining area, and a large great room. The open concept made it easier for the fireplace to heat the whole space.

The stairs hugged the right side of the great room, which was complete with sofa, two stuffed chairs, a coffee table, and a bay window. Patterned

Roman shades were pulled up, allowing a perfectly framed view of the jagged, snow-covered mountains triumphantly reaching into the sky.

They put the groceries away, and their few knickknacks they'd purchased at the Grand Canyon, Mesa Verde, Highland, and gas stations in between on the coffee table.

Stills retraced their steps and put all the discarded clothing in the room, then grabbed two cream sodas and sat at the table while Cassie worked on putting together simple charcuterie to share.

He pulled the binder toward him and began to read:

"The Hideout was originally built in 1883 by Albert Finnes. He came to Colorado for the mining but soon turned his attentions to building and running the local grocery, seeing that there was more money in such an endeavor. He built this very house in 1884 as a wedding present for his bride. Unfortunately, soon after they were married and moved in, they met a horrific end when the grocery caught fire one August evening. Albert and his wife were trapped inside. Town folks came to help fight the flames, but there was no way to help the couple escape."

"Oh no." Cassie gave an audible gasp.

"With no children to inherit, the house passed to Albert's youngest brother, Charles. While Albert was known as a kind man, Charlie Finnes was known for his wild ways and shady character. He came west, not to seek his treasure in the mining of gold, but for the gambling. Charlie became a business owner like his brother, only instead of a lawful pursuit, he opened the Gold Dust Saloon. One of twenty-five saloons in Eden at the time."

A broad grin spread across Cassie's face. "Who wrote this?"

Stills continued reading, "With business booming, Charlie built a small apartment for himself off the back of the saloon so he could be closer to his work."

"Closer to his work?" Cassie mused as she put the plate on the table and sat next to Stills. "The whole town is close."

"What's this one?" he asked of the first slice of cheese he popped into his mouth.

"Smoked gouda," she said then pointed to the rest of the platter, "aged cheddar, Italian spiced crackers, Genoa salami, dried apricots and smoked almonds."

He picked up a cracker and studied it. "You know you make the little ordinary things amazing, right?"

She shrugged. "I try."

He winked and ate the cracker. "Did we buy these in Highland?"

"I made them."

He raised an eyebrow. "Seriously?"

"Are you really surprised?"

"No, just ... I didn't get to see all the things you made and packed at home."

"So we both have our little packing secrets." She wiggled her ring finger toward him.

"I suppose we do."

"And when it comes to me baking, it goes better if I hide it from you; otherwise you'll eat it all in one go." Cassie pulled the binder toward her, found where he'd left off, and continued, "Legend says Charlie often offered this house to various outlaws running from the law. That was how it got the nickname, 'The Hideout.'" Cassie glanced around the room, noticing the color palette had changed since it was originally built. But in keeping with the Victorian theme, the furniture and details were done in maroons and dark blue with a hint of gold. Yet the white walls added an element of brightness. "Charlie's life came to a tragic end when he was involved in a shootout against the infamous Alfred Dale."

"Do you know who that is?"

"Never heard of him." She read on, "When they found Charlie's last will and testament, it began this way: 'This here will is in case my life choices bury me.' It would seem his choices did indeed bury him. The will stated that the Gold Dust Saloon and the house now known as The Hideout, would be inherited by the manager of the Gold Dust, a woman of questionable morals known as Diamond Belle." Cassie wiggled her eyebrows as she glanced at Stills. "I *love* this town."

"A woman of questionable morals ..." he repeated as he paired salami with gouda.

"Diamond Belle ran a successful business for several years before selling her establishment to the railroad. She took her money to San Francisco but left the house to a nephew, Jeffery Wright, who moved to town in 1906 with his wife and child to try his hand at mining. The

Wright family and descendants have owned the home ever since. They are in a contract with The Grand Rose B&B for tourist purposes."

Cassie sat back and looked around the house. "So, whose ghosts do you suppose are here?"

"Albert and his wife, and his brother ..."

"And whatever outlaws were brought here with gunshot wounds that didn't live," Cassie supplied eagerly.

Stills pursed his lips in thought. "I'd say this little house is pretty crowded then."

A sudden loud click sounded— Cassie and Stills froze. The noise repeated, and Cassie had the unnerving feeling she was about to meet a ghost. Thankfully, a whoosh of air accompanied the sound.

"Heater," Stills suggested and pulled the book toward him, flipping to the section about the pellet stove he remembered as 'The damned heater.' After reading a few moments, he verified, "Heater." He took the binder across the room to the freestanding black heating unit. The square glass door shone with a low red glow. He opened a decorative bin behind the unit, then lifted the lid off the top of the heater and began using the small cup provided to add pellets to the stove.

"Where do you want to go to dinner tonight?" he asked.

"I figure we'll stick with what the locals recommend and go to The Western."

"The Western it is."

"Then it's to the Silver Creek Hollow for drinks with the Pines."

"Did I know their last name?"

"I don't think I really ever mentioned it, I keep calling Elizabeth 'the archivist.'"

"I bet she calls you 'the genealogist,'" he said and flipped the page in the binder. Opening the side panel of the stove, he read, "For the best efficiency and to prevent cycling, the convection blower should be left on at all times ..." He pressed a button until a soft whirring sound began. Stills nodded then continued reading aloud. "And for the houseguests to have the best stay, the man should probably take the woman upstairs once again and have his way with her because they are alone and have time and he wants her desperately."

"That book has all sorts of tips, doesn't it?" Cassie called from where

she was sitting at the table.
    Stills held it aloft. "I really enjoy this binder."

Chapter Nineteen

T he only thing they explored before the sun set was the bedroom once more. And once more Tina's laughing comparision to rabbits drifted by. But so what, Cassie thought; maybe they were, but they were also just stupid in love.

They enjoyed each other's company and she was thirtysomething years old and they didn't play games and Stills didn't suffer fools and she'd found someone who saw life as the adventure it was and who allowed her to be herself without restraints; and she hoped she did the same for him.

And she found him sexy as hell and had waited for a man to make her feel attractive *and* attracted for so long … so why the hell did she care that it seemed almost ridiculous that they couldn't keep their hands off each other? And it wasn't like they normally had the time to scratch all the damn itches they wanted.

"We need to stay in shape," Cassie said as they got dressed to go out.

"Okay."

"If we're going to be doing this much hiking and exploration of the world, then tossing sex on top of the equation, we need to make sure we stay in shape."

"Agreed."

Before they left, they consulted the map and found The Western, above which was the description: 'A family-friendly old west saloon with good food and good people.'

"Old west, family-friendly, here we come." Cassie pulled on a pair of blue knit gloves and matching beanie. "Benji, I'm bundling up."

Stills finished zipping up his jacket, held the door for Cassie, but before closing it, called behind him, "No parties while we're gone."

"The ghosts?"

He shrugged. "You never know."

The overcast day had given way to a cold evening and the sweet humid smell in the air meant there was a definite possibility of moisture. And with such low temperatures, it would be snow. Cassie hadn't expected snow, but the probability brought a new level of elation. A new vision of being cuddled up on the sofa, soft jazz playing in the background, a fire, the snow falling out the front window was almost palpable.

The packed snow crunched beneath their feet and Cassie linked her arm with Stills. As they turned onto Main Street, a view brought muttered appreciation from them both.

Old street lamps illuminated the buildings. Spotlights were aimed at various hanging wooden signs that blew slowly in front of stores. A few coffee shops, restaurants and bars had neon signs blinking in windows.

It was as if the whole street put on airs for a night out on the town.

"Have you ever been anywhere like this?" Cassie asked.

"My dad took the whole family to Calico. It was an old mining town, but no one lives there so really it's a ghost town," he offered.

"Is that the one on the way to Vegas?"

"Yeah, have you been?"

"No. The only 'old west town' I ever went to was the Ponderosa movie set in Lake Tahoe ..." Cassie couldn't figure out what to focus on; for such a small town there seemed to be an ample supply of storefronts, signage, and historical markers. "I really do feel like I've stepped back in time."

"But your work is with the past; don't you feel like that every day?"

"Kind of, but none of it has ever been *this* tangible." She stepped toward the nearest bulding and touched it.

They arrived at the restaurant. Above the glass double doors hung a large wooden shingle with The Western burned into it along with two theatrical bullet holes.

They entered and were met with a large, dimly lit, room. The high ceilings had the typical decorative pressed tin most Victorian mining architecture of the time had. A dusty, taxidermy black bear and cougar stood on either side of the entrance; both wore cowboy hats as twangy country music echoed a greeting from hidden speakers.

The dining area was larger than Cassie expected. "Do you think they really get this many people visiting?"

"Well, the binder said Eden gets roughly three thousand visitors a day."

"We should have brought the binder."

A woman wearing a black T-shirt with 'The Western' logo on the pocket greeted them, "Evenin' folks. Two tonight?"

"Please," Stills responded.

They were led through the throng of worn tables while Cassie's attention fell on the long, dark wooden bar that sat at least fifteen.

Old west paraphernalia was nailed to each available surface. And on shelves hanging over the heads of the diners rested old Colorado license plates, warped leather boots, tires, and a stuffed goat, sheep and cougar.

"Here you go." The waitress handed over the menus after they settled themselves. "Can I get you anything to drink?"

Stills looked over at the bar. "Do you have any local breweries on tap?"

The waitress gave a snort of laughter. "That's pretty much *all* we have on tap. As well as Pabst and Coors."

"Do you have a pale ale?" Cassie asked.

"We do, it's a nice one. Place in Telluride brews it."

"Sold," she said, affirmatively.

"I'll take the darkest you have on tap," Stills requested.

The waitress slapped the table and left.

Cassie opened the menu and grinned. "Oh, his menu is amazing. We've got World Famous Wrangled Steak, Wild West Black Beans, Creek Caught Trout and Buckaroo Burgers."

The waitress returned with their drinks. "Any questions about the menu?"

"An odd one;" Cassie said, "there seems to be a lot of green chilies on most of the food ...?"

The waitress laughed as she settled into her right hip. "Welp, that's one way I know you folks aren't from around here." She winked. "You'll find a lot of the food from the southwest here, and New Mexico has fired hatch green chilies. We add em to *everything*."

"Well, when in Rome ..." Cassie closed her menu. "I think I'll have the Buckin' Pork Ribs."

"Trout for me," Stills ordered.

"You bet." The waitress gave another tap on the table then left. Cassie picked up her glass, but before she took a sip, she held it out to Stills, and he tapped his against hers. Then both of their cell phones began to ring.

Stills held Cassie's gaze, raising his eyebrow in question; what did they want to do?

"Ignore," she instructed. They pulled out their phones to silence them but Cassie saw that it was Jessica calling her as Stills commented, "It's Salvatore."

Cassie's finger hovered, but then she hit 'Ignore' with great decisiveness.

"You're interrupting our vacation," Stills answered.

"What are you doing?" Cassie hissed.

He shrugged as he listened, then repeated to Cassie, "Oh, you wanted to give us a heads up that Jessica is going to be calling Cassie to ask if Carlo can stay with us during the week of the wedding because he broke up with Alessandra several months ago and now there's tension …"

Cassie's eyes widened. "What happened? When did they break up?"

Her phone rang again, but this time she answered. "When did they break up? What happened? Is it going to make the wedding weird? Is it going to be weird if Benji and I are engaged now? And of course he can stay with us."

Stills hung up and sat back sipping his beer as he watched Cassie demand answers from her younger sister and plot how to fix the problem. After a few quiet moments, Cassie was filled in and she offered, "Of course they won't make things weird, they're too polite. But if anyone was made for anyone it was those two. That means your wedding is going to be the perfect place to make sure there are plenty of reasons they have to stand next to each other in pictures and sit next to each other at the reception …"

"Dodd," Stills called.

She gave him a guilty smile as Jessica repeated her own theories and plans.

Finally, Cassie found a moment to interrupt her sister. "Look. We have time to figure this out. Carlo can stay with us. I love you. I just got engaged. Now leave me alone." She hit 'End' without waiting for Jessica to bid her goodbye.

"I think we should leave the phones in the glove box of the car for the rest of the trip," Stills suggested as their food was delivered.

"Fine by me," Cassie agreed then thanked the waitress.

She bent over her steaming food and took a deep inhale. "God I'm hungry."

With a shrug, Stills offered, "It's all the fresh air and good sex."

"Can I get you two anything else?" the waitress asked as she cleared the last dish.

"No, everything was wonderful," Stills complimented.

"Can you point us in the direction of the Silver Creek Hollow?"

"So, you're the genealogist come to town to do some research with Elizabeth."

Cassie gave an impressed glance at Stills. "Word really *does* get around fast in this town."

The woman shrugged. "Not much going on just yet. We're still two months away from the beginning of tourist season, so news spreads pretty fast. I'm Stacy, half owner of this restaurant, manager, waitress extraordinaire, and marketing wiz."

"Quite the resume." Cassie held out her hand. "I'm the genealogist, Cassie, and this is my ..." she glanced at Stills as she gave her new favorite moniker for him, "fiancé, Benji."

He winked at her and accepted the hand the waitress offered.

"Nice to meet you both," Stacy said, then asked, "How are you finding our little town?"

Cassie answered, "There are places that sell themselves with the tag line, 'step back in time,' but they often fall short of that promise. But here I really *do* feel as if I've truly stepped back in time."

"Have you been down Belle Street yet?" Stacy asked.

They shook their heads no.

"That's where the brothels and saloons were back in the heyday.

There's been a lot of renovation to make sure the street looks just as it did around the 1890s. You'll feel like you're gonna be in the middle of a gunfight at any moment on that street."

"I can't wait." Cassie was giddy.

"Tonight, though, you're headed in the opposite direction. To get to the Hollow, you want to go back to Main Street, turn right and two blocks down you'll see the fire station where you'll turn right once more and find the bar. Hard to miss."

After paying for dinner and thanking Stacy again, they shrugged back into their jackets, gloves and hats then headed to the Hollow.

Chapter Twenty

As the first caress of cold whispered across Cassie's face, she gave a muttered, "Oof." She hadn't realized how the hominess and warmth had eased her limbs. She sidled up to Stills. "I'm using you as a windbreak."

He pulled the collar of his jacket up and hooked his arm around Cassie's shoulders as they began to walk.

"Only two blocks, Dodd."

They slid down the frozen sidewalk, slipping twice, causing them to separate. The decision was made to hold hands for the remainder of the trek, in case they either needed to steady each other, or bring the other with them if they slipped and fell on their ass.

The lights of the town bounced off the low clouds, extending an eerie illumination to the little valley. Cassie frowned and twisted her lips in disappointment; definitely no chance of stars tonight.

"Dodd, if I didn't know better, I'd think you were upset by the clouds."

"I'm not. I kinda wanted to see the stars. I have a feeling they're amazing up here."

"I'm sure it'll clear up one of these nights; and then we'll go on a starlit hike."

Another gust of wind and she wondered how many more layers she'd need if they went on a starlit hike.

But he was right, they had time and storms passed.

At the fire station, they turned right and found the glowing lights of the bar spilling into the street.

The Silver Creek Hollow was what happened to an establishment when hipsters took over an old miners' bar. The outside of the one-story building had been decorated with dark wood slats, nailed in a vee pattern. A large window with a neon sign stating the establishment's name lit the sidewalk. They pushed open the single door entrance and were welcomed into the large, slightly narrow, long bar. The rough marred wood of the bar had been polished to look artistic and manly. The light was dim and there was a soft brush of smoke in the air, a result of the woodstove in the front corner.

The countertop of the bar ran the entire length of the establishment on the right side, and centered behind it was a seven-foot mirror with glass shelves, backlit in soft, trendy neon blue. The shelves boasted hand-crafted whiskeys, gins and rums. In front of the bartender, was a lineup of tap handles that didn't seem to be the widespread name brands, but a collection of unknown breweries.

The left side of the building was a smattering of mismatched tables and chairs of various sizes and seating options. The wall above the tables held a collection of ten large black and white mining photos, a history of the town told in the faces of the men who'd come to work the area.

And finally, in the very back was a jukebox in front of an open area for dancing and two pool tables.

"Cassie?" A smiling woman was bounding across the room, a bit of a skip in her step.

"Elizabeth," Cassie returned, verifying it was her.

Elizabeth, several inches shorter than Cassie, took the outstretched hand that Cassie offered in both of hers and pumped it enthusiastically.

The first word that came to Cassie's mind as the early thirtysomething Elizabeth greeted her was vivacious. Her blonde hair was twisted into a bun, glasses were pushed onto her head, and she wore jeans, a pink sweater over a white T-shirt, and a glowing grin.

A tall lanky man caught up to Elizabeth and touched her on the shoulder. She released Cassie's hand and gestured to him. "This is my husband, Aidan Pine, he's the town doctor."

"Nice to meet you," Cassie said. "Should we call you Dr. Pine?"

He scratched his thick, sandy blond hair and shook his head, a blush creeping up his cheek. "No, no. Aidan is fine."

Cassie smiled as she put her hand on Stills' arm to introduce him.

"This is my fiancé," she hit the word hard, "Benjamin Stills."

"Fiancé?" Elizabeth asked with a raise of her eyebrow and a tilt of her head.

"He just proposed." Cassie grinned.

"Oh!" Elizabeth wiggled her fingers toward Cassie's hand, an indication to show her the ring, which Cassie excitedly held out. Elizabeth tilted the ring finger toward better lighting.

Cassie mimicked Elizbeth's glowing face as she studied the ring and explained, "You're the first people we've actually told. In person. I told my sister, but we haven't had a chance to let anyone else know yet."

"Well ..." Stills cut in.

Cassie tilted her head. "Well what?"

He gave a shrug and muttered, "My brothers know."

"They do?"

"That's why Dan sounded so ... stupid on the phone, when he asked if we were in Mesa Verde yet."

"You proposed at Mesa Verde?" Elizabeth's voice melted.

"Yes." Cassie glanced back at the glint of the ring. "It was so romantic." A quick furrow crossed her face. "Wait, did your brothers tell their wives?"

Stills rubbed the back of his neck. "I'm not sure, but I suppose I should also tell you that my parents know."

"Your mom talks to my mom," Cassie worried.

"I made her promise she wouldn't say a *word* until you had told your mom."

"Can she be trusted?"

Elizabeth let out a bark of laughter at the same time Aidan poorly covered his with a fake cough.

Cassie explained, "My mother wouldn't be able to be trusted with that kind of secret."

"*My* mom can be subtle when she needs to be." Stills sighed.

"We have a table over here." Aidan corralled the group.

Elizabeth led the way and Cassie leaned over and asked Stills, "Why didn't you tell me they knew?"

"We haven't had time." He shrugged.

She rolled her eyes and playfully elbowed him.

The evening passed with inconsequential details that come about when getting to know someone new. When Aidan asked the polite question of what Stills did for a living; he told the half-truth that Cassie had become so familiar with. He was a business analyst. When the Pines tried to sound interested, Stills bored them with the details.

This was something he explained to Cassie that he did intentionally so people wouldn't ask follow-up questions.

"I document business processes and workflows, to help make sure our company is abiding by logical and efficient business practices," Stills said dryly.

The description almost always brought no further questions.

They shared stories of how they met, Stills and Cassie giving another half-truth of a story. But then she went into great detail about how he proposed, as none of that needed to be fabricated for security purposes.

Elizabeth sighed properly.

"Your turn." Cassie sat forward cradling her beer. "How did you two meet?"

"Oh, that's a long story." Elizabeth waved.

"That she loves to tell," Aidan filled in.

Elizabeth's eyes took on more of a sparkle, if that were possible. "We met in Denver when Aidan was working on his PhD and I was finishing up my history degree. We'd both been set up on dates at the same restaurant and they both went horribly. Really bad. So at the end of the night, we were sitting near each other at the bar attempting to drink away the awful interactions."

"And it was all blue skies and poppies from that moment on." Aidan winked at his wife.

Elizabeth crossed her arms over her chest, shaking her head. "And if you believe that I've got some oceanfront property in Kansas I'd like to sell you."

Aidan grunted in reply and took a long swig of his beer.

Elizabeth jumped to the epilogue of their story. "After we got married, we took a vacation and decided we'd end the trip in Eden that summer and hang out so Aidan could show me where he grew up. But when the Historical Society caught wind of my degree they showed up on our doorstep with a loaf of fresh-baked bread and a job offer."

Aidan took over the story. "I got cookies and a visit from the town council offering me a job. We couldn't see ourselves living here full time, but the idea of dividing our time between Denver and Eden was appealing. So we figured a way to make it work living six months in Denver, then six here."

"Isn't that difficult?" Cassie asked. "Living between two locations? What about work?"

Elizabeth said, "I actually work for the Colorado Historical Society, so they helped create a position for me that allows me to split my time, and the clinic Aidan works for is non-profit, so they're happy for the help when he can give it."

"That's quite the life you've built for yourselves," Stills said, impressed.

The clientele of the Hollow grew in number, the drinks flowed and the volume of voices and music rose. But the warmth and smell of the fire and the need to do nothing of consequence settled into Cassie's bones. She melted against her seat as their conversation twisted and turned around the history of the town.

Stills slung his arm around the back of Cassie's chair and she realized how comfortable he was. Occasionally he'd mindlessly rub her back when she sat forward, excited about another story Elizabeth imparted regarding the wild old west days of the mining town.

Cassie yawned and gave an apologetic wave. "I'm not tired, I'm just relaxed."

"There's also less oxygen at this altitude," Aidan offered. "You're not offending us."

"If you'll excuse me." Cassie decided a visit to the restroom might help.

On the way back, she smiled at the animated locals that had started dancing to the country song with a raucous downbeat playing on the jukebox.

She had to turn sideways and shimmy past a few dancing women, forcing her closer to the pool tables. One of the men playing pool whistled while another smirked and licked his lips. "Hey girl, you new in town?" A third, more inebriated man grabbed her hand and pulled her toward him. "Where you goin' so fast?"

She twisted out of his hold easily, thanks to his drunkenness and the self-defense classes she, Jessica and her mother had taken. "Sorry boys, I'm busy," she held up her hand with the ring and gave it a wiggle, "and otherwise engaged."

"Naw, look at you." The drunkest one grabbed for her again. "A girl like you; you can't be satisfied by one man."

Cassie lost her smile, but easily sidestepped him causing him to trip over his own feet and crash to the ground. She snorted as she commented, "I don't think you're much of a man."

Too late she realized she should have probably kept her mouth shut.

His friends didn't seem to like that she had so easily thwarted the sprawled man and they all turned angry scowls on her as they surrounded her, frowning and feral.

She was shocked, but not scared. She actually saw the futility of their actions and sighed as she glanced from one drunken glaze to the next. "Please trust me when I say this really isn't a good idea boys." And before she even finished her threat, she felt him and *knew* Stills had arrived.

He leveled a gaze at the man closest to him and said, "How about you help your friend up and get back to your game."

But as Cassie figured, it was all a ridiculous testosterone show now.

She watched as space was made beside the group of five, and before any more words were minced, one of the men grabbed her wrist as another one went to throw a punch at Stills.

She twisted her wrist until the man's thumb and fingers were exactly where she wanted them positioned, then anchoring her arm to her side, she moved from her hip and easily pulled out of his grasp. "Hey!" he called and angrily lunged at her; but in the same instance, Stills had sidestepped the punch from the other man, using the guy's momentum to give him a push, shoving him straight into the man trying to attack Cassie and tripping both of them into a sprawl on the ground.

The third attacker gave a growl of anger and leapt toward Stills just as a hand grabbed Cassie's ankle in an attempt to catch her and pull her off-balance. She frowned and pointed her foot to free it. When the hand tried again, she didn't think, but simply reacted by giving a kick of her booted foot, crunching into a body part of the man on the ground.

She stepped back, glancing up in time to watch as Stills twisted out of the way of the last man standing, who was propelling his whole body behind a punch. When the man tripped forward, Stills grabbed him around the neck in a hold that disabled him, keeping him in place.

"That's enough." A loud, burly call came from behind them.

Cassie glanced over her shoulder as the man who looked as sturdy as his voice stepped forward. He was the same height as Stills, had a perfectly trimmed beard, dark hair with the barest of gray starting to show through, and an easy swagger to his walk. He tapped Stills' arm, a request for him to let go. "I'm Cole Clayton," he introduced, "sheriff of Eden."

Stills let the attacker go.

The young man crumbled to his knees, gasping for breath.

Stills held out his hand to the sheriff. "Benjamin Stills."

"Nice to meet you."

Stills turned his attention to Cassie and took her hands in his, narrowing his gaze to see if she was okay.

"I'm fine." She shrugged. "It was nothing, they're just drunk idiots."

Stills let his eyes roam from her feet to the top of her head, a smile pulling at the corner of his mouth as he arched an eyebrow and admitted, "All your hard work in karate is paying off."

She winked at him in reply.

The sheriff demanded all four of the attackers sit at a nearby table and not move. Two of them were holding their faces, and one had his nose pointed to the sky, his hand over it as blood trickled down. That must have been the crunch that Cassie's boot came in contact with.

The bar had silenced during the quick brawl, but now began to return to a loud din.

The Pines made their way over, Elizabeth gushing and apologizing to Cassie for the stupid men, disappointed that this would be Cassie's first impression of the town. Aidan borrowed a clean bar towel and checked on the man with the bloodied nose.

"Sorry about this, folks." Sheriff Clayton sighed. "Would you like to press charges?" The moment he asked the question, two of the men stood and began demanding that they were the ones who had been abused and should be pressing charges. "Bobby, Frank, so help me God ... I've been here all night and I saw you advance first." The men backed down as Cole snarled at them. "Check your alcohol-addled brains; do you really think you have anything else to say in this situation?"

They all mumbled they didn't. Satisfied, Cole turned and ran a tired hand through his hair. "We can go to the station and file a report."

Stills gave Cassie a questioning glance, it was up to her. She shook her head. "I think they learned their lesson." The men were watching her with wide eyes, so she took a moment to glare at each one before loudly stating, "No means no, right boys?"

A resounding "yes ma'am" followed.

The sheriff crossed his arms over his chest and kept an eye on the men as Elizabeth continued to apologize. "I'm so sorry this happened, Cassie. This truly isn't what I had envisioned when I invited you to come for drinks with us."

"It's fine. And if you think about it, I was just in an old west bar fight in an old west town," she said excitedly. "Now I'm really living the history of this place."

"Dodd ..." Stills groaned, seeing how Elizabeth twisted her lips with concern.

"Elizabeth," Cassie touched her arm, "I've been taking self-defense classes for a while now and it was interesting to see that they really work. I seriously never felt like I was in any danger," she explained, leaving out the part that since Stills was nearby, she knew nothing bad would happen to her.

"If you're sure."

"I am," Cassie insisted. "But maybe this is the sign that we should call it a day?"

"I still feel bad."

Cassie waved the apology away. "Don't even give it another thought."

Aidan caught the sheriff's attention. "Cole, I need to reset his nose."

"Go ahead, you takin' him to the clinic?" the sheriff asked.

Aidan nodded as Cole towered above the young man's face. "I know where to find you, so after Doc Pine sees to your nose, I suggest you go straight home."

"Elizabeth, could you help me?" Aidan asked, giving a raise of his chin in goodbye to Stills and Cassie.

"On my way." She turned toward Cassie. "Okay, I'll see you tomorrow morning?"

"What time is best for you?"

"I have a little work to finish up and then I'm yours for the next few days, so let's say ten?" she said slowly, walking backward.

Cassie agreed as Elizabeth waved, gathered up their jackets and her purse, then followed Aidan who was guiding the young man out of the bar.

"So," Cole turned his attention to Cassie, "you're the genealogist?"

"Cassie Dodd." She offered her hand.

"Elizabeth is right, I apologize that this was the way you were introduced to our town. Can I buy you folks a drink to make up for it?"

"Maybe another time," Cassie said. "It's pretty late, I think we should probably head back to the house."

"Did you drive?"

"Walked," Stills offered.

"Then at least let me give you a ride." The sheriff walked over to the men at the table, and gave them a quiet, stern lecture; after which they stood, barely raising their eyes, and with tails tucked firmly between their legs, each mumbled apologies to Cassie before they left.

Bundled once again, they followed Sheriff Clayton out of the bar to find that it had begun to snow. Large flakes, illuminated by the street lamps, twirled lazily down. Cassie grabbed Stills' arm and jerked on it dramatically. "Oh my God, Benji, it's snowing!"

He gave a smile of explanation to Cole. "We're from Southern California."

"Ah, then I hope this is a far better welcome to Eden than anything else."

"Oh, it is!" Cassie tilted her head up and felt the cool flakes land and quickly melt on her cheeks.

Cole pointed out his large truck; a four door, white number with obvious four-wheel drive capabilities. Cassie climbed into the back, so

Stills took the front.

As they drove, Cole addressed Stills, "Those were some pretty impressive moves. What do you do for a living?"

"Business analyst," he said.

Cole laughed and shook his head. "Sure, but before that?"

Stills let a few moments pass before he admitted, "I was enlisted in the military. I served my time then used the GI Bill for college."

"Ah, that makes a little more sense." The truck came to a stop and as he put it in park he waved toward the house. "I assume Marsha told you about the ghosts?"

"She didn't say anything upfront, but it's all in the binder," Cassie supplied.

Cole smiled. "This whole town has ghosts and things that go bump in the night. But I've found that if you don't bother them, they won't bother you."

He got out to apologize and shake their hands once more. "If you need anything while you're here, let me know. My number's in the binder."

Chapter Twenty-One

"I think the heat stopped working." Cassie shivered as she slipped out of bed. If it weren't for a complaining bladder, she would have stayed under the covers with Stills, who was keeping her quite warm.

She haphazardly dug around in her bag for warm socks and a hoodie. Successfully bundled, she rushed to the restroom, being followed by a "Holy shit!" as Stills was greeted with his first blast of cold.

By the time she joined him downstairs, he too was dressed in warm flannel pajama pants, a sweatshirt and slippers; kneeling by the fireplace with the binder open in front of him.

"Is it ..." Her words trailed off as she came face to face with the fresh coating of snow out the front bay window. "Jesus, did you see that?" She was grateful they hadn't closed the blinds last night.

"I did, but I figured I'll get the heat going first, then I'll enjoy the view."

Mesmerized, she mumbled an "uh-huh" as she continued across the room to stand before the window. The heavy clouds and continuously soft falling snow gave off a blue hue, like the blue sky was desperate to be seen even if only as a shadow.

"It's a wonderland," she breathed out.

Branches of the large pine trees that surrounded the house were heavy with the buildup of new snow. Everything wore a coat of fascinating white and it was the most remarkable thing Cassie had ever seen.

"Ah," Stills called, having found the problem, "we didn't add enough pellets last night before we went to bed." A whoosh and whirl was the answer from the persnickety device. Soon, heat was thankfully rushing throughout the room. Stills rolled over onto his back, arms behind his head as the fireplace began to send out a blast of heat over his body.

Cassie shuffled into the kitchen and after opening the kitchen window curtains, called, "Icicles." Long, treacherous multi-numbered spikes hung from the eaves of the house.

She distractedly readied the coffeepot and while she waited, leaned a hip against the counter, mindlessly shaking her head. "It feels like Christmas, doesn't it?"

Stills grunted in reply.

Cassie opened her mouth to say how cool it would be to be in Eden for Christmas when a heavy thud came from upstairs.

Cassie straightened and glanced across the room at Stills; his closed eyes were now open. Another thud followed by a sliding sound and out of the corner of her eye, she saw a slide of snow from the roof come tumbling down.

"Snow must have gotten heavy," she said as she stepped closer to the window and glanced at the small hill of snow that had been created. "Cool."

"For a minute, I thought I was going to have to go fight some ghosts." Stills yawned and pushed himself into a seated position.

"Agent Benjamin Stills: Ghost Hunter."

"It's a new line of work I'm looking into."

The coffeepot was sputtering and steaming to an end as Cassie pulled out eggs, cheese, some veggies, bacon and thick slices of cinnamon raisin bread.

Stills slipped his arms around her waist, and pulled her away from the counter. "Go sit down. Enjoy this. I'll make breakfast."

She gave an appreciative sound as she poured herself a cup and sat down, watching the second most beautiful sight this morning—a handsome man making her breakfast.

After reading through the 'Snow preparedness' section of the binder, they found snowshoes in the coat closet and put on hats, gloves, and heavier jackets. Cassie placed the things she would need for her work at the archive in a plastic trash bag before putting it in her backpack; an extra level of insurance against the falling snow. She shoved her purse in the large front pocket, the pleather wouldn't need any reinforcement.

On the front porch she glanced at the new snow. "We probably need to clear this walkway." Their car had been properly indoctrinated, coated with an impressive shroud of snow. "And do we need to clean the car off?"

"I'll take care of that while you're at work."

"I don't mind helping; I think it'd be fun to shovel snow."

"I think you'll have plenty of opportunities." He referred to the weather report they'd listened to on the local radio station that called for twenty-four hours more of snow.

Cassie arranged her snowshoes on the ground. "Okay Benji, any idea how to put these contraptions on?"

It was easy in theory, but their shoes sunk into the snow and their balance was awkward. Cassie snorted as she fell sideways and ended up on her rear end. She went to the snow-covered stairs and used her forearm to brush off as much snow as she could before she sat down. It was a steadier way to figure out how to adjust the three straps that would hug her shoes into place on the new age skimmers.

Finally standing upright, she brushed the snow off her extremities and attempted taking her first steps as she watched Stills take his; she faltered, bending at the waist in laughter. "You look like a giraffe taking his first steps."

Stills glanced over his shoulder. "Maybe, but I can't even make fun of you yet because you haven't moved."

She gulped air and tried to pull up her right foot, laughing again. "I think I'm frozen in place."

He made a wide circle, and she saw his shoulders, shaking ever so slightly, when he came her way; he was laughing.

She finally pulled her right foot free and began her own wide-legged tromp. Stills watched and after about ten steps, Cassie glanced at him and saw a huge grin. "Newborn elephant," he teased.

"Oh my God." She rolled her eyes but took some more steps. He joined her and the exertion finally helped settle the unexpected amusement.

Since they had time, they decided to travel a few blocks down the street from the house, then come up Belle Street, the infamous area Stacy, from The Western, had told them about. It was going to be a snowy, sightseeing sort of morning.

Steps got easier, and they were able to walk with their feet a little closer together. As their breath came in short bursts, it blew smoke into the air, the cold invigorating Cassie's lungs, or freezing them; she didn't care which at the moment, because she was enjoying this so damn much.

"You've camped and hiked in snow before," Stills said, "did you not have snowshoes?"

"No, just boots. And I've been in snow before, but not this much."

When two women slid past them on cross-country skis, Cassie turned wide-eyed at Stills. He nodded. "Oh hell yeah, we're gonna try that too."

"Have you seen a lot of snow?" Cassie asked.

"A few trips. My favorite was a trip to the Sierra Nevadas when I was a kid, and the snow was cool, but I don't think I've ever been in a place that had this much either. Not enough to require a chapter in a binder called 'Snow preparedness.'"

Flakes continued to fall; lightly, slowly, as if they'd done such a good job the previous evening, they now had all the time in the world to fall and build up.

As they traipsed down the wide street, the snow crunching beneath their feet, the smoke from chimneys twirling up into the sky, and an orange-yellow glow falling out of the windows of the Victorian homes they passed on the dimly lit morning, Cassie was thrilled that she would be hidden from the outside world for a few days.

They turned and passed the post office and The Mining King Hotel. After crossing Main Street, they started going by a small A-line house called the Alpine Café that had chairs and benches, made out of old skis, that had been cleared of snow, along with a flashing red neon 'Cappuccino' sign. Cassie slowed in front of the open café.

"Want to go in?" Stills asked.

She looked down at her feet and flashed a grin at him. "Rain check?"

He winked. "Snow check?"

They continued down one more short block before turning and fully stepping into the past.

"C'mon," Cassie elongated then gave an exaggerated groan, holding out both hands as if she were offering this street up on a platter.

Two blocks of Belle Street had put on airs. Literally. False fronts of wooden buildings in yellows, greens, and red were something right out of a movie production.

According to Stacy and the reading they'd done that morning in the binder, Historic Belle Street was once an infamous dirt street crowded with saloons, bordellos and gambling halls. When mining became scarce, larger operations and more 'moral' families moved into Eden, and the infamous street was left to its own demise.

But when mining production closed and people moved away, two of the buildings were refurbished and served as hotels for the railroad, a few were turned into restaurants, but others were boarded up and abandoned. Strangely enough, it was tourism that brought the street back to life.

Two blocks of buildings had been repaired and upgraded. There was a covered wooden walkway connecting all the buildings on either side. They began to walk down the street, glancing into each of the storefronts. The Mining Car Gambling Hall was now filled with racks of T-shirts and sweatshirts and other kitschy knickknacks. There were several two-story buildings, possible bordellos that wore restaurant monikers and signs in the window that read, 'Closed for the season.'

When they saw a wooden building—dark red, one floor, with a second-floor false front and The Gold Dust Saloon painted on the window—they both called each other's name at the same time and pointed.

Stepping closer, they saw a plaque hanging on a post in front of the building that read:

> "The Gold Dust Saloon was one of the roughest, wildest saloons in Eden. It had two owners, the most notorious was Diamond Belle. It was said she was as beautiful as she was brutal. She was also fair and that was why people flocked to her establishment. In fact, so many people declared they were headed over to 'Belle's Place' that

eventually the very street her establishment rested was renamed after her."

"Can you imagine?" Cassie glanced around the quiet snow-covered street. Sure the town wasn't at its tourist height yet, but in the late eighteen hundreds, this street would have been alive with voices and hopes and dashed dreams. Horses and conversation and new construction.

They moved on toward the archive. "I think I'm just as excited to get to the archive as I am to explore the rest of this town. I feel like we don't have enough time."

"There's enough time," Stills reassured.

Her cheeks had a slight burn to them from the grinning and the cold. Was it possible for a person to be too ridiculously happy?

At the end of Belle Street, the back of the red brick courthouse came into view; it was a dapper two stories topped with a bell tower. They walked around the courthouse to turn onto Main Street again, and right beyond the courthouse building was Eden's small historical museum. Then, tucked back from the road, Cassie caught her first glimpse of the archive.

The building was constructed to resemble an early nineteen hundreds Victorian home; white in color, with three steep gables in a complicated, asymmetrical shape, common during that era. The gables and the steepled portico were all trimmed to look like lace. The porch was completely covered, and a smoky six panel door welcomed visitors at the center of the house, with a large window on either side.

The snow added a particular picturesque quaintness to the whole scene.

In front was parked a snowmobile, now covered, and through the window, Elizabeth excitedly waved as she watched them walk up the front steps.

They untangled their feet from the snowshoes and stomped off the excess snow as Elizabeth swung open the door and hustled them in with the same exuberance she'd greeted them the night before. "Welcome to the Eden Historical Society Archive."

Inside it was evident this structure had been built for research and work, not a living space. The front room was broken into two sides; the right housed the archivist's workspace, coffee station, and entrance to the vault, while the other side had two twelve-foot tables for guests to study over documents and photos. The middle of the room had a gas fireplace and two armchairs. It smelled of lovely moldy paper and hundreds of life stories.

"This is the work space, but the rest of the building, behind the vault doors next to my desk; we have almost two thousand square feet of climate-controlled storage." She ushered them into the vault for a peek.

Cassie shook her head in disbelief at the wall-to-wall shelving. "This is amazing." There were tall tables set out here and there. The air smelled of the humidifier that was in constant use to extend the life of the papers and keep them from becoming brittle. Cassie noticed several sets of handling gloves. "Do you wear gloves all the time?"

Elizabeth sighed. "Handling gloves are a whole thing; they are finding now that it might do more harm than good when it comes to paper. So for our purposes, I just ask everyone to use them when looking at photos."

"Ah."

Stills decided to let Cassie to her work so made his apologies. "If you'll excuse me. I don't want to bother you and I think I have a free breakfast waiting for me at The Rose."

"A second breakfast?" Cassie asked.

"It's free Dodd, and it sounds good after all the snowshoeing we did this morning."

"Took that much out of you, huh?" Cassie joked.

His eyes sparkled as he leaned toward her to brush a kiss on her cheek, whispering, "Not to mention the other activities that have kept me happily exhausted and hungry."

After he left, Cassie turned a wide grin toward Elizabeth. "Are we ready?"

Chapter Twenty-Two

"He calls you Dodd." Elizabeth smiled as she arranged the documents she'd prepared for Cassie.

"He does." Cassie gave a knowing smile as she pulled out her computer.

"It's kinda sexy." Elizabeth wiggled her eyebrows.

"I know." Cassie gave a soft laugh. "I try to explain it to people, but unless you hear it, it's hard to understand how it would affect me."

"And he's all possessive Neanderthal about you, too."

Cassie screwed up her face and gave a snort. "What?"

Elizabeth raised her chin in the air and as if she were giving a lecture pointed, "He rubs your back when you're talking, touches your knee offhandedly or makes sure he's standing close enough to touch you when you're just standing next to each other." She laughed. "Aidan does that, and it was my brother who pointed it out once and said men do that because their old caveman feelings make them want to give physical signals to other people in the vicinity." She lowered her voice in mocking Neanderthal talk, "This one mine."

"Well, it's never been explained to me that way before." Cassie gave a conspiratorial smile. "I'm definitely gonna point that out to Benji sometime."

"Okay Dodd," Elizabeth took a deep breath, "where do you want to start?"

Cassie pushed her hands through her hair. "I suppose I should tell you a story about two brothers who went off to war."

When she finished, Elizabeth was leaning forward over her crossed arms. "All that from various database searches?"

"Yeah."

"Can you imagine what is still out there?"

Cassie grinned. "I can, because I just saw two thousand square feet of storage in a small mining town in Colorado."

"Touché," Elizabeth said.

Cassie rubbed her hands together. "Okay, I think I'd like to start with James Moss. Get his story out of the way and then we can move our focus on to William."

Elizabeth pulled several copies out of the stack she had and began, "I found an announcement from the paper about James' wedding, but as I mentioned, the courthouse caught fire in the late forties and destroyed several years of marriage, birth and death certificates. I'm assuming James' was among those, because I didn't find an actual marriage certificate." She handed the copy of the newspaper article to Cassie.

> James Moss formerly of Chicago, Illinois and Miss M. Buchanan of Pueblo, Colorado were wed on the 5th of June, 1947. The happy couple celebrated their nuptials with Moss' brother, William, and Buchanan's parents in attendance. The small party toasted the newlyweds' bliss at The Grand Rose over an early dinner.

"The Rose? Marsha's Rose?" Cassie asked.

"That's the one. It was a restaurant for years before Marsha and Edwin bought it and turned it into a B&B."

"I love that they kept the name."

"They had to," Elizabeth stated.

"Was that part of the legalities or something?"

"Not exactly." Elizabeth muttered.

When she didn't expand, Cassie sat forward with a smile, waiting for an explanation.

Elizabeth licked her lips before she admitted, "The ghosts insisted, they wouldn't let Marsha change the name."

"The ghosts." Cassie lowered her voice excitedly.

"The ghosts," Elizabeth confirmed.

"There has been a lot of mention of ghosts since we arrived. I figured it's part of the draw; the culture of an old west mining town ... like ghosts help sell tickets."

"It doesn't hurt," Elizabeth said.

Cassie nodded to herself as she reread the page before her, then asked, "Do you believe in ghosts?"

"Yes," she admitted, "but not the kind you're thinking of. Not ladies in white, floating through the air. I've lived here long enough to see that ghosts are stories and lives of the past, and a lot of people live in the past and are haunted by it, and some people can be haunted by stories from a lifetime ago in the same way."

"Oh, that's good. I've never heard it put that way," Cassie said. "I was going to ask if you have any ghosts, but now that's a completely different question."

Elizabeth waved. "We do *not* have time to talk about the ghosts that haunt me now."

"But now that's all I want to talk about."

Elizabeth laughed. "Let's get some work done and then we'll go to lunch at Tilly's Diner and I'll tell you about it," she said as she slipped the next printed article across the table.

"Deal." Cassie began to read.

It is with great sadness that Mr. James Moss was called to the glorious home in the sky this past Thursday. A fairly new citizen to Eden, Moss was kind to all he came in contact with and was never one to be seen patronizing the bars. He will be missed by all who came to call him friend. At this time, the widow will join a sister in Colorado

Springs. The family asks for respect as they mourn their loss in peace.

Cassie looked at the date of the article, January 17, 1949. "Do we know how he died?"

Elizabeth pulled a large book the size of a dictionary from where it had been sitting next to her and flipped to a marked page as she explained, "Twenty years ago, a woman who visited Eden fell in love with the town and began doing research on the cemetery. She compiled this three-volume set that talks about the life and death of each person buried here."

"Whoa, that is quite the undertaking."

Elizabeth held up the book for Cassie to read the title, *The Story of the Paradise Cemetery*.

"Paradise?"

"The first preacher in Eden decided that if this was Eden, then in the afterlife, his flock would be with the good Lord in Paradise."

"Oh, yes." Cassie grinned approvingly.

Elizabeth turned the marked page to Cassie.

James Moss, born 1923 in Chicago, Illinois came to Eden, Colorado after the Great War. He and his brother moved to town to try their hand at mining. James worked at several mines in the area. He was reported as a kind man to all.

On June 5, 1947 he married M. Buchanan of Pueblo, Colorado. (There were three Buchanan daughters, Mary, Maria and Marna. The marriage certificate of James Moss was burned in a fire and the only article to speak of his marriage denotes the wife as M. Buchanan.)

James and his bride were renting a room in the Mining King Hotel while their home was under construction.

On January 16, James had been tending to his ailing brother, William, late one evening. As James headed back to the Mining King, the streets and night were darkened, what little light there was ended up being the death of James.

Peter Syke found out that same night that his wife was having an affair and he went to a nearby bar to wallow in his misery. As Peter made his drunken way home, he saw James and mistook him for the man his wife was having an affair with, he pulled a gun and shot James dead.

James' widow moved back to Pueblo, Colorado. As it was unknown which 'M. Buchanan' married James, it is difficult to say with certainty what became of her.

"Poor James," Cassie muttered.

"I found one photo." Elizabeth took out a photo page in a plastic sleeve. The black and white picture showed two men standing with arms around each other, croquet mallets in hand, and full heads of dark hair combed into place. They were dressed in dark slacks and light button-down shirts, sleeves rolled up, and one of them wore a buttoned-up vest over his shirt. Under the picture read:

James Moss, left in vest, and his younger brother William, sweep the competition in an amiable game of croquet at the 1947 Memorial Day picnic held on the outskirts of Eden, Colorado.

"Handsome ..." Cassie ran a finger along the photo as it was under plastic, "they could be twins."

"I thought so too, and they look like old movie stars," Elizabeth offered.

Cassie clicked open a file and turned her computer screen to Elizabeth. "Theresa went through photo albums, and the earliest photos she found of her father were from 1951 with her mother."

The photo Cassie pulled up showed William with a soft smile on his face, his arm slung around the shoulders of a beaming woman, a few inches shorter, in a fitted skirt and button-down jacket, her hair curled and pinned into place.

Then she pulled up a photo of William. "This was 1951, he's only twenty-eight."

Elizabeth studied the third black and white photo. William, with a serious look in place, wore slacks, a light shirt, and a tie and jacket; the shades were different, so it wasn't a matching suit. Where the photo had been taken wasn't evident, but the palm trees in the background suggested it was far from Colorado.

"He still looks so young, but at that point in his life, he'd seen and done so much." Elizabeth muttered the fact, mostly for herself.

Cassie agreed.

"William seems so serene here." Elizabeth shook her head in wonder.

Cassie frowned at the description. "I suppose."

"You'll see why I put it that way." Elizabeth moved the photo to the side. "Other than these articles, there isn't any other mention of James. Besides the mining documentation you've found."

Cassie tapped a few notes into her document then said, "Okay, then we move onto William Moss."

"*This* is where things get interesting." Elizabeth pulled out several copies of newspaper articles. "Where James was kind to all, William was a drunken hothead."

Cassie tilted her head and frowned. "The old English professor? So beloved by the university system that they want everything he's ever written?"

"Arrested and fined. A lot," Elizabeth emphasized as she handed a copy of an enlarged article to Cassie, who read:

August 15, 1947 – William L. Moss was last evening arrested on a charge of drunk and disorderly, and lodged in the city jail. He filled up on the booze and proceeded to pick a quarrel with John Salberg, and they had a little personal difficulty, resulting as above stated. Mr. Salberg was discharged, once it was found he had not instigated the affair, but had acted solely in defense of his well-being.

Cassie shook her head in disbelief as Elizabeth excitedly handed over two more articles.

> **November 30, 1947** – Fined $15 for being drunk was William L. Moss.
> **April 18, 1948** – William L. Moss was given a 10-day jail sentence for being drunk and disorderly.

"This can't be the mild mannered professor."

"Maybe he was sewing some wild oats ..." Elizabeth theorized as she passed two more articles over, "a *lot* of oats."

> **July 23, 1948** – William Moss, drunk and disorderly, fined $30 by Associate Magistrate M. R. Brennan.
> **October 4, 1948** – William Moss, charged with drunk and disorderly conduct, entered a plea of guilty in the court of Justice of the Peace Daniel Ostberg, who fixed bail at $100. Time for the hearing was set for 10 a.m. today.

As Elizabeth handed the last article over, she said, "This happened a few days after his brother was killed."

> **January 20, 1949** – An altercation in the Hollow Saloon brought a $100 fine and a 15-day county jail sentence to William Moss of Eden when he appeared before Justice of the Peace Daniel Ostberg.
> Moss was charged with assault Monday after reportedly throwing a glass at the bartender in the establishment on Sunday, cutting the man about the eye.
> When patrons tried to step in to lead Moss out of the bar, he became combative and instigated a fight that later became an all-out brawl.

> In addition to the fine and jail sentence, Moss is
> reported to be suffering a nose fracture, inflicted by one
> of the men who later became a participant in the fracas.

Cassie glanced at the photo of William she still had pulled up on the computer, zoomed in on his nose; it might be a little worse for the wear. "I'm looking at this photo differently now," she admitted. "I think I can assume that Theresa and everyone he knew in California had absolutely *no* idea about his youth."

As if to back up her claim, she found the file with William's obituary and read, "An iconoclastic and prolific scholar, Dr. Moss taught classes in early English literature and published numerous academic articles in journals and published three books on a wide range of subjects ..." she scanned the page "... a gentle soul who was formidable in mind and spirit to the very end. He will be missed by generations of grateful graduate students whose careers and lives he helped shape."

"Yeah, that doesn't sound like a man who spent his youth being arrested and jailed for drunk and disorderly conduct," Elizabeth said quizzically.

"Maybe once his brother passed away, he decided to change?" Cassie posed the theory.

Elizabeth shrugged. "People often change after they've lost someone they're close to."

"You know what I find strange?" Cassie began. "William kept journals during his time in the war, then wrote papers on literary topics, and other than the secret letters Theresa found, she claimed there were no other personal journals."

"If he had any others, maybe he got rid of them?" Elizabeth added to the theories.

"His wife got rid of them?" Cassie suggested.

"Theresa got rid of them?"

Cassie looked at the dates of the drunk and disorderly arrests. "Are there any more articles about him being arrested?"

"That's just our local paper, I never checked the surrounding towns," Elizabeth said.

"Maybe James' death finally made him turn over a new leaf."

Elizabeth raised an eyebrow. "That's what I was thinking, that maybe it was a phase?"

"Maybe." Cassie bit her lower lip as she read through the articles again, trying to put together a profile of a man who now seemed to have two diabolically opposed lives.

"My turn, I suppose." Cassie pulled out the faded wedding certificate, yellowed with brown lines from where it had been folded for so many years. "William married an E. Smith on January 22, 1947."

"I looked for a copy, but our records didn't show any results for William." Elizabeth glanced at the certificate. "Ah, okay, this is why. This says he was married in Eden County, which in 1947 encompassed three towns: Eden, Red Creek and Wilson. I bet he got married in one of the other two towns."

"Okay, and how do we find that information?"

"Red Creek was incorporated into Highland, and Wilson no longer exists, but thankfully, all their records went to the Denver archive."

"Okay, that's something. We can search surrounding towns for mention of William."

Chapter Twenty-Three

Elizabeth and Cassie got lost in research, deciding to use the online catalogs of the small towns within a hundred miles of Eden. They came up with one more case of William being jailed for drunk and disorderly in Highland, the date right in the middle of the others.

When their stomachs gave collective growls at two in the afternoon, they took a break. Elizabeth drove them to Tilly's Diner on her snowmobile.

The flakes were infrequent and slow, as the clouds had thinned out. There was more light now, allowing the rolling white landscape to glow.

"It's so beautiful, how can you stand it?" Cassie asked as they entered the diner.

Tilly's was bright and welcoming, painted white and buttery yellows. One wall was filled with old window frames covered in various wreaths while the opposite held old cooking utensils. Cassie shivered, then wrapped herself up in the warmth and smells of fresh baked goodness.

"Cassie, it snows nine months out of the year here," Elizabeth offered.

"Nine months?"

"Sometimes the challenges can get tiresome."

"But you only live here six months out of the year."

"Exactly, I go easy on the challenges."

Cassie was introduced to Milly, the granddaughter of the original owner of the restaurant, Tilly.

Seated and meals ordered, Elizabeth said, "Do you know, the first time I walked into that archive building, after introductions and tours, and the paperwork was done, I was finally alone and had the weirdest feeling; like I was surrounded by ghosts." She shrugged as a blush crept up on her cheeks. "I've only told two people about that."

"Do I look like I'm judging you? I'm on the edge of my seat ..." Cassie gestured to the way she was seated, "literally."

Elizabeth pushed her glasses up on her head and continued, "My working theory is that such a great number of people came to this small town in such a concentrated amount of time, that their stories got caught in the mountains. And when people donate photo albums, or journals, or boxes of various relatives to the archive, they become another ghost in the collection."

"I think I can understand that." Cassie nodded. "I've always loved the work at Ancestry Home. When I started to meet the clients I worked for, passing on to them their family's stories; I felt more connected by helping them become more connected to their own story. The people who had passed on, they were alive again through the telling of their history somehow."

"Yes," Elizabeth hissed. "Exactly."

"Do you know, I've often felt a kinship to indigenous cultures. I think calling upon your ancestors to help you should be part of our daily lives."

Elizabeth laughed. "You don't know the number of times I'm at a loss to find information and after I ask for help, I somehow find what I was looking for."

Cassie shrugged. "Why not? When Catholics lose something, they say a prayer to the patron saint of lost things to help out."

Elizabeth chuckled. "We're going to get in the weeds and be here for days if we start talking about religion and superstition."

"That sounds like my idea of fun," Cassie admitted.

"I'm glad you don't think I'm ... weird."

"I think I'm going to cry when I have to say goodbye," Cassie predicted. She waited a few beats before she asked the question she really wanted. "Elizabeth, have you *seen* ... things?"

Elizabeth tilted her head and waited a moment before answering. "Every now and then, out of the corner of my eye, I think I see someone. Not in a creepy way, it's a more friendly feeling. Like someone is watching out for me and points me in the right direction when I get stuck in the research. But it also doesn't feel like it's one ghost, maybe there really are spirits that aren't able to climb thirteen thousand-foot mountains until their stories get told in some way."

Cassie let out a hiss of breath, her eyes wide. "Jesus, you're a poet."

"I'd be lying if I didn't admit I was writing a book, but I am no poet," Elizabeth said.

"What's the book about?"

"Three Irish men who came to America in 1870 to strike it rich."

Cassie blinked wildly; she didn't know where to start with her questions. Elizabeth burst into laughter. "Unfortunately, we don't have enough time for me to tell you their story and for us to continue the research we need to do."

"We don't have time for any of the topics we're adding to the pile of work I already need to do, but I'll make time."

The bill came and Cassie grabbed her purse. "This is on me. Please." She handed her credit card over to the waitress, then she rooted around for her lotion, but couldn't find it. "This purse is a pit of despair," she mumbled, scratching around once more.

She apologized to Elizabeth as she upended the whole thing on the table. "I just kept adding receipts and crap to it since we left home." To prove her point she held up a keychain from a gas station in Arizona and a forgotten pack of caramels. She exchanged both for the lotion. When she was finished, she started to toss everything back but stopped when she picked up a tiny silver disk, the size of a quarter.

"Is that a battery?" Elizabeth asked.

Cassie frowned. There was no plus or minus sign, but when she turned it over, there was a faint blinking red light. The hair on the back of her neck stood on end as metaphorical ice water doused her.

"Yeah, the battery for my camera." She muttered the lie. "I've been looking for this." She put it back in the purse, hoping her change in attitude wasn't too noticeable.

The waitress returned the check and Cassie signed as Elizabeth and Milly spoke. Cassie was finding it difficult to concentrate as she played out various scenarios of why an obvious tracking device would be in the bottom of her purse. She didn't have to go too far to come to the most reasonable scenario: The man who asked her to marry him was tracking her every move.

Oh Benji, she thought, love me or not, you've got a hell of a lot of explaining to do.

As they drove back to the archive, Cassie decided she wasn't about to allow the tracker to ruin the rest of her afternoon or even the rest of the trip. She and Stills would discuss the intrusion of her privacy, she'd give him hell and they'd move forward from there.

Back at the archive, Cassie shared poignant passages from William's journal and the women wondered if maybe he was a sensitive man. The PTSD was never dealt with after the war, so he came home and drank and got himself in trouble. Of course, they were at the point where they were open to all theories.

Finally, Cassie pulled out the book Theresa had given her with the circled letters and showed Elizabeth how it looked when all written out in sequential order.

"Salerno Wall," Elizabeth read.

"Does that mean anything to you?" Cassie asked.

"Not off the top of my head." Elizabeth pursed her lips. "We can look into that tomorrow. It could be the name of a ghost town no one remembers or a gulch or a stream or a mine ..."

"Oh, good, we've got options." Cassie laughed.

"Tomorrow we can dive into the county clerk and recorder's office records, and hopefully, my friend at the BLM will be able to find some information on the properties with the Moss brothers' names and we'll be able to get the email."

"Why wouldn't we get the email?" Cassie asked.

"When the weather gets bad, we sometimes lose internet and cell service."

"Yeah, Marsha mentioned that." Cassie stretched. "Then I suppose we're done for today."

"Can I drive you home?"

"I don't mind walking, I've got the snowshoes, and I don't get to walk in the snow in Southern California all that much." Cassie smiled.

But what she didn't share was that walking would give her time to reflect on how she was going to talk to Stills about his Neanderthal overprotectiveness.

Chapter Twenty-Four

Cassie took some extra angry stomps in her snow-covered boots on the front porch before she opened the door; readying for a confrontation.

She flung the door open, stepped inside, set her bag down and from the entry rug, she pressed her hands to her hips and frowned.

Stills, on the phone, glanced across the room from where he was sitting at the kitchen table. He shot a tense smile in her direction as he said, "Cassie just walked in. I'll talk to you later."

Something was wrong.

She frowned as she closed the front door and stepped out of her boots. Her argument might have to be pushed to the backburner for a few moments.

"What's going on?" she asked as she made her way to the table.

Stills took a deep breath and scrubbed his face with his hands.

"That good?"

He held his hand out to her when she was close enough and pulled her to stand between his legs. "Cass, you know how we promised each other we'd never lie if we could help it."

Cassie nodded slowly, especially since he'd foregone calling her 'Dodd.' That *definitely* wasn't good.

She steeled herself from whatever bad news was coming as she tried to control a litany of possibilities that were raising her blood pressure with each passing nanosecond. Was it her parents, Jessica, Parker ...?

"Our apartment was broken into."

"Oh." She blew out the breath she'd been holding. Not that her home being broken into was better, but those she loved still had their lives, so maybe it was.

"That was Salvatore," Stills explained, gesturing to his phone. "Our neighbor knew we were gone this week, so when he came home from work and saw the door open, he peeked in and found the place had been upended."

"Upended?"

"He called the police, and since he had Salvatore's number in case of an emergency, called him too."

"Okay. What ...?" She frowned, shaking her head as a dry laugh escaped. "Benji, we don't have anything valuable."

"I know."

"Is it something you're working on?"

"Nothing," he said quickly. "Nothing that would make anyone come looking for me or find where I live and toss our home." He was keeping his frustration in check.

Cassie, however, was not. Her stomach twisted at his choice of words, 'toss our home.'

"Did they take anything?" she asked.

"Salvatore asked Jess to go look around and she said nothing's missing."

Cassie's frown deepened. "Then ... was it ... what kind of person breaks in and doesn't steal anything?"

"Did you want them to steal something?"

Cassie shrugged. "I don't know. The TV at least. That feels more stereotypical. This makes me feel ... violated."

He grunted. "Here's the other thing. The files that were most ransacked were yours. Does that make you feel better?"

With a shake of her head she muttered, "No. But I have a question and now the answer doesn't seem so obvious." She retrieved her purse from her bag and took out the device she'd found. "Did you put this in my purse?" she asked as she set it on the table between them.

Stills' lips were drawn into a thin line as he picked it up, turning it over in his hand. When he didn't answer right away she knew; it wasn't him.

"Benji."

His voice was hoarse when he said, "I didn't put this in your purse."

She opened and closed her mouth, unsure what to even ask, then let the obvious question tumble out. "What does it mean?"

"I don't know. But this isn't a listening device, it's just a tracker."

"*Just* a tracker," she repeated.

"Fuck." The controlled anger flared out of his nostrils.

"This is too coincidental, isn't it? A tracking device and our apartment..."

Stills took her hand and narrowed his gaze. "It is, but we're okay, Dodd. We're gonna figure this out."

"Because you're going to go into badass CIA mode and make sure we figure this out." She needed to state the ultimate fact that she knew would calm her down.

His face softened. "I'm a badass, huh?"

"Not as much as me," Cassie leveraged her claim, "but close."

He kissed her hand and picked up his cell phone to make a call, but receiving the message that his call couldn't be completed as dialed, he used the landline. Cassie watched him, numb.

"I'm calling Salvatore," he explained as Parker must have answered. "It's me. We have another problem. Cassie found a tracker in her purse. It's most likely from an online retailer, nothing military or government issued. No listening capabilities; needless to say I'm not happy about it and it's too much of a coincidence."

Cassie wasn't sure how many more fancy acrobatics her stomach could do, but she wasn't interested in finding out.

"Dodd, when was the last time you remember really going through your purse?"

She already knew the answer to that question as it was all she'd thought about for the rest of the afternoon. Though it was easy to be angry when she thought it had been put there by Stills. Now, knowing it hadn't been was scaring the shit out of her. She swallowed and answered, "When I organized it the night before we left and this afternoon at lunch."

Stills relayed the information.

After a lifetime, Stills nodded. "I checked that number, it was a bot." Another few beats, then he said. "That'll work. Let me know what you find. I'll let you know if I find anything on my end. You have our numbers, but this snowstorm is wreaking havoc on the connection, so let me give you the landline number."

Conversation ended, Stills asked for Cassie's phone.

She handed it over as she asked, "What was a bot?"

"The phone calls you said you got twice a week; I just wanted to make sure. You were right, it was a bot, but I stopped it."

In a small dry voice she repeated his words, "You stopped it."

"Dodd," he waited until she made eye contact and then gave her a reassuring smile, "I would never put a tracker in your purse or on your person without your knowledge."

"Someone did." She swallowed all the questions that statement opened up.

He cursed as he fiddled with her phone.

"What is it?"

"The signal keeps going in and out. I need to download an app."

"Do you think someone did something to my phone? We still don't know if this is about me or you. You have to admit in your line of work, it makes more sense that someone is after you," she reasoned.

He pulled her into his arms and kissed her forehead, and she snuggled against him in an attempt to be soothed.

"It's okay, Dodd. We're okay. We're in the middle of a snowy, isolated town. I don't think too many people would brave that road we came in on in the middle of a storm if they were following us."

"You think someone is following us?!" She pulled away as she made the declaration.

"No, I'm saying that while I don't like that you have a tracker in your purse, it also means whoever put it there is not close."

That did make a lot of sense. "Okay." She tried to gather her nerves, the information and her wits. "Okay. What can I do to help?"

"You're doing it. You're staying level-headed and strong."

She gave a dry laugh. "This isn't level-headed, this is numb."

"That actually works too." He brushed a rough kiss on her cheek and checked her phone as he explained, "I'm going to download an app that can scan our phones and might be able to detect a GPS tracker."

"What do you mean detect a GPS tracker? There's an app for that?" she asked incredulously.

Stills shrugged. "It's merely a precaution."

"Benji," she tilted her head and held out her hands, palms facing up, empty, "what information do I have? That the grandfather of a client was the shoeshine kid for Al Capone? Or maybe it's the fact that I found out one woman's great-grandmother smuggled diamonds out of Russia? Or maybe it's a crazy English professor who doesn't want William Moss' paper on how to properly use a colon to be leaked into the world?!" She had stomped out fear as she listed what she knew, and snorted, happy to be getting angry now.

Stills didn't hold back his smile. "That's exactly what they want Dodd; if the truth behind proper punctuation gets out into the mainstream, it'll wreak havoc on the world." He winked at her then checked on the progress of the downloads.

"Okay," she shook her hands out and rolled her neck, as if the physical act could loosen the afternoon's emotional rollercoaster, "so step one in the official *How to Be a Spy Handbook* is to detect all trackers and listening devices."

"Dodd."

"I bet you're kicking yourself now for not checking out a spy bag for this trip, huh?"

He gave a soft smile and pointed toward the binder. "Call Cole Clayton and ask him if we can take him to dinner."

"Why?"

"Because as we've seen so far, if there is a stranger in town, people know about it. And they talk. And if people are talking, the one person in town who is listening is going to be the good sheriff. So it's not a bad idea to get his eyes on our possible problem also."

"Do you really think we're in danger?"

"No," he said evenly, "I just think it's better to be redundant and protective than sorry."

"Okay, step two in the spy handbook; enlist the local authorities."

"Jesus." He grunted a half laugh.

"Benji, it's calming me down."

"Okay then," he shrugged, "let's write a damn spy handbook, Dodd."

She found the sheriff's number in the binder and asked Stills, "Do you want to invite him here for dinner?"

"No, we'll go out. I want to be out in public where people can see us and we can see people."

As she dialed, she muttered, "Step three, don't hide."

Chapter Twenty-Five

The sheriff took her up on the invitation and suggested meeting at
The Western. Cassie was on her seventh or eighth round of pacing
the front room when Stills finally declared, "Our phones are clean."

"I don't really understand what that means, but I'm relieved."

"It means we have time to get ready for dinner."

In dry clothes, her jacket warmed by the fire, they dressed for the cold
once more as Cassie insisted they walk. "I need to exert as much of this
built-up energy as I can."

"I could have helped with that," Stills muttered with a mocking pout.

"I don't know if even *that* would have helped, Benji."

They strapped on the snowshoes, getting the hang of it, and headed
out into the lightly falling snow. Cassie hoped her nervous system would
get the notice to calm the hell down as she exerted herself.

Stacy, the same waitress from the evening before, greeted them. "The
genealogist, back for some more of our amazing home cooking?"

"Yes, we are." Cassie forced a smile. "And we're meeting Sheriff
Clayton tonight."

"That's what he said, he's in the back right there. Can I bring you two
a drink? Same as last night?"

Cassie nodded, a drink suddenly sounded really, really good. But first
she held up her pair of snowshoes. "What should we do with these?"

"You can stack them in the entryway there, no one's gonna bother
them." Stacy left to put in their drink order.

Cole stood to greet them. "This was a nice surprise, I appreciate the
invite."

Seated with small talk, drinks delivered and food ordered; Cassie took a deep swallow of her beer and then rolled her shoulders forward and back in an attempt to relax before sitting back in her seat. She was rather grateful tonight that they had an out of the way table in the back.

Cole raised an eyebrow as he clocked her actions and when she made eye contact, she pursed her lips then glanced at Stills. How did he want to handle this? The sheriff took the lead. "I had a feeling this wasn't a social call?"

"It isn't." Stills turned his attention.

Cole thoughtfully rubbed his chin as his gaze drifted between Cassie and Stills. After a long moment he sighed and shifted in his chair. "I suppose it's probably best if I start. I may or may not have looked into you, Benjamin Stills."

"I figured."

"You did?" Cassie blinked in wonder.

The sheriff continued, "The way you diffused the little scuffle last night ... no one does that without training."

"I told you, I was in the military."

"Oh, I found your military record, but I couldn't find much else. Your record is impeccable and clean; I'd say you almost don't exist. And the one thing I know about clean records similar to yours ..."

Cassie shifted uncomfortably in her seat, but Stills didn't give anything away, just waited with a knowing smile for the sheriff to continue.

He did. "So this is where I tell you a friend I went to the academy with, who moved into a certain three letter sector of the government, may or may not have verified that I could trust you."

Stills glanced sideways at Cassie and winked at her. She rolled her eyes thinking, spy rule number four: be careful who you verify your career to.

"Sheriff Clayton," Stills offered a good natured smile, "I assure you, you *can* trust me."

"Now, since you invited me to dinner and it isn't a social call, I also have a sneaking suspicion it isn't about what happened last night."

"Your instincts are good," Stills confirmed and without any pomp or circumstance, he calmly explained the current situation regarding their apartment and the tracker found in Cassie's purse.

"Most coincidences are connected," Cole said.

"That's my thought."

"So, you'd like my help ...?" Cole asked the leading question.

"To keep an eye out for any other strangers who might be new to town the past few days."

Cassie had to take another drink for her nerves; it was one thing when she found herself in a situation where her little sister's life might have been in danger—that fired her up and built up her confidence. In that situation she was willing to fight, punch, and kick the crap out of any threat. She was also willing to keep her shit together in order to keep her sister safe. But to be on the receiving end was unsettling.

"I'm pretty aware of the comings and goings in my town," Cole responded.

"I figured as much. And I'm not interested in stepping on toes, so I'll stay out of your way. But if anyone else needs to know about this 'coincidence,' it's you."

"Do you think these two instances have to do with your job, or Miss Dodd's?" Cole asked.

"I don't bring files home and a friend who went to assess the situation alluded to the fact that Cassie's files seemed more ... spread out."

Cole looked toward Cassie. "And the tracker was in your purse," he established.

She gave a single nod in reply.

"I don't want to jump to any conclusions," Stills began, "because maybe I don't have enough information, but if we look at what we *do* have ..." He shrugged.

"Miss Dodd is the winner," Cassie said dryly.

Stills reached out and began rubbing her shoulders. She gave him a sad smile of thanks.

"What are you working on?" Cole asked.

"Genealogy," she said incredulously. "I find people's grandparents and the dates they lived and died, and I put it into historical context. I have five projects I'm working on right now. But I've been doing this job for eight years and nothing I've ever come across was *ever* ... detrimental."

Cole turned his attention toward Stills. "So maybe someone is trying to get to you through Miss Dodd?"

A shiver ran through Cassie.

Stills gave her a reassuring smile. "I won't rule out the possibility, but it doesn't feel right."

Well that didn't make her feel any better.

"I told Cassie, that of all my open cases, none are so damaging or important that someone would want to know my every move."

Cole tapped his fingers on the table. "So we have a lot of nothing to go on but a possible threat."

"That's what we have," Stills confirmed.

"What are you going to do with the tracker?" Cole asked.

"I don't want to destroy it," Stills mused.

"What?" Cassie asked loudly, then lowered her voice. "What do you mean, you don't want to destroy it?"

"Dodd, if we destroy it, whoever's keeping tabs on us will know it's been found."

She blew out a curse under her breath. "But Benji, I don't want to stay in a house with a tracker."

"I think I can help with that," Cole said. "There's an empty house across the street from the local sheriff that would be a hell of a place for a tracker to end up."

"That would." Stills nodded, thinking through his options.

Cassie asked Cole, "You don't mind?"

"It isn't tourist season yet, and if I'm being honest, other than a bar fight or two to break up," his bearded smile grew as he gestured to Cassie, "I don't have a lot going on."

"That's good for us, I suppose."

"I appreciate it," Stills said as he pulled out a paper that had his and Cassie's cell phone numbers written out and handed it over to the sheriff. "Here, although we've been having problems with service. I'm sure you know the number at The Hideout. I think tomorrow we'll go about our business. Cassie can still head to the archive and I'll check in with her at various times,"

"I can do the same."

She glanced between Stills, who she knew for a fact was capable, and the sheriff.

"We have a plan?" It was more a statement than a question.

"We have a plan," Stills repeated.

That was good, because the one thing that helped Cassie the most was when she had an actionable plan.

Chapter Twenty-Six

C assie did a bleary-eyed, half stumble, half shuffle, mostly zombie drag down the stairs to the sofa.

She pulled her feet up under her and gave a loud yawn; but when Stills handed her a cup of coffee a delighted moan emanated as she gratefully hugged the hot mug.

"At least you got a little sleep." He brushed a kiss on her cheek.

"I jumped at every sound," she muttered.

"I know, I sleep with you."

"You didn't sleep either," she pointed.

"I was worried about you."

She frowned into the cup. "He lied convincingly."

"Honey," Cassie's head shot up at the new endearment; Stills didn't hide his smile. "If you'll direct your attention out the front window, you'll see another thousand inches of snow fell last night. And you'll realize that you can't imagine anyone driving in this stuff any more than I can."

Hugging the cup against her chest, she gazed out at the gray dawn and the new blanket of snow. "Okay, that's breathtaking."

"It is, and you're beautiful and according to the binder, the highest mountain peak is called Palace Mountain *and* I talked to Clayton already this morning. He called in a favor to Highland State Patrol and had someone go over video surveillance of cars coming into the area."

"Where are the cameras?"

"At that last gas station before we headed up here," he said, "there is a camera in case someone is reported missing. The highway patrol can check with cameras south and north of Eden, where a snowshed is located."

"Snowshed?"

Stills shrugged. "I guess it's a tunnel that you try to get to if there's an avalanche."

"This is some country." Cassie shook her head.

He continued, "Only forty-two cars were clocked yesterday,"

"Forty-two?"

"Dodd, all except three were caught on camera continuing north of the town. Clayton identified each car; all locals. Which means no *new* visitors in Eden for the past forty-eight hours."

Those were hard facts and Cassie liked facts. She could wrap her head around them and these particular facts were quite helpful this morning. "Okay. That's good, right? Really good?"

"*Really* good," he confirmed. "And now, I have a surprise for you."

Cassie raised an eyebrow as she watched him head to the back room behind the kitchen that housed the washer and dryer. She heard the loud thud of something hitting a wall, a curse and then another thud. Finally, with a grunt, Stills came back balancing two pairs of skis.

"Are those cross-country?"

"I figure you don't have to be at the archive until ten, so why not shake off all the bullshit of yesterday and enjoy ourselves as we get snowed in."

"Do you really think we're snowed in?"

"Dodd, I'm not looking forward to driving these roads out of here. It was wild enough coming in on dry roads; snow-covered is a challenge I'm not ready for."

"Should I call work and tell them I'm not going to be back when I said I would?"

"We still have four days left. Who knows what will happen. Let's plan on keeping to our schedule and somehow, it'll all work out."

"I trust you, Benji."

"Of course you do. How about we ski to The Rose and have breakfast?" Stills suggested.

"Because there are people there?"

"No, because Marsha's husband Edwin is an amazing chef."

"With everything that happened, I didn't get a chance to ask you how your second breakfast was."

He wiggled his eyebrows as he gave his report. "Sourdough pancakes, some magic berry topping, homemade whipped cream and a great cup of coffee."

"Okay then, to The Rose."

Outside, Cassie stood on the porch looking at the cleared walkway, admiring Stills' snow-shoveling skills. "I would have cleared the path," she admitted as she adjusted her wool cap a little lower over her ears and pulled her gloves on tighter.

"I'll let you do it later today and tomorrow if we need it," he said. "I was up early and figured it needed to be done."

He set the skis on the cleared path. Marsha had five different ski boot sizes in the shed, and luckily they each found a pair that fit.

It took them several minutes to figure out the mechanics of the skis and how to clip into them. "How do you know what you're doing?" Cassie asked as she steadied herself on Stills' arm and he helped guide her foot. "Have you had to jump on skis a lot when you're on a mission in Switzerland, after you leave the casino and go running after the bad guy?"

"Yes, Dodd. That's exactly why I know what I'm doing," he answered with amused sarcasm.

"Figured."

When she was secured he handed over her poles. She awkwardly tugged at her hat once more and breathed out into the sky as Stills clipped into his own skis.

"I watched a video online this morning," he admitted.

"Ah, spy trick number five: When in doubt, go to YouTube University."

Once they moved off from the front walkway and were aloft on the freshly snow-plowed road, Cassie took a deep, appreciative breath of the cold morning air. The snow had stopped, but the smell, something in between wood and earth, was an indication that they might not have seen the end of the storm.

They decided to explore the surrounding streets, the snow having turned them into a cross-country wonderland.

Impressive six-foot walls of snow had been plowed in front of various empty lots here and there. Locals who were still in town had shoveled their walkways, creating channels. The pine and aspen trees they passed wore heavy white coats and Victorian homes of vibrant colors bloomed out of the white ground. Smoke twirled out of chimneys, slowly, as if the weight of the gray skies kept the smolder from expanding.

The only sound was their labored breathing and the crunch of snow under the slip of the ski. Cassie felt the fear and worry ease out of her as she exerted herself.

No one new in town.

The sheriff, who admitted he made it his business to know what was going on in his town, was capable and a force to be reckoned with; if she took him on his intimidating, burly build alone.

And Stills spoke in facts—they were safe.

Her thoughts meandered to the first time she ever talked to Stills. It was just after her sister called her from Rome asking Cassie to look up a phone number for her; of course, in the middle of the manic conversation, Cassie found out her sister's life was in danger.

The moment Jessica hung up, Cassie used that phone number to track down what 'help' her younger sister thought she needed. That was when she was put in touch with Agent Benjamin Stills. When she'd told him she was out of her mind with worry, he demanded she go for a run—as fast and as far as she could—to use the exertion and endorphins to help settle her down.

And here she was again, using the same techniques.

She smiled and slowed, glancing over at Stills.

"You okay?" he asked, stopping next to her.

"I love you, Benji," she said simply.

A soft smile grew beneath his well-trimmed beard, his amber eyes sparkled and his jacket gave a soft swish as he moved sideways to get closer to her. "You know," he licked his lips, "I never knew how empty my life was before. I never knew how empty *I* was." His eyes softened as he made the easy admission, "You know you make everything better, right?"

And what could she say to that? Tell him she felt the same way? That she never thought her life could be better? Or admit she never knew what her life was missing either? It all sounded so lame. Instead, she gazed into the eyes that truly saw her for who she was and accepted her for all her flaws. "I do know that. And you know I love you, right?"

"I hope so, you agreed to marry me."

"That I did."

"We're in this together now, Dodd." He winked at her.

Together.

God she liked the sound of that.

Together, she was certain they would be able to face anything that came their way together. Successfully.

She broke the moment and pushed off once again, even lighter than before.

Chapter Twenty-Seven

Marsha was walking past the front door of The Grand Rose when she spied Cassie and Stills on the street stepping out of their skis. She pushed open the door and leaned against it. "Look at you two! I'm so glad you're taking advantage of the skis."

Stills nodded toward the building beside the door. "Can we leave them here?"

"Just prop them up against the wall, no one will bother them."

"We brought other shoes to change into," Cassie said.

Marsha shrugged. "You don't have to change, but if you'd be more comfortable, use the bench inside and you can leave your boots under it," she instructed. As they walked inside, Marsha hugged Cassie around the shoulders. "I'm so glad you came! We missed you yesterday."

"I heard I missed great things." Cassie returned the sideways hug.

"Okay, I'll leave you to it, then come join us in the back. I'll have the coffee ready!"

A hallway to the right of the stairs led around a slight corner and to the entrance of the dining room. A murmur of conversation met them before they entered. Cassie smiled at the welcoming space; the décor from the front room continued into the large area that had at least twenty tables. Dark hardwood floors met walls papered with a gold textured Victorian faux damask. It was warm and the aromatic smells of home-cooked food swirled around them. The entire space was wrapped in the sound of classical music drifting in from invisible speakers.

"There you are." Marsha picked up two coffee cups and a carafe sitting on a side table as she led them to a small table in the corner by a wall of windows, giving them a perfect view of the jagged, snow-covered mountain in the distance.

"It's so busy," Cassie said of the fifteen full tables.

"We open the restaurant to the public for breakfast, but we keep tables open for our guests."

"Do you have a lot of guests staying with you right now?" Stills asked.

Cassie truly understood now why they'd come to breakfast. While the food might have been good, and Lord knew this man was led by his stomach sometimes, it was also another avenue to gather information.

"Right now we only have the Hansen family, here to visit their aunt and uncle who don't have room in their one-bedroom house for the family of six."

"So you make up for the slow season with the restaurant?" Cassie assumed.

"Edwin loves to cook and I like to know people's business," she winked, "so it works out well. Now, I'll tell you that Edwin made fresh sourdough bread last night, so this morning he created a savory strata with sundried tomatoes, mushrooms, spinach, and of course, eggs. But if you want something sweet, he's made sourdough French toast." She poured the coffee and asked, "Cream and sugar?" Cassie said yes to both. "I'll go get those and you can decide what you'd like to have," Marsha finished.

Cassie didn't need time to decide, nodding to Stills she stated, "One of each and we split them?"

"You read my mind."

Orders given, they chatted on and off with Marsha as she traveled between tables.

Cassie decided to use Marsha's small-town gossiping skills for good and softly chided, "Since most people know *I'm* the genealogist here to do research with Elizabeth, I feel like this town has one amazing phone tree in order to pass along such information so you all know who the strangers are and why they're visiting?"

Marsha gave a full body laugh and winked at Cassie. "We only do that in the offseason."

Cassie smiled. "Then who should *we* know about?"

"Sorry to break it to you, honey, you two are the last arrivals, so you're still the big news."

She left and Stills gave Cassie an approving grin. She leaned across the table and whispered, "It's another spy rule, Benji. Get as much information as you can from the self-appointed, local gossip."

Marsha delivered their breakfast with a "bon appetit" and refill of coffee.

Cassie slowly turned the plate of French toast with a caramelized crust, then topped with sliced bananas and a dollop of homemade whipped cream. "It looks so good."

It was the kind of meal that belonged in a snowy mountain town. She took a bite and rolled her eyes; with a mouthful she said, "Why are we cooking on this vacation?"

"Cuz I like your cooking," Stills said, loading up his fork with the strata. After several bites and his own appreciative sounds, he exchanged the plates. "Try this."

She did and gave another satisfied grumble. "Is this guy magic?"

Stills gave a deep nod of his head. "I think so."

Sheriff Clayton swaggered in then wearing jeans, a long sleeve maroon flannel and a cowboy hat. He greeted several locals as he crossed the room.

Cassie felt a flutter of worry in her chest when she saw him, but forced a deep breath and chided herself; *focus on the facts*. No one new was in town except them. Fact. The roads were impassable at the moment. Fact. This was probably one of the better breakfast places in town and the good sheriff simply wanted something to eat. Fact.

"Mornin'," Cole greeted them.

"Sheriff." Stills returned the greeting.

He took off his hat and held it lightly between his fingers, then asked Cassie, "How are you doing today?"

"Better," she admitted.

"Good. And glad you came to The Rose for breakfast, Edwin is an unparalleled chef, in my humble opinion."

"I think Dodd here could give him a run for his money," Stills said.

Cassie grunted in reply to the compliment. "I'm not so sure ..." she admitted.

She loved to bake, and friends and family compared her skills to several cafés and chefs around town, but if Cassie ever made a career out of her hobby, she knew that she'd lose the joy. The baking would turn into a pressured situation, a *job*; the kind that tried to bury a person.

But a bed and breakfast where she cooked whatever she wanted …? Maybe Edwin had cracked the code.

"Wanna join us?" Cassie offered.

"If you don't mind. But I won't bug you for too long." He pulled up a chair.

"It's no bother." Stills glanced at Cassie who nodded in agreement.

"So, was it an uneventful night?" Cassie wasn't interested in beating around the bush.

"I turned a camera from my property and focused it on the house across the street. Watched the feed this morning, and other than snowflakes, there were no visitors."

The confident report allowed for another layer of worry to slip away from Cassie's shoulders. Marsha came with a cup of coffee for Cole, told him the specials, then took his order and flitted away.

"Are you sure I'm not intruding?"

"No, it's fine," Cassie reassured. "Though I might take a page from Marsha's book and be nosy and ask how one finds themselves as the sheriff in Eden, Colorado?"

"It's a valid question." Cole sat back with his cup in hand. "I worked in Denver for several years, but after a while, I wanted a little less adventure. When I began to look around for a new post, I found Eden." He shrugged as if the story was old as time.

Cassie asked, "Is there a wife or a girlfriend at home?"

Stills tilted his head in her direction. "Tired of me already, Dodd?"

She waved his remark away. "I'm making small talk and being nosy. I'm not good at it."

Cole gave a chuckle. "It's just me and a one-eyed cat named Jack."

"A one-eyed Jack," Cassie repeated, charmed at the idea.

Cole hid a smile at the admission. "Seemed appropriate for the atmosphere."

"I bet in a place like this, you get set up all the time."

He gave a soft snort of a laugh. "I've been shown my fair share of photos of daughters and granddaughters."

Stills inclined his head toward Cassie. "That was the one thing she and

I both hated the most when we were single, the awkward setups."

Cassie took over. "Because our friends couldn't imagine that we might be happy alone."

Cole took a sip of his coffee, nodding in agreement.

"However," Cassie shrugged innocently and chuckled, "if you ever find yourself in Southern California, I do have some friends I could set you up with."

Cole politely refused. "I'm off women for a while. I got divorced last year."

"Oh, I'm sorry. I didn't mean ..." She waved her hand to erase the awkward suggestion.

Cole shrugged. "Eh, she left me for my best man."

"Shit," Cassie muttered. "Now I really am failing at this gossipy thing. I didn't mean to bring up any hard feelings."

"Nah, I'm working through it. Besides, she was really unhappy here, small town life isn't for everyone. And, if I'm being honest, I think she wanted to call things off at the wedding, but didn't know how." He ended the story with another sip.

Cassie glanced across the table at Stills, who gave an imperceptible raise of an eyebrow that said, *what should we talk about now?*

"This is some snowstorm!" She rushed the sentiment out and Stills coughed to hide his laughter. She apologized for the outburst and much more calmly, asked Cole, "Is it usual for this time of year?"

The sheriff nodded. "I've only been through two winters here, but the locals tell me there's normally one big storm that kind of finishes off the winter season. And it would seem *this* is that storm. They closed the pass up north about an hour ago."

"The pass? You mean the road?" Cassie asked nervously.

"Yep," Cole replied. "But if the weather reports can be trusted, the snow should break tonight."

"Have you driven these roads when they've been covered with snow?" The concern about being tracked was now being replaced by worry over the ability to drive on the icy snow roads in order to head home.

"Part of the job sometimes."

"It seems unreasonably treacherous."

"It probably is, but it's also part of the way of life up here. This was a tough town, built by tough people who were willing to work to make a living. I think that ideal continues in the folks who choose to live here these days."

"I'm enthralled with Eden," Cassie admitted, "but I can tell that visiting and living here are two different beasts."

"They are," Cole confirmed. "But listen, don't worry about the roads. When this storm clears, the road crews will be out in force. You'll be fine."

There was a lot of that sentiment going around the past few hours, Cassie thought. About her being fine, about everything being fine.

She cleared her throat and decided there wasn't much more to do but lean into it. "We'll be fine," she repeated.

With goodbyes given and full stomachs, Cassie and Stills clipped their skis back into place and headed to the archives.

Chapter Twenty-Eight

"You don't have to stay with me," Cassie said to Stills when they came to a stop.

"I was thinking the same thing."

"You were? Wait, why? What are you going to do instead? I mean, this was supposed to be your vacation."

"I was going to talk to Salvatore," he admitted, "and do a little research."

"A little research. Into trackers?"

He rubbed the back of his neck as he admitted, "And I was going to see about the car."

"What's wrong with the car?"

"Nothing, it's just a modern car and can be tracked. So, I was going to see if anyone was using that service who shouldn't be."

She glanced around at the snow-covered town, such a quaint, quiet place. They should be celebrating and relaxing, but instead, they were trying to figure out an unseen threat. The dichotomy of it all was difficult to put in place.

"Okay, I appreciate the honesty and I'm freaked out. But it's more of a theoretical freak-out," Cassie explained. "And besides, I've been here before."

"You have?"

"Benji, when we weren't sure what was going on with Jess, and you were parked in front of my apartment for months, I was worried then too, but I lived. So, I figure I'll live through this."

"You know, there was one thing that always disappointed me about that assignment."

"Disappointed you?" Cassie asked with a snort of a laugh, unable to fathom something that would have been disappointing.

"I wish you would have walked past your balcony window in less clothing during those days."

She rolled her eyes but smiled. "And I wish you'd done your job without a shirt." She lifted her feet and took large awkward steps so her skis were pointing at the archive. "I'm gonna go get lost in history and shake this crap off. You go find all the answers so we can get back to the romantic part of our trip."

Cassie watched over her shoulder as he skied away. That alone should be proof enough that he wasn't worried about any immediate threat.

Having stepped out of her skies, Cassie stomped her boots on the covered porch of the archive before entering. A smiling Elizabeth greeted her with glasses atop her head, hair in a purposeful disarray, and another graphic T-shirt sweater combo.

"Cassie! I just got a call from a friend at the Pueblo archive. I emailed him yesterday about the family of the woman who married James." Elizabeth pulled a piece of paper and began to read as Cassie took off the boots, changed into her shoes, then hung up her jacket.

"The honorable Mr. and Mrs. Buchanan. He was a judge in Pueblo, Colorado and they had three children; all girls—Maria, Mary and Marna. And each time they were written about in papers it was as Miss Buchanan or M. Buchanan."

"That's helpful." Cassie's lips pulled into a thin line.

"And the mother was Mina."

Cassie gave a dry laugh. "Don't people know that they should have been living their lives for the sole purpose of making things easy for those who would study them a hundred years later?"

"Right?" Elizabeth agreed. "But actually, since the father was a judge, there were more photos and family information than normal. My friend is going to try and see if he can figure out exactly which 'M' married James. And find out what happened to her."

"Thank you, that is helpful."

Cassie retrieved her computer and the papers she'd left in the vault overnight, silently grateful for leaving them in, arguably, one of the safer places in town.

Elizabeth was on the far end of one of the twelve-foot tables unfolding a large, detailed map of Colorado. Cassie turned her computer on before joining her.

"It's time to talk mining claims," Elizabeth said. Cassie groaned in reply. This was why she came to Colorado in the first place, but this piece of the puzzle seemed so daunting and time-consuming, and possibly boring.

Elizabeth began, "There are over seventeen thousand mining claims in Colorado. According to the BLM, only eleven thousand of them are active. And there are abandoned mines that aren't factored into those numbers; right now the best guess is that there are roughly twenty-three thousand abandoned."

Cassie took a deep breath and blew it out slowly at the news which sounded more like a dreaded math problem.

Elizabeth continued, "Eden County has almost seven thousand of those mining claims."

"Well shit." Cassie sighed as she heavily sat down. "Okay Elizabeth, I suppose I can't put this off anymore. Mining Claims 101, please begin my lesson."

"That's a big ask." Elizabeth cleared her throat and settled herself next to Cassie. "So, it's 1858, and in a little place called Pikes Peak," she pointed to Colorado Springs on the map, "they found gold in them thar hills. And the next year, 1859, folks from all around arrived, beginning the second largest gold rush in the history of the US."

"That I can wrap my head around."

Elizabeth smiled. "Good. Now, when they came to Eden looking for gold, the actual process happens in various steps. The first years of gold mining in Colorado were what's called placer mining. That's what you see in all the cartoons; an old guy with one tooth wading in the river with his gold pan. The first miners easily found gold in eroded minerals like sand and gravel. Easy to get to."

She waited for Cassie to nod that she was following her explanation.

"Okay," Elizabeth continued, "so the next phase of gold mining was to find deposits of ore and dig them out using machinery to separate it. And Colorado had extensive, rich lodes of ore deposits. But in the mountains around Eden, the ore deposits are located in the hard rock. Meaning it's more difficult to get to, but by the turn of the century, there were men with technology and tools for extracting the ore."

"Got it."

Elizbeth smiled. "Okay, so now by the time William and James arrived in Eden, there would have been five large mining operations in the area. Each one required about two hundred men to work them and the town had over five thousand residents. Those who didn't work in the mines, but called themselves miners, were still trying to find ore deposits on their own and make their fortune."

"So there would have been people who could have taught William and James how to mine," Cassie speculated.

Elizabeth nodded and explained, "But it isn't easy, or lucrative at first. And here's the thing that I found most interesting ..." She pulled a paper from the ever-growing stack she continued to print for Cassie so she'd have her own documentation. "I got this report from the BLM this morning. Of the seven thousand active mines in our county, the Moss brothers' names were on a hundred and forty-five of them."

"Damnit," Cassie seethed, "I only found mention of fifteen."

"All hundred and forty-five are located all over the map. Not really in a localized area. Suggesting to me, that they were looking for something. But of the hundred and forty-five claims they owned, twenty of them are patented." She gave an excited grin, but Cassie shrugged, not understanding the significance. "Sorry, I forget that people don't spend their days researching mining stories." Elizabeth laughed. "So mining is all about the minerals you can find. The big three are gold, silver and uranium."

"Okay."

"When you own a mine, you own the *rights* to look for those minerals and extract them from the land. There are two types of claims you can make in order to do that. A patented and unpatented."

"Oh my God, I think all I'm hearing is Charlie Brown's teacher, wha wha wha wha wha wha."

Elizabeth laughed, unoffended. "I totally understand."

Cassie took a deep breath and gave a nod. "So, two types of mining claims."

"Yes, a patented mining claim means that the brothers owned the land as well as the rights to all the minerals they unearthed. The Federal Government passes a title to the claimant, making it private land."

Cassie asked, "What does an unpatented claim do?"

"That's where you own the minerals extracted, but *not* the land."

"Okay ..."

"Here's why I think this is interesting; a patented mine requires a yearly fee, like a property tax. And according to this email from the BLM," she pointed to the line of interest on the page she'd handed over to Cassie, "someone has paid the dues on those twenty claims every year since they were claimed."

"Did someone pay for them the past two years?"

"Yup," Elizabeth drew out the word excitedly, "those were paid too."

Cassie shook her head. "I don't think I'm understanding this."

"Cassie, the only reason to pay maintenance fees is because then it won't require an annual assessment of work on the claim. No one will ever go look to see what you're doing."

"Okay, so what does it mean?" Cassie asked.

Elizabeth leaned forward excitedly and wiggled her eyebrows as she said, "I have no idea what it means. But I know we need to find out who's been paying for the maintenance fees."

Cassie rubbed her temple. "Elizabeth, we find out information and I think we're making the water more and more murky."

"I know, it's so cool!"

Cassie pointed to the coffee machine across the room. "Do you mind if I make myself a cup?"

"Of course not."

After making a cup of coffee, Cassie pulled the rolling whiteboard into the middle of the room. She took out an erasable marker and wrote William and James' names on the top. "Let me unwind some information a bit."

James
Born 1923

William
Born 1925

Both
Went to war in 1942.
Came home from the war in 1946.
Eden Colorado. 1946.
Purchased 145 claims.

Married January 1947
Died June 1949

Married June 1947

Arrested 1947-1949
1951 California enrolls in college.
1953 publishes memoir.
1955 married.
1960 Theresa Moss born
1965 – 1970 in Eden.
1970. September. is back teaching.

"So what are the questions remaining?" Cassie asked.

Elizabeth supplied, "What was William doing here for those five years? Which 'M' was James married to? Who paid the fees on the mines in the past two years?"

"What is the point of the cryptic note in the book?" Cassie finished.

"We're doing good," Elizabeth said.

Cassie rolled her head from side to side. "I suppose I know more now than I did before, but I also feel like we're looking for a needle in a haystack; only, I'm not sure what kind of needle we're looking for or if it's even a haystack we should be looking in."

Elizabeth asked, "Do you have a copy of the professor's memoir?"

Cassie retrieved the book entitled *A Torch in the Desert*, and handed it over to Elizabeth.

"Have you read it?"

"Only half so far."

"How is it?"

Cassie shrugged. "He was a young man in a difficult situation and he became an English professor. It's well written and heartbreaking and makes you want to mother the shit out of him."

Elizabeth flipped to the middle of the book and began to read a bit. "Damn," she whispered after a few paragraphs and then asked, "Do you mind if I take this home tonight and read it?"

"Not at all. Maybe you'll find something I haven't yet." Cassie cradled the cup in her hand and turned her attention out the window and watched the snow still falling. "It's a lot of snow."

"Don't worry," Elizabeth tried to reassure her, "I've driven these roads, in these kinds of conditions, but by the time you leave, I'm sure the roads will be fine."

"I'll hold you to that." Cassie smiled.

"Do you have any plans for dinner tonight?"

Cassie shook her head. "I don't think so."

"Aidan and I felt so bad that your first night in town you got into a fight, so we'd love to take you to dinner and show you the classier side of Eden."

"It happens." Cassie waved off the sorrowful look in Elizabeth's eyes. "But we'd love to go. I have to admit, all the food we've had so far has been amazing." As if it were a thought she meant to share earlier, Cassie added, "Do you eat at The Rose often? I can't believe the breakfast I had this morning."

"Edwin is a phenomenal cook, we go once a week when we're in town."

"I would too."

"We'd like to take you to The Mining King tonight."

"Is that the large hotel in the center of town?"

Elizabeth nodded. "It was one of the first structures built when the town was founded in 1882. They needed to accommodate the flood of miners and other visitors that came along with the gold boom."

"And that's where James and 'M' were living after they got married." Elizabeth nodded.

"It would be cool to see the inside." She grinned as she asked, "Is it haunted?"

"Yes."

"Is the food good?"

"Very."

Cassie laughed and shook her head. "What time?"

"Six?"

"Perfect." Cassie put her cup down. "What's next?"

"So I thought I'd start going through a few newspaper databases within the surrounding areas and look for any more information on William's escapades. I also pulled several boxes of photos and articles from 1946 to 1949. Many are of large town celebrations and parades. Maybe we'll find some more random references to William or James."

"Sounds good." Cassie pointed to the three boxes that had been placed at the end of the table, double-checking they were the correct ones.

Elizabeth gave a nod of verification and said, "You know what I should do? I'm going to ask Beverly over tomorrow. She's lived in Eden a long time, I think she got here in the late sixties. Her husband was a native, so she might remember the names or something else that might be useful."

"I'd love that, if you don't mind."

"You have pictures of him during that time frame, right?"

"Yes."

They lost track of time until Stills came sliding up to the front of the archive on his skis.

Cassie stretched her arms above her head, gave a yawn and wondered at the time. "Four thirty?"

"No wonder I'm hungry." Elizabeth scrubbed her face. "We are not good for each other."

Cassie agreed, "Yeah, I think we'd both be happy as could be getting lost in history for weeks at a time."

The stomp of boots on the porch brought a twirl to Cassie's stomach; she didn't realize until he opened the door that she'd been holding her breath. And when he shot her a smile, she slowly let out all the air. Even in his jacket, she could see areas where his muscles pulled the fabric taut—not overly much—but she'd done enough extensive studies of his body and was far from exhausted by her examinations. His jawline and upper lip were filled in with dark hair; it had been a few days since he'd shaved, and the rugged look was growing on Cassie. A lot. It suited this land.

"Benji," Cassie greeted from where she sat.

"Did you two take a break today?"

"Nope, we're all hyped-up on caffeine and history." Cassie grinned. "Wanna go to the oldest building in town for dinner?"

"Of course."

"Elizabeth and Aidan invited us."

"Perfect. What time?"

Cassie looked at Elizabeth. "Does six still work?"

"Yup. I'll close up here. And if you want, we can come pick you two up."

"On snowmobiles?" Cassie asked, gesturing to the snowmobile parked out front of the archive.

"Of course."

"Then yes, that should round out my entire mountain winter experience perfectly."

Chapter Twenty-Nine

Stills meant to ask Cassie about her day and what she'd found, and she had the same intention. But once they were in the house, stripping off their now wet pants and socks, and Stills caught a glimpse of her bare legs—sculpted with muscles from so many years of playing soccer—his train of thought jumped tracks. He crossed the distance between them and pulled off the rest of her clothes while his lips burned her skin. Freeing herself, she stepped away and laughingly headed upstairs as fast as she could go, with Stills hot on her trail.

When they'd exhausted themselves and caught their breath, Stills lay on his side, lightly tracing his fingers across her collar bone. "How was your day, Dodd?"

"Very cool." She laughed. "I was able to search through so many old photos and files ... Benji, there are so many stories in this town, I don't know how Elizabeth handles it."

"But that's what you do for a living."

"I don't have free rein, not that she has free rein necessarily; there are the day to day tasks of running an archive, and the digitization she works on at a snail's pace. I don't think I'd ever get anything done if I came across really cool things on a daily basis. Today for instance, I was going through a newspaper and found this article about how the Gypsies that were camping on the outskirts of town had been run off. I wanted to go straight into researching the history of Gypsies in the states."

He gave an interested hmm. "Did you find any new pieces of William Moss' life?"

"I was given a quick study on the history of mining and types of mining and types of claims in the area and the types of claims the Moss brothers had.”

“Interesting?”

“Nope.” She stretched, and her stomach growled. “Benji, I’m hungry.”

“But not worried?”

She thought about it for a moment and realized she’d been so involved in the work today that she didn’t even think about the tracker or fear of the previous evening.

“No. I’m fine.”

“Good.”

“Did you find anything?”

“I found the best way to get snow off a car when you don’t have the right tools is a broom.”

“Noted.”

“But most importantly, no one has tampered with the car.”

That was a relief. “Shower and get ready to go?”

“Yup, let’s do our part, Dodd and help conserve water.”

Of course, conserving water was the last thing they did in the shower.

They were sitting on the sofa when two snowmobiles pulled up. Cassie gave a snort, and followed it with, “Awesome.” Yesterday, Elizabeth had taken her to lunch on the beast, but it was still a novel experience, so she was still excited.

“Have you ever been on a snowmobile?” Cassie asked.

“Maybe,” Stills answered as he pulled on his gloves.

“‘Maybe’ means you had to ride one for work. Which makes me think of you somewhere in Switzerland again, only this time instead of skis, you had to jump on a snowmobile to chase down the bad guy, and you were driving through a harrowing tree line just so you could retrieve a USB that would somehow save the world.”

“Dodd ...” He tried to sound contrite but the smile ruined it. “I was in Montana visiting a friend one Thanksgiving and it snowed and *he* had snowmobiles."

"That's a very boring story," she said as they closed the door behind them.

Aidan greeted them and told Stills he could drive the machine if he wanted, but Stills let Cassie take the front instead. He thought he made the right decision as he pulled her against his body and wrapped his arms around her waist, leaning his head close to hers so he could give her a few instructions as to how to drive.

The warm air and tickle of his short beard on her ear sent shivers up her arm. She leaned into him, trying to get more.

When the Pines took off, Cassie didn't move.

"You okay?" he asked.

"I kinda like this situation," she said.

When Aidan stopped up the road, thinking something was wrong, Cassie launched the snowmobile into motion.

They weren't going at high speeds, this was simply a jaunt a few blocks down the road, but Cassie felt alive and so very cool. As if she were the first person to ever use a snowmobile. The snow still fell, and the cold on her face shocked her hungry stomach into a temporary calm. The excitement of doing something new, with Stills holding her, was sheer delight.

The whir of the snowmobile and the flickering light of the headlamp against the dark gray dusky sky, along with the beginning shadows of all the buildings was pure magic. And a handful of blocks later, the drive was over; all too quick.

She slowly pulled up in front of The Mining King Hotel to park on the cleared area of the street next to a handful of other cars and snowmobiles. Yellow light spilled onto the sidewalk, inviting and warm. From the street Cassie spied the full restaurant.

"For the 'tourist season' having not started yet, this town is hopping," she muttered.

In the entryway of the grand hotel, they shook off the snow that'd collected on their boots and coats, then hung up their jackets on one of the several tall coat trees strategically placed around the room for guests.

On the left, the giant reception area had a large mahogany desk where guests could check in; then to the right was a grand staircase with a gold filigree banister. The carpet throughout was the Victorian maroon with a gold paisley pattern that Cassie was growing quite accustomed to and found she rather expected now. The carpet filled the length of the room and stairs, and the walls were decorated with white and gold embellished paper.

A sofa and two matching armchairs sat next to a grand piano in the farthest corner and on both sides of the staircase were four leather and wood chairs angled toward each other for visiting.

Cassie wondered at another feeling of stepping back in time to the proper Victorian Old West; the only thing missing was proper clothing of the time

In the back of the reception area was the entrance to the fine dining establishment. The restaurant was on par with the rest of the establishment she'd viewed so far. Hardwood herringbone floors, simple matching tables and chairs, white tablecloths with a candle in the center of each.

The bar took up one whole wall and was an intricately carved mahogany showpiece. Hand-carved leaves, branches and filigree trailed around five arched and antique mirror backed alcoves that had been upgraded with lighting to illuminate the bottles of liquor that sat upon glass shelves.

Hanging from the pressed metal ceiling were recreations of floral Victorian pendants that gave off a soft, romantic glow.

Cassie walked behind the Pines and was strangely envious of the way most patrons greeted them as they passed, with a respectful, "Doc. Elizabeth." Some would nod or add a bit of information as to how they were personally doing: "That heat pad sure is helping my arthritis at night." Others simply complimented or asked after the couple: "You look good, glad to see you're back."

What must it be like to be in the thick of a community like this? Of course, Cassie knew herself well enough to realize that if she had to be the center of gossip for too long, it would end with her intensely offending *a lot* of people. She liked her privacy.

Seated, with drinks and food ordered, they fell into conversation about the research Cassie and Elizabeth had been doing the past two days. Aidan and Stills weighed in on the possible reasons William would change his ways, theorizing about what life must have been like for men all those years ago.

"Do you think you would have been a miner?" Cassie asked Stills. "Would you have felt the urge to go West and find your fortune?"

"I've never thought about it. I'm not sure." He shrugged. "It doesn't sound like much fun, but the idea of striking it rich probably held a lot of pull in those days."

"I think I would have still been a doctor," Aidan surmised.

"Who knows," Stills gave Cassie a knowing look, "I might have been a peace officer."

The idea caused Cassie to ask, "Did any of the famous robbers or gunslingers come to Eden? I can't believe I didn't think to ask that. I mean, according to the binder, The Hideout might have had a few men and women of ill repute as guests; but did Wyatt Earp or Doc Holliday ever ride through town?"

Elizabeth shot Cassie a wide grin. "If you ask a lot of the locals, they'll claim Wyatt Earp, Billy the Kid and a whole list of famous gunslingers and gamblers came through. Even Lincoln."

"Lincoln?"

Elizabeth pursed her lips and gave a shake of her head. "The dates don't line up. But there's an entry in the ledger of this very hotel for Doc Holliday, though it hasn't been authenticated. But it's fun to think they might have come through, and it's not out of the realm of possibilities. They both loved Colorado and Wyatt Earp spent years traveling through the gold mining camps."

"I would have been a gambler and traveled with Earp and Holliday," Cassie announced.

Stills tilted his head as he studied her, sizing up the possibility when the bartender rang a bell above the bar.

The sound brought a smile to Cassie's face, but as the mood in the room tensed and everyone became eerily quiet, the smile faded.

The bartender cleared his throat before loudly announcing, "There's been a slide south of town, just before the pass, a car's been spotted nearby."

Several men and women stood and began to gather their coats.

"Unfortunately, that's my cue," Aidan said. "Search and rescue is being assembled and since there's a car nearby, I'll need to be available just in case."

Cassie felt a chill run down her spine—this was not what she expected when she imagined her and Stills on vacation.

"What can we do?" Stills asked.

He held out his hand to Stills. "I appreciate it, but avalanche search and rescue in this country requires several months of training. This town has a well-oiled, well-trained group, but if there's anything we need, I know where to find you and am grateful for the offer."

Aidan caught the attention of one of the men walking past. "Hey Tom, can I ride with you and do you mind stopping at the clinic first?" After an agreement, Aidan turned his attention to Elizabeth and gave her a quick kiss. "You okay to take the snowmobile?"

"Of course." She patted his hand.

He nodded to Stills and Cassie. "And why don't you two take the other one. You'll be here a few more days and it's the best way to get around town, so you might as well use it."

They agreed as the young man who would be giving Aidan a ride patted him on the shoulder that he was ready.

Still standing, as the handful of people part of the rescue left, Cassie glanced uneasily at Elizabeth. "Should we go?"

"No, we'll finish dinner," Elizabeth said as the noise in the restaurant regained its loud murmur.

"Okay." Cassie's forehead creased and she examined the room; there was still a slight air of worry. "Elizabeth, this might be normal for you, but I feel weird," she admitted, causing Stills to wordlessly rub her back.

"Well, since we don't have all the information yet, I've learned that it's best to keep going until we do."

"Is it normal to have avalanches this time of year?" Stills asked.

Elizabeth shrugged. "Yes and no, it normally depends on the amount of snow we get. This year, Eden had a pretty wet, cold winter. You see, when the snow freezes and melts then refreezes, the built-up layers are uneven, and when there's as much snow as we've had the past three days, it creates perfect avalanche conditions."

"And this is just a normal, accepted part of life up here?" Cassie asked.

"For the most part, it's merely another aspect of what made the people who lived in Eden so stalwart and strong."

"I guess."

When their food was delivered, the waitress told Elizabeth she put the doctor's in a to-go container and would bring it before they left.

Elizabeth turned her attention to Cassie and Stills with an apologetic smile, and wanting to soothe their obviously rattled nerves, she calmly said, "There's nothing we can do. So we'll finish our dinner and our visit. If there *is* something we can do, someone will come knocking."

The tension in the room seemed to release, then after several bites, Stills asked, "So how long does it take to clear an avalanche?"

"It depends on the size, but road crews here in town will start working tomorrow, as well as crews from Highland. It usually doesn't take more than three days."

Cassie glanced at Stills. "If it's more than three, we need to talk to Marsha."

"She'll prorate the rental, it's not like anyone else is going to be using the house. She also only charges fifty percent of the normal fee; as she says, 'no one ever expects an avalanche.'"

Suddenly they were both making mental lists of who they needed to notify for their jobs, and what it meant to be stuck.

"What happens to the town?" Cassie asked.

Elizabeth smiled. "Life goes on. Restaurants will still be open, and if there is something you need, they post a list at the grocery store so we can help each other out."

"Have you been stuck in town before?"

Elizabeth nodded.

"What's the longest you've been stuck?"

"Eight days."

Cassie's eyes widened. "Eight days?"

"The people of Eden rally, and no one went without." She patted Cassie's hand. "That time, though, it was a larger avalanche and there were problems with the equipment on our end. So they couldn't do their fair share of the work. This won't be like that."

Stills winked at Cassie. "It's another part of the adventure."

"People in Eden say that we aren't snowed in, it's the rest of the world that's snowed out." As Elizabeth took a bite, Stills narrowed his gaze at

Cassie and raised an eyebrow; the rest of the world being snowed out wasn't such a bad thing.

After dinner they took a cold snowy ride back to the house, only this time it didn't feel liberating. It was a bit more sterile, mainly because Cassie was trying to shake off the worry.

The landline was ringing when they entered the house. "I can't remember the last time I heard a good old-fashioned landline ring," Cassie said as she answered the phone.

"Hello dear, it's Marsha."

"Marsha," Cassie greeted cheerily, as Stills went about adding more pellets to the fire.

"I don't know if you've heard or not, but we are now snowed in. There's been an avalanche south of town."

"Yes, we were at dinner with the Pines when they made the announcement."

"I just want you to know that you have The Hideout as long as you need. No one ever factors in an avalanche on their vacation. And in cases like this, I give a discount, so don't you worry about anything. And if there's anything you need, give me a ring."

"We will, thank you."

"And come by for breakfast tomorrow. Edwin is in a frittata mood."

After thanking Marsha again, Cassie passed the information along to Stills as she heated water for some tea.

With the fire roaring to life and three candles set on the coffee table, they turned out the rest of the lights and snuggled on the sofa with their tea as they watched the outside world, lit only by the reflection of the town's few lights against the low clouds.

"The good news is that no one is getting in." Stills repeated Elizabeth's sentiment from earlier.

Feeling soothed by that thought, Cassie said, "I should email work and call Jess; in case we can't get out when we're supposed to."

"Tomorrow, Dodd. There'll be plenty of time tomorrow."

"I suppose I just got a few more days to continue working, and you can relax now."

"You could start on a side project, who knows what else you'll find."

Cassie grunted, not wanting to admit that she had secretly jotted down several side projects she was going to look into once she was back in LA.

Chapter Thirty

Something woke Cassie. She blinked her eyes in the darkness of the room, but stayed frozen as consciousness cleared her senses. The sound came again, someone knocking on the door.

She bolted upright, her stomach in her throat. At the same moment Stills was slipping out of bed and pulling on his flannel pants, followed by a stranded shirt flung over the end of the bed. He glanced sideways at Cassie as he pulled it down and reassured her, "Bad guys don't knock, Dodd."

That was true. And since they were snowed in, chances were it wasn't someone who meant them harm.

"Another item to add to my spy training list," she mumbled while getting dressed.

He smiled at her, but it didn't reach his eyes; bad guys might not knock, but it *was* still one in the morning, and whoever was knocking was not here for a social visit. As they headed downstairs, Stills leading the way, she tried not to focus on his tense shoulders and careful movements.

The Roman shades were drawn, keeping the identity of the knocker hidden, so Stills placed his foot and body in the way of the door before he opened it to greet the midnight caller.

Cassie didn't realize how apprehensive she'd been until Stills relaxed completely and opened the door all the way, revealing Aidan and Cole.

"Sorry for the late hour," Cole said, his deep voice laden with exhaustion. Both men looked haggard and edgy.

Stills swept his hand in invitation. "C'mon in."

Cassie joined Stills' side. "Is everything okay?"

Aidan took off his thick gloves and slapped them lightly against his thigh, giving a nervous glance to Cole as he admitted, "Not really."

Cole shot a look at Stills, removed his wool cap and twisted it in his hands, "We pulled a body from the avalanche."

Cassie took an instinctive step closer to Stills and he slipped his arm around her waist as Aidan explained, "In cases like this, I can keep bodies at the clinic until I can properly transport them to Highland. As the town doctor, it falls to me to declare the time of death along with the cause ..." He glanced again at Cole, pursed his lips as if he'd been instructed to tell them what was happening, but utterly confused as to why.

"I take it the cause of death wasn't an avalanche?" Stills led.

Cole nodded for Aidan to continue.

"He was shot," the doctor said softly.

Cole continued, "The body was found on this side of town. And since the north road is also closed ..."

"I thought they already closed that?" Cassie said.

"They did close the road because of dangerous conditions. But while we were working on recovery, word came in that there was another avalanche north of here closing off the only roads in and out," Cole explained.

"So whoever killed your victim ..." Cassie couldn't finish, so Cole completed the thought, "Is still in town."

Stills continued. "And you've got a limited amount of time to figure out who did it."

Cole blew out a heavy sigh in reply.

"What am I missing?" Aidan finally asked.

Cole didn't answer, but instead said, "There are defensive wounds on his arms and the trajectory of the bullet suggests the victim was shot from behind, maybe while trying to run."

"Jesus ..." Cassie breathed.

Aidan glanced confusedly between the two men, so Stills took pity on him and directed his question at Cole. "And did you tell Aidan why you came here in the middle of the night to personally give me this information?"

Cole Clayton furrowed his brow. "Because Agent Stills, I'm all alone here and you're CIA."

"CIA?" Aidan whispered in disbelief.

"I'll put some coffee on, sounds like it's gonna be a late night." Cassie turned on lights as she made her way across the room, followed by the three men.

Seated, Stills aimed a half smile at Aidan. "In my career I'm not encouraged to tell people what I do for a living."

Aidan nodded. "I understand."

After everyone was settled, Stills started by asking, "Do you know the man who was killed?"

Cole nodded. "His name is ... was, Art. Mid-seventies, local man, quiet, kept to himself. He's lived here a long time, so he knows better than to drive out in this weather. But from the wounds, I don't think he had much choice."

"Can you establish a time of death?"

Aidan was still a little shaken; he had to clear his throat a few times before answering, "Best conclusion I have, is that by the time we found Art, he'd been dead about four hours."

Cole took over the explanation. "The slide happened around six eighteen this evening. Once we gathered everyone and started looking, we found Art's body on the side of the slide, his head and arm sticking out."

"When we were at the restaurant, the bartender said there was a car near the slide," Stills recalled.

"It was Art's car," Cole confirmed. "By the time we arrived, the car was stil on but it had swerved into the side of the mountain. Both driver's and passenger's side doors were open, suggesting he wasn't alone. And it is a possibility that whoever shot at Art caused the avalanche."

Cassie shook her head in disbelief as she slipped in the chair next to Stills, the coffee beginning to gurgle as it brewed.

Stills began to question and run theories. "Was he the kind of man who someone would want to harm? Did he have an angry wife, pissed off kids? Was he the kind of guy people would hold a grudge against?"

"Never had kids," Cole informed. "He married late in life, lost his wife a few years back. He was a nice, upstanding citizen. Quiet is all. Showed up to every community event, first to lend a hand when it was needed."

"But someone wanted him dead." Stills shook his head and stared across the room as if he were starting to place all the information on an invisible board. "Did he have valuables? Was he wealthy?"

"No, as far as I know, he was on a fixed income." Cole slouched, the weight of the situation pressing down on him. "This is why I came here, I need help on this one."

"Benji'll help," Cassie volunteered at the same time Stills gave a soft smile and agreed, "I'll do what I can."

Cole took a deep breath and some of his stress seemed to slip away. "Okay, I contacted the Highland Sheriff's Office and explained the situation. This storm is causing problems for them as well. They want to try and fly someone in tomorrow, but with nowhere to land, the current idea is to send someone in via heli-skiing. But they're just spitballing, it's not a good idea."

"Heli-skiing?" Cassie asked.

Aidan explained, "We have a popular ski mountain for extreme sporters. You take a helicopter to the top, jump out and ski down."

"No." Cassie shook her head, appalled at the idea.

Cole gave a gruff laugh. "Yeah, let's just say it's not the most ideal way to get support into town right now."

"And it takes two or three days typically for crews to clear an avalanche?" Stills asked.

"That's right," Aidan replied.

Stills frowned. "So, we have two or three days to find a killer."

A shiver ran through Cassie at the use of the word 'killer.' She stood to pour four cups of coffee, then delivered them.

"I asked Highland to slow down the DOT," Cole said. "And on our side, old Ben Wilson, who runs the crew, is gonna help me by making sure most of the equipment is broken."

"What kind of time does that leave us?" asked Stills.

"Four days. Max."

Aidan's hands shook as he brought the cup of coffee to his lips. Cassie gave him a tight smile; she wasn't feeling very well herself.

Cole rolled his cup between his hands. "I'm sorry you folks came to town only to find yourselves embroiled in this mess."

"To be fair, we brought a bit of mess to your town too." Cassie frowned and then raised an eyebrow in question at Stills. "Do you think this is a coincidence?"

"This time, I do," he reassured her. "Okay, the way I see it, we all need to go to breakfast tomorrow. And coffee and lunch," Stills affirmed.

"Why?" Aidan asked, confused.

Understanding Stills' idea, Cole nodded in agreement while giving Aidan an answer. "Because people are going to be talking about Art and we want to hear every word of gossip they have."

"Exactly," Stills said. "If you have one thing working for this town, it's the refusal to keep secrets. We need to use that to our advantage."

"Okay." Aidan nodded.

"Was there anything strange about the car? Prints around it or something left behind?" Stills was in proper CIA mode now.

"There was too much snow already built up, so I had it towed to the gas station on the edge of town; haven't had time to look for prints or anything yet," Cole responded.

"What was Art wearing when you found him?" Stills asked.

Aidan frowned as he answered, "A light flannel, jeans, hiking boots, but only one was on his foot ... I assumed the other fell off due to the trajectory of the slide."

"Was the shoe tied?"

Aidan sat back and frowned, unable to remember. Cole pulled out his phone and after a moment, turned the phone to Stills and zoomed in on the foot with the shoe, the laces undone.

Stills raised an eyebrow and shared the first assumption he could make. "Not prepared to be in this weather, but rather hastily dressed. That fits with the theory that someone was forcing him to do what he didn't want to do. If the car crashed, maybe he caused it, trying to get away?"

"Maybe," Cole said.

Stills took a deep breath. "So, you don't have a suspect because the man who was killed was a nice guy. You also don't have a motive. And you came here in the middle of the night because you don't want anyone else to know what I do for a living."

"That's the tall and short of it," Cole admitted.

Cassie glanced at him as the realization and confirmation from the sheriff washed over her.

"Do you have pictures of the scene where you found the body, and a preliminary coroner's report?"

Both men nodded as Cole found the photos on his phone and handed them over.

"There is a slight chance the avalanche began and Art swerved into the mountain, but the way his body was found buried in the snow, it isn't the best theory. The airbags didn't deploy, so he couldn't have been going very fast. And like I said, the car was still running when we arrived." It looked like the green Subaru had lost control on the ice and slid into the side of the mountain. With the doors open, snow had gathered on the top of the car door and inside on the seats and floorboards. As Cole said, any tracks going from the car had been covered already with snow.

On the passenger side were several newspapers and other trash. In the back seat, all the excess garbage and items had been moved to the seat behind the driver.

"This is interesting," Stills pointed out. "If I had you at gunpoint, and I was forcing you to drive, what's the best place to be?"

"Back seat, passenger side, better angle," the sheriff stated.

Stills raised an eyebrow. "What if the suspect who did this was caught in the avalanche too? How do you know there isn't another body out there?"

"We use avalanche probes and dogs."

Cassie felt like she was losing her mind. What world had she walked into that avalanche probes and dogs, who could locate people in mountains of fallen snow, were ideas thrown out so cavalierly. "Dogs?"

"Yup," Cole replied. "There are about five dogs in town that have been trained to be avalanche rescue dogs. If we can't find the person buried in time, at least the dogs can help bring closure. They can sniff out anyone who might be buried under several feet of snow."

"So chances the killer was caught in the slide are slim," Stills surmised.

"Especially based on the trajectory. If the killer's gun was the catalyst for the avalanche, he would have seen it coming and run away, behind the car. He probably would have been clear of it," Cole suggested. "We had the dogs sniff the car and follow any tracks, but they just made circles."

"Another car?" Stills muttered. "Someone else following and helping?"

Cole shrugged. "Another possibility."

Aidan handed over his photos. "There is also some bruising around the temple; he was hit with something."

Cassie glanced away from the phone; while the car information was intriguing, she wasn't interested in this part.

After a few moments of study, Stills handed the phone back. "Hit with the butt of a gun? To prod him into doing something?"

Cole gave a curt nod at the conclusion.

"When would be a good time for me to see the car?" Stills asked.

"Let's do it now while the town is quiet. We'll take my truck," Cole said. "Doc, I'll drop you off on the way."

"I suggest we all accidentally meet for breakfast tomorrow at The Rose, about eight," Stills said, then stood, holding his hand out to Cassie. "Give us a second to get some warmer clothes on."

"You want me to go with you?" Cassie asked, surprised.

"I don't want you to worry," he said, then whispered, "And I think we really are starting some sort of spy training now."

"But suddenly, I'm not so interested in it," she muttered.

Chapter Thirty-One

Cassie yawned as she pulled her jacket on. "I wanted to be exhausted on this trip for a different reason."

Stills pulled her to his side and brushed a kiss on the top of her head, but she turned her body into his and wrapped herself around him.

"Cass?" Stills whispered, concerned.

"I'm fine," she told his neck, where her face was buried.

"Are you?"

"No," she muttered.

"What do you want to do?"

"Talk it out," she suggested, but the disdain coming through made Stills laugh.

He tilted his head so he could rest it against hers. "What's really bothering you?"

"How are you going to find this person who did this with nothing to go on? In four days?"

"Dodd, if this was all theoretical, and on paper, how would you go about it?"

She grunted. "Not the same thing."

"Humor me."

She scowled. "I'd look into Art's life; he might have known the person or left behind some indication of who kidnapped him."

"Exactly."

She took a deep breath and began talking through the truths they did know. "No one knows what you do for a living."

"Fact: I'm *just* the boyfriend of the genealogist," he supplied.

"Actually, that's a half fact."

"How do you figure?"

"You're the *fiancé* of the genealogist."

Stills gave a rumble of a laugh then continued. "Fact: You've taken a year and a half of self-defense classes, liked it so much it's led to karate classes."

"Shotokan Karate," she muttered.

"Fact."

It was Cassie's turn. "The tracker was placed in another house and nothing has happened there."

"Fact."

"This avalanche and murder, it's not related to us. We happen to be in the right place at the wrong time?"

"Fact." He cupped her face. "And I too have had extensive training in the job of keeping people safe."

"Fact." She actually *was* feeling better. It always helped when she could reason things out. And of course, Stills never scoffed or disparaged her for worrying, but instead helped her find solid footing and factual ground to look at the world.

"Better?"

"Maybe." She slipped out of the hug.

"Good. Now, I'm hungry and want whatever Edwin has cooked up."

"Fact," Cassie said.

"You wanna drive the snowmobile or want me to?"

"I'll drive. I love that thing."

At The Rose, the Pines were already seated. Cassie waved at Elizabeth but was intercepted by Marsha. "Mornin' darling, I'm so glad you came by. Edwin outdid himself with an asparagus, sundried tomato and feta frittata, and then he went and made white chocolate, cranberry, oatmeal cookies."

Cassie's stomach gave a grumble of approval. "Marsha, if you don't mind, I think I'm going to need to borrow a few ingredients. Since we're going to be here a few more days, I think I need to do some baking of my own."

"Really?" Stills asked, his excitement palpable.

Cassie gave a wobbly frown, trying to convey the message that of course she was going to bake; it was the number one thing she did when she felt life got on top of her.

He didn't pay her any attention and instead told Marsha, "She's an amazing baker. It's one of the reasons I proposed."

Marsha laughed. "Oh I understand sticking around for the love of food darlin'. And I'm sure Edwin'll give you whatever you need." She hugged Cassie around the shoulder. "Now, the Pines are here, and Elizabeth is waving you over, so how about we push two tables together so you can visit? I bet you two have dug up some fascinating stories the past few days. Do you like working at the archive?"

Cassie nodded. "I do. Normally I can do most of my research from my office at work, but there is something intimate and very cool about being able to grab the physical copies of pictures and newspapers when I need them."

"I bet you feel like Nicolas Cage in *National Treasure.*"

"Ummm ..."

Stills corrected, "She's more like Lara Croft from *Tomb Raider.*"

Cassie frowned at him over her shoulder while Marsha laughed, giving her another squeeze before letting go to reorganize the tables and pour coffee for everyone.

"Marsha," Elizabeth caught the woman's attention, "how are you doing this morning?"

"Oh, I'll miss Art, that's for sure. The fool must have been slipping in his old age. No clue what he was thinking going out during this storm." She put one hand on her hip and let the carafe of coffee hang limply from the other.

"I don't know," Aidan commiserated, "we're all going to miss him."

"Did you know him a long time?" Cassie asked.

"As well as anyone could know Art. He was an introvert but came to all the dances and parades. I served with him on the Friends of the Library Board, he was really passionate about books." She straightened. "That's what we'll do. We'll have a memorial donation to the library for Art. He would have loved that. Okay kids, I'll put your order in but I've got a few phone calls to make." She winked at the table and turned to leave.

Elizabeth let out a shaky breath as her smile faded. She swallowed and glanced around the room before she leaned across the table and whispered, "Aidan told me ... about how you spend your time at work,

Ben."

Stills gave an understanding smile. "I figured he would."

"I feel so weird," she admitted.

Cassie shot her a reassuring look. "Don't, he's still Benji my fiancé and you and I have work to do and everything's going to be okay."

Stills draped his arm around the back of Cassie's chair, looking bored as he asked about the six tables that were filled. "You know everybody here?"

"All local," Elizabeth said as Aidan sat up straight, nodded to Stills and waved a greeting across the room to Sheriff Clayton as he entered.

Marsha came back with plates as Cole arrived at the table. She looked at him, concern etched on her face. "How you doin', Cole? Long night?"

"Unfortunately," he said wearily.

"I'm glad it wasn't Edwin who found Art." She explained to Cassie and Stills. "Edwin's on search and rescue, and he and Art played cards every second Friday of the month. He's pretty upset."

"I'll come visit with him later, if you think it'll help," Cole said.

"Of course it will. Now, I'm going to impose on all of you and make Cole sit with you this morning." She pulled up a close-by chair as everyone gave various verbal invitations.

She patted him on the shoulder once he was seated. "I'll get you coffee and put your order in."

As she walked away Stills said, "Do you think Edwin knew Art enough to know if he was having any problems?"

"That's what comes to mind," Cole agreed. "I'll follow up on that lead later today."

"So now what happens?" Elizabeth breathed out the question.

"Life as normal," Cole suggested.

Stills leveled his gaze at Cassie as he said, "You two will go to the archive and work on an old case and we'll start putting together the new one."

Cassie muttered, "He says his job and ours are similar in that we piece together information and ..." When she trailed off, Elizabeth frowned in question, but before Cassie could explain, Stills let out a laugh. "You see it now, don't you, Dodd? The similarities."

"Our jobs are not the same."

"I never said the same, I said similar sometimes in the execution of events."

"He thinks the way *we* research, and the way someone in his line of work would research ... a horrible event," her pause was obvious as to what she was talking about, "are basically the same."

"Oh," Elizabeth nodded, "I can see that."

Cassie shook her head. "You're not supposed to agree with him."

Cole joined in. "Actually, I can see similarities."

"Sheriff Clayton," Cassie tisked.

The rest of breakfast was spent debating the differences and similarities in the way law enforcement and a historian would work a case.

Chapter Thirty-Two

The group made a small parade down Main Street to the archive. The snow continued to fall in soft quiet sheets from the low, gray clouds. As Cassie stomped her feet on the porch, then climbed out of her jacket and hat and gloves once again, she had an inkling of how the snow might be challenging.

Of course the biting cold, after being in the cozy warmth of The Rose, was different this morning. There was more of a stark reality to the situation as she took in the daunting mountains that surrounded them on all sides; with no way out, the idea of being snowed in lost all of its romance when you were stuck with an unknown killer.

The men followed Elizabeth and Cassie into the archive. Cole left his coat on, but took off his hat and began, "As you can see from the continued snow this morning, it isn't safe for anyone from Highland to get here. But it also means no one is leaving either. It would be stupid to try and pack out, either with a snowmobile or cross-country skis."

Elizabeth licked her lips. "So we're really snowed in with a murderer?"

Cole's gruff demeanor softened. "No, whoever did this is stuck; and doesn't know that I've got more manpower helping me out." He slapped his hat against his leg as if to reiterate how important that fact was. "I'm a hundred percent convinced you're safe. But keep the door locked as an extra precaution today."

"We can see who's coming and going anyway," Cassie offered.

"Exactly," Stills said.

"What will you be doing today?" Cassie asked him.

"Aidan will go back to the clinic, but Clayton is going to give me a tour of the town."

Cole grunted. "Which means we're going to drink a lot of coffee and shoot the shit with a lot of folks."

"Kinda like a stakeout?" Cassie gave Stills a knowing grin.

"Kinda."

"Okay," Elizabeth said.

Aidan hugged his wife. "You'll be fine."

She smiled up at him. "I will. What will you be doing?"

"Benjamin asked me to go over my work once more," he said tactfully.

"Then I suppose Cassie and I will be right here, doing what we do best."

Cassie elbowed her softly and grinned. "Hell yeah."

Elizabeth and Cassie gathered the papers and files from the locked vault and settled with fresh cups of coffee as an older woman with short gray hair, a scowl and thin lips stomped into view of the window, heading toward the porch.

"Oh damn," Elizabeth blew out. "I completely forgot I invited Beverly to come talk to you this morning."

"I can't imagine why."

"I can tell her to go away," Elizabeth whispered as the woman stomped across the porch and tried to open the door.

"Nah, it's fine. It might help jumpstart our focus," Cassie said.

The woman knocked three quick, demanding raps before Elizabeth could open the door. "Good morning, Beverly."

"The door is locked." Beverly's voice was scratchy, from age and a possible youth filled with cigarette smoke.

"We have a lot of valuable material for the project we're working on spread around." Elizabeth gave the lame excuse.

"Hmm ..." The woman made quick work of hanging up her jacket, patted the front pocket of her oversized denim overshirt and then openly eyed Cassie as she gave one more stomp of each foot.

Cassie crossed the room. "I'm Cassie Dodd."

"Beverly." The woman shook hands and then tilted her head to the side, taking in Cassie with a squint of her eyes. "You do work like Elizabeth?"

"Yes." Cassie figured it was the easiest answer. "I work for a company called Ancestry Home, I'm a historian there."

Beverly grunted. "Everyone wants to know who they are and where they come from." Whether Beverly thought that was a good or bad thing, Cassie couldn't tell.

"Well, thank you so much for taking time to meet with me. I really appreciate it."

"What else do I have going on? Did you hear about Art?" She sat down at the head of the table on which Cassie and Elizabeth were working.

"I did," Elizabeth said. "He'll be missed."

Beverly sighed. "Damn shame."

"Did you know him well?" Cassie asked.

"As well as you can know a man who keeps to himself. I knew his wife better." She shrugged. "You get to my age in a town like this and there's comfort in seeing other old fools who decided this was the way to live." She pursed her lips, making them almost disappear among the weathered wrinkles, and then sighed the conversation away, sat up straight and nodded at Elizabeth. "So, offer me some coffee and I'll take it."

"Of course, cream or sugar?" Elizabeth asked as Cassie rested her fingers in front of her mouth, hiding a laugh. Beverly's abruptness was refreshing and entertaining as hell.

Once the coffee was delivered, Beverly gestured to Cassie. "Ask me what you want to ask."

Cassie cleared her throat through a widening smile. "I'm researching the life of William Moss. He lived here between 1946 and 1951, and then again from 1965 to 1970. I was curious if you remembered him or anyone who knew him." Cassie pulled up several photos on her computer of William in 1965. Elizabeth passed along the photo from the paper of the two brothers at the picnic.

Beverly pulled out a pair of glasses from her pocket and studied the photos, snorting as she did. "Yeah, I knew who Bill Moss was."

Cassie felt a thrill run through her body.

Beverly continued, "Bill, that's how he'd introduce himself. A rather cocksure man; I remember that much. Mind you, we weren't friends, but I remember him."

Cassie explained, "Theresa, Bill's daughter, found letters between her parents when he was living here between '65 and '70. But we don't really know what he was doing here. The letters weren't very forthcoming; really only notes about how much they miss each other with questions and reports on how their daughter is doing. If you can remember anything about him at all, I'd appreciate it."

Beverly leaned forward and held up a finger. "When a man leaves his wife and child for five years, it's a safe bet he's philanderin'." Her voice squeaked out the word.

There was laughter in Elizabeth's voice when she said, "It's one theory we've considered."

Beverly nodded. "He was a man who thought he was better than everyone else. I remember that, but like I said we weren't friends and never talked to each other."

"That's alright," Cassie soothed.

"I said we weren't friends, honey, I didn't say I didn't have a story or two about the old bastard."

Both women didn't try to hide their laughter that time. Beverly grinned, her sunken eyes lost with the action. "My husband used to say I had an uncanny recall for local connections; probably why Elizabeth said you should talk to me."

"You are my encyclopedia of this town's history," Elizabeth agreed.

Beverly took a sip of her coffee and sat back in her seat. "So here's the story that comes to mind when I think of ole Bill Moss. He got in a helluva fight in the middle of The Mining King dining room one night. My husband and I were there for dinner, and if we were there, it would have been Sunday night; because that's what we did in those days. So the place would have been full. Bill was there, I don't remember who he was with, but I remember Elmore Smith came in, walked right up to Bill, jerked him out of his chair and slammed his fist into his face. Nothing will ruin your appetite faster than two men being stupid."

Cassie felt like she was being hypnotized by Beverly's commentary, and she truly enjoyed it.

"Elmore yelled that Bill had killed his sister, and they scuffled for a time until some of the men pulled 'em off each other and the sheriff showed up to excuse both men. We took our food home that night; first time I ever had a doggie bag."

Cassie glanced wide-eyed at Elizabeth, so many questions and comments racing between them. But she started with the most obvious. "Do you know who Elmore's sister was?"

"Hmmm," Beverly screwed up her face as she glanced around the room, "Eleanor or Evelyn ... I know it was one of those."

"Do you know why Elmore would have accused Bill of killing his sister?"

"Of course I do. On the way home I asked my husband what he thought about the fight and he said when he was a kid, maybe twelve or thirteen, Bill was in town and always getting arrested for being drunk, but he married a girl from Wilson; that's a ghost town now. But Elizabeth knows about that. Anyway, my husband said that Bill and his wife were a mess and a lot of gossip went on when they were around because she was a woman of ill repute." Beverly wiggled her eyes at Cassie. "Did you know there were still women who plied their trade in Eden in the forties? Can you believe that?"

Cassie didn't have time to comment.

"Well, they got married, but two drunks don't stay married long. I think there was a divorce and my husband said he remembered hearing that the woman drank herself to death." Beverly shook her head sadly. "We figured Elmore thought it was Bill got his sister hooked on drinking. I don't know if Elmore ever knew his sister's chosen profession, and my money's on the fact that she learned to drink a long time before Bill came into the picture."

"Wow." Cassie shook her head in wonder. "You've certainly given us more information than we had before. Do you recall anything about Bill's stay from '65 to '70?"

"Not much, he never showed up at any town events. Kept to himself. Had a beat-up pickup and was out of town a lot ..."

She squinted as if she were trying to remember something. "Oh! He wasn't drinking then. Overheard someone at the grocery store once, when Bill had come and gone and I was in line, say they were surprised he was sober as a minister."

"So he was just mining then?" Cassie frowned at Elizabeth.

"Probably," Beverly shrugged, "but if he wasn't finding anything and needed money, he might have picked up some jobs at the mines."

"That's a good idea," Elizabeth said. "We have some of the payroll registers from the mines during those years. If he got a paycheck from them, it'll be recorded."

"Well, that's all that comes to mind at the moment. I'll keep thinkin' on it. If I come up with anything else, I'll holler." Beverly finished her coffee then set the mug down and slapped her hand on the table. "I have to go, lots to do today."

They followed her to the door and after she'd put her jacket on, she turned abruptly to Cassie, held out her hand, and narrowed her gaze again as she gave a resounding, firm shake. "Nice to meet you, honey." Then she patted Elizabeth on the cheek. "I have some muffins for you and Aidan, I forgot 'em this morning, but I'll drop 'em off later tonight."

She didn't wait for replies, just opened and closed the door, then marched back the way she came.

"And just like that, she was gone," Elizabeth whispered.

"Holy shit!" Cassie exclaimed and turned a wide grin at Elizabeth. "That was amazing. She was amazing. I could listen to her all day!"

"That's what I meant when I told you there are ghosts and their stories everywhere in this town."

Elizabeth pulled the payroll registers for the biggest mine in operation during William's stay. She handed the year 1965 to Cassie and began going through 1966 herself.

After an hour, they each found several entries with his name, Elizabeth commented, "It's a verification that he was here, but what was he doing? I can't imagine, with a wife and a child and a good job waiting for him back home, that he was dying to do manual labor in a mine."

Cassie pulled out the letter found in the back of the geology book that was now in a plastic sleeve and held it out. "I think he was looking for whatever had been hidden."

"Do you want to continue going through the payroll?"

"No, I don't think so. We know where they are and that they exist."

"Okay then." Elizabeth stood and motioned for Cassie to follow her into the vault. "While I was waiting for Aidan to get home last night, I read William's memoir. You were right, it's heartbreaking and insightful and well written."

"Not a man who was cocksure and a drunk, huh?" Cassie frowned at the descriptions most associated with William Moss in this town.

"No," Elizabeth agreed. She opened a file on the computer in the back and pulled up the archive database. "I did find a few interesting things in the book. The first, a name. William said one of the men he served with, Jacob Hines, used to tell great stories about his life in Colorado. The reason I found this interesting is because there was a Hines family in Eden, often in the history books about the area."

Cassie watched as Elizabeth typed in the family name 'Hines.' Having found what she was looking for, she crossed the room to the location and pulled out an archival box, then returned to the desk in the vault and opened it. She pulled out the Hines' family tree. "Here it is," she said excitedly. "Jacob Hines, died 1944 in the service of his country."

Cassie raised an eyebrow. "That's something we can add to the backburner, find out how many Jacob Hines from Colorado served. But it's a good possibility."

"I think so too. It was one of the things that's bothered me about this story."

"One of the things?" Cassie gave a dry laugh.

Elizabeth smiled. "I was curious why they would have chosen Eden. If it's the same Jacob Hines, the boy who told such great stories, then after the war, when the brothers found themselves broken and disheartened, maybe Eden sounded like a good idea."

"So that's another little piece of the puzzle. You said there were a few things you found?"

Elizabeth smiled as she retrieved William's memoir and opened it. "Whose copy was this?"

"Theresa gave it to me, she never said."

"Whoever it was circled numbers in the index." Elizabeth pulled out a paper where she'd written the numbers, and slid it across to Cassie.

"What are these?"

"I think they're latitude and longitude. Mainly because whoever circled the numbers, also circled a decimal."

"Have you checked it yet?"

"No, I was waiting for you."

Elizabeth plugged the coordinates into a computer program. They both held their breath as the earth turned, slowly zoomed in on the United States, then when it continued to zoom in on Colorado, Cassie grabbed Elizabeth's arm. When it finished pinpointing the exact location several miles east of Eden, Elizabeth grabbed Cassie back.

"So, that's something," Cassie said. "Do you know what it means?"

"No." Elizabeth laughed. "But this morning I saw an email sent from my friend at the BLM. Might as well see if that helps."

Chapter Thirty-Three

S tills jumped out of the passenger side of Cole's truck and quickly made his way to the door of the archive. As she opened the door for him, Elizabeth called out across the room to Cassie, "Your Neanderthal, my dear."

"You okay?" Stills asked.

Elizabeth nodded. "We're fine."

He glanced over at Cassie. "You sounded weird on the phone."

"Oh, hell yeah I did," she scoffed. "We just unlocked the damn motherload, Benji."

Cole followed Stills in, slapping his hat against his leg, as Aidan was pulling up.

Once inside, Cassie said, "Okay, everyone settle in." She pushed the whiteboard in front of the window.

The board still had the dates and pertinent information about the Moss brothers. Cassie uncapped the marker and as the fumes raced into her nostrils, making her dizzy, she admitted with a shake of her head, "This gets pretty convoluted."

She took them through the simple facts, births, time in the war—adding that it was a man named Hines who inspired their move to Eden—and William's arrest record, or at least most of what they'd found to date.

With nods all around that they were following, she wrote the number 145 on the board. "The Moss brothers purchased one hundred and forty-five claims. Most of them don't matter, but Elizabeth's contact at the BLM answered a few questions we posed yesterday, giving us some interesting information about several of the claims."

Elizabeth took over the explanation. "Some of the claims James and William jointly owned always had an anonymous person paying the fees on the claims, up until the past two years. Those fees were paid by a man named Lewis Treat."

Cassie wrote the name on the board as she continued the story. "Treat has purchased a lot of claims in the past, which is nothing new. It's what some people do. However, Elizabeth's contact thought we'd be interested in the fact that about twenty of the claims he bought were previously owned by the Moss brothers."

"And," Elizabeth added, "Lewis Treat's purchases are being contested."

Cassie wrote another name on the board while announcing, "By Art Buchanan."

"Art?" Cole sat forward, very interested.

Cassie quickly added, "Everyone kept referring to him as Art, not Art Buchanan."

"I didn't think about it," Elizabeth said. "It was right there in front of my face and I think I was too shocked to put it together."

"Is that why you asked me when Art was born?" Aidan asked about the call he'd gotten earlier from Elizabeth.

She nodded in reply. "It's sad ... Art was so much a part of the fabric of Eden. I didn't know much about him, just assumed he'd been here forever."

"When Elizabeth looked up his birth certificate, we found that he was born in Pueblo, Colorado." Cassie wrote it on the board. "The mother listed was Mary Buchanan and his father was J. Moss."

"What?" Cole frowned.

"James Moss is Arthur Buchanan's father!" Cassie exclaimed.

Stills met Cassie's gaze.

"Art Buchanan is the cousin of the woman who hired you?" The crease between Stills' eyes deepened.

"Not much of a coincidence any more, huh?" Cassie acknowledged.

"Just wait," Elizabeth muttered.

Cassie continued, "In the obituary it said the wife went to stay with her sister and asked that everyone respect their mourning period."

"We figure it was now because Mary was pregnant."

"But she went back to her maiden name. Why not keep the name Moss?" Cole asked.

"Something had to have happened," Cassie suggested, "because it was the late forties, and in those days a woman was better off being a widow than she was a mother out of wedlock."

Stills asked, "Did Art even know who his father was?"

Elizabeth shrugged. "But if he was a normal kid, he would have asked questions."

Aidan tapped his fingers against the table as he threw out his own theory. "He must've known something to have moved back to Eden."

Cassie surmised, "I don't think Theresa knows she has a cousin in Eden, and I don't know if William ever knew his brother had a son."

Elizabeth shared some of the theories they'd already wondered aloud. "We're not sure Mary even wanted William to know. He was known as a drunk and not a good man. If she gave her son her maiden name; that isn't someone interested in extended family."

"That's very plausible," Aidan said.

"So how do we find out when Art moved back to town?" Cole asked.

"We need to check the county recorder's office, but they just started digitizing; and began with the most current years. The way I understand it, they're only in the 1990s at this point."

"We added that to our list of questions." Cassie cleared her throat. "So, you ready for more?"

Stills raised an eyebrow in interest; Cole narrowed his gaze as Aidan cocked his head to the side. Cassie continued with the timeline: "So James is dead. Mary gives birth. William moves to California. In 1965, he came back to Eden, possibly due to this letter." She picked up the note and handed it around. "While he's here, he's sober, doesn't get into trouble, but he does work in a few mines."

"We found payroll evidence today," Elizabeth informed.

Cassie circled the name Lewis Treat. "So our next question was: Who is this man?"

"I found two entries in the archive," Elizabeth said as she opened an album to show everyone the first picture. It was a photo from the eighties, with a caption written under it: "Costumes made by Amelia Treat, here with her husband Bud, and son Lewis."

Elizabeth glanced at Cassie as she opened the next album and turned to a photo labeled "The Treat family enjoys the Labor Day picnic." The son was older, maybe early twenties.

"What the hell ...?" Stills breathed, his frown deepening as he studied the photo.

"What?" Cole asked.

"This man," Cassie pointed, "is the younger version of a man who introduced himself to Stills and me as Lou Macon. He claimed to be an insurance salesman in Highland."

"Fuck," Stills added again.

Before any more questions could be asked, Elizabeth brought out a page they'd printed off the internet as Cassie continued, "We searched for the birth certificate of Lewis Treat, using his mother's name."

On the board next to Lewis' name, she added his mother's name: Amelia Macon Wright and his father's: William L. Moss.

"Jesus Christ," Cole breathed out.

"In the newspaper archives we found an article in 1972 that announced Amelia Macon Wright and Bradley 'Bud' Treat's marriage."

"Lou Macon also used his mother's maiden name," Aidan said.

"Lewis Moss Treat. William's son," Cole hissed.

"Theresa Moss' younger half-brother," Cassie added.

Stills shook his head. "And Art Buchanan's cousin."

Aidan wondered aloud the question they all had. "Do you think any of them know about each other?"

Cassie offered, "Lewis might know, even if Art didn't?"

Cole shrugged. "If Art was contesting Lewis' purchase of one of his mining claims, at least that's something; it would be a motive."

Aidan shook his head. "But why kill Art over a dispute of mining claims?"

"The main three motives for most murders are vengeance, jealousy or money," Stills responded.

"William and James must have found something and hid it in one of the claims they purchased," Cassie reasoned. "And my bet is that Lewis Treat somehow knows and has narrowed it down to these final twenty claims."

"It makes as much sense as anything," Elizabeth agreed.

"Dodd, he must have planted the tracker," Stills said.

"What tracker?" Elizabeth asked.

It was the first thing Cassie thought too when she saw the photo and recognized the man. "When he helped me pick up everything that spilled out of my purse," she offered.

"That's when I'd do it," Stills verified.

Cassie frowned. "So who trashed our apartment then? What were they looking for?"

"What?" Elizabeth asked even more emphatically.

Cassie explained about the tracker and their apartment being broken into. She was still struggling to figure out how the work she was doing here and the recent unsettling events were connected.

"They were looking for the books," Elizabeth said wide-eyed.

"What?" Cole asked.

Elizabeth continued, speaking directly to Cassie. "You said that's the only thing Theresa gave you of her father's. Do you think she knows everything? Or maybe she gave the books to you unknowingly?"

"I don't know anymore." Cassie heavily sighed as Cole asked, "The books?"

Elizabeth slid the geology book across the table explaining, "This one has letters circled that spell out Salerno Wall." She then slid the Moss' memoir over. "And this one has numbers circled that create a latitude and longitude; we found the coordinates several miles from here."

Stills took the books and flipped through them quietly, then sat back and gave Cassie a pride filled smile. "This is amazing Dodd. Maybe you should come work with me."

"I could keep a better eye on you then," she admitted but waved the idea away. "For now, I think maybe we should focus on all of this before I go making any career changes."

"Do any of you know a Lewis Treat or Lou Macon?" Stills asked, looking around the room.

Everyone shook their heads no.

"Can't we find his driver's license photo or something more current? Now that we know who we're looking into, can you find out more?" Elizabeth asked Cole.

Cole took out his phone and frowned. "No signal."

Elizabeth pointed him to the landline, her voice shaky as she asked, "So what's the next step?"

"I think it's safe to say that for now, we can assume we've found our number one suspect," Stills stated. "Now, we find him and bring him in for questioning."

Cole finished giving details to his contact in Highland, then returned to the conversation. "I feel better having a suspect, but until we can get a signal, the only two who can identify him are Benjamin and Cassie."

Cassie's skin crawled at the thought.

"And the second problem;" Cole continued, "if Lewis Treat had family in this area and came around over the years, folks don't think of him as an 'outsider.'"

Cassie groaned. "So all the times we asked if there was anyone new in town ..."

Stills shrugged. "It was just us."

Cole glanced around and gave a few murmured grunts as he seemed to make several unspoken decisions. Finally he said, "I have some work to do. I think we should meet for dinner."

"Strength in numbers?" Elizabeth asked.

Cole nodded. "And who knows what epiphanies you'll have between then and now."

"Do you think Lewis or Lou will make an appearance?" Aidan asked.

"He hasn't yet," Stills offered.

"I don't think so," Cole assured while fitting his hat to his head. "And while it's a good lead, we don't have any concrete evidence that he's the one who killed Art."

Cassie felt lightheaded. "But ..."

Cole shrugged into his coat. "I'm not saying it isn't him either; I'm just saying we need to continue to work as if he is a suspect, but we also need more evidence."

Elizabeth and Cassie glanced at each other, sharing the same feeling of their elation falling down around them.

"How about we meet at The Western at seven?" He didn't wait for an answer as he turned and left.

Cassie turned her face up to the sky and closed her eyes as snowflakes landed and melted, cooling her heated cheeks. "So, regardless of if Lewis, aka Lou Macon, killed Art, he was the one who put the tracker in my purse and it would seem that all of this is related somehow to the Moss family."

"We don't have all the details," Stills said offhandedly.

"But we do have some really good details, Benji." She was frustrated.

"Dodd, I never said you didn't. What you've pulled together has been incredible."

That was what she needed, a little pat on the back. "Okay, there's nothing more we can do," she declared. "I think we should run by The Rose."

"To see Edwin?"

"I need to bake something," she muttered.

As they climbed on the snowmobile he asked, "What are you thinking of making?"

"Brown butter blondies."

"I have no idea what those are, but I've been dreaming about 'em ever since you said you might bake today."

"No you haven't."

"Dodd, have you met me? Ever since we met, I started dreaming about the things you bake." As she wound her hands around his waist, he set his hand on top of them and over his shoulder added, "Most of the time though, in the dreams, you're naked."

"That doesn't sound sanitary."

He faced forward and loudly stated, "Dreams aren't supposed to be sanitary, Dodd."

Chapter Thirty-Four

"And now the power is out?" Cassie reiterated the obvious in an angry whisper from the kitchen. The overhead lights had flickered twice and then shut off. She was horrified at the creepy nightmare mingling with Christmas weather; the combination of which had *not* been filled with catchy, upbeat musical numbers.

"Dodd, why are you whispering?"

"Because of everything. And it just occurred to me that we don't know if this place is bugged."

"I'm pretty sure it's not bugged."

"Pretty sure? What about cameras?"

"Dodd."

She mindlessly took a large bite of another brown butter blondie, which was, as she explained to Stills, a brownie made without chocolate. With a full mouth, she said, "Benji, I'm gonna spin out of control for a second and you're going to let me."

He lit candles in the living room and after a moment, glanced over to where Cassie was pacing. "Wanna have some fun?"

"How can you think of sex at a time like this?" she demanded.

"I was thinking about something else, but since you brought it up ..." He caught her around the waist and suggestively rotated his hips against hers.

"We are tracked, bugged and have cameras on us!" she hissed.

"If you think about it, Dodd, that would make this kinda hot."

She shook her head and pushed him away, but he kissed her on the cheek before letting go.

"Okay, what do you think we're going to do for fun in this situation?

There's snow everywhere." She took another bite and let herself spiral a bit as she stated the obvious. "The power's gone out and now I'm really worried. I mean, I was worried before, but I think it's okay to say I'm now properly freaked out."

No sooner had the words come tumbling out of her mouth than Stills had her hoisted against his body again and was nuzzling her neck, while slipping one hand around her behind and the other under her shirt.

Still having a mouthful of brownie, she grunted and pouted, but tilted her head to give him easier access.

After finally swallowing her bite, she breathed out, "That's not fair."

"Then don't be so easy," he whispered, nipping her earlobe. She snorted a laugh as he continued across her collar bone to the other side of her neck, brushing a few more kisses before whispering, "Let's go break into Art Buchanan's house."

"What?" She pulled away and saw how his eyes were sparkling in the dim candlelight. "Is that really what you think is going to be fun right now?"

"You're right, fun might be the wrong word."

"Why?"

"Why is *fun* the wrong word? I suppose, because technically it's a crime to break into someone's house."

"Benji."

"And since his house is currently a crime scene, it's super illegal; but I suppose I could get Clayton's approval."

She lightly slapped his arm. "Why do you want to break into his house?"

"I have a hunch."

"A hunch."

"A hunch," he confirmed.

"So, what, you want to drive right up and park in front of his house and go in?"

"We need to be a little more inconspicuous."

"In case someone is watching?"

"No one's watching."

"How do you know? We don't know if Lou or Lewis is here in town and we don't know who is working with him and you said we can't drive up to the house because we need to be inconspicuous but you don't think anyone is watching ... pick a storyline and stick with it Stills."

"You gotta trust me Dodd."

"Isn't this something you and Cole should do together instead?"

"Maybe," he reached around her and grabbed one of the blondies, "but I don't necessarily know what I'm looking for. I need your help."

"You don't need my help," she muttered, then widened her eyes as she realized why he wanted her to go with him. "You don't feel safe leaving me here alone."

"I actually feel fine leaving you alone. The truth is that you're the one working this case. You know what you're looking for."

"This case?"

He shrugged. "I maintain that our jobs have a lot of crossover."

"What am I looking for?"

"I don't know."

"Benji."

"I'm serious, I don't know what we might find at Art's house, but if there is something to be found, you'd know what it is."

She licked her lips, starting to get intrigued by the idea. "So ... how do we do this?"

"Snowshoes I think."

She glanced around the room, opening her mouth and closing it several times, swallowing a lump in her throat. "But how ...? How do we hide our tracks? Should we tell the sheriff what we're doing? Did you bring any night vision goggles I don't know about? What if someone is watching his house? What if someone is watching *this* house? Should we grab the flashlights out of the camping gear?"

"There are flashlights in the front closet. We'll go through the back door, and there is a path no one would be on at this time of night."

Cassie squinted at Stills. "You were going to talk me into this even if the lights hadn't gone out."

"You didn't need to be talked into this. You think it's going to be fun."

"Whatever."

Dressed and bundled in several layers, Cassie put her boots on. Then she stood and swung her arms around and did several kicks with her legs.

Stills stopped zipping his jacket and asked, "What are you doing?"

"Making sure I can move if I have to throw some asshole over my shoulder," she said as she did a squat.

He gave a chuckle. Tensing her shoulders she glanced at him from across the room, but he wasn't making fun of her; he was giving an impressed nod. "Good call, Dodd."

"It's all part of the training, Benji." She was trying to embrace what they were about to do, because mounting fears and the variables of what could go wrong were closing in fast. "Spy training," she verified.

He gave a grunt in reply.

Cassie held out her hands. "Benji, we're about to break into a locked house and keep to the shadows and I don't know what else, but somehow, being ridiculous and thinking this is all spy stuff is making me feel better."

"I *never* said you were ridiculous."

"I know. I'm the one who said it."

He gave a thoughtful scratch of his beard. "Keeping to the shadows and breaking in is also what a thief would do."

She scrunched her face at him in response. "Stop. You know I'm trying to hold it together; so let's get going or I'm going to cry and freak out."

He took a step toward her, but she put a hand up. "I'm fine, just on edge. But so help me Benjamin Stills, if you hug me right now, I'll start crying. So let's get moving, roll those endorphins around my body to calm me down and hope your hunch is right and I can find something to help finish this whole mess sooner rather than later."

"Yes ma'am."

The cold pressed in on Cassie as she stepped onto the back porch, a large area that probably held a table and chairs and grill in the summer months.

The loss of power, low clouds and soft falling snow set her immediate surroundings in an eerie glow.

Stills pulled out two headlamps, turned them both onto the red light setting and handed one over to Cassie.

"Red?" she asked, slipping the band on top of her woolen covered head, thinking the glow added too much of a spooky element to Stills' 'fun' adventure.

"It'll protect our night vision, so if we have to turn it off, our eyes won't have to work so hard to adjust to the darkness. It helps to see finer details actually."

A shiver ran through her as she slowly turned her head, coating the landscape in an unnatural hue and opening the door to all sorts of nightmarish scenarios. She stomped her feet, a physical attempt to stomp out the thoughts, and went to work on clipping the snowshoes into place.

Stills led the way out of the unfenced yard and away from the other houses to the very end of the street from where The Hideout was positioned. Then he turned toward the hill, answering Cassie's question of how they were going to get to Art Buchanan's house.

A walking trail wound up into the slight foothills, traversed the distance between the east and west side of town, and would eventually drop them down a few houses away from Art's.

Chapter Thirty-Five

In the low light and buildup of snow, the state and color of Art's house was difficult to ascertain.

Cassie followed Stills around the side of the house, toward the back, watching his careful movements as he glanced into the window off the kitchen. Cassie tripped over her shoes but caught herself on Stills' arm as she leaned in and whispered, "How do you know this is the right house?"

"Clayton," was his quiet reply.

She followed his footsteps up to the flat area that led to the back door. He glanced over his shoulder and his face looked disarming in the red light—of course, it could have been his instruction to "wait here" that caught her off guard.

"Why?" she called softly, but he'd already disappeared around the other side of the house.

Cassie stood wide-eyed under the porch covering. There was no sound. No hum of electricity, no television, no traffic. She realized she had probably never been in a situation where it had been this quiet before; this natural. The snow was soft as it fell to the ground, and her head bobbed back and forth at any perceived noise. The silence was deafening, leaving adrenaline to hum loudly in her ears.

She jumped when the thunderous crunch of Stills' feet rounded the corner.

He narrowed his gaze, a silent question; was she okay?

She nodded and bent to take off her snowshoes.

"Now what?" she whispered by the back door.

He put his hand on the handle, turned it, and the door opened.

"Did you know it was open?" she whispered in surprise.

"Spy 101, Dodd. Check the door first; you never know."

She pressed her gloved hand against her mouth to hold back the adrenaline-fueled laugh.

Inside the air was cold and stale, whatever heat that had been there was long gone.

They entered through a mudroom that led to the kitchen, a large space with a round table in the middle. A half-eaten meal was sitting next to an upended chair.

"He was forced?" Cassie whispered the question. Stills nodded in confirmation. "What do we do now?"

Stills shrugged. "Look around. I'm not quite sure."

"You're not quite sure?" she said loudly, then slapped a hand over her mouth and waited until the perceived echo of her voice stopped and brought no movement from elsewhere in the house.

"I told you, I have a hunch and if there's something to be found, and if anyone can find it, you'll know its importance."

"I thought you were joking."

In the red light she aimed at him, Stills glowed and winked at her. "Look for anything ... historical or that might have to do with the Moss family tree," he suggested. "Or something that you simply *feel* is right."

"I don't remember the 'look for something that feels right' part of *Spy Games*," she muttered.

He replied with a tisk.

"Well, let's be methodical about it," she mumbled and pointed to the fridge. There were only receipts for an oil change and a coupon for The Western held under a dancing cat magnet. "The Western has coupons," she said. "That fact should go in the binder."

"We'll make the edit." He was opening and closing cupboards.

"Oh, where's his junk drawer?" Cassie started opening each drawer, quietly and slowly. "Everyone's got a kitchen junk drawer." And Art did. It was full of old matchbooks, a wrench, hammer, eyeglass cases and rubber bands.

They moved on to a hallway that led to the living room, the tired wooden floor creaking under their weight.

Photos were crowded on the wall. A man, maybe mid-fifties—Art she assumed—stood with his arm slung loosely around a smiling woman's shoulders. "This must be his wife." She wasn't looking at the woman though, she was squinting to see if there was any resemblance between Art and the photos of James she'd seen. She thought there was one, but she couldn't be sure if it wasn't a trick of the light or her wanting there to be one.

There were more pictures of the couple; several scenic shots, and old black and white photos, but the one that interested Cassie the most was in an ornate gold frame. It was a professional black and white photo of a woman. "I bet ..." she whispered, taking the photo down and turning it over. A piece of faded tape on the back read Mary Buchanan, April 1950.

She turned the photo again and studied the soft smile of the woman's face. "Mary," she said as she ran her fingers across the frame before putting it back.

There was a coat closet opened in the hallway; several jackets had fallen to the floor. Cassie pulled a wicker basket off the top shelf, but it only held gloves and hats.

A half bath was opposite the closet. Stills went through it, then returned with a shake of his head; nothing of interest there.

The living room boasted a semicircle of furniture around an oval coffee table: green sofa from the late 80s, two worn stuffed chairs and a recliner, but no television. There were two mismatched smaller tables next to the recliner and sofa. Whatever papers or books had once been stacked in neat piles, were now strewn across the floor.

"Is it safe to assume whoever did this was looking for something?" she whispered.

He gestured at the room. "Sometimes there is a deliberateness to the mess, a mess for the sake of a mess to throw us off the scent. But this has the look of someone searching for something."

And, Cassie thought to herself, someone had caught Art unaware, the poor man. She tried to shake the lump forming in her throat. The bookcase and all its contents had been upended too. She knelt next to the books and picked them up one by one, glancing at the titles before she began to shake them free of any secrets that might be hidden inside.

After several books she paused. "Shit. Don't we need to keep this scene intact?"

Stills shook his head. "Clayton's already taken pictures."

She frowned. "Have you been here already?"

"No, he showed me photos. But I thought if you were here ..." A frown creased his forehead as he glanced around; what was he missing?

Cassie went back to work, and once she finished going through all the books, she said, "There's no books on mining or geology. No copy of William's book."

"Did you think there would be?"

Cassie shrugged. "If he knew who his uncle was, maybe."

Her search of the living room only ended up producing receipts, four bookmarks and a two-dollar bill. Stills came away with out-of-date manuals, insurance information, the title to the car, but nothing that would point to murder.

They decided to move their search upstairs, but when Stills stepped on the second stair, causing it to squeak loudly, Cassie reached out and pulled him backward, throwing them both off-balance, resulting in their tripping to the floor among the sounds of various curses.

"Sorry," Cassie said, having landed on top of Stills as he'd turned his body to take the brunt of the short fall.

"What were you trying to do?"

She started laughing and hid her mouth against his chest as she admitted, "Save you."

"From what?"

"I don't know."

He pulled her body up and in the red light his half-smile looked sexy and menacing. "Thank you for trying to save me from the squeaky stairs." He brushed a kiss against her lips. "Should we try that again?"

She rolled off him. "Did you get hurt?"

"I might have a bruise or two."

"Ah, Benji," she snorted, "I'm sorry."

"Don't worry Dodd, later I'm gonna make you kiss them and make them better." He pointed to the stairs. "Once more into the breach."

They arrived at the top stairs without any further problems. The second floor had two rooms and a bathroom.

The first room must have been Art's, as the contents of his armoire had been heaved onto the floor and the closet had also been unceremoniously cleared out.

Cassie began to shake clothing out and pile it as Stills reached onto the shelving at the back of the closet.

Cassie's frown deepened as she continued piling clothes, having not found anything useful. If someone wanted to hide something, they normally tried to do it away from places someone else would think to look.

So far the home was simple in décor and lifestyle. So where would someone who was a minimalist hide something?

"Oh!" She stood abruptly.

"What?"

"I don't know." She cleared a path in front of the armoire and stood to look at it. "This is an older piece, from the turn of the century," she explained as Stills joined her. She began running her hands along the details and inside walls of the piece as she went on, "The top was for hats, the left side was for hanging clothes and the shelving on the right was for folded items." The lower four shelves had carved wooden valances. "I read an article last year about turn-of-the-century furniture and hidden compartments." She began to push on the sections of the arches that made up the valances. "A lot of the time, the builder would create a secret compartment hidden in plain sight. It was common knowledge when these items were first made in the late 1900s and brand new, but not now." Cassie was on the last shelf, on the center arch, when a click and a scrap gave way. She gasped in reply.

"Dodd, you're amazing."

The compartment was big enough for the two letters it housed. Cassie began to open them, but Stills stopped her. "We'll read them back at The Hideout."

An unladylike grunt of a laugh escaped. "What the hell have we gotten ourselves into, Benji?"

He helped her up. "Where else would you hide things?"

"Let's look behind the armoire."

They muscled the heavy wooden beast out from against the wall but found only ancient spiderwebs and dust balls.

They looked in the nightstand and under the mattress. Nothing.

The last room had been turned into an office and storage space. It had also been ransacked into a nightmare of a mess.

"You know, whoever did this knew what he was doing and what he was looking for." Cassie chewed on her lip. "So maybe we can assume nothing of value was found in the papers on the ground."

"Okay."

"Shit," Cassie muttered beneath her breath.

"What?"

She scrubbed her face. "I don't know, I feel like I need to do something miraculous so I can really impress you."

He gave a warm, gruff laugh. "Dodd, you don't need to impress me. But if you want to know the truth, you *have* impressed the hell out of me today."

"Was it the baking?"

"Yes." He gave a mischievous grin.

She shook her head and glanced around the room. "Okay, if the stuff that's out isn't important, then we're still looking for hidden items."

"Got it." Stills went through the filing cabinet as she shifted a small bookcase out of the way. They peeked in boxes that said Christmas and Fourth of July; the contents were indeed decorations for said holidays.

Cassie pulled open the drawers of the desk, the last item in the room to check, but nothing looked historical or like it had 'hidden mine' or 'estranged uncle' written on it.

Frustrated, Cassie gave a grunt and slammed the top drawer closed, but it didn't close all the way. She paused, pulled the drawer open as far as it would go, hoping to dislodge it, but it was built into the desk. So she crawled underneath and glanced up, finding a manila envelope.

"Benji!" she called as she began to free the worn, tattered, faded envelope that had been taped to the underside of the drawer. When she had it in her hand and crawled out from under the desk, she was glad she was sitting as she read the scrawled word on the front: Moss.

"Holy shit!" The brittleness of the old paper was chalky in her hands.

"Didn't I say that I had a hunch and that you're amazing?" he asked excitedly.

She took a deep breath. Stills pulled her to his side and asked, "Does anything else look promising?"

"I think we've gone through everything we can," she admitted. "But let's look under all the drawers and furniture now, just in case."

They did and came up empty-handed. But having found the two items was more than they'd started with.

"We should probably head back, we've been here longer than I expected," Stills said.

"I want to get a plastic bag to put this stuff in before I put it in my jacket. I don't think we can afford to get any of it wet."

In the kitchen they found several plastic bags and secured the papers.

They were getting ready to leave when Stills' light shone on a heavy winter jacket hanging on the hook by the back door. Cassie touched the lapel, angry for the man described as good and kind. She tapped the coat, for reasons she didn't quite understand except to say a kind goodbye; but when the tap became a thud of something against the wall, she paused for a moment.

"Dodd?"

She didn't answer, but swept the jacket out of the way and found a reusable bag hanging on the hook. When she peeked in and came face to face with a familiar book, she took several steps back, blinking wildly and shaking her head.

"What?" Stills asked.

After a deep breath, she retrieved the book and held it up for Stills to see; *Subsurface Geologic Methods*. As he stepped closer to look at the book she opened it to where a letter had been sticking out. She kept her finger in the book as a place saver and scanned the letter, hissing, "What the fuck?"

Stills looked over her shoulder and when he saw the signature—Theresa Moss—he gave a low whistle.

Cassie's anger was difficult to keep quiet. "She knew about him. What the actual hell? Did she use me? Does she know about Lewis?"

"Dodd," Stills said calmly, "this isn't the time to be indignant. You can do that the moment we get back to our place."

She gave him a curt nod, replaced the letter where she found it, retrieved the plastic bag, added the book and tucked it back inside her sweater.

"Ready?" Stills asked.

As quietly as they had before, they put their snowshoes on and followed the path back that had led them there.

Chapter Thirty-Six

What the hell?!

The thought followed Cassie out the back door of Art's house and onto the low foothill path. Her calf muscles and quads burned as she created a hurried, awkward pace, much faster than the first trip they'd made.

She snarled as the thunder of possibilities and storylines kept pace with her.

What the ever-loving hell?!

Illuminated in red light were the faintest of indentations from their first trip, and Cassie frowned and cursed at those too; frustrated with the turn of events, with the relentless snow and the betrayal.

She was pissed off for the sake of Art Buchanan and when she thought about tripping over Lou Macon ... would he have tripped her if she had been watching which way she was going?

What would she find in the letters?

If it was something important, what were they going to tell the sheriff?

And if their prints could be hidden so quickly, what other tracks were being covered tonight?

She picked up her pace and tried to rid herself of the endless, tumultuous slide of thoughts and tried to count instead: the way she did when she ran at a fast pace. Through her breathing, she focused only on the count of four.

Inhale: One, Two. Exhale: Three, Four.

A strange math problem involving snow presented itself to her—maybe she could tell how long they'd been at Art's house and how long it would take to cover certain depths of prints if she could figure out how much snow was falling...

One, two, three, four...

The only answer she could come up with was *a fucking lot of snow*. She hissed then gave a snort of anxious laughter. She covered her mouth, not glancing over her shoulder to see if Stills had heard, but why wouldn't he? Her exerted breathing was already filling her ears and echoing off the surrounding mountains.

It was one thing to be snowed in with nowhere to go when you had a fireplace, a handsome man and some romance ... but a completely different thing when murder and midnight break-ins were part of the activities.

She brushed at her face as she tried to think of something productive to focus on.

One, two, three, four ...

The Moss brothers.

She started with their births, their enlistment, their marriages, and their children. Soon, though, her mind drifted to the notion that if it was Lewis who bugged her, Lewis who killed Art, then it was her life that was in danger.

She had to blink several times when Stills reached out and stopped her. She'd been so angry and so lost in thought she didn't realize they were back at the house. Not waiting for Cassie, Stills undid his snowshoes with record speed, and by the time she entered the house she realized why he'd been so quick.

He was doing a sweep of the house.

Fuck.

A mixture of anger and fear and resentment and all the weird stress from the past few days bunched together between her shoulder blades, along with the thought of what she'd do if someone was upstairs and attacked him.

She was across the room and headed for the stairs as he appeared on the top step in the red light of her headlamp; his carefulness replaced by his easy swagger.

Cassie watched him come down, but her breathing never normalized. She quickly but carefully placed the plastic bag holding the book and documents on the coffee table. Then the second Stills was within reach, she grabbed for him, crushed herself against him, and pulled his head down so she could sear a kiss to his lips.

He lifted her up so she could wrap her legs around his waist as she used him to release every last emotion that had been building.

Of course she couldn't get to him with all the clothing, so she slipped down his body, a tangled, grunted argument playing out with hands and fingers as coats and clothes and headlamps were discarded.

Cassie's bloodstream was heated with need. She walked Stills backward toward the sofa, then pushed him into a seated position. Straddling him with her knees, she slowly lowered herself as matching Cheshire grins were illuminated in the red light from the floor as they came together.

The loud drumming of exertion that had rushed to Cassie's head had been replaced by irregular panting.

"I was angry," Cassie muttered against his neck.

"If that's what you need to do with your anger, I'm *always* here for you."

"I appreciate it." She brushed a kiss across his lips before she moved off his lap and fell to his side. "I'm hungry."

"Me too."

She stretched and gave a grunt of satisfaction before she suggested, "Pjs, tea, blondies and let's see what kind of treasures we stole from Art's house."

"I'll light the candles."

Thankfully, the house had a gas stove and, according to the binder, there was a battery backup for the pellet stove to keep it heating the house.

Cassie went in search of more candles but found a camping lantern instead. "Jackpot!"

Stills had a blondie in his mouth and set the remaining four on the table along with two cups of tea.

"I made twenty-four of those," she pointed.

With his mouth full he mumbled, "They were good."

"Benji ..."

He patted her backside, wiggling his eyebrows as he sat down. Pulling her chair out dramatically, she grunted and sat next to him. He licked his lips with a laugh. "Okay, Dodd. What's behind door number one?"

She pulled the documents from the bag as a soft knock came at the front door.

Bad guys don't knock.

She didn't have the same fear she had last night, but as it was past twelve, she had a very good feeling the midnight visitor was Sheriff Clayton.

Stills pulled open the door, revealing Cole, then nodded in greeting and gave a jerk of his head; the international, unspoken sign of 'come in.'

"Everything went okay?" Cole asked as he took off his beanie and gloves.

"It did," Stills confirmed.

"What?" Cassie sat back slowly, a frown darkening her face. "Did he know we were going to Art's house?"

Stills shrugged.

"You didn't want to tell me?" she asked sharply.

Stills wrinkled his nose, not making eye contact as he mumbled, "I thought you'd have more fun if you thought we were breaking and entering."

"Benji," she called incredulously, then glanced at the sheepish way Cole was rubbing the back of his neck, so aimed her next question at him. "Were you the one who left the door unlocked?" She didn't wait for an answer as she asked Stills, "Did we even need the flashlights?"

"Actually, those we did need. We didn't want anyone else knowing you and I were searching through the house. And the power was out." Stills said.

"Did you shut the power down to the town?" She asked the ridiculous question of Cole.

He gave a soft laugh. "Not even I have *that* kind of power."

She wasn't sure if she should be angry or relieved or really pissed.

"Dodd, I really did need your help and we really did need to be secretive," Stills offered in way of explanation. "Clayton told me about the path and he did leave the door open."

"I was scared to death," she muttered.

"It was still dangerous," Clayton stated. "I've been asking the more close-mouthed, trustworthy folks about Lewis Treat, and so far he's a ghost."

"Well ..." She let the word echo throughout the kitchen and watched two grown men shift from foot to foot before she stood and asked, "Cole, do you want some tea? We were just about to see exactly what we found."

Chapter Thirty-Seven

Cassie carefully took the book, the manila envelope and the letters from the bag. The first thing she did was open the book to the page where the letter had been kept, and replaced it with a napkin, in case that particular spot was important.

She scanned the letter then began to read it aloud:

Mr. Buchanan,

I am afraid you have the wrong William Moss. My father was a well-respected, tenured professor in the university system in California. He was a good father, a kind man, and of unwavering fortitude.

While my father did have a brother named James, this is mere coincidence. My uncle was killed in action in the war. So as you can see, there is no way your father and my uncle could be the same person.

If you contact me again, I will have no recourse but to file a cease and desist order.

Theresa Moss

Cassie turned the letter over, there was no date, but thankfully Art had kept the envelope with the note. "She wrote this a month before her father passed away," Cassie supplied.

Cole wondered, "If she received that letter, I wonder if she asked her father about it?"

"Did she think her uncle died in the war?" Stills asked.

Cassie shrugged. "Now I don't know what to think. Maybe the university didn't really want his letters and she tried to find answers, but came up with so many unsolvable questions she hired our company."

"Do we think she knows Lewis?" Cole mused.

Cassie turned the letter over in her hand again. "How did Art find her address?"

"There are plenty of paths to get someone's address; it might have been as simple as sending it to the university in the hopes they would forward it," Stills responded.

"When did she hire your company?" Cole asked.

"Several months ago. I'm not sure of the actual date, just that after the initial meeting with a representative, she then claimed she wasn't ready to begin and put the project on hold. A month ago, I finally started the work." Cassie inclined her head toward Stills. "She knew; when I met with her last week, she already knew all the information I gave her. She must have, why would she threaten to file a cease and desist?"

She handed the letter over to Cole and began to leaf through the pages in the book; but there was nothing of importance on the page where the letter had been.

She flipped back to the beginning again, looking at the inside of the front flap and found an old library sign-out card and holder. Cassie pulled it out and shook her head at the elegantly scrawled name. "I should be surprised, but I'm not."

James Moss was written next to the date, January 14, 1947.

"Okay, this isn't a coincidence." She shook her head as she explained, "This is the same mining book Theresa said was on her father's bedside table when he passed away."

"I'm with you Dodd." Stills said. "At this point it really does seem as if everything is connected."

She flipped through the book mindlessly as she tried to douse her anger when the first flash of a circled letter caught her attention. "Oh, shit."

"What?" Cole asked.

She reached for the pen on the table and another napkin, went back to the beginning of the book and jotted down circled letters while Stills, seeing what she was doing, explained to Cole.

Cassie wasn't surprised when the letters spelled out 'Salerno Wall.'

"I mean that's great, but what or where is the Salerno Wall? Why the hell is it in a book with James' name, and in the book found by William's bedside? And why the hell does William's memoir have a latitude and longitude circled ... we're just adding more questions," she said, frustrated.

"Let's put that aside for now," Stills suggested.

"I think I found all the hidden messages anyway." She picked up the two fragile, faded envelopes and explained to Cole, "We found these in the armoire upstairs."

"In a secret compartment." Stills smiled, his pride in Cassie's find evident.

Setting down one of the envelopes, she saw that the other she still held was from Mary Buchanan to James Moss, with a stamped date of 1946.

> My Dearest James,
>
> I can't imagine the cost of the deeds that you carried out in the name of your country that now weighs so heavy on your soul. But I do not begrudge you what you had to do in order to stay alive. I love you. Now, forever, and always.
>
> I want to marry you, but as you say, we have mountains to overcome to find a way to that path.
>
> I will wait while you work on separating ties from your brother and will rest forever in the hope that you imparted to me. The hope that one day you will be free of obligation from him and we can live happily together.
>
> I wish you haste with all my heart. Your Mary

"Whoa," Cassie blew out.

Cole shook his head. "So the relationship between the brothers wasn't all rosy and glowing."

She opened the other yellowed envelope, which wasn't addressed. Inside was a small piece of paper wrapped around several clipped newspaper articles. The paper had a hastily written note:

Mary,

If anything ever happens to me, leave town and don't look back, ever. Then show these to your father.

"What the fuck ...?" Cassie whispered as she turned the paper over. Finding nothing else written, she set the small articles out in front of her, counting fifteen in all.

With a frown she began to read the one on top.

Two men robbed the First Bank of Highland late Tuesday of $10,000. Stealing a car outside the bank they made their way south. While the bandits were not found, the abandoned car was.

Cassie looked up and frowned at Stills and Cole before she began to read the next article.

The bank of Pagosa Springs was held up and robbed shortly after noon today by a pair of bandits who escaped with the cash in the change tray, amounting to $13,000. The robbers selected an ideal time for the robbery, when the business men were attending the chamber of commerce luncheon at the Denver Café and the streets were practically deserted at the noon hour.

Doctor Sloan was the sole customer in the bank at the time and was being waited upon by Mrs. Debbe Nowakowski, assistant cashier. The vice president of the bank was attending the regular chamber of commerce luncheon as well. Doctor Sloan was at the window when two masked robbers calmly walked in the main entrance. One stood lookout while the other, using a heavy colt's automatic revolver, walked up to Mrs. Debbe

Nowakowski and Doctor Sloan, and insisted this was a 'stick up.' While the man keeping watch pulled all the blinds, the other was polite when he asked Mrs. Nowakowski and Doctor Sloan to get into the vault. Once he had them locked in, the robbers escaped without being detected.

"Do we think the two men are the Moss brothers?" Stills asked as Cassie began to read the next article, unable to stop the ice cold chill from creeping up her spine.

> Two masked bank robbers, north of Gunnison, Colorado, bore a burlap sack bulging with a reported stolen $13,000 in loot. As the robbers fled the scene of the crime, they first stopped at a filling station across the street from the very bank they robbed, purchased food and cigarettes and then handed out wads of money to Betty and Rusty Knapp, whose automobile they stole. The robbers eluded the police.

Cole gave a low whistle as he gently took the first article in his hand and looked it over.

Cassie cleared her throat and continued:

> Two masked bandits, using a stolen car, executed at 3 a.m. Monday what police termed the duo's tenth successful robbery in eight months.
>
> Police Chief C. Smith said they have located the abandoned car, and according to the bank manager of the Bank of Delta in Delta, Colorado, they stole approximately $16,000. A manhunt has been escalated for the pair.

"How did you say James was killed?" Stills asked.

"He was mistaken for someone else after coming home late one night from taking care of his ailing brother." She shook her head. "If these robbers were the Moss brothers ..."

"Then maybe he wasn't really 'mistaken?'" Stills mimicked Cassie's head shake as Cole picked up the next article in line and began to read:

Two masked bandits held up and robbed the Royal Bank in Telluride and fled with $50,000 in cash in what Telluride police described as a "beautifully planned" holdup. Police were immediately mobilized and set up a blockade on all roads leading out of town amid hints that the bandits might be trapped in the city. However, after a long search, the bandits were not found and theorized to be far out of town before the police could ever get mobilized. The sheriff has verified that this was indeed the work of two robbers who have been wreaking havoc on banks throughout the southeast of Colorado for the past year.

The bank manager said that one man carried a sub-machine gun and looked young, around twenty-five years old.

The bandits forced five employees and nine customers to kneel on the floor while the bandit holding a luger went through the till, picking up the cash.

The police said that the bandits had planned the robbery with great care. Each walked in by a separate door at exactly one minute before 3 p.m., the usual closing time. Each closed the doors, pulled the blinds and locked them, so that it would appear the bank was closed for the day. They then seized the cash.

Cole, careful of the aged pages, looked through them, his frown increasing until he finally said, "If these are all the same men, they stole a lot of money."

Cassie shook her head in wonder. "It would be worth more than that today."

Cole gave a sarcastic snort. "I don't think the brothers were very good at mining."

Stills grinned. "If these masked robbers are the Moss brothers, then they found a much more lucrative business."

Cassie scrubbed her face with her hands. "Okay ..." She sat back and glanced down at the table. "Okay, James would have told Mary to take these to her father because he was a judge in Pueblo and he could have brought William to justice. So, we know she left after James was killed and the family asked everyone to stay away so they could mourn. But did William stay away? Did he threaten her family? Is that why she didn't show these to her father? Or if she did, maybe William somehow convinced her father to stay silent? But bringing a scourge of bank robbers to justice would have propelled his career into great heights." She shook her head and pursed her lips as the different scenarios played out. "Dammit, there are too many variables. Did William know Mary was pregnant?"

"Is that why he came back?" Stills asked.

"To find a big old bag of stolen money?" Cole ascertained.

"The letter, in the back of the book Theresa gave me, said, 'He hid it. And now that I'm dying, you'll never find it.' Could that have been from Mary?"

"Did the note have a date on it?" Stills asked.

Cassie shook her head, but then suddenly declared, "We need to go to the archive. I have the note in the vault. Now that we know this one was written by Mary," she held up the letter to James, "maybe we can compare the handwriting."

"It's one in the morning, Dodd."

"Trust me, I am quite aware of what time it is. You two seem to prefer doing these things under the cover of night."

"So how does all this fit into the big picture?" Cole asked.

Cassie shrugged. "A bastard child and old secrets and I'm the schmuck at the middle of it all who could piece the puzzle together and get answers for someone who would kill for a lot of hidden money."

Cole gave a sad laugh and asked, "Then where's the money?"

"At the Salerno Wall." She meant for it to be a smartass comment, snide and flippant; but as she said it, her eyes widened in the same moment that Stills tilted his head. She repeated the theory, "The money is hidden at the Salerno Wall!"

"Where's the Salerno Wall?" Cole asked.

Cassie shook her head and added glibly, "Italy." But as soon as the word was out she stood up abruptly and laughed. "Fuck me."

She paced in a big circle and pointed to the bookcase in the living room, then drew her finger across the titles.

"What do you need, Cass?"

"The power to go back on and an internet connection," she mumbled, but then gave a click of her tongue. "Marsha, you beautiful weirdo and your great house." She pulled out an atlas of the world book and turned to Italy, then set the book on the table.

"The only reason I'm remembering this is because I *just* wrote this part of the research for Theresa about her father's time in the war." She pointed to the northern coast of Tunisia. "The allies had this area under control and when they made their move, they went from Tunisia to Salerno in September of 1943." She drew her finger across the map and nodded. "I don't think naming a possible location for the hidden money Salerno Wall is a coincidence." She frowned and asked, "But why wouldn't James let the location die with him?"

"It was a lot of money," Stills offered. "Maybe he thought somehow he was helping his wife. Maybe he knew she was pregnant and was doing it for his child?"

Cassie screwed up her face. "The house we 'broke into' didn't look like someone with a lot of money."

"It was a lot of money, but not a lifetme's worth. He could have spent it in his youth ..." Stills was playing devil's advocate.

Cole stretched his arms and brushed the back of his beard with his knuckles. "So we have a motive and a suspect. We don't know Theresa Moss' role in any of this, but the fact that your apartment was ransacked doesn't bode well for her, and we don't know where Lewis is."

"Where do you stay in a snowstorm?" Cassie asked. "He *must* have friends in this town; I'm sure Eden has its shady characters, just like anywhere else."

"We do." Cole frowned. "I suppose that's going to be on my list of things to do later today, check in on the ne'er-do-wells."

"I don't know where else you'd hide during a snow storm," Cassie said, "though I like the idea that he tried to get away and might have frozen to death."

"I understand that, but from my point of view, I'm hoping he's hiding out with someone in town; that would take care of an arrest and get this all wrapped up sooner than later." Cole stood up and held out his hand to Stills and Cassie. "I'm grateful for the help, even though it feels like this crazy mystery continues to be one step forward and two steps back."

Stills walked him out and came back to stand behind Cassie, where he began massaging her shoulders. "We need to try and get some sleep."

"I don't think I can."

He leaned down and brushed a kiss on her neck. "You're safe," he promised.

"It's not that, it's all this ..." She gestured to the table then turned the paper she'd used to decode the book over and began to scribble a to-do list:

-Check exact dates of banks being robbed in newspaper archives.
-Check handwriting examples.
-Look into Mary Buchanan's father and his career.

Chapter Thirty-Eight

Cassie's alarm went off, jarring her out of a deep sleep. She blindly slapped at her phone on the bedside table until it slipped onto the floor, happily singing from under the bed.

She groaned as she slid out of bed and onto the floor in a prone position, retrieved the phone and glanced at the screen through the one eye she forced open.

7:00 a.m.

She was having trouble recalling why she set the alarm for so early, given that she and Stills had only crawled into bed at two thirty.

She rolled over onto her back, stretching her arms above her head as she tensed all her muscles and gave a loud yawn before she released the exertion and felt better.

A whiff of coffee filled her nose, along with something else that smelled scrumptious.

As if she was a rag doll, she hung her head and limbs as she pushed herself into a standing position; legs sore from the late night snowshoeing.

She pulled on a sweatshirt and dragged her body into the kitchen where Stills was cooking; the power having been restored in the past few hours.

He might enjoy when she cooked, but she was equally thrilled to be waited on.

He greeted her with a singsong, "Morning, Dodd."

She grunted in reply and shuffled to him, wrapped her arms around his waist and rested her head against his back, eyes closed. He gave the eggs he was cooking a quick stir and patted her hand. "You should have slept in some more."

"Too much work to do." She yawned.

"Sit down."

She did, then laid her head on the table and propped a hand nearby, ready for the coffee cup he slowly slid into her grasp.

"I need to get to the archive."

"I know."

"I have so much to tell Elizabeth."

"You do."

"What are you gonna do?"

"Help Clayton. We have some good leads. I think he's right, if Lou Macon, aka Lewis Treat, is in town, he's staying with someone. And if he made an excuse to run into you in Highland, then he knows me, so I think I'm done playing."

He dished up toast with jam and scrambled eggs with mushrooms, spinach and feta.

Cassie sat up and took an appreciative deep inhale; 'mmmm.'

"It stopped snowing," Stills said as he sat down.

She glanced out the front window. "Do we think that's a good or bad thing? Do we know if it's going to start up again?"

Stills shrugged as a heavy stomping of boots on the front porch preceded knocking.

"Three guesses as to who that might be." Cassie took a sip as Stills went to answer the door. "Do you know, the only friends we've made so far are with a sheriff, a doctor and an archivist."

"Said the genealogist to the CIA agent."

"I think I can make a board game out of all this."

Stills opened the door to Cole who greeted him with a stiff smile and an apology. "Sorry for the early call, hope you got a few hours of sleep."

"We got enough." Stills waved him in.

Cole was wearing a cowboy hat this morning, jeans and a heavy insulated green and black flannel jacket.

"Coffee?" Cassie asked.

"Please." He wiped his feet and set his gloves by the door. He didn't beat around the bush as he made his way to the table. "I got a call from the office in Highland. They've gotten pushback from CDOT; crews are hoping to complete avalanche mitigation work tomorrow, probably late afternoon."

Cassie put her fork down, her stomach churning with the news. On one hand, the joy of having an open road and being able to go home was liberating, but allowing Lewis Treat to leave and possibly continue to harass her was out of the question.

"In other words, we need to work fast." Cassie stated the obvious as she caught the slight rise of an eyebrow Stills aimed at her. She shrugged. "I'm not going back to our home to have another round of worrying about some ghost trying to hurt me or my family."

"But it'd be like old times; I could keep an eye on you, you could cook pastries for me." He winked at her.

Cassie tilted her head and explained to Cole, "He's talking about our origin story, but it's too long. So," she straightened in her chair, "what's the plan?"

Cole sat down heavily, accepted the coffee Stills handed him and rolled the cup between his hands. "I don't like this time constraint," he admitted.

"We can run the prints this morning and since I've been able to get a signal, we can print out copies of Treat's photo," Stills offered, hoping to put the sheriff's mind at more ease. "It's going to be quick and dirty, but I think we're in a good position."

Cassie found herself entranced by his congenial comfort. It's what had gotten her through the difficult times when he was parked outside her apartment and an unknown threat was lingering; his constant, unwavering calm.

Cole pulled on his beard. "So we'll push forward with our plan."
Stills nodded.

"What plan?" Cassie had been so focused on what they'd found the evening before, that when she was rereading the material she'd missed the hushed tones and quick conversation between the men.

"We're gonna pick up a gentleman who has an outstanding parking ticket in Highland; there's a warrant out for his arrest."

"You can do that?"

"Dodd, we're going to intimidate the shit out of him as legally as we can and find out where Treat is so we can end all this."

"Oh, I'm not worried about logistics and legalities right now," she shrugged, "I just didn't know you could bring someone in on an unpaid parking ticket."

Stills winked at her in reply.

She frowned. "You know you wink a lot when you're feeling cocky, right?"

"Do I?"

She pursed her lips at him. "Well, while you have fun, I'll be in the archive. Not worrying." She said the words to ward off the fear that was trying to settle over her now that the coffee was beginning to kick in.

"You won't worry," Stills said matter-of-factly, trying to bait her.

"I *said* I won't worry." She was baited.

"Dodd..." his voice dipped low, a damned caress, "you won't worry."

"Whatever." She hid a smile behind her coffee cup.

"Finish your breakfast, we'll drop you off."

"Don't tell me what to do." They stared each other down for a moment before Stills gave a grumbled laugh and winked at her once more.

Chapter Thirty-Nine

With the internet working, Cassie brought Elizabeth up to speed as they both scoured the Colorado Historic Newspapers Collection to find the original articles about the robberies. It took them less than an hour to find all fifteen, this time complete with dates, all having occurred between June of 1946 and May of 1947.

"We still don't know if this was the Moss brothers," Elizabeth said.

"Yeah, but the coincidences are building up. But I know what you mean, we can't jump to conclusions. Innocent until proven guilty, right?"

Of course that didn't stop Cassie from plugging the dates of the robberies into the timeline while Elizabeth did an extended search using some of the verbiage from the articles.

When Elizabeth called her name excitedly, Cassie abandoned her chair to stand behind her as she began to read aloud:

> "Federal authorities said Friday that the two men wanted in connection with eighteen bank robberies across the state of Colorado were believed to still be alive and living in unsuspecting communities as respectable citizens.
>
> M. Tomlinson, special agent in charge of the Denver, Colorado division of the Federal Bureau of Investigation, said the men had never been identified. "The problem is that they are of very average looks." Each customer and bank teller that was present during the robberies was interviewed and all have reported the same standards.

That the men seemed to be aged in their early twenties. They barely said more than one sentence during their interactions, so no one knows if they have an accent. And with only their eyes ever visible and their hair in the fashion of working men -tidy and combed into place- is it any wonder there is a worry that the men will never be caught and brought to justice.

The three eyewitnesses who saw the men without hats and scarves, said they were average looking; dark hair, dark eyes but nothing in particular that made them stand out.

The bank manager from the last job in Telluride shared his views with the paper, that he was certain of one thing; the men were calm, collected, highly intelligent and organized.

To date, the bank robbers have stolen a total of $500,000 dollars. And while the Federal Bureau of Investigation continues their manhunt, the duo seem to have retired or possibly absconded with the money to another country."

Elizabeth printed the article and Cassie began to pace and run through theories. "Maybe it really is all coincidence, and they had nothing to do with it. But what did 'he bury?'"

"Maybe one of the robbers killed James," Elizabeth added. "Maybe James knew who the robbers were, one of the men found out and killed him for it."

"Then why not kill William? And if that was the case, William would have left town immediately. Instead he stayed for three more years."

The women took turns suggesting different scenarios; poking holes in some theories and expanding on others in an attempt to get to the truth.

"So maybe William was working with someone else, and James found out?"

"Dammit, we're two steps forward and ... an avalanche back," Cassie hissed.

Elizabeth stretched her neck from side to side and blew out her own frustration.

"Okay, facts," Cassie stated, then stopped pacing. "We know when and where the Moss brothers were born. We know when they joined the army and that they were part of the allied movements into Italy that landed in Salerno. That takes care of the circled letters."

"That can't be a coincidence," Elizabeth said assuredly. "We found the mention of a man who is from Eden in William's memoir. We found circled latitude and longitude of a place close to here."

This was good, Cassie thought, these were the facts. "So we know why they chose to come to Eden. We know how long they stayed here based on James' wedding announcement, William's jail time and when he joined the university system in California.

"We know Mary named James as the father of her son, Art Buchanan. And the date on the birth certificate and the date of James' death are *well* within the realm of possibilities that he was indeed the father."

"The only other way those dates work is if she had an affair," Elizabeth said.

Cassie laughed. "Oh good, more possibilities to muddy this whole mess."

Elizabeth shrugged. "We're taking Mary at her word on a birth certificate."

Cassie squeezed her eyes closed then opened them. "Okay, new facts based on letters. James and William weren't bosom buddies." She picked up Mary's letter. "Mary says *I will wait while you work on separating ties from your brother* and *one day, you will be free of obligation from your brother.*"

"Being forced to rob banks with your brother might cause some bad blood," Elizabeth offered.

"James is older, he joined the military to protect William. William said in his memoir his older brother was always looking out for him."

"And add the fact that their parents were dead and their sister passed away while they were overseas, you get a man who is going to do anything for the only family he has left." Elizabeth raised an eyebrow. "Even if doing anything for family involves robbing banks or keeping quiet about the identity of the bank robbers."

Cassie scoffed, "That's good, throw it on the stack with all the others."

"Okay," Elizabeth said, "the note telling Mary to run, it's from James. He's scared. So what is he scared of?"

"That whatever secret he has will be found out." Cassie gave an unladylike snort. "That was the lamest obvious answer ever."

"But the truth."

"James wrapped the note around the clipped newspaper articles, so we can assume he's scared of the bank robbers and what he knows about them." Cassie pulled it toward her and reread it, then she slid the letter from Mary and said, "Shit. Where ...?" She pulled the threatening note out found in William's book and put it next to Mary's letter to James.

Elizabeth joined her and they were quiet for a moment while they scoured the lettering. At the same moment they both pointed to the letter 'y' in different places on each document.

"You see it too?" Elizabeth whispered.

"All of them are disconnected with an extra loop at the bottom."

"I'm no handwriting expert," Elizabeth said, "but that looks the same to me." Elizabeth grabbed Cassie's arm.

"I see it."

"Damn, you go Mary." Elizabeth breathed. "So, she sent the letter that said 'he hid it.'"

"When did Mary die?" Cassie asked.

"Adding it to my list of questions right now."

"Okay, so more assumptions; William was the one who *it* was hidden from," Cassie began. "The '*he*' that hid it, might have been James."

"*It*, might be a shit load of money," Elizabeth added.

"A shit load of money at Salerno Wall."

Cassie began to pace as the muted sound of a snowmobile hummed outside the archive. Elizabeth glanced out, saying, "It's Benji."

Stills was closely followed by Cole in his truck.

The men entered, Cole carrying a to-go bag. He held it aloft. "Sandwiches from Tilly's."

"Oh good." Elizabeth pointed to the other table that had free space and Cole began to pull items out.

Stills asked, "Find anything interesting?"

"We were able to find all the articles and put them in order; also found an article that said the FBI were on the case but as they had no leads, they were worried they would never find the bank robbers."

"Do you think it was the Moss brothers?"

Cassie shrugged as she opened a bag of chips. "I can't prove that they were the men who robbed the banks, but they sure as hell seem wrapped up in the whole drama of it."

"Have you found Lewis?" Elizabeth asked.

Cole rubbed the back of his neck. "I have an informant cooling his heels at the station."

"Has he said anything?"

"Nothing important yet," Stills replied. "But he knows Lou Macon and Lewis Treat are the same person."

"That's something at least."

"We have pictures." Cole pulled out a printed picture of Lewis from his driver's license and showed it to Elizabeth. She studied the photo for a long time, then finally shook her head. "I want to say I recognize him, but I truly don't."

"That's alright, we've shown a few folks and they know him and have given up some information," Cole reassured.

"We know where he lives in Highland and the police there are getting a warrant together to go search his house today," Stills informed them.

"This is good. Really good." Cassie grinned at Stills.

"I agree," Cole said. "That's why we thought you wouldn't mind the company for lunch. Since we came bringing better news."

Elizabeth locked the door after the men left and turned a beaming smile at Cassie. "I feel so much better. Lighter. Is that weird?"

"I know what you mean, I feel like a fog has been lifted from my brain."

"We're not working out of fear anymore," Elizabeth realized.

"Exactly." Cassie patted her on the shoulder as she headed to the coffee maker. "Now we can get back to being fueled by history and caffeine."

"I have that printed on a T-shirt." Elizabeth laughed.

"Of course you do."

They spent the next hour marking the twenty mining claims the Moss brothers owned on a map and cross-referencing the latitude and longitude found in the book with each of them.

There was no overlap.

"Dammit." Cassie shook her head. "The Moss claims and Art Buchanan and Lewis Treat are all connected. But we're a little off. Like, we've been looking right, when we need to look more left. Does that even make sense?"

"He hid it *good*." Elizabeth muttered the droll joke.

Cassie frowned. "Is there a way to see if this latitude and longitude is located at a mine and if it is, who owns it? And can we find the holdings Art had that Lewis was contesting? Did the email from the BLM contain that information? Is that even something we can do?" Cassie shook her head. "I think I'm spiraling a bit."

"I have an idea." Elizabeth moved to her work desk and picked up the phone to make a call. "There's this website where active claim records are stored. I don't have an account because I'm not sure how to use it, however–" Whoever she was calling answered. "This is Elizabeth Pine with the Eden Historical Society. I need to talk to Todd Sumer please."

She covered the receiver. "I'm done being polite and waiting for return emails. Todd works for a small archive in Telluride and writes a lot of histories about Colorado, but he also knows how to use all the online mining information stuff and has accounts everywhere."

Cassie rested her hip against the front desk as she listened.

"Todd! It's Elizabeth Pine. Listen, thanks for taking my call. I need help, and time is of the essence. If you'll help me out, I promise, once we figure everything out, I'll tell you this story; and trust me when I say, you'll love it, and I think there's a book in it."

Cassie wondered if that was enough for someone to give up his time. Apparently it was, given the victorious fist thrust in the air by Elizabeth. "Okay, I need help with the active claim records; actually Todd," she chuckled and admitted, "I want you to do my homework for me."

She gave him the names of Art and Lewis, the latitude and longitude, and explained the information she wanted. After a few moments a wide grin spread across her face. "That'd be great, just email it to me."

Cassie watched Elizabeth wait for Todd to accomplish whatever magic he could do.

"Okay, you're sending me screenshots of the information," she verified, then after a few seconds of clicking around on her computer said, "Yes, they came through."

Cassie knew that whatever he sent was helpful as Elizabeth's eyes widened and her voice squeaked as she declared, "You're the best Todd, I'll be in touch." And Cassie was sure Elizabeth hadn't waited for him to say goodbye as she slammed the phone down.

"Look!" Her hands were shaking as she zoomed in on the graph across the top of the document Todd had sent. There were lines about Legacy Serial Numbers, File Numbers, Claim Type, but the most intriguing was the Claim Date, May 4, 1947.

"That's a few days after the Telluride job," Cassie whispered, her skin tingling with expectation.

Elizabeth clicked over to the Claimant and they both read the name: Mary Buchanan. The next column denoted the Claim Name: Salerno Wall.

"Elizabeth," Cassie said softly, "do we think there's half a million dollars of stolen money in that mine?"

Elizabeth nodded, answering in the same tone, "We sure as hell do."

Neither of them moved for the longest time, until finally Cassie righted herself and exclaimed, "Holy shit!"

Elizabeth didn't hold back her laughter as she said, "This must be what archeologists feel like."

"So did Art know about the mine? If it's in his mother's name ..." Cassie shook her head. "Did he cash in? But we found the latitude and longitude in William's book."

"Did William find out after Mary sent the letter and she passed away?"

"Oh my God, we found Salerno Wall but we still have more questions ..." Cassie trailed off but smiled, letting her mind ponder those questions further.

Elizabeth caught Cassie's attention again. "There's a column for payments. The next payment due date is a year from now. Someone knew, and someone was paying the fees."

Cassie rubbed her hands together quickly. "But Lewis doesn't know about it. Or maybe he does now? Why was Art killed? Did he know?"

"Maybe everyone had a fraction of information to the story, but no one has been able to put it all together yet."

Knowing she was putting it together, a chill ran through Cassie; chances were she had more information at this point than any one person had had for years.

That comfort she'd gotten after talking to Stills began to slip once again.

Chapter Forty

Outside they heard a snowmobile. "That should be Aidan," Elizabeth said. "He had a few house calls to make and said he'd stop by this afternoon to check on us." Elizabeth unlocked the door.

"It must be so different being a doctor in a small town than in Denver," Cassie said. "He seems to love it. He's such a calm man."

"My sister says he's so laid back he's almost horizontal." Elizabeth laughed.

A bundled form passed the front window, quickly opened the door, then shut it and stood with a gun leveled at both women.

He slipped his hood off and blindly locked the door behind his back as a steely grin crossed his face.

"Good afternoon, ladies."

Elizabeth gave a strangled sound as she tripped backward, holding the table behind her back to keep her upright.

Cassie seethed and asked, "So would you rather be called Lewis or Lou?"

His salt and pepper hair, which had been combed neatly the first time she met him, was now askew; his brown eyes were dark from beneath the skin they were folded into, treacherous and menacing.

He winked at her and a rumble of disgust twisted in her gut as he said, "I knew you were smart and could figure this all out."

Cassie took a few steps, trying to get to Elizabeth and figure out how to make a secret call on her cell phone that was in her backpack, all while separating Lewis from the gun. But she wasn't given much time to make any moves as he stepped toward Elizabeth, leveled the gun and ordered, "Where are your cell phones?"

Elizabeth pointed to her desk and when he looked at Cassie it took her several tries to say, "In my bag."

Keeping an eye on the women, he retrieved the phones and stepped on them with his boot, mangling the technology.

Elizabeth let out a soft groan of despair and if it were possible, his grin grew and he pointed to the back of the room. "Vault. Go."

When she didn't move, he shrugged. "Vault or I shoot you. It makes no difference to me."

Cassie was prodded into action; she reached for Elizabeth's hand and pulled her toward the vault.

When they were inside he pointed to the lock. "The vault door won't open from the inside without the batteries. Take them out," he instructed Elizabeth.

"No." Cassie breathed out the helpless word.

He snarled and took a step closer to Elizabeth, pointing the gun directly at her, causing Cassie to immediately hold up her hands in apology.

She watched Elizabeth's shaking hands as she removed the batteries.

"Toss them into the other room," Lewis demanded.

Cassie couldn't think, she couldn't focus on anything but the pumping hot fear that was pulsating through her body; but that heat soon froze to ice when he changed the direction of the gun and sneered. "Cassandra Dodd; with me please."

Instinctually, Cassie's hand found Elizabeth's; being in this situation together was a lot better than apart.

"Cassandra, I can leave Elizabeth dead or alive in this room, you choose."

Cassie nodded her head. "Okay," she said and repeated it as she gave Elizabeth's hand a squeeze. But when Elizabeth didn't release her, Cassie turned apologetic eyes toward her new friend as she shakily untangled their hands. When she was a slight distance from Elizabeth, outside the vault, he pushed Cassie out of the way so she was farther than arm's length and closed the door.

Cassie righted herself, and turned to make eye contact with Elizabeth, trying to force a smile that said everything was going to be okay. But Elizabeth already had tears streaming down her cheeks, her feeling of utter helplessness contagious as the door shut her in with a scary finality.

Lewis turned the handle to make sure it was locked, then sized Cassie up. "I believe you have a story to tell me, but I don't think this is a very good place. Your boyfriend and sheriff friend are busy, but they won't be for long. Put your coat, hat and gloves on. We're going for a ride."

Cassie swallowed as the memory of taking a gun out of an attacker's hand flashed before her eyes, but they'd only covered the lesson twice in class and she didn't remember the details of how to accomplish the task.

"I'm not a patient man. I can still open that door and kill Elizabeth."

With her heart hammering violently in her chest, she tried to hold fast to one coherent thought as she shakily reached for her windbreaker, but she dropped it, opting for Elizabeth's heavier winter coat instead, along with her thick gloves and hat. She left her own lighter weight options on the ground.

As an extra precaution, Lewis took out a knife, went to the phone and cut the cord. Then he stood at the table and waved at the pages laid out. "What details do you need? We're going on a gold hunt."

She frowned at him. "What do you mean?"

He gave a scoffing laugh. "Do you really want to play this game?"

She pointed at the computer screen that was still pulled up as her mind was quickly attempting to focus on any sort of actionable steps she could use to get out of this situation. When she couldn't see a way out, her fear pushed aside cognizant reasoning.

He walked over and glanced at the screen then said, "Print this out."

She did so and when she was finished, he asked, "Is there anything else on this computer we need?"

She shook her head so he also cut the cords on the monitor and computer tower.

His gun still trained on her, Cassie stood nervously in the middle of the room with the printed page.

"Where did you find the latitude and longitude?"

"William's memoir."

His eyebrow shot up, perhaps surprised. "Where is it?"

She pointed to the table.

"Get it."

She retrieved the book and he asked, "Is it written down anywhere else?"

God she wanted it to be, how was Stills going to find her if he didn't know where she was going? She pointed to the whiteboard.

He studied it for a moment and gave an almost approving nod. "You've been busy, that's a lot of information. So why don't you erase it."

She hated the way her hand shook as she followed his directions.

He pointed to her bag on the floor. "Put all the papers and that laptop in that bag."

When she was finished he tossed two sets of handcuff zip ties to her. "Put the backpack on and then put each wrist through one of the zip ties."

Once that was accomplished, he gestured to the door with the gun and an almost amenable tone. "Let's go for a ride, Cassandra."

The archive was part of a group of buildings and homes at the edge of town, on a road that led to ghost towns and higher elevations. A road that was not traveled in weather like this. So the chances of someone seeing her with Lewis Treat were a hair shy of slim.

She opened her mouth to ask where they were going but it wouldn't do any good. It wouldn't even stall time, it was really an excuse to work her mouth in the hopes that her mind would catch up. And that was all she needed. "Where are we going?"

"I'm not a patient man nor am I stupid and I know you're not stupid. I am, however, calculating. I'm also a wanted murderer. So now that we have that out of the way, do you have any more questions?"

She actually had a litany of questions, but none that she was about to pose to this psycho.

She opened the door and he locked it before pulling it shut. He stayed close to her and leaned forward so she could feel the pointed end of the gun against her left shoulder as he whispered, "Slowly."

She jerked her head away from the foul breath that tortured her ear but did as he said, and shakily walked to the side of the building where the snowmobile was parked out of sight of the street.

As they approached, he commanded, "Sit on the back." She did as she was told. "Now with your left hand, zip tie your right hand to the passenger grip." Her hands shook so badly, it took her several attempts, but when it was done, he nodded, put the gun in a holster on his hip and attached her other hand to the other side. She would be able to hold onto the grip, but as for falling off or trying to roll to safety, the zip ties made sure that trick was out of the question.

The luggage rack on the snowmobile had two gas cans and several boxes. She assumed they were supplies and she hated everything about this snowmobile that foretold a long journey.

He pulled on a helmet and with a sneer said, "Only one helmet, sorry girly."

He turned the starter and drove slowly. He was calm and collected, and Cassie thought this was worse than any deranged, frantic lunatic. This man was fully cognizant of his faculties and decisions.

It was nearing dusk as they drove, the shaky light of the snowmobile making more of a path as the sun set. The snow had started again in earnest, and once they were out of town, he sped up and Cassie blinked back a few stray tears as she bent her head down so Lewis Treat's body shielded the cold from her. She tried to remind herself that Elizabeth would be found. She could contact Todd and he would have the coordinates saved. The sheriff knew this area, and Stills would not rest until he got Cassie back to safety.

That was something.

It had to be.

Chapter Forty-One

At some point, the cold and fear played equal parts in numbing Cassie. The surrounding darkness nipped at her with icy fingers, and the headlight chased off large, falling snowflakes, but left them to swirl up around her and whisper disparaging threats regarding her current situation.

Lewis drove so far for so long. Each passing tick of an imaginary clock that kept time with her pounding heart and each length the snowmobile ate up, left her more and more desperate.

Finally, he slowed and made a hard right turn onto a nonexistent path between tall trees and bushes. He crawled around a few curves and finally up a slight hill, cranking the steering column and taking them down into the front of an overhang where the opening of a cave suddenly appeared.

He pulled into the darkened space then stopped abruptly on the slight amount of snow that had flown into the mouth of the cave.

Even though he'd stopped the snowmobile, he left it running for the light until he could retrieve a nearby lantern that was sitting at the base of the cave. Cassie tried to put her nose and mouth into the top of her jacket, the smoke from the diesel engine making her lightheaded. The lamp shone, and Lewis reached across the steering to stop the vehicle. He held the key up for Cassie to inspect, and then as if hypnotizing her, held her attention the entire time he stepped to the open mouth of the cave and tossed the keys out into the snow.

She stared wide-eyed at the action, to which Lewis sneered in appreciation. Thankfully, the shock of being abducted and trying to calm herself down for so long helped dull the shock of this latest atrocity.

If the long drive and lost keys weren't enough, Lewis stepped to the right side of the cave, close to Cassie, and reached up as far as he could, where a wad of material had been placed in a naturally formed nook. When he pulled the material free, it became a giant drape of white camouflage strung across the opening, completely disguising the entrance; releasing the last drops of Cassie's hope.

She knew Stills would move heaven and earth to find her, but this had created some seriously tough odds.

Lewis cut her hands free and started to hand her the lamp, but when she reached for the handle, he kept ahold of it and leaned forward. "You might want to smash me over the head with that lamp, but then you'll be walking out of here, girly. And it's cold and you're lost. So let's just play nice and once I have what I want, I'll let you go back to your nice little life."

The gun he leveled at her didn't validate that he was going to let her live.

She wondered if she could make it on foot, in her jeans and hiking boots, without skis or snowshoes. But she was smart enough to know that the last thing you did in weather circumstances such as these, was take off in the wrong footwear.

But maybe it was worth losing a toe or two if it meant she would live.

Believing that she had a worst-case scenario plan if she needed it, she gave a nod that she understood, and he released the handle then motioned with the gun for her to head deeper into the cave. After a slight distance, he stopped her and pulled the starter on a generator. The echo wrenching of a motor and flickering light bulbs made her jump. He pointed to a spot next to the generator. "Turn the lamp off and put it down there."

There was a uniform distribution of fluorescent light bulbs hanging along the cave walls as they walked; time and distance were distorted with her heightened adrenaline and fear. The shadows looked like ghosts, mocking her with knowing smiles and reaching for her with spindly, gaunt fingers.

She didn't know how far they had gone when a spark of calm screamed into her brain to count the steps.

She physically stumbled on the thought.

"Go," Lewis hissed.

She took a deep breath and used every ounce of concentration she could to count the remainder of the distance. Four hundred and thirty-two steps later, the tunnel ended in a large circular room where it was apparent Lewis had been living for a while.

A camp stove was set up along one of the walls on a wooden table that had a cutting board and plastic tub; for washing dishes, she assumed. On the floor were boxes of food and an amount of water jugs that can cause a person who is being held against her will to physically shake with raging fear.

Another side of the circled outcropping housed a cot with a sleeping bag. And in the middle of the whole room was a camp table.

Lewis turned on a portable heater the size of a box fan, and Cassie realized then that she wasn't as cold as she had been. It was warmer in the cave.

He motioned to a camp stool on the other side of the table as he opened one for himself to sit on.

She glanced around her once more, blindly staring at the black and gray cave walls, the eerie way the light played with the shadows. The sound of wind, coming from so far away, gave off a dull, soft whistle, and the dirt floor was covered with boot prints.

Cassie's stomach lurched as she fell against the table, holding herself up. "Snake." She pointed to the boot print with the snake in the center.

Lewis looked at the floor and frowned. "Stupid goddamned boots."

She gave him an astonished gaze but he growled his instructions, "Sit down."

She didn't remember sitting and tried to gather herself, not caring now that she was breathing so deeply in and out.

You're important to him. The same voice that demanded she count her steps demanded she believe this too.

She sat up straight and continued the deep breathing. *I'm important.*

She might be important but he was in charge; though that didn't mean she couldn't prepare herself for what was to come.

She forced her voice to not shake as she asked, "Are you going to rape me?" She figured she would go big with the first question.

He snarled, "The worst I'll do is shoot you in the head." He raised an eyebrow as if asking if that was threat enough.

She nodded, ridiculously comforted by that fact. "You're not unhinged." It was more of a fact.

"I want what I'm owed," he said calmly.

"The money that's been hidden." Cassie was verifying the assumptions she and Elizabeth had made thus far.

"*My* money."

She went through another few rounds of breathing until she finally stated, "So you know William was your father."

"William Moss was a sperm donor," he seethed. "He knocked my mom up, but they were just fooling around, at least that's what she told me. She never wanted anything to do with him, never asked him for help. Never told him about me. It was my stepdaddy told me I wasn't his. Never found out until I was in college and had a copy of my own birth certificate and the sperm donor's real name."

"So I'm here …" She couldn't get her heart to regulate or the fog of fear to clear. "So I'm here to help you fill in the missing pieces?"

"That, and you're my get out of jail free card. I'm sure the sheriff you and your boyfriend have befriended will be more than happy to give me a head start if I offer up your life in exchange for mine."

Cassie was strangely thrilled he didn't know what Stills did for a living. And as long as she was a bargaining chip, her life would be spared.

You're important.

But at what point would she stop being of value?

"Are you working with Theresa?" Talking was helping her thoughts shuffle back in order, helping her body back into some semblance of passable rhythm again.

He shrugged and mocked, "I'm merely her long-lost little brother that she didn't know about. We're each other's last family and I'm simply trying to make a connection. But out of respect for our father's memory with the university, I don't want to tarnish his name with a bastard son."

"So you knew about the money and needed to see what information she had."

He nodded triumphantly. "I planted a few ideas in her head; wouldn't it be fun to research good ole *Dad?*" He growled out the word. "Dad's whole life, his whole story. That way at least if I wasn't known to the rest of the world, I could finally know my own heritage. I suggested your company, which goes 'above and beyond,' then all I had to do was bide my time. Theresa told me Cassandra Dodd was the name of the woman working on our story and that she was going to Eden for research. Finally, you were being brought to me."

"You followed us?"

"Actually, that was my buffoon of a cousin."

"Art? Did he know you were related?"

"You really are good at this family history stuff."

"I don't understand; he was following us? So you did know each other? Were you working together? Did you kill Art?"

Lewis gave a gruff laugh. "Look at you, little Sherlock Holmes, you really do go above and beyond. Art helped me set this whole place up." He gestured around the cave. "Pretty good, huh? But then he wanted to call the police because he didn't like the idea of kidnapping you. I tried to calm him down, thought we'd take a little ride, but he tried to run away ..." He tilted his head, did Cassie understand?

"How did you find us in Highland?" She mumbled the question because she was still reeling from the fact that this kidnapping had been premeditated; and for a while.

"Art followed you from California to the Four Corners. He actually wanted to talk to you and tell you who he was, but he couldn't find the nerve, thank God. The damned idiot would have ruined everything. He went back to Eden from the Four Corners."

Ice cold fingers crept up her back at the memory of boot prints outside their cabin. So they had been Art's? When had he been there?

"Once I knew you were on the way, I greased a few palms to keep an eye out for your car. When you stopped in Highland, our interaction was serendipitous."

"If you knew I was going to Eden, why did you put a tracker in my purse?"

"I just wanted to know where you were going to be at all times. But I suppose I didn't take into consideration you aren't the kind of woman who doesn't take a purse everywhere, or that you'd find it and hide it in an abandoned house." He smiled, almost as if he admired her attempts.

"Who broke into our apartment?" she asked.

He frowned and shook his head.

"Did Theresa hire someone to break in?"

Another confused shrug. "I don't know why she would, all she knows is that we're related. But I didn't have anyone break in."

"A coincidence?" Cassie rubbed the back of her neck, she was getting a headache.

"Must be. I tripped you, bugged you, stalked you and killed Art, but I didn't hire anyone to break into your apartment."

She stared disbelievingly at Lewis, her original theory that he wasn't unhinged was unraveling.

"Okay, time to swap stories and figure the rest of this out," her captor said.

Chapter Forty-Two

"We have a long night ahead of us." Lewis moved to the stove and began to make coffee.

Cassie's head was swimming, maybe from the sudden fumes of the gas stove that didn't have any decent ventilation, but probably from the situation.

He retrieved granola bars and a bag of beef jerky. Tossing the snacks on the table, he gestured to the offering. "Brain food."

She thought about not eating, for the sake of contempt, but she also knew she had to keep her energy up and be ready for anything if she found a window to escape or if Stills found her.

When, a voice whispered in her head.

She liked the word so much, she allowed it to linger and repeat itself over and over again.

When.

When Stills found her.

When Benji found her.

Lewis slopped the coffee into two camp mugs and slid a cup toward Cassie. "If you take cream or anything you're shit out of luck."

She took a sip and watched as he pulled out a plastic shoebox from one of the tubs stored around the edges of the cave. He set it on the table, settled himself behind it and took a deep drink of his coffee. As he lowered the cup, eyes squinting in the dim light, he studied Cassie.

She forced each of her cells to focus on being angry. He might be insane, but he'd admitted he'd rather kill her than rape her, and that was something. So why not focus on being angry now?

Finally, he pulled out the contents of the box and stacked a bunch of papers on the table. To the side of the papers, he placed a laminated map and a red wax pencil.

He didn't explain himself, but of course he didn't have to.

He simply handed the first page from the top of the stack to Cassie.

Her hands shook as she took the letter, then stared for a long time, trying to convince her eyes to make sense of the letters on the page and marry them together to create words. Finally, she was able to focus.

James,

I took the train yesterday to Highland and spent most the night drinking, course you know that's what I do best. Mining Eden is a bust. I give up, but we both know you gave up a long time ago.

I did a thing, James. Maybe it was stupid, maybe it was enlightened. But ol' Jacob Hines was right, there is gold in these mountains, just not the kind we thought there was.

James, you spent your whole life keeping me out of trouble, one way or another. I hate that I didn't see you when we enlisted, I was angry and hungry and the army seemed like a good idea. I didn't see your keen mind then, and you should have stayed out of infantry and maybe you should have gone the way of the aviation mechanical line. But we went into the army poor and hungry, we were put in danger only to stay poor and hungry, and now we're here in the middle of nowhere with no valuable learning, still poor and hungry and not suited for civilian life. The war made sure of that.

Truth of the matter, James, is that I'm mostly tired of being poor. So I have an idea. This one last time, I'm asking you to follow me and help me. I'll be back to Eden soon.

Your brother, Bill

"Where ...?" Cassie hated the fear in her voice that seemed to delight Lewis. She tried again, "Where did you get all this?"

"My dear cousin. Had boxes from his mom and never looked into them after she passed away. Just kept them closed up in the closet."

The next item in line was the Highland Standard, the entire paper from April 3, 1946. Lewis took it and opened it, shook it out and slid it in front of Cassie. He pointed to the pertinent article that reported a bank robbery. "The concealed man absconded with $2,000."

Cassie compared the dates of the letter and the article. "William robbed the banks?"

"Of course, you found this out already," Lewis said as he laid out full page articles from all the bank robberies in front of her, one after another.

She touched the top corners of them. "I found clippings from Art's house, but none of them had the dates; we had to search the newspaper database to find those." Was that this morning that she'd done that work with Elizabeth?

"Eighteen banks in one year," Lewis smiled, "nineteen if you count the first one in Highland."

Next was a xeroxed copy of Art Buchanan's birth certificate with the name J. Moss highlighted. Then, as Lewis handed over an envelope he said, "The stupid oaf, this letter was right under his nose his whole life."

Cassie gently pulled the letter from James out of the envelope.

> My dear child,
>
> I don't know if I'll ever get to see you brought into this world or grow into adulthood. Life has a strange way of standing in a man's way, even when a man tries his best to do what's right, there's always something.
>
> I'm not proud of who I've become. I'm not proud of what I've done up to this point in my life.
>
> I have one source of pride. It's my marriage to your mother and you. And it isn't fair. Rarely is. That's what I've learned of life, but that is far from the lesson I want for you.
>
> I wish you a life filled with all the love and laughter you

can get. A lifetime of a million rays of light having shone on you.

I'd like to say what I've done was for you, but it wasn't.

What I've done, what I continue to do has always been a family obligation.

It wasn't until I met your mother that I realized what love was. How big it could be, how it could grow and encompass two people and become a place of solitude all its own.

I wish you that love and peace a million times over. Your mother brought the peace that eased my heavy soul. But I have these damned family obligations that pull at me, tear at my compass of right and wrong. In the war they tore us down and built us back up, only I don't think I ever recovered. I think I've only continued to sink lower and lower.

Therefore, I write to you, an idea I can't even fathom right now. And if you are reading this, then to you, I am the same idea. We are two specters who will have to wait until the afterlife to meet. And for that I am sorry, but I fear my sorrow will be of no comfort to you.

I robbed eighteen banks throughout Colorado, New Mexico and Utah with my brother William this past year.

Forgive my shaky writing, I've never put such a confession to paper and the only other person I've said these words aloud to has been your mother. And even she says she'll forgive me my trespasses, though I don't deserve it. But for you, I feel the need to wash away what grime I can and try to be a better man. For you. For your mother.

I've looked after my brother and sister my whole life. Our parents died early, our sister took in laundry and sewing to make ends meet in Chicago. We weren't doing much more than surviving. When the Japanese bombed Pearl Harbor, William saw a way forward for all of us. Not for love of country, I'm ashamed to say, but a way to be fed and send home money to our sister.

We enlisted as infantrymen. It's what you do when you have no skills or decent learning. They call infantrymen 'cannon fodder' and there's a reason for that. We ended up on the front lines.

It was a difficult time, and as you grow older, you'll find mention of the war and what men went through. I don't need to spill that confession here as well.

William wasn't a man when we entered bootcamp, and he was barely a boy. That's why I went with him. To protect him. I think something happens to you when you become a man in the middle of the horrors we faced. William came out of the war lost and broken.

We came to Colorado to find a new life. But that didn't work either. Then William robbed a bank in Highland. He returned and came back to the bunk we lived in and hid for two weeks. When no one came knocking on the door and it seemed the authorities didn't know it was him, he told me he was going to rob another bank and he needed my help.

I tried to talk him out of it, but William is hotheaded and said he was fine if I didn't want to follow through. He would still go on without me.

When you fight with your brother halfway across the world, when you watch his eyes die, when you know you were supposed to keep him safe and when he's your only family in the world ... you find that solidifies your obligation and brotherhood. I would do anything for my brother.

He is bright and showed a scary aptitude when it came to researching and plotting the robberies. I helped too, I am not innocent of that. But we were so methodical and smart about the whole thing that we pulled off each robbery without any hardship.

I lived looking over my shoulder, worried for us both. Scared at how easy it seemed, and knowing that any moment we might be gunned down.

William was living the high life. He started drinking, carousing, and flashing the money around. I talked sheriffs out of arresting him more than I care to admit, but he still ended up in jail for being drunk and disorderly.

I realized I wanted out. I had an idea that if we had enough to live out the rest of our lives comfortably, then I could stop and put all this behind me.

It was a dream. I know that now. But it turned out that William's love of money was the root of all his evil.

I understood why, having grown up with nothing, we'd never been in the position we found ourselves. But my arguments and pleas to save the money and use it over time and build an actual life for ourselves or build a business, fell on deaf ears.

I had fallen in love with your mother after we'd robbed our ninth bank.

I wanted out. I wanted to get a job at one of the mines in Eden and build something with her. Something safe and sustainable, I suppose. I was willing to do anything to be with your mother.

I tried to live two lives until finally William was amiable to a new deal. He asked me to give him one year, from the date we robbed our first bank. If I would plan and rob as many banks as we could until the one year anniversary, he'd part ways with me.

I proposed.

Your mother should have turned me down.

We married and began to build a life while I tried to release the grip my brother had on my old life.

Our last job was in Telluride. The papers said the cops called it well planned, and it was. But William was near unhinged, it felt as if he wanted to stay and get caught or be gunned down.

That night we came back to Eden and agreed to lay low. Go fishing for a few days. But he went drinking and it was a friend who came knocking in the middle of the night to tell me William had been buying drinks all night for the patrons and talking about how he'd finally hit it big in the mountains.

I didn't go retrieve him from the bar the way I usually did when his mouth began to write more checks than it was good for.

You see, I hatched a plan when I proposed to your mother. The first thing I did was purchase a few claims. I put half in William's name, and half in mine. One of the claims I worked in my free time. I told no one, not even your mother. But that night, when William was arrested yet again, I packed up all the money we'd stolen, all of it except enough pocket money for about a month, and properly hid it.

My only thought was to save William from himself. When I returned to town, William had been arrested, but his mouth had run afoul. There were whisperings that we might have started another gold rush. People were excited and wanted answers, if we had indeed found a gold vein.

I purchased even more claims, in case someone looked into the claims in our names.

William left for Albuquerque to get some sun. He wrote me a letter saying as much, and ended the note explaining that he understood the time we'd agreed upon was finished. He trusted me with the money until he returned.

We are happy, your mother and I. But I'm worried what will happen when William returns to town and asks for his half of the money.

That's why I felt compelled to write you this note. A confession from the grave, or perhaps I'll burn this letter.

I wish for you a multitude of good things in this life, my child. Don't follow in my footsteps. But if you do, go about it legally, maybe check out subsurface geologic

methods. I'm sure you'll find the earth, its formation and
composition, as interesting as I found it.
Your adoring father forever, James

Chapter Forty-Three

Cassie sat back and shook her head several times.

"I'm not a bad man," Lewis smiled, "I just come from an alcoholic thief."

"Oh, is that all?" Cassie bit her lip, having forgotten for a moment where she was and what was happening around her. She held up her hands as if to fend him off and excuse herself. "So, James hid the money. Mary must have known because she sent the letter to William that she was dying and that he'd never find it. That must have been why William came back to Eden in '65."

"I figured as much," Lewis said.

Cassie frowned and shook her head several times, hoping it would help loosen all her thoughts from the exhaustion and fear and adrenaline, so she could organize the storyline properly. "All of these were in Mary's possession?"

He nodded in answer. She gestured to her bag and reached for both copies of the geology book.

"So James left the coded message in the library book. But William must have known about it because he had the same book with the same letters on the same pages circled. And when did Art find it?"

"What do you mean Art found it?" he asked angrily.

She pushed the book forward. "I found this hanging in a bag on a coat hook at Art's house, under his jacket. There was a letter from Theresa in it." She turned to the front page where the library card was. "This was the most interesting part of the book."

He laughed, the sound short and clipped, the laugh of a man who didn't think he could be bested.

Cassie's frown deepened as she tapped the books. "But the latitude and longitude, we found those in William's memoir."

"What do you mean?"

"Theresa gave me two books that had been on William's bedside table when he passed away. One was the geology book with a letter in the back that we now know was from Mary." She pushed that copy of the book forward and slid the note found in the book out and placed it on top. She then retrieved William's memoir and set it on the table. "The second book was this copy with numbers circled, the latitude and longitude of the mine we just found out was under Mary's name."

"Called Salerno Wall." Lewis shook his head and muttered, "So ridiculous."

Cassie raised an eyebrow. "Did you know that Salerno is where the allies landed when they went from Africa to Italy."

"I didn't, but thank you for the history lesson."

"I brought it up because there's a possibility it meant something to them both. An inside message."

He inclined his head and Cassie cleared her throat, then hid her fluctuating nerves behind another drink of coffee before she continued the narrative. "So, William returns from Albuquerque after four months and probably needs money. He went to James who has a happy home and a child on the way and he gets mad when James tells him the money is gone?"

He shrugged and slid over the next letter on the stack.

It was the notice in the Eden paper about the death of Peter Syke.

"The man who killed James?" Cassie mumbled as Lewis grunted in reply.

> Eden county Sheriff, said Saturday night that Peter Syke, 27, mechanic at the Eden Stage Stop, who has been under house arrest awaiting trial for his murder of James Moss, took his own life.

"When was this ...?" She glanced at the top of the page, three months after James' death. "Why didn't this come up when we searched James' name?"

"Because technology is flawed, girly."

"But the woman who wrote the cemetery book should have been able to find mention of this."

He handed over the next paper, the sheriff's report on Peter's death.

> In the left hand of the victim was a M1911 and the shot verifies self-harm. Syke was left-handed. However, I did the personal walk through to make sure no weapons were on the premises when Syke was put under house arrest. Only Deputies Cale, Walters and myself have been keeping watch over Syke. No signs of foul play, but there were two shot glasses on the table and a bottle of half-empty whisky. He was not allowed visitors. Could it be foul play? A last joke from Syke to have our department chase our tail? There was no other sign of tampering, Syke's home was always in a state of disrepair. The window out of the kitchen was half open upon arrival. It was a cool evening. But perhaps drinking had made Syke heated. The gun was the standard-issue sidearm for the United States Armed Forces. Syke was never enlisted.

"Where did you get this?"

"I have my ways."

She thought about pushing the subject, but instead stated, "So the sheriff thought something was off. Did he do any more about it?"

"If he did, it wasn't on any other reports. It seemed that the good sheriff decided to let sleeping dogs lie."

"What do you think?"

"I think William might have been angry about the money but he loved his brother a lot more." The answer shocked Cassie, the continual pendulum swing of cognizant intelligence to sneering maniac sent another shiver through her.

She narrowed her gaze on the pages in front of her, trying to see them and clear her head of threats that were attempting to seep in. "So ..." she led.

Lewis shrugged. "William was a drunk, his brother was dead, the man who did it was within reach and he was still fresh from the war; it's all within the realm of possibilities, Cassandra. And the firearm used was a military issue. I don't think we need to go too far afield to decide William vindicated his brother."

"William was in and out of jail after James died. The sheriff would have had time to talk to him about it."

"Maybe he did, but there's no documentation proving it."

That was true. "Okay, so after James was killed and William got drunk, Mary went directly back to Pueblo with her family and was never heard from again. I found letters in Art's house." Lewis' jaw tightened again at the mention, so she shakily pulled out the letters she'd found in the armoire and showed them to him. "Mary ran, but I don't think she ever passed any information over to her father."

After a moment, he took the next letter in front of him and handed it to Cassie. "Next letter."

This was an official looking letter, with an embossing across the top that read "The Court of Common Pleas," and under that was the moniker Judge Buchanan. It was a copy of a handwritten note meant to look official and daunting.

> Sir,
>
> It is for the gracious character of your brother and my precious Mary that I write to you. I have more than enough information needed to put you in the back of a deep, dark jail cell and throw away the key for the remainder of your days.
>
> Mary and her child have passed.
>
> My advice to you, leave Eden. Start over somewhere far away from Colorado. If I hear of you in the state again, or if you ever pose a whisper of a threat to my remaining family, I will come after you with all the force of the law and the fires of damnation.
>
> The Right Honorable Judge Buchanan

Cassie blew out a breath. "Holy shit."

"I think that's what sobered up good ole Dad. He saw the light after that."

"And hightailed it out of Colorado," she mumbled. "Did you ever read William's book?"

"Nope, can't say I cared enough about dear old Dad's life until my mom told me there was money at stake."

"Did he … tell your mom?"

There was a long silence, and then Lewis shrugged, as if it didn't matter now what he admitted. "She passed away twenty years ago. When she was given some powerful drugs to make her comfortable, she told me my real father hid a lifetime's worth of money in a mine. But he forgot which one. And if there's money, it's mine. I want what I'm owed."

Cassie soaked in all the new information and the dangerous gleam in Lewis' eye and tried to focus. So she took out William's memoir and turned to the dedication page, then slid it to Lewis.

For James, who saved my life more than once, was always the brains of the operation, and whose death changed the entire trajectory of my life. It was difficult to move on without him.

Lewis wasn't moved. "It would seem, Cassandra, that I've told you what information I have; would you like to fill in some of the parts I'm missing?"

She pointed to the coffeepot in question, and he nodded his approval for her to move. She stretched and shook her hands, trying to alleviate the physical shaking that was growing from lack of sleep and over-caffeinated senses. After she poured herself a cup she pointed to the water bottles in question and he agreed to that with a wave of his hand.

Once seated again, she took out everything from the backpack and laid it out on the table, then began her side of the story. She tried to figure out how to hold the one piece back that she knew he was most interested in. Not able to come up with an idea quickly enough, she desperately thought of other ways to stay important to this situation.

When she finished, she gripped her hands together under the table and said, "There are still a lot of holes, but it's as complete as we can get it."

"True." He pushed all the papers aside and put the map in the middle. "Can I please have the latitude and longitude?"

She tried to steady her breathing as she pulled out the paper and handed it over.

He found the location and began plotting a route.

"What does this mean for me?" she asked, her voice barely a whisper.

"We're working against time to get there before the sheriff does. Of course, that all depends on your friend at the archive and when they find her and if she can remember the area we were heading to. I figure we're a few hours ahead. So as soon as I get this plotted, we're heading out."

He continued to study the map and Cassie had a sinking feeling that someone who was this open to sharing the plan of action, was not the kind of person who would let her live.

"When you find it … when we get there …" She needed to get control of herself. The 'what if' questions starting to race through her mind were not helping.

Lewis still answered the unasked question. "Once we find the money, I'll leave you in the mine and if you're lucky, someone will find you before you freeze to death."

She had to swallow the urge to cry. Being left behind in a cave didn't sound so bad at this point.

She glanced at the granola bar and jerky on the table, but Lewis caught her and pulled them away. "Now, if you take some food with you, chances are you might try to escape before this partnership has reached its natural conclusion." His smile distorted his face, wrinkled it, drew the shadows of the cave in on it, and revealed the true villainous state of the man.

"Okay girly, let's get going."

She *wanted* to leave, just not with him. She also wanted to know what had truly happened between him and Art. And *did* he know Theresa? But she wasn't about to ask Lewis about his familial ties at the moment.

"Way I figure," he said as she pulled her jacket and hat, shoving the gloves in the pockets, "we'll take a little drive, find the mine; you'll help me pack up my money and I'm gone."

Was it that simple? She wondered, because sometimes, one's best-laid plans do *not* work out.

And he was off-kilter enough that if there wasn't any money, if they never found what they were looking for ... well, Cassie wasn't in the mood to be around this man if he found out the father who bastardized him, also ripped him off.

When Lewis wasn't looking she slipped the paper with the latitude and longitude into her hand, wadded it up as slowly and quietly as she could, while trying to make the scuffing sounds of her shoes match the times she balled up the page.

When they reached the generator, he pointed to the lantern again. After she turned it on, he turned off the lights and instructed her to continue walking toward the cave entrance ahead of them.

When they arrived back at the snowmobile, she stood meekly by as he put more gas in the tank, then pulled out another set of keys from his pocket and grinned. "You didn't think I was that stupid, did you?"

Stupid wasn't a word she'd use to describe Lewis. Dangerous, disturbed, and insane were becoming her new favorite adjectives.

He handed her another set of zip ties then strapped a large bag of tools and flashlights, along with several different shovels that had been sitting in the cave entrance, onto the back of the snowmobile. He checked his map again, then after a few nods, pulled off the screen covering the cave, letting in a blast of cold air that straightened Cassie's spine. Not a fit night for man nor beast was the first description that assaulted her.

She tossed the wadded paper into the center of the cave, hoping that if someone found this cave, maybe they would also find the information she left behind. She put on her gloves and couldn't bring herself to put the zip ties back on. She stared at her hands and the black plastic.

"Cassandra," Lewis growled and the crunch of earth and snow beneath his feet as he crossed the distance between them screamed in her ears. It was the cold press of metal against her temple that caused her to find the energy to begrudgingly affix the zip ties.

He gestured for her to get on the back and she shivered as her hands were zip tied onto the handgrips once again.

His helmet back in place, with no concern for keeping her from the elements, he slowly retraced the path they'd used to get here, flakes flew and twirled about. She strained her eyes in the darkness and couldn't find any traces of the tracks they'd made a handful of hours before.

Fear for Stills and Cole began to sink into her imagination. What if they'd taken off without planning and something happened to them in this storm?

"No," she said aloud and clenched her teeth together. Stills wasn't that kind of man. Emotional or not, he would look at all the facts, all the reasonable avenues he could travel to help her and make the best decisions in order to save her.

Sure Stills is smart, she thought, *but this fool who tied you to a snowmobile in the middle of nowhere in the middle of the night has already killed someone over what he thinks is in a cave in southeastern Colorado.*

"No," she said aloud again. *I'm valuable.* She screamed the words in her head and fought the evil little voice that whispered, *you* were *valuable.*

The wind and cold and snow slapped at her face. The flickering headlamp laughed at her. Cassie dropped her head into the top of the jacket in an attempt to block the frigid conditions, closing her eyes and forcing herself to mentally go through the actions she'd learned on how to disarm someone who was pointing a gun at her.

She issued all the strength she could muster to mentally plan each move she could take to turn the tables. Because it wasn't up to Stills to save her now. While that would be really, *really* fucking nice and helpful, it wasn't plausible. What she needed was to calm herself down. Stills wasn't here, she was. She'd worked hard to be able to take care of herself amid difficult situations, and one hell of a difficult situation was presenting itself.

She thought of the plastic gun they used in class; and the instructor who stated that the odds a person would end up with a gun pointed at them was less than ninety-eight percent. She squeezed her eyes harder and snorted a laugh at the ridiculous thought that arose: *Spy rule 15: Use your time wisely.*

She shook her head and focused again.

First she would need to grab his arm at the wrist, spin the gun away from her body, then using momentum and force she could either flip him to the ground as she spun and held his arm; or, if she had enough momentum and the element of surprise on her side, she could twist the gun out of his hand in such a way that she could break a finger in the process.

The goal is to reposition the gun and then twist it from his hand.

And then you have to commit to possibly using it.

She swallowed a forming lump. Commit.

If she decided to go through with this action, it would be life or death, and *Cassandra Leigh Dodd, you have a lot to live for.*

Chapter Forty-Four

As the snowmobile once again ate up more miles and the distance from Eden grew, the hope Cassie so desperately fought to hold on to slipped away. The only way getting the gun from Lewis would be of any help to her was if she could also get the snowmobile—keys included—and the GPS device he had.

Another round of savage trembling seized her. The helplessness at being anchored to the stupid machine made her jerk her wrists angrily against the zip ties, cutting off circulation from the bare movement that was available. She was spinning, as out of control as the snow in the lighted path ahead of her.

She tilted her head back and gasped, even though the bitter cold rubbing her cheeks raw was suffocating her with dark, icy, hopeless fingers.

She needed to find something to hold on to, a thought, a glimmer of some damn thing.

Then get fucking angry.

A blink of a thought formed, and she narrowed her gaze on Lewis' back and nodded and repeated it again and again, until she muttered the mantra aloud, "Get fucking mad."

And she was.

She was mad at the fucking cold, mad at Lewis, mad at Theresa and mad at zip ties and snowmobiles. She was mad at her jeans and hiking boots. The anger began to build, like a fire in the pit of her stomach. She heaped William and James onto the flame; and for extra measure, she tossed another load of resentment on the snow.

She tucked her head back down into the top of her jacket, closed her eyes, and leaned closer to Lewis to use him as a human shield.

And she let the rage and anger grow.

The snowmobile stopped on a flattened area and Lewis pulled out a handheld GPS mapping device. As Cassie looked around, she realized there were new shades of dark and light around her; it was almost dawn.

And that changed everything. Didn't it?

If Cassie had some damn daylight to work with, if she could get ahold of that GPS and the gun and the keys and subdue this asshole ... not *if* she could, she reminded herself.

That was what she was going to do.

"It's up there!" he exclaimed excitedly. Lewis pointed to the right, where Cassie could see an area under a substantial cliff overhang that had been spared from a buildup of snow. He drove as close as he could get, stopping a few feet from the covered area. He cut Cassie free, no gun held on her this time; probably because they were too far from anything and if she tried to run, she'd most likely freeze to death.

And he was underestimating her.

And that is your greatest power right now, Dodd.

She watched as he slipped the keys in the right pocket of his jacket but didn't have time to plot a way to get them as he quickly handed a bag of tools over for her to carry. He took the shovels and led the way.

They didn't have to wade through high snowdrifts. The natural covered area had only a small dusting of snow, and the further back they went under the overhang, the less snow, until finally it was only a flat dirt area in front of the rock face. It was reminiscent of the cliffs and structures built in Mesa Verde.

At first glance, they couldn't find a possible entrance, but when they reached the end of the outcropping, they found an illusion—a dark interior just beyond a five-foot, oval-shaped hole.

Cassie stood open mouthed as Lewis' heavy breathing accompanied his flashlight that spanned around the shape of the entrance.

"There!" His voice let loose his eagerness.

Cassie narrowed her gaze on the area where his light stopped. Sloppily carved into the brown gray rock at sharp angles was the word *Salerno*.

"Holy Shit." The cold and fear lessened as even her anger slipped slightly.

When Elizabeth first mentioned the 145 mining claims in the area, and as Cassie studied the life of the people whose hopes and dreams were made and dashed in these mountains, she realized how vast the land was.

And she couldn't fathom this life and what James and William had gone through themselves.

But now, standing in front of *the* one mine, it made tangible the world she'd been researching the past few days.

"All this kidnapping bullshit aside," she muttered, "this is amazing."

Lewis aimed a squinty smile at her, but she returned a frown of disgust.

He put the shovels and pickaxe a decent distance from her reach, then motioned for her to put the bag down as he pulled out a headlamp from his pocket and handed it to her. She fixed the elastic band over her head and turned on the red light.

When she faced him again, he had the gun back in hand. "Ladies first."

She scowled at the gun for several moments, this was the opportunity she'd been waiting for ...

... and she didn't take it.

As she turned in slow motion to begin walking into the cave, an internal scream called her a litany of names as she hung her shoulders in shame; she wanted to see what was inside the fucking cave.

It better be life changing.

And let's be honest (she continued the internal dialogue she was having with possibly four different people in her head), chances were good he'd level the gun on her again.

So there's that.

"Go," he growled.

She had to crouch to walk inside. The carved space was only big enough for one person to walk through at a time.

"He blasted it," Lewis informed her, pointing his light at the jagged edges and uneven shape of the cave. As if to verify the fact he continued, "In the letter he said he worked on it for months."

And it was many months' worth of work they walked through. The size of the cave never changed, but after another hundred feet, the tunnel ended in a room big enough for both of them to stand upright and for Cassie to put several arm's length distance between her and Lewis.

She didn't need to scan the cave. Right in front of her was a large burlap tarp covering a form that reached just above her waist.

A strangled sound came from Lewis as he lunged for the cover and pulled it off like a magician pulling a tablecloth from a full table.

Eighty years of dust and debris floated in the rays of the headlamps, a trick of its own as it revealed two stacks of suitcases, eight in all, made of dark brown leather with brass luggage locks.

Lewis caressed the suitcase on top, wiping the dust from it in wonder. Cassie stood stunned, her mouth agape.

When he attempted to open the top case, and finding it obviously locked, he holstered the gun and pulled out his all-in-one tool from his pocket and began to hit it against the frail lock. When the first one broke, he worked the second. When that popped, he stopped and took a deep breath.

Cassie inched forward, adding her light. Slowly, he raised the lid and the contents shone before them. An animated growl erupted from Lewis and the breath Cassie hadn't realized she was holding rushed out.

Hundreds of dollars.

Stacks on stacks.

"It's real," Cassie whispered.

"It's real!" Lewis called giddily. He shuffled through the money and repeated, "It's real."

Cassie picked up a hundred-dollar bill. A bright green, Benjamin Franklin smirked, looking frustrated in the dim lamp light. She touched the date on the bill. "It's from 1934 ... This is worth a lot more than a hundred dollars now."

"Hot damn!" He grabbed the bill back and put it in the case and shut it. "Okay. Okay." He turned in a circle as if he couldn't decide his next actions. "Okay, we need to get these suitcases loaded onto the snowmobile."

There was momentary comfort in the word 'we' but it wasn't going to last long; best-case scenario, she had four trips to commit to whatever life saving tactic she was going to take.

Commit.

No matter what you decide to do, Cassandra Leigh Dodd, when you make your move, you need to commit.

Because now, the money was real and there was a lot more than five hundred thousand dollars at stake. And there was no way this man who wanted what was owed him was going to let her live.

Cases were strapped to the back of the snowmobile and as they brought the last two out, she knew it was now or never.

She faked a trip in the direction of the shovels, dropped the case, then as she stood, grabbed the first shovel she came in contact with. As quickly as she could she turned, swung with all her might and caught Lewis in the right shoulder.

"Fuck!" he screamed, but instead of grabbing the sore shoulder, he went for his gun.

Cassie swung again just as he pulled the gun out and flung it from his hand into the snow.

She was so surprised at her success she let her attention follow the gun for a moment, giving Lewis enough time to lunge at her. He caught her around the waist, knocked the shovel out of her hands and used the momentum he'd gained to slam her flailing body into the rock wall, catching her head and back against the jagged rock. He released her and she fell to her knees, the wind knocked out of her.

"That was a good trick. I didn't know you had it in you, but that's all you get."

When he picked up his foot to kick her, she somehow managed to roll out of the way, and with his one foot in the air, she kicked at his leg from the ground, sending him careening off-balance with a curse and stumbling several feet from her.

She scrambled to her feet as he regained his footing and pulled his all-in-one tool from his pocket and quickly opened the knife.

Her gaze shifted between his face—pulled in deathly anger, eyes blackened with rage—and the gleaming, sharp knife.

He was standing between her and the shovels; she had to get to one. It was her only option.

When he lunged at her, she bent low to center her gravity and as if she were playing soccer, sidestepped and hip checked him.

He yelled and brought his fist down, nicking her, but she got past him and was able to grab a shovel. They turned at the same moment to face each other. His unhinged anger was driving him, and if she wanted to live, her only option now was to knock him unconscious.

She waited for him to make another manic move and when he lunged again, she swung the shovel with every ounce of energy and force she had in her and caught him at the temple. With a grunt, his body went limp.

She took several staggering steps backward, and tried to both steady her breathing and hold back the tears that had started.

"No." She madly shook her head.

That was step one; disable her opponent.

Step two was to get away.

She needed keys and the GPS.

Her hands shook as she pulled the keys and GPS from his pocket, fearful that he would move at any moment. But as she watched his blood pool, another sickening thought twisted her stomach. She'd killed him.

She took a step back and faltered, her leg feeling strange. She glanced down and found that she wasn't the only one who'd gotten in a lucky strike. The nick she felt in her leg was actually his knife sticking out of her left thigh.

She stared at the knife for several long seconds, slowly realizing she hadn't noticed he didn't have a knife in his hand when he'd lunged at her the last time.

As bile rose, she bent at the waist and let what little she had left in her stomach loose into the snow.

She shook her head and again seethed, "No." It was a weak noise, so she repeated herself, stronger now. "No."

She thought she would pull the knife out but had a vague memory from somewhere that suggested leaving a knife in a wound was better; you wouldn't bleed out as fast.

She went back to Lewis, pulled up his jacket, found he was wearing a belt, and with shaky hands, unbuckled it, then tried to stamp down another rise of bile. She pulled the belt and as the motion rolled his body, she heard him groan.

Not dead.

Which meant Cassie needed to get going.

She put the belt around her leg, above the knife wound, and took a shaky breath before she tightened it as much as she could. Grunting her pain, it echoed around the canyon walls.

She gingerly climbed on the snowmobile, her hands shaking as she put the keys in. "C'mon Dodd. You've got this." She started it, pulled on her gloves and then very carefully, she began to back out, then turned the snowmobile back in the direction she'd come. She wanted to get a decent distance from Lewis before she checked the GPS.

Cassie didn't feel good. It was too cold again. It was biting into her, but now she had another problem. She needed medical attention. Because she wasn't sure how long she really had before the knife sticking out of her leg wouldn't cause more problems.

She should have grabbed the helmet, but the urgency to get away was more important.

Now, she was exhausted, because whatever adrenaline she'd used to get through the past few hours had faded.

She stopped to check the GPS, and saw she was heading the right way. The road she was on would connect her to a road that would take her back to Eden. But it looked so damn far away.

She shook her head. It didn't matter. She was headed back to Eden and she wouldn't stop until she got there.

She began to drive and used all her remaining energy to focus. She told herself that Stills was probably already out looking for her so she'd come across him before long. It was light now and the snow had stopped.

That would help everyone.

She could do this.

She could get to Stills.

The hand grips of the snowmobile continued to grow heavy, heavy to hold on to, heavy to turn. Even holding her arms up and herself straight on the slippery snow was getting more and more difficult. And even though the snow had stopped falling, the white that covered the land in the gray light continued its attempt to flow into tunnel vision.

When it did that, Cassie yelled aloud for herself to stop and slow the snowmobile. Then she'd blink and rub her eyes and try to keep herself from looking at her leg and the growing bloodstain.

She started and stopped, looked down, and shook herself out of self-pity and into action so many times even that was growing too heavy.

Everything was too much now.

She forced her eyes to stay open as wide as possible. Then at one point she became aware that the snowmobile was slipping off the road. She cranked the handles as hard as she could but the overcorrection sent the snowmobile one way and her the other. Cassie closed her eyes against the pain that was coming but the slipping felt so good she let the darkness claim her.

Chapter Forty-Five

S omeone was touching and shaking her. Roughly.

She didn't like it and gave a groan while trying to roll away and stop it, but that hurt.

Another shake.

Then something was invading her space, trying to move her, but she didn't want to be moved.

She should open her eyes and stop the intrusion, but her eyelids were glued shut. She felt another movement and pain.

She tried to open her eyes, but it was so hard and going back to sleep sounded so much better ...

"Cassandra." This time a demanding voice accompanied the shaking.

She didn't like that either, so she fought to open her eyes once more, just to give the angry voice a piece of her mind. But when she was able to open her eyes ever so slightly, focus was now an added difficulty as everything around her was so white.

"C'mon Cassandra." Another harsh demand.

She frowned up at Stills as he came into view, bending over her. She was on her back and remembered why she didn't want to wake up; she was so, so cold.

"Cold." Her voice cracked on the word and sounded so far away.

Suddenly Stills was drifting away from her. She reached out her hand to touch his face, but he was pulling further and further away.

"Cassie, stay awake." He shook her slightly and with pinpoint precision, he jumped back into close-up focus and her hand came into contact with his warm cheek.

"Justcold ..." she muttered.

"It's okay baby, you're gonna be fine." Stills' typical calm demeanor flickered. His forehead creased with worry and his eyes were narrow beams, his face drawn.

Cassie's eyes widened at his words and the fear painted on his face; he was lying to her. It was bad. *Really bad.* Tears welled up and burned the cold from her eyes.

"I've got you," he insisted vehemently.

She heard yelling coming from somewhere.

"Okay, listen honey, you're in a small ditch off the road, we need to get you out, and there's a lot of snow. So we're gonna put a rope around you, under your arms; it's attached to Cole's snowmobile. He's gonna slowly pull you up onto the road."

She shook her head as the heated tears singed a path down her cheeks.

"Honey, we found you, it's going to be okay."

"Notgonnabeokay," she said through sobs, "callmehoney ... isreallybad."

Stills gave a gruff laugh and brushed the tears away. "Okay, listen Dodd. You fell off a snowmobile and I'm worried about blood loss from your leg and I don't know if you have broken bones or a concussion." His voice went dry with the laundry list. "But we can deal with all that later. First we need to get you out of here."

"Gotstabbed. Left the knife, did tourniquet." She shakily reached out to touch her leg, but the knife was gone. "Blood loss." Her eyes widened.

"You did so good, baby."

"Baby?" More tears.

"Dodd," he said sternly.

Swallowing her tears, Cassie gave a half-nod and tried to focus on his face, touching his cheek again. He put both his gloved hands on top of hers. She had to give him a rundown of how she was feeling so they could get her back to Eden.

"Feel feet, toes," she began but her teeth began to chatter, "thighs," she grunted in pain from tensing her leg muscles, "hips," she wiggled slightly on the ground, "shoulders, arms," she twisted her head left and then right, "head good."

Another loud call came from above them and Stills stood, leaving Cassie's view. She began to sit up and felt the world tilt, so she stopped and let a few more tears fall. Stills was lying—nothing was okay.

He returned with the rope and made quick work of tying it then helping Cassie put it around her chest, right under her armpits.

He yelled up to begin, and slowly, her body was dragged up the snowy side of a deep ditch, away from Stills.

He clambered up the slope next to her and when she arrived at the top, he took the rope off and Cole came running through the snow to help.

"She's awake," Stills offered.

"She's awake," she repeated, blinking up from her prone position on the ground.

Cole nodded as he took in her leg and chattering lips. "We need to go. Cassie, this is going to be a helluva uncomfortable ride," he said gruffly.

She gritted her teeth as both men helped her into a standing position. Cole continued to keep her steady as Stills climbed on the front of his snowmobile. She gave a loud yelp of pain when Cole helped her to get on behind Stills.

"Cassie, hold on to Benjamin," he instructed. "We're gonna tie you to him, so even if you pass out it should be fine; but we can't have you falling off another snowmobile again."

She winced in pain as she shifted her weight against Stills, finally resting her cheek on his back as he pulled her exhausted arms around his waist. But instead of linking them in front of him, he put her hands in his pockets, his warm, warm pockets.

Cole took off the scarf he was wearing and wrapped it around her neck and face. She tried to fight back the tears, coming from having something warm on her.

Cole hurriedly and awkwardly tied Cassie to Stills. Finishing, he said, "I'll follow. If you hear me honking, it's because she's slipping." The instructions over from Cole, Stills didn't wait for anything else. He started the snowmobile and began to drive as quickly and safely as he could.

Cassie tried to suck as much warmth as she could from him, but she was still so cold. She couldn't recall ever being this cold before in her life. It kept her awake for the rest of the agonizing ride back into Eden. Stills drove directly to the clinic. Cole already had a knife out and was cutting Cassie free when Aidan, with a gurney, rushed out to the bottom of the snow-cleared ramp. The scarf slipped off her face as the sheriff started to help her get off the snowmobile.

Elizabeth appeared as Aidan gave instructions on how they were going to all put her on the gurney. He didn't wait for questions, but counted to three. The world twirled and tilted, then Cassie was on the gurney, with Elizabeth by her side, holding her hand. She was wheeled into the warmest, most welcoming building she'd ever been in.

Stills began reporting to Aidan what he knew. "She has a tourniquet on her left thigh, and possibly a concussion. We found a snowmobile up the road; she must have fallen off. Not sure how long she was in the ditch, but she's been in the cold since last night ..." His voice, rough with the details, trailed off.

Cassie was dizzy and felt like she was drifting through a cold fog. "Benji ... found the mine. Found the money." Her voice continued to sound far away. She opened and closed her mouth several times, as if she could make silent echoes.

"We'll talk about all that later." Stills patted her hand.

"I killed Lewis." She whispered the confession.

Aidan began to calmly call out to each person what he needed them to do.

"Elizabeth, get the electric blankets." She took off to do his bidding.

"Cole, Mrs. Edgar is on her way. Can you make sure she gets here a little faster?" He was speaking of his nurse.

They rolled into the examining room. "Ben, please help her out of her gloves, jacket, shirt, shoes and socks."

Stills' hands shook as he did what was requested. She was left in her jeans and bra.

Elizabeth returned with the blanket, which she carefully laid on Cassie's chest before plugging it in.

Stills stood to the side and took Cassie's hand in his.

"Elizabeth, cut the jeans away." She and Aidan put on gloves and once she'd cut the jeans away on the right side, she folded the blanket carefully to cover that side of Cassie as well. Aidan took the scissors and cut the jeans on the left, then he gathered a few items on a mobile tray. "Elizabeth ...?" he asked and handed her a large pad of gauze.

He took off the tourniquet then finished cutting the jeans to the top.

Elizabeth pressed the gauze to the area.

"Ben, can you start rubbing her feet to get them warmed up? Not too hard, just kind of hold her feet and rub gently," Aidan suggested as the door opened and a woman with gloves already in place wheeled in a tray with all the needed tools to place the IV bag that also sat atop the tray.

"She's hypothermic, possible concussion, deep laceration on the left thigh," he reported. The woman nodded in understanding as she and Aidan began to work together like a well-oiled machine.

"Cassie," Aidan said to focus her attention, "you did really good with this."

"Didn't take the knife out," her teeth chattered, "kept it in, but fell …" Her head felt floppy as she tried to find Stills and focus on him. When she found him, he was smiling encouragingly at her, but his face was shadowed with concern and worry.

"The snow you fell in actually helped," Aidan explained calmly.

Needing to help Stills, she grinned at him. "It's okay," she said as she closed her eyes, then using all her strength, opened them and asked, "Should I try to stay awake?"

It was the last thing she remembered.

Chapter Forty-Six

Cassie was aware that she was awake, but her body and eyes were too tired and exhausted to act on the information. After several attempts, she finally forced her eyes open, then shut them quickly due to a burning sensation. She tried again and felt heavy. In fact, her whole body felt heavy, but there was also something else; she felt warm. So warm.

She gazed around the room, and saw it was a small hospital room. But where? Stills was asleep in the chair next to her, his legs stretched out in front of him, arms crossed over his chest, head dipped down.

"Benji ..."

His head shot up at the sound. His eyes cleared and Cassie came into view. Fully awake now, he stood and took her hand in his. "Hey baby."

All the warmth seeped out of the room, and her lips trembled as she swallowed and tried several times to ask what was wrong but couldn't quite get the words out.

Finally, she whispered, "What happened? Did I lose ...?" She reached out and touched her left leg; it was still there.

"No, you're fine, Dodd." Casssie took a deep breath, hearing what she needed as Stills chuckled with relief. "It was only a flesh wound. You were so damn brilliant. You did everything right. The tourniquet, getting away, keeping your wits about you ..." He cleared his throat as he brushed a possessive kiss across the knuckles of the hand he was holding. "I, however, did not do very well seeing the woman I love in the condition I found you."

She let her heavy eyelids close for a moment. She was feeling stronger now, but her whole body was sore. "I'm sore."

"I bet. You've been in and out of consciousness for two days."

She opened her mouth and eyes in surprise and took in Stills' ragged appearance. "Have you slept?"

"I'm fine."

"That's a no."

"I was worried," he admitted evenly. "You had hypothermia, your face is blistered from the wind and cold," he lightly touched her hairline, not wanting to hurt her, "not to mention the stab wound in your leg."

"Who stabs someone in the leg?" she asked as she tried to sit up; it took all her energy and Stills' help.

"Assholes mostly," he offered.

Assholes.

She swallowed and whispered, "I killed him."

"Actually, you didn't." Stills sat on the side of the bed. "Which is good; it means the asshole now gets to stand trial for murder *and* kidnapping *and* attempted murder."

"Oh." Cassie shook her head as scenes from her ordeal swirled around her. "I was scared, Benji."

"I know honey."

"I was scared, but then I got mad and I kept running through the steps to get a gun out of an attacker's hand, and I was waiting and knew I'd find my moment. And when I did, I was lucky enough to have a shovel and I swung as hard as I could."

"Of course you did, you're Cassandra Dodd."

She let a few tears fall now that the threat was over and everything was in the past. "I didn't know if you would find me. I didn't know if you *could* find me. And I realized I was the one who was going to have to do something."

He allowed her the space she needed to talk through her nightmare of events.

"There was a lot of blood the second time I hit him. I thought ... and then he moaned when I pulled off his belt to use as a tourniquet."

"Aidan said the snow he was laying in probably saved his life."

She nodded and glanced around the room blindly, not seeing where they were, but stuck in a looping replay. She mindlessly reached out and touched her leg, then shot a panicked look at Stills. "Will I be able to run again?"

"You'll be able to run and hike and swim and snowshoe and bike ..."

Cassie blew out a relieved, shaky breath and gave a slight smile.

"And you'll be able to have Olympic-style sex with me."

"Olympic-style?"

He winked as he continued, "Also, I contacted your work, my work, your sister and your dad. I will admit this one time Dodd, that I chickened out when it came to the idea of talking to your mom."

"And when Barbara Dodd called you back?"

He blew a quick snort of a laugh from his nose before he cleared his throat and muttered, "I ignored it, called Jessica and made her talk to your mom. Then I called her back and told her everything was okay. And talked her out of rushing to Eden."

Cassie narrowed her gaze. "Is she somewhere else in Colorado?"

"No. She's home and waiting for you to call her."

Cassie laughed and moaned from the few sharp pangs that radiated through her body.

"God, I can't tell you how much it means to hear your laugh again." He brushed her hair away from her face.

"Benji, we found the mine and the money." She shook her head. "It was *so* much money."

"I've seen it."

"What?"

"When search and rescue went to get Lewis, they found two suitcases near him; then they retrieved the snowmobile you fell off of, that had the rest strapped onto the back. We have all the money, Dodd. And Clayton pretty much swore everyone involved to secrecy, put it in the vault at the archive and contacted the FBI to see how they'd like to deal with this whole situation."

"It's been a busy few days." She was surprised. "I'm going to have a lot of testifying to do, huh?"

He shrugged. "Only if you want to."

"Where's Lewis?"

Stills paused for a moment before he revealed, "There are only three rooms in this clinic. He's down the hall, handcuffed to a bed and under sedation." He found it difficult to contemplate that the guy was so close to Cassie.

"How did you find him?"

"GPS had the last coordinates. Dodd, you were amazing."

She felt a little more centered; a lot of information was still floating around, but she was coming back to the ground. "How soon until I can go home?"

But instead of Stills answering her, Aidan, who she suddenly saw standing in the doorway, said, "I'd like you to stay in town for at least two more days if you don't mind. I did a CT scan, and things look clean, but we should watch for increasing pain, redness around the wound, swelling or fever. I think you're out of the woods, but just to be on the safe side, maybe you can humor me."

She nodded, her throat thick with the realization of what the doctor had done for her. "So should I walk on my leg, or ..."

"Crutches for a few days, keep your legs elevated when you aren't moving." Aidan smiled. "But you're in great health so really, take it easy for ten days and see a doctor when you get home. They'll probably prescribe a bit of physical therapy, but other than that, you're already out the other side of this."

She pointed at the floor of the room. "Do I have to stay here for the next two days?"

"Nah, I don't see why you can't recuperate at The Hideout." Aidan pushed himself away from the door and said to Stills, "If you want to get her some clothes, I'll find some crutches and you're out of here."

Chapter Forty-Seven

C assie was grateful for finally being released from the hospital to finish recovering at The Hideout. Once Stills helped her get settled on the sofa, she looked out over the bright snow-covered landscape. The light bouncing off all the white was almost blinding.

She snuggled into the couch, holding a cup of hot tea with two hands against her chest, as soft classical music from the only local radio station drifted around the room. So she had a front seat view when Cole pulled up in his truck.

"It's the sheriff," Cassie called.

Stills came downstairs. "Probably wants to check on you," he said, opening the door.

Cole nodded a greeting, took off his cowboy hat as he entered and crossed the room to hand Cassie a jar of raspberry jam.

She smiled up at him approvingly. "Did you make this?"

He grumbled, "of course," then accepted a cup of coffee from Stills and sat, resting his hat on his knee. "The house I bought has a ton of raspberry bushes. There's so many of them, and every year I think I'm gonna rip 'em all out, but then I don't; and I hate for the raspberries to go to waste, so I learned how to can and make jam."

"Oh. Thank you," Cassie said.

"I figure it'll go well with all the homemade bread you're about to get."

"I'm about to get homemade bread?"

"Folks in this town love to dote on someone who's ailing." A smile lightened his gruff face. "And they think homemade bread has magical healing powers."

"We really don't know anyone in town."

Cole gave a chuckle and reiterated, "You'll see."

Cassie realized as he sat back with a deep sigh how tired he was. His eyes were slightly sunken in with black rings surrounding them. He had the same drained look as Stills.

"Cole …" She nodded her head several times, as the words burned and stuck in her throat. It took a moment before she could finally say, "Thank you. For saving me."

He waved it away. "It's me who needs to be thanking you; both of you."

"Do I need to give a statement?" Cassie asked, glancing between Stills and Cole.

"Yeah, but we can do that tomorrow or the next day. Lewis isn't going anywhere, and your law-abiding fiancé understands paperwork. He won't let you leave town without doing your due diligence."

The crunch of a car pulling up caught their attention and Cole glanced out the window. "That's Edwin and Marsha."

"It is?"

Cole winked as Stills answered the door. The couple was a jumble of feet stomping and greetings as they balanced containers and brown paper bags.

Cassie put her cup down and moved to stand up, but Marsha called out, "Oh no, you don't. You stay right there." She handed her bags to Stills then marched over and carefully arranged Cassie's feet back up and covered her with the blanket as Stills showed the loaded down Edwin to the kitchen.

"Oh honey," Marsha pressed her hand to her chest, "my heart almost burst when I heard what happened to you."

Cassie glanced over at Cole, a silent question: What did Marsha hear happened to me?

"Edwin is the director of the Avalanche Recovery and Safety Team," Cole explained. "They were the ones that recovered Lewis."

"I just don't understand it," Marsha picked up Cassie's cup and handed it back to her, "how greed can drive a person mad." She pulled a chair from the table next to the sofa and gave Cassie's hand a pat. "Enough about that. What do you need?"

"A place to stay for the next few days?"

"Of course. Already arranged that with your handsome man there."

Stills gave Cassie a knowing smile as he and Edwin joined the group.

Marsha patted Cassie's arm. "And you two are going to try and pay for the extra days, but I don't have anyone scheduled to stay here for two more weeks, so I won't hear about it." She narrowed her gaze at Stills, a quiet reminder that they'd had this argument and she'd won.

He held up his hands in surrender and Marsha nodded her head once.

Edwin pointed to the kitchen. "I started the chicken noodle soup yesterday, homemade noodles of course, and today I made some strawberry Danish. And my sourdough starter is doing so good this year, I decided to make some baguettes to go with the soup."

Cassie glanced at Cole who gave her an 'I told you so' look.

"Thank you so much. You didn't have to do that, but it's really appreciated," Cassie said.

It was as if there had been a bat signal put up that people were visiting The Hideout, because another car came to a stop in front of the house.

Cole continued to keep her apprised of who was arriving. "That's Beverly."

Beverly didn't wait for anyone to answer the door, simply burst in with her no-nonsense manner and a towel wrapped package under her arm. She greeted everyone and patted Cassie on the shoulder as she passed. "Looks like the gang's all here. I'll get myself some coffee, if you don't mind."

Cassie whispered, "Benji, you might have to make another pot."

He winked at her, already on his way to help Beverly, who was asking, "What did you bring Edwin? Sourdough something I suppose. So, I made you a loaf of cranberry bread. It was my mother's recipe, keeps nicely in the fridge. Don't worry about the towel, Marsha'll know it's mine and get it back to me later." She came and stood at the edge of the group and squinted down at Cassie. "Ya shoulda asked me about Lewis Treat, I knew the family."

"We just found out, I didn't have time."

Beverly pursed her lips. "I figured, smart girl like yourself; of course you wouldn't go and put yourself in the middle of danger without a reason."

Cassie glanced over at Cole as she heard the whir of a snowmobile stop in front of the house. "Stacy," he supplied.

Cassie couldn't recall the name and frowned.

"Works at The Western," Cole filled in.

Since Stills was standing, he greeted Stacy. She had a tray in her hand and Cole further explained, "She also works on the avalanche team."

"Ah."

"Howdy, howdy. I don't mean to intrude, but saw Marsha drive by and knew she was heading this way, so I figured I'd throw my bread in the ring." Stacy held out a foil-covered pie tin in Cassie's direction. "Cheddar bacon rolls," she declared before continuing to the kitchen.

As the din of conversation grew, Cassie glanced wide-eyed at Stills.

Another crunch of tires and Cassie began to laugh at the parade.

"The Pines," Cole offered.

She sat up taller now as she realized she should have had Aidan call Elizabeth before she'd left the clinic.

Elizabeth smiled politely as she entered the house, handed the tray over to Aidan and made a beeline for Cassie's side.

"Are you okay?" Elizabeth asked.

"Are *you* okay?" Cassie met her concern with her own.

They both nodded and broke out in laughter as their eyes filled with tears. "It felt like forever before Aidan found me in the vault. Thank God I taught him how to open it if the batteries died. And then it took so long to track down Todd to get the coordinates ... I'm so sorry."

Cassie was shaking her head. "*I'm* the one who's sorry, it was my research that brought all this here."

"I would have been a part of it even if you weren't," Elizabeth reasoned. "Who knew this kind of work could bring life or death situations?"

"Not me," Cassie breathed, then studied Elizabeth's face that looked drawn with worry. "I'm okay," she insisted.

Elizabeth took a deep breath as the tears began to fall again. "I was so worried, and it was so cold and snowing–"

"That's why I stole your hat and gloves and jacket."

"I'm so glad you did." Elizabeth laughed. "When Cole finally called in that they'd found you and you were safe ... I'm shocked that I didn't faint."

Cassie took Elizabeth's hands in hers and gave them a thankful squeeze that she hoped relayed everything she wanted to say to the woman who had become a true friend in such a short amount of time.

"I made you brownies. Try them with some raspberry jam," she suggested. "I think you'll be surprised."

"How do you all know what each other is going to bring?" Cassie laughed.

Elizabeth shrugged, holding back a smile. "The ghosts tell us."

After everyone had another cup of coffee it was Beverly who clapped her hands loudly. "Okay, let's all get out of here. Miss Cassie needs her rest."

There was a swirl of quick dishwashing and a refill given of Cassie's hot tea. Marsha double-checked the blanket tucked around her, Edwin checked the fireplace, and Elizabeth bent toward Cassie's ear and whispered, "Tomorrow, you have to come to the archive. There's something pretty cool you should see in the vault."

"Deal," Cassie said.

A final wave of goodbyes and the parade was over.

Stills pressed his back against the door after he closed it.

"That felt a little bit like the end of *The Wizard of Oz*," Cassie admitted.

"I was going to compare it to the end of *It's a Wonderful Life*; but instead of money donations, it's baked goods." Stills grinned.

"So many baked goods."

He wiggled his eyebrows. "I know. C'mon Dodd, let's eat."

Chapter Forty-Eight

Cassie napped on and off for the rest of the afternoon, then woke to the smell of homemade chicken noodle soup being heated on the stove.

"Yes please," she called in the direction of the fragrant air.

Tired of sitting on the sofa, she hopped over to the table. The action radiated through her leg, so that when she sat down, she could still feel her pumping heartbeat throbbing in her leg.

Stills helped her prop up her foot, and by candlelight and the last rays of daylight, they dipped fresh sourdough baguettes into the hot broth, both rolling their eyes from the care and devotion that was used to make such a savory marriage of flavors.

"I feel weird, like I was in a nightmare, and when I woke up safe in my bed, I'd still suffered the actual wounds inflicted in the dream." She touched his hand and began to trace his fingers with hers. "I know you want to ask how I'm doing."

"I do ..."

"But you don't want to push me or anything."

"I don't."

"I'm okay. I feel capable. Does that make sense?"

"It makes a lot of sense," he responded. "The real measure of your capability right now, Dodd, is do you feel like calling your mom?"

"Not that capable."

They sat next to each other on the sofa after dinner. Stills pulled out a book to read, and Cassie was happy to sit in the silence and allow her thoughts to float in and out of the information and reality she'd been faced with the past few days.

After her fifth yawn, Stills laughed as he marked his place. "I think it's time for bed."

She stretched her arms above her head and let out a dramatic sigh. "Okay, but there's something we need to do first."

He looked at her expectantly as she pushed herself into a standing position with one of the crutches. He stood to assist and when she had the crutch in place, she insisted, "We need to go outside on the porch real quick."

"Why?"

"I want to look at the stars."

"We can see the stars from the upstairs window."

"Benji," she leveled a smile at him, "we have to go outside."

"Fine. But you need slippers and a sweater."

Once they'd bundled up, he helped her onto the porch.

The cold was a shock and Cassie sucked in a breath then blew out the smoke. She held all her weight on her right leg, the crutch on the left, and she studied the sky for a long time until her hand whipped out to point up. "There!" she yelled as her hand accidentally slapped against the back of Stills' head.

"Ow."

"Finally!" she exclaimed.

He rubbed the back of his head. "What, the stars?"

"Benji, see the handle of the big dipper?"

"Yeah ..."

"On the handle of the big dipper, there is a bright star at the end, it's called Arcturus."

"Arcturus," he repeated.

"Do you see it?"

He nodded. "I see it, Dodd."

"Okay, count five stars down from that ... south."

"Dodd ..."

She shifted her weight and touched his arm. "Benji, five stars directly down from that, do you see it?"

He counted. "I see it."

She took a deep breath. "Really? You do?"

"I really do." As if to humor her he pointed and counted, "One, two, three, four, five. I see it."

"Good, now go two stars to the right."

"One, two."

"Five down, two over to the right?" she confirmed.

He chuckled. "Yes honey, I see it."

"Good, cuz it's yours."

He looked puzzled. "Mine?"

She gave a relieved sigh. "Yes. I've been trying to give it to you this whole trip."

"Mine?" he repeated with an uncertain laugh.

Her smile was wide as he turned his attention to her. "Benji, when we went on our first date, you gave me the stars."

"Le Stelle." He whispered the name of the restaurant.

"You talked about making love to me under the stars in Mesa Verde for so long, and when we planned this trip ... I never imagined you'd propose. But that didn't matter, because I was so focused on trying to give you the stars in return." She swallowed, this was more difficult than she thought. "I wanted to give it to you when we were finally camping there, but it's been cloudy every night of this trip."

"I don't know what to say." His gaze drifted back to the sky and a swell of joy expanded throughout Cassie.

"I love you, Benji."

He turned toward her and nodded. "I love you too, Dodd. More than you'll ever know."

"I named it ..." she trailed off, suddenly a bit self-conscious about this part.

"What did you name it?"

"Benjamin," she admitted, with a soft chuckle.

His face beamed as he looked up once more at his star. "I love it."

Chapter Forty-Nine

"**Y**ou ready?" Elizabeth asked as she keyed in the code to the vault. "To see what half a million dollars from 1947 looks like? Hell yeah."

Cole suggested Elizabeth and Cassie have a few quiet hours at the archive before they were inundated with investigators and FBI asking for statements and information.

The roads were cleared, the snow had stopped, and the picture Cole painted was that the town would soon be overwhelmed with law enforcement.

Elizabeth picked Cassie up and Stills went to help Cole; the two wanted to take a final look at the mine Lewis had been hiding in, and the cave where the money had been found.

Elizabeth swung the vault open wide, and both women stood for a moment, trying to erase the last time they'd stood there together.

"Before we open the cases, want to see the newest addition to the archive that was put in over the past few days?"

She led Cassie to the back corner where a table held an organizer of various papers and plastic covers, some tape and scissors. She pulled on the organizer to reveal a hollowed out space and a phone. "Aidan and Cole were insistent that I wasn't allowed to come back to work until the safeguard had been added. Other than them and the man who put the phone line in, you're the only other person who knows."

Cassie gently touched Elizabeth's arm. "Was it awful?"

"The helplessness was. I *knew* someone would find me, I just wasn't sure how we'd find *you*. I used my time coming up with a plan of action for the second I got out, from contacting Todd to Cole and Benji."

"Of course you did."

"Okay," Elizabeth wiped at her eyes, "we could both get all weepy and maudlin, but we're not going to. We're going to go look at some old money."

The first thing Cassie noticed was that the locks were all undone on the suitcases. She raised an eyebrow at Elizabeth. "Those were locked the last time I saw them."

"Cole wanted to be sure of what he was reporting to the FBI."

"So you've already seen it."

Elizabeth opened the top suitcase in reply. On top of the stacks of bills was an envelope.

"What?" Cassie muttered as she gently picked up the envelope.

"We went through it all, each suitcase, this was the only other thing that was in them." Elizabeth gestured to the front room. "Have a seat and read it."

Cassie sat in front of the gas fireplace with her leg propped. Elizabeth sat next to her and smiled as she pulled out a letter of several pages and opened it.

"1966?" she asked, shocked at the scrawled date.

Elizabeth nodded and pointed, a wordless instruction to read.

August 9, 1966

Dear James,

You hid it good, big brother. But I found it.

I couldn't believe it at first, when I found the cave and the damn name carved into the rock above the opening. I couldn't believe how much blasting you had to do, and how many lies you had told me.

And I cursed your name.

I never understood why you did that to me, all those years ago. Why would you hide the money we risked everything for?

I am angry.

But you know what? I've been so angry for so goddamn long.

Angry that our parents were taken from us so soon, angry that you had to become an adult overnight. Angry that we slept on the streets. Angry that we went to war. Angry when we came home with only the clothes on our backs and our sister dead and that we were barely shells of the boys we once were.
Nothing in this life seemed fair and it made me angry.

And I watched you work your fingers to the bone, watched you bleed for me time and time and time again and it unmanned me.

I should have been more help, but I was drowning in anger; and the only thing I could think to do was drink my sins away and try to steal something I thought would make me happy.

All I did was steal the last little piece of happiness you had with Mary, and because you came to see me in my fevered state, I took your life too.

I was numb after that, after you abandoned me James. I didn't want to be the last one standing. I didn't deserve to live.
But I did.

I have a wife and a daughter and if you can believe it, a career. I don't deserve any of it. I thought I had healed all my past transgressions but here I am, running back to Eden, willing to throw everything away again looking for the long-lost treasure that you hid.

I thought Mary died. Until I got a letter from her two years ago. Her father knew everything, she must have known everything too.
I killed Peter Syke.

I've never told anyone. But I wanted retribution for your death and I didn't trust the courts to do right by you.

Somedays I think I should turn myself in; not just for his death, but for all my sins. Then other days, when my Theresa smiles up at me with her mother's eyes, when a student writes me and tells me of their accomplishments, I go on.

Those days, when I find some semblance of a smile, the past seems so damn far away. It feels like it was someone else, another man in another body with another life all those years ago. Damn but it feels like it was a hundred years ago, that shadow of a life lived.

But being back in Eden has dredged up so much pain that I packed away. I can't go back to my life with all of this baggage.

There were good times here, but they are shadowed by the suffering and my stupidity and forcing you to continue to look out for me.

When I read the letter Mary sent me, her last jab at me, the anger resurfaced. For my family's well-being, I took a leave of absence from the university and I've been in these mountains living like a madman, crazed, searching and buying a few new claims and putting them in both our names. It was a fluke at the recorder's office, when I was filing, that I had an idea to search for a claim in Mary's name.

That was smart big brother.

It took me almost twenty years to figure out such a simple solution.

And I finally found the cave and the money and I've been brought to my knees.

I now see that I must do what I've never done. I must truly pay a penance; and I must spend the rest of my life paying it. I see that now.

I never deserved you as a brother, you who did everything to look out for me, who did nothing for yourself except think awful things about how you were always thwarting me at each turn.

I'm the man I am because you planted the seeds. When we were in Africa you found that journal for me and told me to just start writing. I don't know why you did that, I don't know why I needed it. For reasons none of us understood, I wrote and wrote and wrote. I wrote a book about the war.

I brought the other journals though, the ones I was too scared to show my wife, the ones that show the man I must pay a fine on this life for. I burned them last night, outside this very cave that you built.

After I got angry, after the pain subsided, I burned them and sat next to the flames and looked up at the scarred wall with the carving Salerno and I finally understood.

When we were in Salerno that night that I wanted to run away, I was packing and in a frenzied state. I was losing myself, going crazy and you pulled me back into myself. Told me it was natural for every man to hit a wall now and then. But you were there to save me from myself, to bring me off my ledge, to help me climb off that wall.

A stupid metaphor of two boys who were so far from a home they didn't have.

I think I understand why you hid it.

So now here I am.

I can't take this money with me. And I can't destroy it.

So it looks like the only option I have left is to leave it.

I wish the sentiment 'I'm sorry' was able to hold a lifetime of regret and repentance. It doesn't.

William L. Moss

Cassie wiped the tears that had continually fogged up her vision and lowered the pages to her lap. She stared quietly into the fire, knowing the letter brought a needed finality to everything.

"There are still holes," Elizabeth said softly, "but I think the story of William and James Moss is as complete as we can get it."

"I never understood why the latitude and longitude were in William's memoir. Now I do," Cassie whispered.

Elizabeth asked, "What do you think will happen to Theresa?"

"Benji said she'll be interviewed to see if she had any knowledge that Lewis was planning on killing Art."

"Do you think she did?"

"I think she knew about Lewis and wanted a family connection. I don't think she knew about the money or that Lewis was slightly off his rocker."

They let the afternoon sounds envelop them; the click of the fireplace, the drip of the melting snow off the eaves, the wind that whistled against the window panes.

Cassie took a deep breath and slowly, ever so slowly, let it out.

"You know," Elizabeth tilted her head, "I believe this has been one of the most intense avalanche seasons I've ever been through." A subtle raise of her eyebrow accompanied her sentiment.

Chapter Fifty

"You sure about this?" Stills asked, standing next to Cassie in the hall of the clinic, right outside Lewis Treat's room.

She tapped the photocopied letter in her hand and gave a nod of her head. "It's okay."

He held the door and slouched against the doorjamb as Cassie hobbled over to the side of Lewis' bed.

He was laying at a reclined angle, a hand was cuffed to the bed, and he was staring out the window, squinting into the brightness. When he turned to face Cassie, she smiled at the black and blue knot on his temple.

"I misjudged you," he muttered.

"I'm glad."

He shrugged. "No hard feelings?"

Cassie scoffed at the declaration. "A lot of hard feelings, actually."

"Fair enough."

She unfolded the letter, placed the pages side by side on the rolling tray and slid it in front of him. "I brought you something. Just thought you'd like to see how this all ended."

He squinted at the page, then used the control to raise the bed and was quiet as he read the whole letter.

When he was finished, he grunted and sat back.

"It's a slippery slope, livin' a life full of resentment and thinking finding what you're owed will make it all better."

"Do you still feel that way?"

"I don't know if I'll ever stop."

She tilted her head and opened her mouth, then shut it and took a step back.

"Don't stop speakin' your mind now, girly."

"I was thinking that the only person who ever cheated you out of a life was yourself. You could never control William or your mom or stepdad and the decisions they made, but you could control how you came to terms with it."

"I'm too old and it's too late now."

"It is."

She took a step away and he muttered, "You could have let me go."

"I thought you were going to kill me," she admitted over her shoulder.

"I was." He shrugged, looking as defeated and deflated as a man could.

When she reached the door he called out, "Thanks for letting me see this letter. It doesn't help. But thanks anyway."

It was another gathering of new friends outside The Hideout that came to offer their goodbyes.

"I don't know what I'm going to do now that we're done with this research. Nothing is going to feel this exciting again," Elizabeth said as she lingered in a long hug with Cassie.

When they pulled away from each other, Cassie shrugged. "I don't know, I think I'd rather not have my life in danger while reliving the past; if it were up to me."

Elizabeth grinned. "I agree. You'll keep in touch, right?"

"Of course, especially now that I know what kind of contacts you have."

Elizabeth wiped a tear from her eye and settled into her husband's side. "Of course. And now I'll be adding you to my list as well."

"Anytime."

"And maybe I could even get an invite to the wedding?"

"Top of the list."

Cole shook Stills' hand, then slapped him on the back with his other. "I've said thanks too much, I think. But this time the thanks is for helping me weather that damn storm of agents in my town."

"Anytime," Stills returned.

Marsha dragged Stills into her arms next. "I enjoyed meeting you two so much and am so sorry things went the way they did. Come back and give us another chance one of these days, okay?"

"It wasn't all bad," he tried to soothe.

Cassie shook Cole's hand, wrinkling her nose as she admitted, "Look, I'm gonna open my mouth and hear my mother, so we'll ignore that; but once again I'd like to say that if you're ever in our part of the world, come say hi and let me introduce you to some nice girls."

He laughed and patted her on the back. "I don't think so, but thanks just the same."

Beverly shook her hand, her sharp voice declaring, "That's quite the engagement story you have now. Better than 'he proposed, and I said yes.' Now you get to say, 'and that was just the beginning.'"

Cassie laughed and had to press her lips together because she was about to declare to Beverly, *I think I'll miss you most of all, Scarecrow.*

They packed the car with the new loaves of bread and muffins that were given as parting gifts. Once settled and ready to go, Cassie turned and waved to everyone as Stills pulled down the road. They turned onto Main Street, and once more passed the colorful storefronts of the early 1900s before heading away from the old west mining town.

They didn't talk until Stills had driven up the most harrowing of switchbacks and hairpin turns, though it did feel a bit safer having the side of a mountain hugging the car as they climbed.

"You okay, Dodd?" he finally asked.

"I feel like I'm coming out of a dream."

"I think I feel the same way."

She let the build-up of snow that had been plowed and pushed off the road in various areas hypnotize her as her thoughts swirled and floated. "I wonder if this was how William felt when he left town, as if it had all been a waking nightmare of a dream."

Stills shrugged in reply. "We'll never know."

"We'll never know," Cassie sighed.

"You know, you're pretty amazing at research and connecting the dots."

"I know."

"I've been thinking; maybe you would want to do some freelance work for the CIA?"

"Research is a special skill set?"

He rolled his eyes dramatically. "Don't you ever listen to me?"

"I listen," she muttered.

"Okay, let me put it this way. As a historian and a genealogist, there are some files that the public aren't privy to, but the CIA is; and oftentimes they need help researching some more historical files."

"What?"

"You'd be considered a civilian consultant."

"Holy shit. You're not kidding."

"What part of this made you think I was kidding?" He frowned.

"I don't know."

"Dodd," he repeated the question, "do you wanna do a little freelance work for the CIA?"

"I really like my job."

"I'm not asking you to quit your job."

A smile spread across her face. "So I'd get to see where you work and learn all your secrets?"

"A few of them."

"Would I get to take spy training classes?"

He rolled his eyes as she laughed.

"The offer is there if you want it."

"Can you live with that? With me putting my life in danger?"

"Dodd, you wouldn't be putting your life in danger. And need I remind you, it wasn't *my job* that put your life in danger."

She waved the fact away as he continued, "I saw how you handled difficult situations and it was enlightening to see how you work. I think you have a lot to offer."

"I'll think about it."

"That's all I'm asking you to do."

"We have bigger matters to tackle though, Benji."

"What's that, Dodd?"

"We have to figure out how we're going to tell everyone that we're engaged."

And as if she had heard the declaration from over eight hundred miles away in a different time zone, Barbra Dodd picked up the phone to call her oldest daughter.

Book Notes

T hank you so much for reading *A Simple Avalanche.* I truly hope you enjoyed the time you spent with Cassie and Benji. I know I did!

One of the things I like to do is to give my readers some fun trivia about these books I write. So without further ado...

1 – This was the story I tried to tell when I first met Cassie and Benji. But when I started to write, they told me a completely *different* story. And it wasn't until the end of that one, *Simply Protocol*, that they smiled and got in the car headed for Colorado and gave me permission to write the story I wanted to write.

So if you've ever wondered how characters might waylay a writer, it's like that!

2 - Of course I've hiked the Grand Canyon. I loved it there. I can't wait to do it again.

3 - Where does the love of history and archives come from? I have a degree in history, worked in an archive for five years, and have written several historical articles over the years. However, I would say it truly started during Christmas break my Junior year of high school. I had to do a history report on the life of a relative who lived during WWII. And that year we just happened to be visiting family in Georgia. My Grandpa Sharp told me our family history and about his time in the war. He too lied about his age to enlist. In thirty minutes I had all the information I needed for a paper. After four hours, I filled a notebook. The following summer we lost Grandpa Sharp, and the information I have, that he passed on to me, has become priceless.

4 – I lived in Colorado for five years after college and worked for a

museum and archive in a small town. Eden, however, is an amalgamation of several different old west mining towns I studied and visited during that time.

However, each building, restaurant, menu item, and décor I mention in this book, were inspired by places I traveled in Colorado. The characters are made up. The historical characters are all from my imagination; which wasn't too hard after spending years reading fascinating histories of characters of the Old West. The scenery is based on memory, how it felt to stand in the buildup of falling snow, alone in the early morning hours, with no noise but the crunch of soft white beneath my feet.

5 – The newspaper articles I wrote are "kind of" real. I wanted to get the cadence of the late 40s newspaper writing correct, so I used my local library's online newspaper research tools. (Your library has them too, and I highly suggest you check it out.) And I searched several of the drunk and disorderly articles from the Idaho Statesman Newspapers, I used some of the language, changing all the names and locations of course.

6 – The <u>Colorado Historic Newspapers Collection</u> is a REAL database. It is a service of the Colorado State Library and I wasted so much time perusing the collection. "3.6 million digitized pages, representing more than 715 individual newspaper titles published in Colorado from 1859 to 2023."

7 – Grandma's Fry Bread is a real location. I found mention of her stand online and then found an article in the Boston Globe from November 2, 2022 about 'Grandma' Daisy Kady, who learned to make Navajo fry bread from her mother. And I did use her words from a quote in the article: "... she does know the secret to fry bread: entering into the right frame of mind. "You just gotta be calm and put love into it. If you're mad and doing it wrong, it won't come out right.""

8 – When I visited Mesa Verde, I remember the ranger telling us about the sacred space, and the history of the people and asking us to honor those that came before. In doing my research I came across an article that summed up some of the things I think were most important about the Mesa Verde area:

"When I enter a modern-day kiva, I ask permission out of respect and cultural tradition," says T.J. Atsye, who is Laguna Pueblo and a one-time ranger at Mesa Verde National Park. "I do the same thing when I enter a cliff dwelling. I ask permission to pass by." Atsye, who often calls Mesa Verde the place "where the ancestors whisper to you," explains that Pueblo people believe their ancestors are all around them, like many people feel the presence of their departed family members at a cemetery or maybe in a loved one's favorite spot. Atsye understands not everyone has the same beliefs, but she suggests taking a quiet moment to address those who have passed on but whose spirits can still be felt in these sacred places. "Be sincere, be genuine, be respectful," she says. "Let them know you are here to see their beautiful homes. They will listen to you, and you might feel their warmth wrap around you." <u>Here's the article that inspired me</u>.

9 – I have no idea if the star "five down and two to the right from Arcturus" is available for purchase.

10 – Support your local libraries and archives!

Cassandra Dodd's list on "How to be a Spy"

1) Detect all trackers and listening devices.
2) When shit goes down, enlist the help of the local authorities.
3) Don't hide!
4) Be careful who you verify your career with. If you're actually in the CIA, you don't wear a badge that says 'Ask me about my job' or have a bumper sticker that declares: 'How's my driving? Call 1-888-theCIA.'
5) YouTube University is a viable way to learn how to do the things you don't know how to do.
6) Use the local information tree to the best of its ability.
7) Get as much information as you can from the self-appointed local gossip. Start at popular bars and wherever the best food is served.
8) Bad guys don't knock!!
9) Make sure you wear clothes you can fight in, or "throw some asshole over your shoulder" in.
10) Check the door first, you never know, it might already be open.
11) Use the red light setting on your headlamp to protect our night vision, so if we have to turn it off, our eyes won't have to work so hard to adjust to the darkness. It helps to see finer details and doesn't interfere with night vision technology.
12) No matter what Benji says, demand night vision technology. Selling point: might make the bedroom fun.
13) Use your time wisely.
14) Commit to the actions you're about to take when it comes to defending yourself.
15) Trust your gut.

Acknowledgements

The last book in the *Simply Trouble Series*.

Phew.

Putting this first series to bed seems like a dream.

In this book, Cassie tells Stills, "I feel like I'm coming out of a dream."

That's what it feels like to be finishing up the final late night notes that will be put in this book. A dream.

You see, I put my head down in June of 2021 and got to work. Found a book coach, a group of like minded writers, a support system, and mapped out what I wanted for my career. And for some reason, in the back of my mind, I decided I wouldn't look up until winter of 2023.

And here we are, and I'm looking up and I can not begin to comprehend what I've accomplished.

It's been *A LOT* of work, and the gears haven't always turned the right way, but friends, I must admit, I'm proud of my dreams that have come to fruition.

Have you ever seen those gothic buildings that use an architectural design called flying buttress to stabilize the structure?

I've got a support system of friends and family that hold me up like that. So a heartfelt, overwhelming amount of thanks to:

Ariane Kimlinger, my grammatical guru and friend. She not only brings out the best in my writing as an editor, but she brings out the best of me as a human.

My Mom and Dad who continue to be an example of how to live life to the fullest.

My sister Katie, who knows that there aren't enough adjectives to describe how much she means to me.

Amy, Gina, Sophie, Ashelee, Jewell, Shannon ...badass pillars, each and every one of you! I love you.

Tammy, Bryan, Jeremy, Celeste, Leslie, the Sharp cousins who read and send me encouraging messages -thank you, *thank you* for your continued support and encouragement.

Eliane, Crystal, Adam, Amy B., Allona, The Italian Group, Barbara, my Star Wars gamers, Connie, Janell, my book club, Jeni, Karen, Melinda...and all those I'm forgetting, thank you for your kind words, for checking on me, for the coffee dates and for reading my words.

Stephanie George an amazing historian and friend. Thanks for letting me talk this book through with you!

Michele, the alpha reader. Ever since someone pointed out that was what she did, as she's the last one to read the book before it goes live, I've loved it. Thank you for your friendship.

Jessica and Cami at Soul Self Defense, again, thank you for your insight and help.

Freda Peterson the true author of a two volume book about everyone who was buried in The Hillside Cemetery.

Kristi, a friend and amazing book coach who believed I could get to this point when I was too scared to believe it myself.

My husband and child whom I love with all my heart.

My extended family **Cameron and Daniell and Piero**. And **my little brother** who hasn't read one of my books yet.

TIRAA (The Independent Romance Authors Association) who is always there to support and help! I truly appreciate it.

And you, my dear reader. Thank you for your time, I know how truly valuable it is in this day and age; and I appreciate that you spent it on my words and story.

HERE'S A SNEAK PEEK AT

Chapter One

And then there was more snow. Falling in large sheets, covering the city once again. Metaphorical shoulder rolls and cracking of knuckles could be heard all over; the response of a whole city readying itself to endure the newest layer of snow that would be added to the already record-breaking layer.

The reactionary groans of frustration that rose into the cold air were palpable as people shoveled driveways and walkways, swept off cars, and tried to figure out how the hell they were going to get where they needed to go.

Needless to say, it had been a rough winter. And the snow, which had been fun in December, had lost its magical luster by mid-January when stores ran out of ice melt, the Department of Transportation reported a desperately low sand supply, and there wasn't a spare snow shovel for sale anywhere in town.

The good news was that work had, again, been canceled.

The bad news was that work had, again, been canceled. Because I lived off of tips.

My phone notification sounded, and I opened a picture of my smiling roommate who'd been happily stranded in Oahu for work during Denver's bad weather. I snarled and tossed the phone on the table, shuffling across the kitchen floor to the only real friend I had left, Mr. Coffee. Together we went through the ritual of making an entire pot for one. After a lap around the kitchen I glanced at the sofa by the front window, where I'd spent the past four day staring down the snow and realized I didn't have another staring contest in me. So instead, I settled for trying to find something to watch on TV.

The news showed some poor intern bundled up in front of a downtown parking lot turned designated snow dump that had grown to an impressive height. Meanwhile, clips of snowplows, attempting to clear the snow as well as find a place to put it, made up the rest of the morning show news.

I wasn't interested in watching more "snowmageddon" programming. I could write, but lately, all that had turned into was a story about snow and depression. I settled on another round of cleaning the already clean apartment, which didn't take long. So, with nothing better to do and food running low, I decided to take a twenty-dollar bill and attempt the three-block walk to the store; a journey that would no doubt prove a tedious exercise in winter calisthenics.

It was that day, somewhere between telling my reflection in the living room window for the hundredth time that 'the snow lost its charm weeks ago' and the second pot of coffee, that I made a plan. I checked my bank account, did some creative math and decided I didn't care how bad debt collectors could be.

So, we're talking and I say, 'Valentine's Day is so commercial.'

To which my sister counters, 'If you had a boyfriend you wouldn't say that.'

I remind her, 'I've had boyfriends on Valentine's and their in-action was even more depressing.'

So she offers, 'You should come visit me for Valentine's Day.'

And that's when I decided to pay two bills, buy the cheapest ticket I could find, and pull out the rest of my life savings: three hundred and fifty dollars – and hightail it to Florence, Italy (by way of Rome) to see my sister who's studying abroad!

I imagine the businessman I'm squished next to on this last leg of my journey, from Chicago to Rome, wants to hear the story of how I ended up in this exact seat beside him two days before Valentine's Day. I glance at him several times, in reply he shakes his newspaper as if I'll take the hint and stop my imitation of a bothersome fly. Or stop staring.

To be fair, he does have the window seat, but the passing clouds and bright blue sky lost their appeal a while ago, and he's right to be annoyed, because *I am* studying him.

He's debonair in that way that screams educated but not stuck-up about it. His head is shaved, possibly making sure some slight bald spot isn't a distracting attribute. He smells good; not drowned with cologne, but like he knows how to apply it just right.

I take a deep breath. *Whoa*, warm rosemary and desert winds. Was that a thing?

I bend my head nonchalantly toward my left armpit and inhale, hoping I don't smell. I have a favorite perfume but even if I drench myself in it, I don't think people can smell it. It wears off somehow, like my skin is in such dire need to smell good, it soaks up the scent and internalizes it.

Mr. Business is well-pressed; black slacks and a light blue button-down accenting a sleek dark blue tie. His coat jacket had been handed over to the flight attendant when he boarded. The question, '*why isn't he flying business class?*', is quickly replaced by my grandmother's complaint, 'people don't dress up to fly anymore'. I wore my trusty dark jeans, a white tank top under my zippered black hoodie and sensible walking shoes. I think if the seats still had room and people weren't treated like cattle, maybe we would still dress up.

Case in point, the seat is too small for Mr. Business. His knees are pressed against the seatback in front of him, and his broad shoulders are spilling over the edge of the arm rests. I mean, his shoulders pull impressively at his shirt when he moves to rearrange the paper. He's solid. Emanating authority, he's a force to be reckoned with. He's good-looking, in an intimidating way, or maybe it's just his size in that seat.

Another rattle of the paper.

Fine.

I turn my attention away from him, put my complimentary earbuds in and mess with the small TV screen embedded in the seat in front of me. I tilt the screen up and down, going through its entire range of mobility; which is less than my seat's ability to recline. I adjust the earbuds and take several deep breaths as I scroll through the movies being offered. I want to watch about five of them, so that should help the time go quickly.

But how much time do I need to waste?

I slip an earbud out and ask my seatmate, "How long is the flight?"

He sighs; the kind of sigh that verifies his annoyance with me. But still, he reaches over and presses a button on my screen. The flight tracker comes into focus, giving me our location, how fast we're going, our altitude, how long we've been in the air and how much longer we have until we reach our destination.

Seven more hours.

A flutter of excitement kicks at my gut and I rub my chest to catch my breath. This is my first solo international trip.

"I'm going to see my sister," I burst the information forth. "She lives in Florence."

He waves his paper at me once again: Shoo fly.

She's been there for the past five months. I internalize what I want to say: *She studied the language before she went, took classes for three years. She lives with a bunch of Italians. It's the most courageous thing she's ever done – such a cool ass adventure, so far from family.*

I live in Denver. Well, by way of Oregon, California and Virginia. I'm a sort of gypsy. My sister planted roots in San Francisco while I traveled. We don't get to see each other that much; but still, we're sisters who've become best friends over the years and the miles.

"I'll be there for two weeks." The phrase is a release of steam from a screaming teapot. I'm too excited.

The businessman lowers his paper a bit. "That's wonderful. I'm sure you'll have a nice trip. Good luck." He gives another defiant shake of his paper and creates the barrier once again.

"Are you going to Rome?"

We're landing in Rome and I have to find a train to Florence. I have no idea how to go about it, but I've never allowed things like that to cause me any undue stress. The excitement and anticipation...well, those two things might kill me.

"Are you going to attempt to talk to me the entire flight?" he growled from behind his paper.

"Maybe," I answered honestly.

He lowered his paper again. "I am going to Rome to visit a friend," he offered, then raised an eyebrow in question: Would that bit of information appease me? Could he please go back to reading his paper now?

"A woman friend?" *Not gonna happen buddy.*

He put his paper down as a slight smile pulled at the corner of his mouth. "Yes, a woman friend. She's in Rome, I'm flying in to spend Valentine's Day with her." He nodded – was *this enough* information?

I tilted my head and narrowed my gaze.

"Yes?" he asked.

"That's pretty romantic. Does she know you're coming?"

"Yes," he said.

"Do you love her?"

"Do you interrogate every stranger you sit next to on a plane this way?"

"I'm really excited," I offered; then because it was the truth, repeated, "*Really* excited."

With a gracious, resigned sigh, he folded his paper and stuffed it in the seatback in front of him then offered his hand. "I'm Lorenzo."

"Keats," I reciprocated.

"Keats?"

"My parents love literature." I got the question enough that I was always ready with the answer. "Lorenzo." I tested his name out. "Do people call you Enzo? Are you Italian?"

He raised that eyebrow again at my questions. "My parents are from Southern Italy. Some family calls me Enzo, everyone else, Lorenzo," he explained. "So, Keats...if your parents loved literature that much, what's your middle name?"

I paused, but then shrugged, it was just a middle name, information anyone could find on a driver's license. "Keats *is* my middle name. Olivia is my first, but I never acted like an Olivia, so they called me Keats."

"And what do you do, Olivia Keats? Are you a student like your sister?"

"No, writer."

That eyebrow raised again, interested in the answer. "Would I have read any of your work?"

"Do you read any literary journals or local magazines from the Denver area?" I asked somewhat jokingly, having had this conversation many times before.

"I can't say I do."

"Then you've never read any of my work."

"Do you write under the name Keats?" he asked.

"Nah, too pretentious. Olivia McCall." I smiled.

He laughed, and the slightly intimidating manner he'd been exuding over the past hour melted. His face softened with his laughter and his shoulders relaxed. "Has anyone ever told you that you're a whirlwind?"

"Most of my life." I smiled. "How long are you going to be in Rome?"

"Not sure," he admitted.

"Don't you have a return ticket?"

He shook his head no in answer.

Wasn't that expensive? I opened my mouth to ask but suddenly felt shy about my ineptitude in situations with people who could afford open-ended tickets to foreign countries.

"Is your woman friend picking you up?" I asked instead.

"If her meetings haven't run too late."

"God, that will be romantic, won't it? Rome with someone you love..."

Surprising someone you love in a foreign country sounded like a lovely idea. Especially after the hell I'd just come out of with a stupid boyfriend of three years who had, it turned out, cheated on me for the latter part of the relationship. One and a half years and I never saw it. I was blindsided by the breakup, and it cracked my confidence and my heart. But I was scrappy. I was working through it.

It was nice to hear that a man could still surprise his girlfriend in a romantic way, that there was still love out in the universe.

Lorenzo didn't respond to my posturing about the surprise, but his study of me took on an intensity. I wanted to lean away from his intrusive stare, but forced myself to stand my ground and keep my smile steady. After all, I had spent the last hour studying him and I interrupted first.

He moved then, thankfully breaking the strange moment as he rummaged around in the soft briefcase at his feet. "Ah..." He turned back and produced a small velvet box, took a deep breath and then proceeded to open the box slowly, reverently. His hand was shaking just showing me the ring.

"Oh...wow," I whispered. "It really *is* going to be a romantic trip."

He looked down at the ring and his shaking hand, frowning. "I was thinking about doing it on Valentine's Day." He cleared his throat. "I haven't really been able to talk to anyone about this..." he excused as we both continued to silently contemplated the ring. He nervously cleared his throat again, then quietly asked, "Does that seem too...cheesy?"

"No," I whispered, then reached out and gently touched the ring. I couldn't imagine a world where someone flew to a foreign country to propose to me with a gold ring that glittered and blinked. But that was the insecurity brought on by the recent breakup. Of course, I couldn't imagine that world because my ex-asswipe hadn't even been able to bring himself to go to the store and get my antibiotic filled when I was really sick.

"It's beautiful," I verified. Though how could anyone question the breathtaking beauty of the large oval diamond encircled by a halo of smaller diamonds. It was truly stunning.

"It took me two weeks to choose one," he admitted.

"What's your girlfriend's name?"

"Annabella."

I smiled and pointed to the ring. "So, it would seem that *you* are just as emotional and anxious as I am about this trip."

He gave a soft laugh. "I am excited," he turned the ring toward him so he could inspect it at a different angle, "and anxious..." he admitted, then cleared his throat once more. "I would argue, however, that some of us are better at handling our emotions than others."

I finally met his eyes as I exclaimed, "I can't help it! Excitement works me up...it flips and kicks in my gut. It makes me wear my emotions on my sleeve."

"Well–" He might have been meaning to say more when a passing flight attendant's gasp interrupted, "Oh, oh! Did she say yes?"

I blinked up at the flight attendant and then glanced over at Lorenzo; we frowned at each other.

A woman across the aisle leaned over and when she saw the ring, added her own gasp. "I've never been on a flight where someone proposed."

"Oh, no..." I started.

Lorenzo shook his head and emphatically pointed. "No no, not her."

"Gee, thanks," I muttered over my shoulder at him.

"No, sorry. You seem...interesting," he tried as he closed the ring box.

I leaned across the aisle and explained to both the passenger and the flight attendant, "He's going to propose to his girlfriend in Rome. He was just showing me the ring."

They were evenly disappointed.

"Such a shame, you make a cute couple," the flight attendant said, then continued down the aisle.

I gave a snort of disbelief and muttered, "You know, going to Rome to propose on Valentine's Day is just as exciting."

As Lorenzo put the ring back in his bag, I touched his arm and reassured, "*That* is beautiful. Good job. All around."

"I feel..." He stared over the seats stretched in front of us, trying to find what he was feeling. A shake of his head, he asked once more, "Do you think it's trite to propose on Valentine's Day?"

"Not at all. It's going to be perfect."

"I'll hold you to that," he affirmed.

There was a lull in the conversation, but the anxious excitement continued to permeate. I bit my tongue on the urge to ask if we were there yet, and instead asked, "Why aren't you flying business class?"

"I should have. I could have read my paper in peace." He winked at me.

"I'm *excited*." I repeated my mantra for this flight.

"I flew standby, this was the only seat available," he explained. "So, is this your first time on an international flight?"

"I act like it, don't I?" I gave a snort of laughter. "Actually, and you might be shocked to hear this, this is the seventh time I've been to Europe."

"Have you always gone alone?"

"No." I grinned. "That's why I'm a little overzealous. The first four times I went to Europe with tour groups, then twice with my family. But this time...it's just me."

"Ah, the open road is all yours."

"Yes. I'm *alone*." The word was a confession. An enlightenment. I was still afraid that at any moment, a missing friend or tour group leader would come to collect me and fold me into their structured trip. This time, the dream trip was mine. *All* mine. "Italy will be all mine..." I trailed off dreamily.

"But you're going to see your sister."

"Yeah, but...it just feels different. Like, a grand adventure." Now *that* declaration sounded lame.

"Do you know the language?" he asked.

"About ten phrases." It was my turn to rummage around in my bag; I pulled out a small *Italian for Idiots* book and waved it in triumph. "But I have this."

"You know there's an app on your phone you can use to translate for you."

"Where's the fun in that?" I put the book back. "Besides, I can't afford the international plan. Do you know Italian?"

"I do. And I speak a southern dialect." My confused look prompted him to explain. "In different regions of Italy, there are different dialects spoken."

Well shit. And here I was trying to learn a little bit of a language I thought was universal. To Italy.

"Is anyone going to understand my ten phrases?" I asked.

He nodded his head. "Of course. Years ago, the country took on Dante's Italian as their united tongue. That's the Italian you'll find in your book."

"Ah." I was vaguely discouraged and mildly intrigued. "Grazie," I thanked him for my first Italian language lesson.

"Prego," he offered. I knew that one, it meant 'you're welcome'.

That one little word of Italian, spoken by a handsome man on his way to Rome, kicked the butterflies back into gear.

"Where are you going to propose? Have you picked a place yet?" I asked.

Instead of answering my question Lorenzo asked, "How old are you?"

I frowned. "Thirty-two. How old are you?"

"Thirty-five." He smiled. "I didn't mean to offend you with the question. You're just very...vibrant."

I laughed and nodded. "That's a very nice way of putting it."

"Putting what?"

"That I act like I'm younger."

"It's not a bad thing." He rubbed his hands on his thighs. "I didn't mean to offend you, truly. I just think...you act like you haven't been beaten down by life the way other thirty-year olds I know have."

I shrugged. "Oh, I've got scars. Plenty. But he...the ex, and any others...they don't get to win, you know? The trips to Italy, they can win. A gorgeous sunset, the sound of the waves crashing on the shore, finding five bucks on the ground– those moments can shape me. But not the bullshit." I wrinkled my nose and peeked at Lorenzo. "Sorry, was that too much?"

"Not at all." His intensity was back. "I like that idea."

"Good." I nodded. We were interrupted by the announcement of the dinner service. I lowered my tray then watched Lorenzo try to do the same, but his knees kept the tray at an angle. "Would it be any better if you were on the aisle?" I asked.

"Are you trying to get a free window seat?"

"Yes."

He smiled. "Actually, it might help. I could also try and trip people as they walk down the aisle," he joked.

We performed an awkward exchange of pillows, blankets, earbuds and bags. Lorenzo bumped his head twice, definitely putting his height in the six something range.

Once settled with dinners and complimentary bottles of merlot, our conversation continued.

"So what do you do for a living, Lorenzo?"

"I'm a financial advisor," he responded.

"You do have a bank-y look about you," I said.

His eyebrows furrowed in question. "Is that good or bad?"

"It's nothing. It's just..." I shifted in my seat and squared my shoulders toward him, "if I were going to write you, I'd write you as someone with a bank job. Maybe a...commodities broker?"

"Do you often write people you just met?" he asked.

I shrugged. "I write people I've just met, people I've known for years...people I glimpse across the street..."

"I've never understood the artsy type," he confessed.

"Don't worry, we artsy types have never understood the business types." I smiled. "But I'll admit, there are times I wish I were more business minded. There seems to be stability in that world."

"Yes and no," he offered.

"Okay, let me ask you this; do you have a 401k, a retirement plan, money in the bank and a savings account?"

"Of course," he answered suspiciously.

"Do you have your own apartment or house?"

"House," he supplied.

"Do you *own* your house?" I clarified.

"Yes."

I nodded and continued with my inquiry. "Car?"

He raised an eyebrow at the line of questioning, but nodded in answer.

I laughed and explained, "Okay, I rent a room from a friend. I don't have a steady job. I don't have a car. I had enough money to buy this ticket and managed to scrape together three hundred and fifty bucks for the next two weeks. I have no way to pay my bills when I get home and every last bit of my energy goes towards trying to find an agent so I can make a career out of the only thing I've ever really wanted to do my whole life, which is write." I grinned. "So you see, business minded seems like it comes with a lot more stability."

He was quiet for a moment, then shook his head and picked up his drink. "No. I don't think you want security at all."

"What?"

A slow grin spread. "Your starving writer's life," he pointed at me with his cup, "you like it. You wear it like a badge of honor. You even talk about it with overflowing pride. You aren't looking for people to feel bad for you."

Well, he had me there. "Fine, I love the starving writer's life...sometimes." I held out my hands in admittance. "Sometimes it *is* hard and I do wish there was a bit more stability."

He nodded. "I think I can understand that."

We took the lull in the conversation to eat a few bites and talk about how it wasn't 'that bad' for airplane food.

"Why are you only staying for two weeks?" Lorenzo asked.

"Because that's the trip I planned."

"Yeah, but if there isn't anything to go back for...why wouldn't you just stay?"

"In Italy?"

He nodded easily as the weight of the question pushed all the air out of my lungs. *Why wouldn't I just stay?* Because...well shit, I don't know why.

A list of my worldly possessions flashed before my eyes along with the list of goods that were lacking: no job, car, house, mortgage, boyfriend, kids. No obligations. Hell, even my roommate was just taking pity on me until I 'got back on my feet'.

Dear lord, if I wanted to, I could stay in Italy.

Couldn't I?

Where would I live?

With my sister in her rented room? Maybe. Maybe we could find a place together.

But...

"It's something to think about..." I whispered.

"That's the way I'd write it." Lorenzo winked.

I had been so busy writing adventures for made up characters, that it never dawned on me to write myself into such possibilities. So far, I'd written myself as a supporting character. But maybe Lorenzo was right; if I was trying to create something bigger than myself, and I was willing to sacrifice anything to get there, then why not write myself into an adventurous expat life in Italy?

"That's really something to think about," I reiterated.

TO
CONTINUE
Reading

Go to:
NicoleSharpWrites.com

Legend has it that Nicole Sharp was born to hippies during an ice storm in Stone Mountain, Georgia. While confirmation of said events cannot be agreed upon, one fact is for certain, it was a Tuesday.

By age twelve, Nicole was sure of two things: 1) She wanted to be a writer and 2) She wanted to travel. She begged her parents to allow her to voyage alone to exotic lands. They permitted her to go from California to Boise, Idaho to visit a great-grandmother.

After muddling through her college years, Nicole graduated with a Bachelors in History (think Greeks and Romans). Why not study English if she wanted to be a writer? There were better stories in history class.

Nicole is Italian. According to Ancestry.com it's a rather low percentage, but she feels she is at least 51% Italian. She's visited the homeland a handful of times, studied the language and loves the Italian cappuccino.

Nicole's first concert was to see the bluegrass group The Seldom Scene when she was a fifteen-year-old, thanks to her parent's bluegrass phase. However, she never admits it, and instead tells everyone that They Might Be Giants, whom she saw in college, was her first real concert.

Her first car was a yellow Chevy Celebrity and her favorite job was working as a docent at a museum in an old Colorado mining town. She has written extensively about both.

Visit NicoleSharpWrites.com for more entertainment.